ANGEL ✍ ——
IN THE PARLOR

By Nancy Willard

Children's Books
The Well-mannered Balloon
Strangers' Bread
Simple Pictures Are Best
The Highest Hit
Papa's Panda
The Marzipan Moon
The Nightgown of the Sullen Moon

Fantasy Trilogy
Sailing to Cythera, and Other Anatole Stories
The Island of the Grass King: Further Adventures of
    Anatole
Uncle Terrible: More Adventures of Anatole

Short Story Collections
The Lively Anatomy of God
Childhood of the Magician

Poetry
In This Country
Skin of Grace
Nineteen Masks for the Naked Poet
A New Herball
Carpenter of the Sun
A Visit to William Blake's Inn: Poems for Innocent and
    Experienced Travelers
Household Tales of Moon and Water

Critical Essays
Testimony of the Invisible Man

Nancy Willard

ANGEL &
IN THE PARLOR

5 Stories and 8 Essays

With an Introduction by Robert Pack

Harcourt Brace Jovanovich, Publishers
San Diego New York London

Library of Congress Cataloging in Publication Data
Willard, Nancy.
Angel in the parlor.
1. Willard, Nancy—Addresses, essays, lectures.
2. Authors, American—20th century—Biography—Addresses,
essays, lectures. 3. Authorship—Addresses, essays,
lectures. I. Title.
PS3573.I444A83   1983   818'.5409   83-4307
ISBN 0-15-107181-0

Designed by Dalia Hartman

Printed in the United States of America

First edition

B C D E

For my mother and in memory of my father

Contents ✍

Stories

1. Her Father's House   3
2. Animals Running on a Windy Crown   32
3. The Doctrine of the Leather-Stocking Jesus   55
4. The Tailor Who Told the Truth   76
5. Amyas Axel, His Care and Keep   111

Essays

6. The One Who Goes Out at the Cry of
   Dawn: The Secret Process of Stories   171
7. Becoming a Writer   190
8. Angel in the Parlor: The Reading and
   Writing of Fantasy   201
9. The Well-tempered Falsehood: The Art of
   Storytelling   222
10. The Spinning Room: Symbols and
    Storytellers   240
11. The Game and the Garden: The Lively
    Art of Nonsense   258
12. The Rutabaga Lamp: The Reading and
    Writing of Fairy Tales   283
13. "Who Invented Water?": Magic, Craft,
    and the Making of Children's Books   308

Introduction ✐ ─────────

Astronomers, evolutionary biologists, physicists, no less than storytellers, are compelled to ask themselves how the universe and life began and what are the causes of change. And therein lies a story. In fact, many stories. One might say that man is the storytelling animal. In the deepest human sense, we are, and we become, the stories that we tell about ourselves to explain ourselves. We never tire of retelling each other into each other's lives.

True storytelling begins with the sense of wonder. Why does the universe exist rather than nothing? Why did he meet her by the willow tree that windy day? What happened next? Did they get married? Did he die? In this remarkable collection of stories and essays, Nancy Willard wonders her stories into form and wonders about the art of wondering. In effect, her essays are stories about stories, how they have their roots both in experience and in invention. If her childhood seems to have been magical, it is because she has not lost her sense of enchantment in its recounting. In her retelling of the Cinderella story from the point of view of the rat-turned-coachman, she is able to project herself into other characters who also value their histories and speculate about what is to become of them. Unlike the children in e.e. cummings's poem who "down they forgot as up they grew," Willard cherishes the origins of astonishment in the child's curiosity about herself and her world. Willard says:

The teller tells the story he has made out of bits he has seen and pieces he has heard. His telling brings these fragments together, and in that healing synthesis, he gives the wasted hours of our lives an order that they don't have and a radiance that only God and the artist can perceive.

The universe that Willard's imagination inhabits is enchanted because everything in it has its story, everything is touched with the animation of her own delight in the thoughtful act of looking. In this book the reader can witness the products of Willard's imagination in their completed form and at the same time glimpse the resources of her particular experiences that she has shaped into stories. And therein lies her dominant theme—how people either fail or succeed in inventing the lives that finally they must call their own. Their fictions of themselves must bear the weight of what they feel, just as the lovers, Nicholas and Janet, must define their chosen love against the fantasy of their benefactor, Amyas, who wishes he could fly. The story that Willard creates is a fabric of the fictions each character creates for himself or herself, and this composite fiction is the "lie" that enables the reader to see into the representative truth of her characters. That is what Willard means when she concludes her essay, "The Well-tempered Falsehood": "Yes, to tell the lie. But in the telling, to make it true."

Willard is right in assuming that the fictions we invent, the life of the imagination, are an essential part of the reality of human life. And so the supernatural in her work, the aura of enchantment that often surrounds her objects and people, must be seen as what the mind adds to the perceived world of events and images. A dreamlike or impressionistic sense of things gives expression to the feelings that inevitably are associated with what we call the actual. Even the most recalcitrant realist must acknowledge the existence of human fantasy, of wishing and making believe. It is as if we live in two worlds at once, and these worlds of the literal and the imagined are always merging or clashing, each contending for our allegiance.

In the world of the actual the universal law is that everything is causally connected, and therefore description is essentially linear. Explanation or interpretation must show how things connect in sequence, motivation causing action, one action leading to the next. But in the world of imagination such necessity may be suspended briefly to allow an imaginative premise to take the place of a cause. In Willard's hands, the real and the imagined are joined and enhance one another. That is perhaps one of the many reasons why her lectures on the craft of writing given at Bread Loaf Writers' Conference over the years have been so important to other writers.

Willard's writing demonstrates that the spirit of fiction is never far from the spirit of childhood recollection, of the fairy tale, and of myth. Such narration possesses the freedom to reject explanation for presentation, to apprehend an image or an action in the intensity of the moment in which it is witnessed. For example, in a poem inspired by a literal reading of a newspaper headline on a sports page, "Buffalo Climbs Out of Cellar," Willard restores the life of the buffalo by making him a four-legged buffalo again. She gives us his predicament and his story. We know how he must feel, and so we care. But as artist she does not tell us, nor does she have to, how he got there in the first place, for that would be another story.

Robert Pack
Director of the Bread Loaf Writers' Conference

5 Stories

1

Her Father's House

————————————Over the loudspeaker the stewardess's voice disintegrated, crackling like cellophane. Erica stood up and herded Anatole into the aisle.

"Goodbye," said the stewardess. "My, you're real big for three years old. I'll bet your grandma's going to give you a big hug."

"I'm going to hug my grandma," said Anatole. "My old grandpa died."

The stewardess smiled. Erica's husband, Theo, made a space for them, carrying the suitcase, and they all three hurried through the carpeted tunnel into the terminal. Erica saw John, looking more bald than she had remembered him and paler, wiping his glasses on his T-shirt the way he always did just before he lifted Papa into his chair at the table or took Papa the paper. She wondered if he was looking for a new job or if her mother would let him stay on to take care of the house. Perhaps he'd already put his advertisement in the newspaper—the same advertisement that had brought him into their family three years ago.

Then she caught sight of her mother at the gate and ran forward and hugged her, astonished at how small she had become.

"Mother, you've gotten thinner since I saw you at Christmas."

"I *am* thinner," said her mother. "I didn't sleep a wink all night. I know I won't sleep tomorrow night, either."

"Your sister and her kids got in yesterday," John said.

"Kirsten's here?"

"But not Harold," added her mother. "He couldn't get away. I've got to make a reservation for Kirsten and the children at Grubb's for Saturday. Joan wants to go there for her last free birthday. After your tenth you have to pay for the cake and ice cream. Danny went there for all his birthdays."

"I thought you said the funeral's on Saturday," said Erica.

"Funeral's tomorrow. This dragging it all out, I'm a wreck."

"I'll get the car," said John as Anatole and Theo joined them. "I'll meet you outside the baggage gate."

The four of them watched him hobble down the escalator.

"How's his foot?" asked Theo.

"It turns all dark in the morning," Erica's mother said. "It's his circulation. And he keeps on smoking. And he won't have an operation. Yesterday he cut the toes out of his shoes. Too bad his room is on the third floor. It takes him forever to get there. And he can't lift as well as he used to. But he was so good with Hal."

John turned onto the expressway and opened the window. The warm winds of May blessed them. Traffic at this early hour was not heavy; the air smelled fresh. In the front seat, her mother turned around and talked to the space between Erica and Theo, just over Anatole's head.

"Hal had such a good day Monday. He ate a big lunch——"

"Not quite as big as the day before," said John.

"Why, he ate some nut loaf and a bowl of yogurt and a dish of prunes. And he shaved all by himself. The bridge club was coming over, so I got him dressed in his best suit. He looked real nice. I asked him did he want to go downstairs and watch TV, and he said no, he'd rather read in the study. All the ladies came to see him when they went upstairs for their coats, and he talked to them."

"Did he talk?" asked Erica. "He hardly spoke a word to me at Christmas."

"He did. He showed Mrs. Nordlund his book on the Grand Canyon. He used to read it every night. I'd sit up with him when he couldn't sleep. I can still see him reading that book, the tears running down his face."

"Was he in pain?" asked Theo.

Erica's mother shook her head vigorously.

"No," she said. "He told me his grandfather used to cry too, for no reason. They called it sunstroke in those days. Look at the new shopping center that's gone up since you were here last."

Over a drive-in restaurant a giant chef balanced a hamburger on his upraised palm and turned slowly on a pedestal. Erica tried to recall what had stood there before. An open field? Stands of oak and hickory, holding the twilight like a cup?

"I used to tote a tray like that," Theo said quietly.

"You worked as a waiter?" asked her mother, surprised.

"Six months."

"And now Erica tells me you're working with birds for some research project."

Theo nodded. "Only till my teaching fellowship comes through."

"I didn't know you knew anything about birds," said John.

"I don't," said Theo. "I was only hired to feed them and clean their cages."

"What kind of birds do you work with?" asked John.

"All kinds," answered Theo, suddenly vague, as if he had very nearly divulged a great secret.

Her mother blew her nose.

"And after dinner I took him into the sunroom to watch TV, and then I took him upstairs to bed and got his nightshirt on, and he said, 'I have a bad pain,' and I said, 'Where?' And he pointed to his heart. And I said, 'I'm right here, Hal'—he always liked to know I was there—but his eyes were going all funny and I ran downstairs to call for the ambulance."

"I'd already called the police," said John. "They came right away."

"I had the downstairs looking good for bridge club but I'd thrown everything into the bedroom. And that's where everybody came. The police, the ambulance, the rescue squad. All the kids on the block were lined up across the street. The doctor gave Hal oxygen all the way to the hospital."

John turned off the highway, down Norfolk Drive.

"I shouldn't have had bridge club," said her mother, rolling up the window. "I shouldn't have gone to that college reunion with Minnie. It was my fiftieth. After that you don't get any more."

Far ahead of them, Erica could see the pear trees blossoming on both sides of the front walk like a wedding procession, spangling the grass with petals.

"He was ninety-two," said John. "He had a good and fruitful life."

"I never knew his age when I married him," her mother said. "I was twenty-six. He didn't look forty-five."

"The trees," said Theo. "They're beautiful."

"They carried him out on the stretcher under the pear blossoms," her mother continued. "I remember that shock of white hair sticking out of the blanket. You know, he had so much hair. Oh, those doctors, they all lie! There was a nice young intern who told me, 'His heart is getting stronger. He's going to make it. He'll be fine in a few days.' "

John drew up to the curb. Her mother opened the door for herself, still talking. "Kirsten and the kids are in Hal's and my room. Kirsten can sleep in my bed and Danny can sleep in Hal's, and I've put up a cot for Joan. I'll sleep on the couch. It's awful for me, looking from my bed over at Hal's empty one. The night he died I had to push the dresser between them."

"You should have moved into the guest room," said Erica.

Her mother shook her head.

"No. I knew if I didn't sleep there right away, I'd never sleep there again. Anatole can have the cot in Hal's study. When Kirsten comes back, she can help us pick out a suit for Hal. She went downtown to get some ice cream with Joan and Danny."

Standing in the upstairs hall, Erica looked for a place to unpack. The house seemed smaller every time she returned to it. The walls in the hall were done in diplomas; whenever her mother uncovered a new certificate she added it, and now the plaster was almost invisible. There were baptismal certificates and marriage certificates; certificates stating that long ago Erica and Kirsten had finished a summer program here, a Bible program there. There were Papa's chemistry awards and his Ph.D. diploma.

Her mother puffed upstairs with the laundry.

"Where's Theo?"

"Outside."

"He has his B.A., doesn't he? Why didn't he pick up his diploma?"

"He says he doesn't need a diploma."

"Of course he needs a diploma. Who will believe him if he doesn't have a diploma?"

. . . And an enormous certificate on shriveled parchment stating that somebody—the name could not be read—was Bearer of Dispatches to Denmark. There were Kirsten's certificate of graduation from the Powers modeling program, Aunt Minnie's Dale Carnegie award, Erica's mother's fiftieth-reunion certificate, an Arthur Murray diploma that came with the house; and then the wall turned a corner and there were the photographs, the family and the family and the family. . . . But her father's family was notably absent, having died long before the births and marriages celebrated in this house.

Erica could hear Theo counting to ten outside and Anatole and the other children calling him.

"Hide, hide!"

"Here I come—ready or not!"

Her sister's suitcase lay open on the floor. A dozen navy socks and Danny's eighth-grade yearbook spilled out of the corner. And whose wristwatch and bikini pants lay folded together on top of the clothes? Joan's? At ten years old? At ten, Erica was wearing undershirts suitable for either sex and she still couldn't tell time, having been sick the week it was taught in second grade. And then one day she was too old to admit she did not know how.

But what difference did it make? Her father owned no watch. Yet he was always punctual, home for dinner at five-thirty and back to the lab by eight. For half an hour he listened to Lowell Thomas and Drew Pearson; for half an hour he read the newspaper with such concentration that he didn't notice the time that Kirsten and Erica combed his hair and wound it in curlers. It took him ten minutes to straighten the curls. He never looked at a clock; it was as if these events measured themselves. Beyond the front door lay his work, of which Erica understood nothing until one April day her mother said:

"Your father has been given an important award. I want you to see the presentation and to hear his acceptance speech. I know you will not understand it, but I want you to hear him."

In the auditorium, her mother led Kirsten and Erica proudly past papa's students and colleagues to the front row. For Kirsten, always a lady, her mother had not brought so much as a single crayon. For Erica she had brought ten "Little Lulu" comic books.

The crowd applauded. Her father stood at the podium. The microphones leaned toward him, a field of cattails. And then he began to speak.

Erica put down her comic books. She tried to listen. If I listen hard enough, she thought, I will understand him.

Growing old, he almost never spoke to her. Age had eroded the rich soil of his learning and exposed the bedrock of his childhood. He dozed all day, interrupting his long naps for the enormous meals his wife prepared for him and for George Pereau's television trips to Africa.

Coming to visit on her father's ninety-second birthday, Erica was appalled at her mother's haggard face.

"Mother, you sleep in the guest room tonight. I'll sleep in your bed and keep an eye on Papa. I can listen for Anatole from there."

Her mother was tucking fresh pillows under Papa's head. The old man watched her wistfully, a child who did not want to sleep.

"Don't let him get out of bed. The bedrail won't stop him. Remember Marie Hetchen, who climbed over the rail and broke her hip? He sleeps pretty well till around two. Then he wants to get up. I'm the only person who can lift him. And he likes the light on, don't you, Hal?"

"Yes," came a voice, tiny as a cricket's.

"The purple lamp?" asked Erica, anxious to please him. "You like it on?"

In the circle of its twilight shone the bottles of lotions and pills and piles of clean handkerchiefs neatly arranged on the bureau. Her mother bent down to adjust the dials on the electric blanket and then motioned Erica to the door.

"I've got the two beds tied together. If he tries to get up, you'll be right there. My sunglasses are on the dresser if you need them."

"Sunglasses?" asked Erica.

"I can't sleep a wink with the light on," said her mother.

Erica climbed into her mother's bed and gazed attentively at the sharp features of her father's profile and the shock of white hair on the pillow so near her own. Under his freckled skin, veins lashed the bones of his hand together.

"I want to get up," he whispered.

"Oh, Papa, you can't get up. It's the middle of the night. Shall I read to you?"

She looked wildly around the room but could find nothing except two books he had written himself.

"Papa, let's sing. Remember how we used to sing in the car whenever we went on a trip?"

He gave her a puzzled look. She hesitated, uncertain of the words, and then started bravely:

"Cruising down the river on a Sunday afternoon
The birds above all sing of love . . ." His voice piped up, faint but exactly on pitch.

". . . waiting for the moon."

And then they both remembered the old accordion playing a sentimental tune and Erica saw the river very clearly; it was the Detroit River, which long ago they had crossed at a family reunion so large that a boat was hired for the occasion. It chugged slowly past the marinas of

Grosse Pointe, past the elegant houses of those whom Mother called the "captains of industry," and whenever a new house, always bigger than the last, glided into view, everyone rushed to the rail for a look. The distant relatives from both sides called each other "Cousin" to save confusion, and when the captain's voice over the loudspeaker announced a message for Mr. Widholm, men hurried to the captain's cabin from all quarters of the ship. Queer to find strangers with your face and your name.

"After the ball is over, after the break of dawn——"

"You did not sing that correctly," admonished her father. "You should have sung, '*After the break of day.*'"

She listened while he carried the song alone, and when he had finished the verse, neither of them spoke for a long time. At last he said, "I want to get up."

"Oh, Papa, let Mother sleep."

"I want to get up," the old man repeated firmly. "This bed's full of salt."

Erica bounded out of bed and met her mother in the hall.

"Mother, he won't stay in bed."

Her mother hurried into the room. "Hal, do you want some orange juice?"

He nodded happily. "I want to get up. I want to get off this boat."

"Oh, Hal, how could you possibly be on a boat? Look—there's your mother's picture right over your bed."

Cautiously the old man turned his head. "Why, so it is!" he said.

"He told me the bed had salt in it," whispered Erica.

Her mother laughed. "Now, Hal, how could there be salt in your bed? There isn't a body of salt water in the entire state of Michigan. Erica will sit with you while I run down to the kitchen and make your juice. Come. Lean on me."

She sat down on the edge of his bed, put his arm around her neck, and rose unsteadily, bearing his full weight on her shoulders.

"Grab the bedpost, Hal. Then the doorknob."

They lurched into the hall—her father in his blue pajamas, her mother in her long, purple nightgown—like a conspiracy of sleepwalkers, he clutching woodwork and doorknobs and she easing him past the diplomas and photographs into his study and letting him down into the overstuffed chair. Then she arranged the afghan around his knees. The tears ran slowly down his cheeks.

"Hal," shouted her mother, "Hal, here's Erica come to see you for your birthday! Is that something to cry about?"

"I don't want to die," he said, weeping softly.

"Oh, Hal, what makes you think of such a thing? You're not going to die. Who do you love?"

"You," he answered at once.

"You're my sweetheart," his wife told him, kissing his ear. "You know that? Erica, you can go to bed now. Everything's all right—I have some letters to write and some bills to pay. Look at this from the phone company. A fifty-dollar call to Hawaii! I never called Hawaii."

"Oh, Mother," said Erica, "I was going to let *you* sleep tonight."

Her mother shrugged. "A lot of people have it worse. What important business do I have? The one who gave us the time didn't charge us for it. Our real life comes later."

"We'll need a tie and a shirt and underwear, everything but shoes." Her mother's voice from the closet. "Kirsten, you pick a tie. You've got good taste. Erica, can you find some B.V.D.s?"

The crashing of hangers applauded the search. Erica kicked a Monopoly board and a pile of dirty sheets under the bed and opened the bureau drawers. Handkerchiefs. Razor. Shirts. Socks. All I could ever think of to give him was socks, she thought.

"A bolo tie," said Kirsten's voice, muffled. "He always wore bolo ties. I suppose that's too informal for the occasion."

"Oh, I hate to bury his bolo tie. Danny should have it, Kirsten. Indian jewelry has got so expensive," said her mother.

Clump, clump: John limping down the third-floor stairs. Kirsten stuck her head out of the closet. Her face was flushed, but her blond hair was immaculately curled and combed under a headband.

"Erica, tell John to see what the kids are doing."

"Danny's making gunpowder," John called back. "For his invention."

"What invention?" called Erica.

Her mother and her sister emerged from the closet looking like salesmen, their arms draped with trousers.

"His rocket," said John. "Go see for yourselves."

"Erica," said Kirsten, "run down and tell Theo to watch them."

"He *is* watching them," said John.

Erica dropped the B.V.D.s and ran across the hall to the bathroom window. The wisteria hung over the broad roof but the wind blew her a glimpse of three children in the yard below, clambering over a huge box. Danny, blond and large for twelve, was lifting Anatole into it. Joan was clapping her hands, her red hair shaking like fire.

"What are those droopy things on the side?" asked Erica.

"Wings," muttered John. "Theo brought him that box of feathers, and now Danny figures he's ready to fly. He got the idea from a man on television who jumped out of a window in a glider. Killed himself."

"My God," said Erica.

"He's rigged them up to your dad's foot vibrator," said John gloomily. "These kids, they think nothing can hurt them. They think they're immortal."

But when she reached the backyard and they all stopped playing and stared at her, Erica could not remember how she had meant to scold them.

"Theo," she said. "Mother doesn't want anyone making gunpowder."

"Just what I told Danny myself," Theo said. "Didn't I? A rocket is a very second-rate mode of travel. Come on, kids—let's play!" he shouted.

Just as if this were a family reunion instead of a funeral, thought Erica. Then she heard her name called and she ran into the house. Her mother was standing on the back porch with Hal's clothes lying over her arm.

"Does this suit look okay to you? Hal paid two hundred dollars for it in the days when you could get a good suit for fifty. He picked the material himself."

Erica remembered her father bending over the little swatches of cloth and asking them all did they like the red stripe on gray? When the suit arrived six months later, the stripes looked enormous and the shoulders sagged and he could have hidden a machine gun in the sleeves. But he continued to order his suits from the tailor and his shoes from a shoemaker in England until he walked so little, he ceased to wear things out.

"There's a moth hole in the back," her mother said, her mouth close to Erica's ear, "but it won't show. Does Theo have a good suit? We need one more pallbearer."

"I thought Hank Anderson was going to be the sixth pallbearer."

"Hank? Why, he can't even lift a telephone book since his hernia operation."

"Mother," called Kirsten's voice, "are you ready?"

Their mother wiped her eyes with the back of her hand. "Can Theo watch the kids while we pick out the casket? John is soaking his foot by the TV."

"I'll stay," Erica said quickly.

"No. We need you," said her mother.

When they arrived at the funeral home a thin rain was falling. The tiny green blossoms from the maple trees crunched underfoot and gave off a heavy sweetness. Her mother, cradling the clothes, opened the door and motioned first Erica and then Kirsten inside.

"I've done this twice before—once for my mother and once for my father," she announced proudly. "When my father died, all the rooms were filled. We nearly didn't get one. But I'm glad that Hal's funeral will be in the church."

They entered the vestibule. A dull light rose from the bronze bowls of the floor lamps that lined the corridor, peculiar trees of an underground kingdom. As they started upstairs a large, silver-haired man sneaked up behind them.

"Mrs. Widholm? I'm Mr. Metzger," he said, pushing his horn-rimmed glasses up the bridge of his nose. "And you've come about the casket. Right upstairs. Just make yourselves at home. My office is across the hall if you need me."

"Thank you," said Kirsten, and they all three reached the landing and stepped over the threshold into the fluorescent noon of the display room. The windows were papered over with caged birds, so steeped in stillness they seemed part of some fabulous household under enchantment.

Her mother walked down the first aisle, fingering the caskets that stood open-mouthed like gigantic shells, price tags and guarantees lying inside like pearls.

"The wood is nice," her mother said, "but I don't like green ruching, do you? It's too fancy."

Erica touched the wooden lid, marveling at the workmanship. The thing could as well go into a living room as into the ground.

"Here's a rosewood one," Kirsten said. "It looks like Grandma's old piano."

"Maroon velvet," her mother said. "That's nice. It's the color of the bathrobe I gave Hal before we were married."

They all bent down to examine the price.

"Two thousand dollars," Kirsten said.

For several moments no one spoke.

"The first one is fifteen hundred," Kirsten said.

"Let's think about it," said her mother, "while we pick out the vault."

"The vault?" repeated Erica.

She followed her mother to a table set with three

17

boxes, the first painted bronze, the second silver, the third gold, and each of them cut away to show the structure, like a classroom model of the pyramids.

"What's the difference between them?" asked Kirsten.

Mr. Metzger appeared as if summoned by their ignorance. In the bright light his lips looked heavy, his hands huge; two ruby rings ignited his knuckles.

"The vaults are lined with asphalt or plastic." He touched first the silver model and then the gold. "Now, if it was me, I'd prefer the plastic. I've seen the tests. It's specially sealed."

"But are they waterproof?" asked her mother anxiously. "I'd hate to think of Hal floating around down there."

"The plastic ones are guaranteed. Guaranteed. The asphalt . . . well"—he opened his palm toward Kirsten—"you can't be absolutely sure. The bronze-plated model is ordinary steel. It runs about a hundred dollars less."

"We'll take the plastic one," her mother said. "Will it look just like the model?"

"We paint them to match the casket. Have you found one you like?"

"That wooden one over by the wall," Kirsten said.

Mr. Metzger strolled over to it and studied it gravely.

"Now, if it was me, I think the interior is a little too fussy for a man. The rosewood one behind it has a very simple interior. Very masculine, I think."

"Why, my goodness," said her mother, as if caught in an embarrassing mistake. "I guess we'd better take *it*."

They followed Mr. Metzger into his office and sat in three chairs drawn into an intimate arc around his desk. Her mother laid the clothes on the papers and pads that littered the desk. Mr. Metzger slid into place like the last piece in a simple puzzle. Erica watched his hands as they glittered among documents.

"This is the death certificate. The doctor will fill it in. The first one costs two dollars. There's a fifty-cent charge for the others."

Her mother and Kirsten touched it, bewildered.

"You should have some for all legal purposes. It's not the expense—it's the inconvenience of not having one when you need it."

"I'll have twenty-five," her mother said.

Mr. Metzger rubbed his eyes. "Well, that's quite a lot of them," he said.

"How about ten?" suggested Kirsten.

Mr. Metzger wrote "10" on his pad.

"And then there's the minister," he said.

"How much does he usually get?" asked her mother.

"From fifteen to fifty dollars."

"I'll give him fifty," her mother said.

Mr. Metzger wrote "50."

"And the organist. Fifteen or ten," he said.

"Fifteen," said her mother.

"And the flowers," he said. "A blanket of roses runs fifty-two dollars. Carnations run a bit cheaper."

"Roses," said her mother. "They're more sentimental."

"For two dollars more you can have a ribbon lettered with 'Husband' or 'Father.'"

"I'll have both," her mother said, "so people will know they're from the family."

"For fifteen you can also get half a dozen sweetheart roses and a small white satin pillow lettered with 'Grandfather' in gold script."

"We'll take one," said her mother

He wrote "15" and then he reached into a drawer and pulled out a folder and a package of vellum cards.

"The plaque you can pick out later. I understand you have your lots on Sunrise Hill. They don't allow headstones there. Spoils the landscaping, they say."

"No headstones?" said Kirsten.

"Just bronze plaques. Mrs. Widholm, was your husband a Mason?"

"A Mason?" her mother said.

"Or an Elk? You can have any emblem you want put on the plaque. Any emblem at all. And if you pick out a plaque for yourself at this time, we can match the bronze and give you a cheaper rate."

Mr. Metzger fanned the vellum cards across his desk.

"Some people like to have these by the register for visitors to take. Inside you'll find the Twenty-third Psalm embossed in gold. You get a hundred for twenty dollars."

"Kirsten, you'd like these, wouldn't you? I'll take a hundred," said her mother.

"We'll send a car for you at ten tomorrow morning," Mr. Metzger promised. "The First Congregational Church, isn't it? Oh, one more thing. Would you like the casket open or closed?"

"Open," Kirsten said. "I haven't seen Papa for a whole year. I want to say goodbye."

"Here comes Minnie," said Danny, standing at the front door. "Is it time to eat?"

Erica and Kirsten crowded behind the children and

they all pressed their faces against the panes. A short, sprightly woman in slacks and a tweed coat was ransacking the trunk of a Volkswagen parked in the driveway.

"Aunt Minnie's hair—it's so white," Kirsten said.

And her mother, who had trained herself to hear through walls, called out from the kitchen, "She's let it go natural. But she's got a wig for the funeral. Wait till you see her in it—she looks just like she always did. At the reunion everybody knew we were sisters."

"Look at her big suitcase," Joan said. "Is she moving in?"

"No, that's her vitamins," said Erica's mother, coming into the hall.

Minnie let the door slam behind her and dropped her suitcase in the hall. The mirror over the telephone table rattled.

"I *knew* I'd be coming here!" Minnie announced. "I got myself weighed at Woolworth's, and the card said I'd be taking a trip very soon."

"It's your ESP," Erica's mother said, taking Minnie's coat and hanging it on the rack. "Dinner's on the table. Come and eat."

They trooped into the dining room and everything around them tinkled—the cups and plates stacked unevenly in the china cabinet, the silver set out on the sideboard as if for a consecration.

John had already found his usual place and was unscrewing the lid from a bottle of pickled cherries.

"I can't take Hal's chair," her mother said. "I just can't."

Everyone looked at the empty chair. Of all the dining-

room chairs, her father's alone had survived two genera-
tions of children; it was still upholstered in its original
horsehair.

"Let me take it," said Theo. "Pass me your plates."

They seated themselves while her mother brought in
the salad.

"Anyone want one of my pickled cherries?" John
asked. "I marinated them myself."

Silence.

"Or some dandelion wine? No?"

He poured himself a glass.

"I'll have some wine," Theo said.

John hobbled over to the china cabinet and rummaged
among the cups for a goblet.

"You and I are the only hard drinkers around here,
aren't we, young man?" John said.

"Mother, stop waiting on us," Erica pleaded, following her into the kitchen. "Sit down."

Her mother was looking into the open refrigerator and
wiping her eyes with a dish towel.

"Look at those custards I made for Hal. Erica, you
always loved custard. I made them the night Hal went to the
hospital and I forgot to turn the oven off, but they don't
look too bad."

"I'll taste one," Erica said, taking a spoon from the
drawer. She touched the spoon to her lips. She thought of
her father's mouth. She put down the spoon.

In the dark living room after dinner the movie projector
clattered to a halt, and the image on the screen vanished.
The children, sprawled on the floor, sat up. Erica cocked

her head and listened for Theo, hoping he had not gone to bed.

She felt across the end tables for the lamp. Click. Click. Nothing happened.

"You've got to jiggle it," her mother said.

"Mother, where's John?" asked Kirsten, who hated the absence of anyone at a family gathering.

"Upstairs, soaking his foot."

"I'm ready," said Danny, turning on the projector.

Nudging close to Erica on the sofa, Minnie put on her glasses.

The projector hummed. A throng of shades came into focus.

"It's my wedding!" Kirsten cried.

"Why, there's Mrs. Corkin," her mother said, genuinely pleased. "She died last year. How nice to see her again. And there's my mother!"

"And there's Jack Teal. And Harold Bitterjohn," said Kirsten. "Funny how many of Papa's students are dead now, isn't it?"

Grandma Schautz was shaking hands with Reverend Lemon; both of them were dead now. It seemed to Erica she was watching a pageant in which the actors wore a makeup that erased time. Her grandfather stood rigid and smiling under the pear blossoms.

Joan reached out and touched Erica's knee.

"Where are *your* wedding pictures?"

"In my head," said Erica. "We eloped."

"I hope you had a ceremony," said Minnie.

"I want a cartoon," said Anatole.

"Look!" said Kirsten sharply. "There's Papa!"

Erica caught her breath. For there before them stood

her father, walking through the rock garden, on the sunny side of the house, which the weeds had long since over-taken. Young, dark-haired, slim in his white flannel suit, he smiled at them engagingly.

"Is that the old grandpa who died?" asked Anatole. "Did he get new again?"

All the next morning the sound of bath water running up-stairs drowned out the cries of the children playing by the TV. It was Theo who first noticed they were gone.

"Wouldn't you know they'd disappear," said Kirsten, peering out the front door. "With the car coming in half an hour, wouldn't you know!"

"We'll fan out," said Minnie. "I'll check the basement. They were looking at the old Christmas decorations this morning."

"I'll check upstairs," Erica said. "Theo, you check the yard."

She glanced perfunctorily into the guest room, the study, the bathroom. The door to her mother and father's bedroom was closed. She knocked gently and then turned the knob. The door did not open, but as if by some con-fusion of cause and effect, the telephone rang.

Erica rattled the door. The phone rang again. She raced into the study and snatched the receiver off the hook. "Hello?"

"This is Mrs. Hanson, across the street. I see the chil-dren are out on your roof. I hate to butt in, but I thought you should know."

Though she flew downstairs, Erica was the last person to reach the yard. A little crowd of neighbors had joined

Kirsten and Minnie and Theo and her mother. The children were dancing at the edge of the roof that slanted over the sun porch. Anatole fanned the air with his arms; a giant patchwork of feathers, scarfed to his wrists, rippled green and scarlet and blue.

"My turn," yelled Joan. "My turn to fly."

"Don't jump!" called Kirsten. "John's bringing the ladder."

A clatter silenced them all. The top of the ladder leaned itself on the opposite edge of the roof. As John's head appeared over the eaves Joan shouted, "Fly, Anatole! Here they come!"

Anatole gave a loud yell, and flapping his useless wings, he sailed off the roof into the evergreens below.

"Not a scratch on any of them," said her mother. "Not a scratch."

The weasel-faced young man driving the limousine shook his head.

"Kids have nine lives," he observed sagely.

Erica felt faint, as if locked in a capsule. A warm breeze rocked the heads of the trees outside.

"Where's John?" said Anatole.

"He never goes to funerals any more," her mother answered.

The car turned onto Washington Avenue and Erica sat up, alert. Her father had always taken this route when he drove Kirsten and her to school, past the Presbyterian church, past the turreted houses on Mansion Street and the gardens gone to ruin around them.

"I don't suppose you saw the write-up about my husband in the paper?" her mother asked the driver. "All the children's names were in it."

"I missed it," said the driver tragically.

And then, after a silence, he said, "The corner of Market and State streets, isn't it? I'll let you off at the front entrance."

The car drew up to the curb and the driver scurried to let them out. They huddled awkwardly in their dark clothes in the middle of the sidewalk while shoppers eddied around them. The doors of the church stood open. Students lounged in the park across the street, and over the drugstore a rock band wailed. It was a bright, sunny day. Erica looked nervously at the children, washed and combed and sweating.

"I guess you kids haven't seen a dead person before, have you?" Kirsten said.

"I have," said Danny. "On TV."

"That doesn't count," said Joan.

"Come on," Erica urged her mother. "Let's go in."

As they entered the church even the children grew quiet. From the vestibule Erica could see the coffin, heaped with red roses.

"We're early," said Kirsten. "Nobody's here."

Erica took Theo's arm, and they moved in procession down the aisle.

"Why, look—over by the window," her mother whispered. "There's Frank Pederson."

They all looked. A slim, gray-haired man was just sitting down.

"Who is it?" asked Minnie.

"Frank Pederson. He's not anybody important, but he

always loved Hal. He only took one course with him," she chattered nervously.

They arrived at the steps of the altar where Erica had knelt, angel-winged, in Christmas pageants. She dropped Theo's arm and looked into the casket, past the white satin pillow with its gilt inscription, "From the Grandchildren," pinned to the lining of the lid. She looked at her father's face, her face close to his face, both astonished.

"It's Grandpa, all right," whispered Joan, "but he looks like a dummy."

"I want to touch him," said Erica's mother. "I'd never forgive myself if I didn't touch him."

Her hand caressed his cheek. In the light of the stained glass her silver wedding band winked. An old notebook ring, Erica always called it after the engraved flowers had worn off. Her mother had let her wear it sometimes for a treat.

Erica reached out and touched her father's forehead. The makeup on his skin had rubbed into his hair. Over her shoulder she saw the guests arriving. The music pumped out from an invisible place behind the pulpit, and a large, bald man in black robes stood up at the lectern and snapped on the light.

Her mother motioned toward him. "That's Reverend Hurd," she said.

"Theo, stay with me," said Erica, but Mr. Metzger stepped between them.

"Pallbearers on the right, family on the left. The front row."

Sitting next to her mother, Erica rested her chin on her son's head and fixed her eyes on her father's profile, the sharp nose and the high forehead jutting above the satin lining.

" 'In my father's house are many mansions; if it were not so, I would have told you,' " the minister intoned.

Erica listened. Yes, there was enough room in her father's house, always enough for whoever wanted to sleep there.

Reverend Hurd closed his Bible.

"Is that all?" whispered Anatole.

"Now he says the Meditation," Erica whispered back.

In the world of clocks, the carillon was chiming the half hour.

" 'We live with death, and die not in a moment. But the long habit of living indisposeth us for dying. We cannot hope to live so long as our names, as some have done in their persons. Our fathers find their graves in our short memories.' "

The pages sighed, fluttered, and turned. Her mother was staring stonily ahead of her.

" 'The greater part must be content to be as though they had not been, to be found in the Register of God, not in the record of man. The night of time far surpasseth the day, and who knows when was the equinox? There is nothing strictly immortal, but immortality.' "

The voice rose on all sides of her. Erica felt people leaning forward to hear him.

" 'But all this is nothing in the metaphysics of true belief. To live indeed is to be again ourselves, ready to be anything, in the ecstasy of being ever.' "

———————

From the car they observed the mourners leaving the church, walking quickly past them.

"There's Mrs. Bergman," exclaimed her mother, and waved. "And Mr. Nutt and Mrs. Hanson!"

She waved again. They all waved except Theo.

"Nobody notices us," Minnie said.

"Is that Frank Pernell? Let's call to him," said Kirsten.

Ahead of them, a policeman gunned his motorcycle and the hearse slowly pulled out into traffic.

"Time to go," Theo said.

The family passed the park. Students on the curb waiting to cross glanced at them with mild interest. An old man in a slouch hat grimaced impatiently.

"In the old days," said Minnie, "men would have taken off their hats when they saw a hearse."

Like actors in a theater of silence, the family glided through the busy streets, past the farmers' market and the trading-stamp redemption center, past the railroad station, past the cement works, past the broken houses and dirt yards of the poor. A black man leaning on a shovel gazed at them.

This was the edge. of town; now they drove high into the green hills. The dogwood flared like white fires built all through the woods, their trunks so thin they seemed a shower of petals caught in the act of falling. Forsythia and honeysuckle burst forth on both sides of the road, and far off the black willows were marching across the field, marking the path of the river.

"When I die," said Theo, "throw my ashes in a mountain stream."

"I'd like an angel on my grave," said Erica. "I don't

care what happens to me, but I want to be all in one place."

Suddenly Danny began to sob. Kirsten folded his head against her shoulder.

"Don't cry," she whispered. "Grandpa lived a good life. A good life. And he's gone to heaven. I know he has."

As the black car drove out of sight her mother gave a little gasp.

"I forgot to buy anything to drink! People will be stopping by." She mashed five dollars into Erica's palm. "Theo, run out and get a bottle of something fancy."

"You can take my Volkswagen," Minnie said.

"Erica," her mother whispered, "go with him and make sure he doesn't speed."

"We'll get the best," said Theo. "You can count on me."

They drove down the quiet street into the green cathedral of the elms, turned onto Washington Avenue, and passed the drugstore and the bookshop.

"Let's try Paccino's," said Theo. "It's the closest."

Though she did not drink, Erica loved to study the bottles: the golden fish on the bottles of Moselle, and the blue nuns, the red barons, the kings bearing grapes and wands on the bottles of Liebfraumilch. The mysterious city, yellow as an old map, on the squat green flasks of Mateus rosé.

"Where's your best sherry?" asked Theo.

The man eyed him up and down.

"The imported sherries are on your left. A fifth of Harvey's Bristol Cream sells for about eleven dollars. It's the best in the world."

"We'll take a gallon," said Theo.

"Did you say a gallon?" the man said.

"A gallon," repeated Theo. "Didn't you say it's the best in the world?"

As Erica laid her mother's five on the counter, she saw that Theo was emptying his wallet. The senselessness of it filled her with sudden anger.

"Theo," she exclaimed, "that money is all we brought with us. How will we get home?"

But the salesman was already wrapping the sherry, medallioned with gold lions, elegant as a reliquary.

Animals Running on a Windy Crown

I

At morning prayer on Whitsunday, Father Martin is taken ill. See how his hands shake and his old legs buckle under him. Peter Beasley, the deacon, has to help him out of the sanctuary. For six weeks his name is read at intercessions, and prayers are murmured for his speedy recovery. But there comes a day when the congregation hears the visiting priest intone Father Martin's name among the names of the departed; may God's light shine upon them forever. Dozens of hands make the sign of the cross. Outside, the forsythia bushes are dropping their yellow bells on the wet sidewalk, and the bare elms stand misted with the promise of leaves.

Two months later, the vestry submits a list of suitable candidates for the new rector of St. Joseph's to the bishop, who rejects them all and after a long delay sends a young man from a parish in Syracuse. He has wheat-colored hair, a red beard, and remarkably small hands. When he blesses the elements, his hands seem wax, his fingers tapers. He is unmarried, which many consider regrettable. Father Martin had a jolly wife and three daughters who took turns minding the nursery during the services.

The new rector, Father Hayden, is installed with great pomp, but not until All Souls' Day is he persuaded to move from the boardinghouse, where he has rented two furnished rooms, into the rectory, where he has the care of twenty. Mrs. Stout, who cleaned for Father Martin and Father Legg before him, complains she can find nothing to do. Father Hayden's furniture fills half the living room and one bedroom—he has chosen for himself the cook's room off the kitchen—and he shows no inclination to buy any more. Nor does he order curtains for the windows. He pulls the shades in the evening and he raises them in the morning.

If it is Saturday morning, you can look into the rectory kitchen and see him baking bread, which he will distribute tomorrow at the ten o'clock service. If it is afternoon, you will find him at his desk in the parish house, answering letters and drinking great quantities of tea, a special blend of hyssop, skullcap, lemon grass, and the flower that is called life everlasting. All day long he keeps a pot of water boiling on the stove of the parish house kitchen, as one might maintain an eternal flame on the grave of a hero. During his first two weeks in residence, he has already burned the bottoms out of two teakettles and quietly replaced them.

At any time of the day you can hear him singing. Even the choir mistress says his singing could charm the devil and convert a dog. Hear him this morning, the first Sunday in

Advent, standing behind the holy table, hands lifted like white birds:

The Lord be with you.

And the people answer him:

And also with you.

A small, dark-haired man wearing a windbreaker and a fur cap and carrying a duffel bag steps into the vestibule of the church. He removes his cap, stands swaying from side to side, and glances about him as if uncertain how he arrived here. He allows the usher to show him to the back pew, but he lets the mimeographed service sheet slide to the floor, and he sits, open-mouthed, kneading his cap, and watches row after row of men and women move forward and kneel at the communion rail.

When the last woman has returned to her seat and the deacon is wiping out the chalice, the little man walks carefully down the center aisle as if he were stepping around an arrangement of traps that he alone can see. Now he stands at the rail and he waits.

Father Hayden glances up from the prayer book, which lies open to the postcommunion blessing. Their eyes meet. The little man whispers without ceasing.

"Jesus, Jesus, Jesus."

The deacon nods at the head usher, who takes the stranger gently by the arm and draws him into Father Hayden's office.

And after the service, it is there Father Hayden finds him, warming himself by the empty fireplace, still kneading the cap in his hand. Catching sight of the rector in the doorway, Peter Beasley, still vested, springs forward.

"I offered him the bread and wine you had reserved for the sick—it was all we had left—but he didn't want any."

The man nods and crooks his thumb and index finger to shape a wafer. Seen at close range, everything about him seems exaggerated, his pointed chin, the comic black tufts of his eyebrows, his sharp nose, and the size of the duffel bag which rises over his shoulder as he gestures toward the pictures of Jesus on the Christmas cards ranged along the bookshelf behind the rector's desk.

"Jesus, Jesus," he repeats tonelessly.

Father Hayden reaches for the nearest card and hands it to him, but the man shakes his head no, and motions to show that he wants a smaller picture.

"Some people don't know when they're well off," snorts the deacon.

"Perhaps he's Roman Catholic," muses Father Hayden. "All that business about not wanting the bread and the wine. If I could find him one of those little prayer cards—you know, the kind they give to the children at Saint Mary's—" And seeing how easy it is to make this man happy, Father Hayden takes his arm. "Is it a prayer card you want? Come back later. I'll try to find you one."

Now see him that evening, when a full moon silvers the cloister that joins the back of the rectory to the parish house and the church. Frost sparkles on the ground, and the grass around the broken sundial lies long and sparse like an old woman's hair. He goes into his bedroom and has just started to remove his collar when he hears a knock at the front door. Assuming it's the sexton stopping to remind him of the vestry meeting—though later it strikes him that the sexton, coming from the church, would have knocked at the back door—he shouts.

"I'm coming!"

He pauses in the kitchen to snap on the vestibule light. Though he feels sure he locked all the doors a few minutes earlier, he enters the hall and sees standing before him the small dark-haired man, wearing the collar of his windbreaker straight up under his chin, like a priest's. The filigree shade on the overhead lamp spatters him with a shining skin of light as he closes the door behind him. He is about to speak when he drops the duffel bag, and a dozen miniature boxes of breakfast cereal tumble out. Involuntarily Father Hayden kneels down to gather them up but recoils from the little man's hands, snatching this way and that as if they were picking pockets.

Tomorrow, he reminds himself. I'll stop by Saint Mary's tomorrow.

Seeing his visitor is about to take off his coat, Father Hayden hastily opens the door for him.

"Where do you live?" he asks gently.

The man only shakes his head.

"Let me drive you to the Salvation Army. You can stay there for two nights, and perhaps by then something will turn up for you."

They walk briskly across the front yard to the garage, and Father Hayden helps the old man into the red Volkswagen which gleams in the light from the street. Unaccustomed to owning a car, he backs out with great caution into Mansion Street. They pass the churchyard where angels and obelisks poke through the grass like the ruined monuments of a sunken city.

"Jesus, Jesus," whispers the little man dreamily.

Father Hayden busies himself cracking open the vent, and he hears, very clearly, the long bleat of a tugboat on the Hudson a mile away.

He turns into Main Street, brilliantly lit, empty of people. A huge Christmas tree shines in front of the public library, its gumdrop-colored lights winking randomly.

He passes under the greenery stretched across the intersection of Main and Market.

He passes the big department stores whose windows show various winter tableaux, then he passes the used furniture store, and he comes at last to a small door marked with a red shield. Paper bells hang in the windows to the right and left of it.

Father Hayden stops, but the little man does not move. Frightened, the priest touches him and, seeing him stir, he reaches across and opens the door. Slowly the man climbs out. He looks around him for a moment like a fox nosing the wind, then he crumples to his knees and touches his forehead to the pavement.

"Here," exclaims Father Hayden, springing out to help him, "stand up now. I'll ring the bell."

But the little man shakes his head no and bursts out laughing. The noise dies and renews itself again and again, filling the empty street like a parade. Masks of amazement peer from behind the paper bells. The man laughs and pulls out a handkerchief and flourishes it, as if preparing for some tremendous feat of conjuring. Father Hayden again reaches for the doorbell but the little man pushes him back, still laughing, still waving the handkerchief.

"Goodbye! Goodbye! Goodbye!"

"Good night," says Father Hayden, stiffly. The handkerchief flutters in the rearview mirror like a flag of truce all the way down Main Street, and only by turning onto Mansion Street can he push it out of his sight.

When he has parked his car in the garage, Father Hayden hurries up the steps of the parish house, reminding himself that he will very soon have a railing installed here for the old people to use in icy weather. But can he order the railing before he orders the repairs on the roof? So many people have complained about the unsightliness of the great crocks which the sexton puts in the chancel to catch the water on rainy Sundays.

Father Hayden hangs his coat on the rack in the dark corridor and steps into the comfortable warmth of his office. Peter Beasley, the deacon, is fanning the logs in the fireplace, which show no flames but send forth a pungent smoke and much crackling. He is a stocky man with a rosy, cherubic face and dark curly hair, and as he bends over the logs the rector notices with some surprise a purple flowered patch on the seat of his trousers, where the seams meet.

Tom Croft, the Sunday school superintendent, has drawn a folding chair opposite the door, so that he can watch for Father Hayden's coming, and now he stands up respectfully. He is as trim as the deacon is robust. He lives alone in a room on Mansion Street. The deacon lives in the suburbs and has a wife as large and good-natured as himself, and five children.

"Well, let's get down to business," says Tom Croft, and he draws up the swivel chair for Father Hayden.

A long silence follows, as they all watch the fireplace hopefully. Father Hayden says, "What did you do last year at the Christmas Eve service?"

The deacon takes a large loose-leaf notebook from the coffee table and begins leafing through it, pausing to study one of the mimeographed programs collected there.

"We opened with a festival of lessons and carols. We omitted the confession of sin. And there was an anthem instead of a sermon. Ah, the fire's started."

They watch the red tongues leap up from the logs, and move their chairs closer. Father Hayden remembers, with a pang of guilt, the good Samaritan.

"Do you remember how Father Martin hated to give sermons?" says the deacon. "Remember how he always wanted a sermon hymn?"

"That's against the new council," says Tom Croft.

"I've already started writing my sermon," Father Hayden assures them.

Tom Croft's face brightens.

"And what's the topic to be?"

"The fragility of the Word in the modern world," answers Father Hayden. Seeing that the deacon is staring intently at the chandelier, he glances at it too, but sees nothing amiss.

"What I'd like," says the deacon, "is something really high church. Incense, to start with."

Silence.

"No incense," says Tom Croft. "Prudence Barry doesn't like it."

"Oh, but her sister does," says the deacon, "so they cancel each other out. Remember how Father Clair loved to swing the censer at St. Margaret's? If that chain had broken, it would have hit the back choir. 'We never use the bought stuff,' he told me. 'It's too sweet. We always mix our own.' "

"You can't use incense without a reason," says Tom Croft.

"I fear we must abandon the incense," says Father Hayden firmly. "Don't forget the Bishop has ordered us to use the new rites printed in the green book, not the old rites in the Book of Common Prayer."

The deacon looks round with an injured smile.

"Well, I should hate to see the old rites dropped entirely," he says. "Why, people have nothing in common any more except the doxology."

"The old rites are passing," says Tom Croft quietly. "No one knows what they mean anymore. They've taken out all the saints' days and put them on weekdays, and given Sunday the prominence."

"A pity, a pity," sighs the deacon. "But I'll bet if I went back to the home church in North Carolina I could still find ladies who curtsied at the name of Jesus. In those days, you crossed yourself to show you were a Christian. My aunt used to cross herself as she passed the church, whenever the priest was raising the host inside."

Father Hayden sits up straighter in his chair; he feels the evening's purpose slipping away from them.

"Peter, read us the lesson for the Christmas service. We'll start from there."

"Where's the green book?" asks the deacon.

"Isn't it on the table? Ah, then it's been borrowed."

"Stolen," says Tom Croft, crisply.

The deacon picks up the Book of Common Prayer and opens it at the crimson ribbon. Then he puts it down.

"Excuse me," he says, reaching for the Bible on Father Hayden's desk. "The lesson is from Titus two. Oh, you've got a marker in it." And he reads very slowly.

"The grace of God that bringeth salvation hath appeared to all men—"

A passing ambulance drowns his voice but his lips continue to move, as if someone has turned off the sound which returns as suddenly as it has gone.

"—and our Savior Jesus Christ who gave himself for us, that he might redeem us from all iniquity and purify unto himself a peculiar people—"

"Peculiar!" repeats Tom Croft.

The deacon hesitates.

"Do you want me to read the Gospel?"

"Never mind," says Father Hayden, "we all know the Gospel."

"But shall we have a Gospel procession?" persists the deacon. "I have to schedule the acolytes well in advance. We can use the six gold candles by the font. And I hope we'll have our crêche again, for the children."

"God willing the dead bishop doesn't knock it down," adds Tom Croft.

Father Hayden starts.

"I beg your pardon?"

"Bishop Legg," explains Tom Croft. "When he was rector, he hated anything to do with Christmas legends. And now every time we set up the crêche, he knocks it down. There's not a breath of wind in the sanctuary, yet every morning, right on through Epiphany, the sexton finds the figures scattered on the floor."

"How curious," exclaims Father Hayden.

"It was the wise men that offended the bishop," continued Tom Croft. "He loved to remind us that the three wise men didn't come to the stable at all. They stopped at a house. It took them two years to reach Bethlehem."

"They didn't have jobs," adds the deacon. "Or vacations."

A knock at the door startles them all. The sexton sticks his head into the room.

"Father, there are no more garbage bags. And there's an awful lot of garbage."

"Well, put it out in the cans, then," says Father Hayden, slightly annoyed. To his own surprise, he stands up to signify that the meeting is closed.

The clock strikes eleven. Closing the door behind him he goes into his bedroom, takes off his collar, sits down on the bed, and pulls out a letter from his mother. He opens it very carefully. He has carried it all afternoon, waiting for the leisure to read it. She wishes him good holiday from his four sisters in Yarmouth and his cousins in Halifax. The weather is nippy, the grandchildren are well, thank God. Her letters sound very formal, now that her sight is bad and she has to dictate them to someone else.

His mother has never visited the States, and now she is too blind to travel. But when she was younger, what fine walks they took together along the marshes at low tide. The rushes shone bright green at their feet, lupine and morning glories lit the hill at their backs. And when the fog burned off, they arrived at the mud flats, where kelp and gull feathers lay scattered on the sand. He filled his pockets with little gray whelks and watched for porpoises on the horizon.

Easter morning before sunrise his mother fetched her best carafe and walked far out on the flats to fill it with water, which she believed was always holy at that hour and powerful against measles, gout, falling hair, and general misfortune. By the end of the year, her holy water looked so muddy that Papa said it would sooner give the gout than cure it, and he already had more patients than he could handle. His patients often invited him to dinner, and he always consented, too kindhearted to refuse though he had a horror of gaining weight. Returning home, he would retire to the bathroom and tickle his throat with a feather. The children, lying awake in their beds, heard gagging, then silence, then singing as he climbed the stairs to kiss them goodnight.

> Here's to the thistle,
> The bonny Scotch thistle,
> The home of the free,
> The badge of my country,
> The thistle of Scotland
> Is aye dear to me.

Papa never went to church; Mama went all the time, to the communion service on Sunday morning and morning prayer at midweek. Sunday morning she called out from the kitchen, "Who's coming with me?" The girls slouched over their toast in silence. "Heathens!" she shouted. "All of you except James!"

Father Hayden, even as a child, liked to go to church. He especially liked the churchyard, for many of the graves had small porcelain photographs fixed to their markers. The widow of an admiral, hero of many battles in World War I, had all her husband's medals engraved and enameled in color on his tombstone. He liked to run his fingers over those bright stars and crosses.

Inside the church, the boy did not go to Sunday school but stayed with his mother through the regular service. God the Father, wearing a beehive on his head, glittered in the window over the high altar (Mama called it a table); sometimes the shadows of birds darted over the glass as if God were dreaming them. The ring of candles above the communion rail was lowered and raised for special occasions. Each Sunday in Advent, the curate added another candle. Once, during the reading of the Gospel, a candle hurtled down from the ring like a falling star. The deacon sprang forward and stamped it out, fixing his eyes on the three remaining candles throughout the rest of the service. But old Father Jackson did not miss a syllable of his text.

"And that's because there's a special devil who picks up the words we drop in our prayers," his mother warned him afterward. "His name is Titivillius, and he keeps all our lost words in a big bag. He has a bag for each one of us, and when that bag is full—watch out!"

But she never writes of this in her letters, only of the weather and births and marriages. Father Hayden folds the letter and puts it on the table by his bed. When he has finished his prayers, he undresses and lies down, and as soon as darkness settles on his eyes he sees clearly in his mind a little man in a windbreaker shuffling through a pack of cards. But now he does not look particularly lunatic, only unhappy, and Father Hayden watches his features shift like oil on water into the features of his schoolmaster, Duffey Kidd, a large, kindly man who in his spare time built a replica of Westminster Abbey out of matchsticks. He never married; he wanted to be a priest but had no money for divinity school. He earned, instead, the title of licensed chalice bearer, which allowed him to serve at communion and to walk in the litany processions. See him coming into the classroom on cold mornings, biting the fingers of his gloves, each in turn, to loosen them, then pulling till the gloves came off in his mouth, like a dog worrying a mitten. Oh, the steam on the windows, the red-hot scolding of the tiny stove which warmed only those who sat in front of it and left the rest to huddle in their wraps!

And Father Hayden laughs. And he remembers with keen pleasure walking downtown on Saturday nights. In the shadow of the Grand Hotel, young people promenaded up and down, the girls on the inside walking one way, the boys on the outside walking the other. On that sidewalk he fell in love with Helena Blackstone and brought her for Christmas a box of candy which, when she lifted the lid, let fly a blizzard of moths. She burst out laughing. He was sixteen; he never spoke to her again. Now it strikes him as marvelous that he is loved by so many women in the parish, young and old. They knit for him and bake for him, they all want to sit beside him at potlucks.

The moon peeps in at the window. He hears carolers singing far away, perhaps as far away as Montgomery Place. He wishes snow would fall and lighten the trees and the dark streets.

Coming by here? He raises his head from the pillow to listen.

No, no. The sound is moving farther off.

A passing car slides its shadow on the wall opposite his bed. He remembers as a child watching the shadows cast by the candles in church, and he hears his mother say, as she said so many years before, "Why do all the flames have such long haloes on them? They didn't used to."

Neither of them knew that she was just starting to go blind.

—————————— II ——————————

The third Sunday in Advent, women from the altar guild stay after the ten o'clock service to decorate the church. Now a sharp smell of pine and resin fills the sanctuary. Branches green the windowsills, and the cold flames of poinsettia ignite the spruce boughs on the steps below the pulpit. Father Hayden kneels on the first step arranging the crèche, which the sexton finds scattered every morning and which Father Hayden, smiling to himself, sets to rights. The dead bishop troubled Father Martin too, throwing all his books about at night till the old priest was obliged to move them out of the rectory into his office, untenanted by any lingering spirits.

In the evenings Father Hayden works on his sermon. The ragged music of the choir practicing in the library pleases him, though he hates to hear them start a hymn he especially loves and then break it off in the middle.

O, praise the Lord, all ye heathen!

He tries to recall the Christmas sermon he gave before his fellow students at the seminary. What was the topic of that sermon? Why can't he remember his own? He only remembers the face of his teacher and a sermon on the Last Judgment, given by Bartholomew Kelly, who died in a car accident last year. *Do you think Christ the servant, born in poverty, will come in glory to judge the living and the dead? Holy and gracious Father, teach us to judge ourselves.* Father Hayden writes it down.

Then he stands up and wanders over to the bookcase and pulls out the history of the parish, careful not to lose the bookmarks he keeps there. He resolves to remind his flock that not so long ago the rich rented the front pews and had them upholstered to their own taste. Yes, he will revive the history of the first black communicant, the rector's cook, who sat on a bench provided for her at the back of the sanctuary.

And he'll tell them about the church where he conducted his first services, at Milltown, not far from Yarmouth, and how during the Christmas offertory, the people brought the fruits of their labor—chickens, bread, fish—directly to the altar. A rooster, its legs hobbled, crowed once, twice, three times during the sermon, and Father Hayden motioned the deacon to take it away. Not until he turned to bless the bread and the wine did Father Hayden discover that the deacon had wrung its neck.

A knock at the door makes him jump. The sexton, not waiting to be invited, pushes it open and stands there clasping a large duffel bag which Father Hayden recognizes at once.

"Pardon me, Father, but as I was emptying the garbage, I found this."

"Where did you find it?" demands Father Hayden. His voice sounds louder than he intended it to.

"In the furnace room, Father. Shall I throw it away or keep it?"

For an instant there splashes across his mind the image of the old man lying dead under the everlasting arms of the furnace, like a trapped animal.

"Did you find anything else?"

"No, only this."

"Well, put it back where you found it. Whoever left it will surely come back for it."

The sexton shifts his weight from one foot to the other.

"Shouldn't you call the police?"

"I can't telephone the police about a bundle of old clothes. How on earth did he get in, I wonder, without anyone seeing him?"

"I leave the door open on Thursday nights for choir practice, Father."

He waits attentively for his orders. Father Hayden sighs.

"Put it back, put it back. If you see any suspicious persons, come and tell me. Don't call the police."

The sexton nods. Father Hayden turns back to his notes, but they reveal nothing to him now.

He goes to bed earlier than usual and does not drop off to sleep until early morning. And then he dreams that the sexton is chasing him round the sanctuary with a broom, shouting, "Do not loll on the altar! Keep your elbows close to your sides! When you make the sign of the cross, make crosses, not circles, and make them high or you'll upset the chalice."

Then he dreams that he wakes up. And in this two-storied dream, he sits up in his bed and hears music on Mansion Street, as from a parade far off. Running to the living room he throws up the shades and opens the great window that looks out on the street. From where do I know this tune? he asks himself, for it teases him like the smell of soap or tea when the memory of the smell has outlived the memory of the place it belonged to.

The street shines, paved in silver.

And now he sees the animals, the foxes beating their tambourines, the bears juggling firebrands, the goats tossing saucers and drums on their horns. The camels sing in thin, reedy voices. The hares and the marmots walk on their hind legs, paw in paw, all their grossness purged away as the souls of hunted and useful things must be, permanent as ivory, yet touching as flesh and fur. And he recognizes them at once; they walked on the silver lip of the tide on the first mornings of his childhood, before he learned to speak. Holding his mother's hand, he often watched them pass. And now he knows they have been walking all these years, looking for him.

But are they real animals or men in animal masks? he asks himself. For what animals could create such a radiant presence?

At once the whole company vanishes, and he wakes up, ready to weep at the loss of them. He runs to the front door and unlocks it and stands for a moment blinded by the white brilliance of Mansion Street, empty but glazed with last night's rain. Rain in December! He wishes that he might spend the morning walking that street, but he has four sick calls to make, and he has promised to visit Bertha Wells, the oldest living parishoner, who is bedridden and cannot attend the Christmas services that night. She lives in the Episcopal home across from the rectory. The others live in places less convenient to himself. Ah, he tells himself, someday there will be money to hire a curate who can make some of these visits for him.

Later that afternoon, he enters the sanctuary and pauses by the steps to choose a poinsettia for Bertha Wells. He lifts out the smallest pot, hidden among the spruce boughs. He stands up, hesitates.

Someone is watching him. He feels the skin on the back of his neck prickle. But looking out over the empty pews into the darkness, he sees nobody.

Is somebody watching me?

Nobody.

Holding the pyx in one hand and the pot in the other, he crosses Mansion Street and climbs the steps to the front door. Behind the frosted oval glass, the shadow behind the desk rises to meet him. And for a moment he feels like his father, calling on the sick, and he wishes he had the power to heal bodies as well as souls. To make the lame walk and the blind see.

The door opens and a young woman in a white uniform admits him.

"Father Hayden," she smiles. "How wonderful to see you. Won't you come with me?"

He follows her across the empty lobby. The sound of his footsteps sinks into the carpet. A TV set flickers soundlessly in front of a huge leather sofa. Hearing a clatter of dishes and voices to the left, he turns, but the young woman motions him to the elevator. They ride up smiling at one another.

"Flowers," remarks the woman. "How nice."

"Has Mrs. Wells had many visitors?"

"Hardly any. But she gets lots of cards. She's outlived everyone in her family, you know. Her husband died five years ago. Her daughter died two years ago of TB. There were no grandchildren."

"TB? I thought no one died of that anymore," says Father Hayden.

Leaving the elevator, he walks close behind his guide down the corridor. When she holds a door open for him, he enters without hesitation.

"Bertha, you have a special visitor."

In a bed against the far wall lies—is it a man or a woman? The figure is nearly bald. Father Hayden sets the flowerpot and the pyx on the bedside table. The bed nearest the door lies empty, immaculate. He puts his coat on the foot of it, and comes forward, extending his hand.

"God bless you, Bertha, and merry Christmas to you!"

The old woman's blue eyes study him. Then she leans forward and whispers, "Just look at those people in the corner, Father. And they aren't even married."

Glancing behind him, he discovers that the attendant has vanished, and in that instant the door across the hall opens and he sees an old woman in a bathrobe peering into the drawer of her table and scolding somebody.

But Bertha still stares into the space behind him. Touching his arm, she draws him lightly toward her.

"I know they're not real, Father, because you walked right through them."

Hastily he takes his prayer book out of his pocket.

Hearing the familiar prayers on his lips, the old woman lifts two fingers to receive the host. Arthritis has crumpled the others.

"Here," she says in a scratchy voice, "between these two."

When she has received his blessing, she seems all at once to come alive. She sits up, stares at Father Hayden, and says, "Are you the curate?"

"I'm the new rector," said Father Hayden.

"The rector?" she repeats, surprised. She studies him,

as if she hoped to unmask an imposter. Then, satisfied, she says, "We had a curate when Father Legg was rector. But it was Father Legg I always wanted to serve me. Still, you couldn't tell which side he would serve on. And if I sat on the right side, then I had to go to the right rail, and if I sat on the left side, then the left rail. And if the curate served me, I confess I felt as if I'd hardly taken communion at all. And then I had to wait a whole week to take it again."

Father Hayden laughs in spite of himself.

"And we young girls, we always got our hands folded just so, long before it was time to go up."

She closes her eyes. She is silent so long that he fears she has forgotten him. He takes her hand. Outside, snow is falling at last, draping the gravestones in the yard, the roof of the rectory, the steps.

He feels the warmth of her hand like a lining in his glove all the way back to his own door. And it's there the sexton takes his sleeve and whispers, smiling.

"That bag of old clothes I found—it's been taken away."

And Father Hayden thinks, he's been waiting for me to tell me this.

"Taken away? Who took it away?"

"I don't know. It was gone this morning. Taken away," he repeats, as if he has done nothing his whole life but bring old clothes together with their rightful owners.

"Well, that's fine," says Father Hayden. "A merry Christmas to you."

"And to you too, Father. Peter Beasley tells me you'll be taking dinner with his family tonight, before the service."

Father Hayden nods. He unlocks his door and steps

inside. The sexton is padding across the snow back to the sanctuary which is already aglow with candles for Christmas. Darkness comes now at four o'clock. Time! Time! There is not much time. Father Hayden remembers he must wrap the puppets he has bought for the deacon's children, but a growing uneasiness has paralyzed him.

Can a man be living in this house and I not know it?

He hurries through all the rooms downstairs, turning on the lights. Then, standing in the vestibule, he snaps on the light in the second floor hall. Then he ascends the stairs, making as much noise as possible. He whistles. He bangs his feet. He sings a little. He reaches the top landing.

Now he goes into the first bedroom. Turns on the lights.

Nobody there.

Into the second bedroom and the third. Empty rooms he has forgotten ever existed, rooms painted colors he never chose or papered in fruits, ships, and flowers. His footsteps shake the floorboards, his shadow follows him, gigantic, inhuman.

Nobody there.

At the foot of the stairs leading to the third floor, he turns on the light. His chest tightens, he can hear the thump of his heart. How frail a thing the body is! That his heart continues its work without a word from him amazes him, that his limbs move in spite of his doubts and confusion fills him with a peculiar tenderness toward them.

Noisily he marches up the stairs. Into the first room. Nothing but dead flies in one corner, thick as sand. Now the second room. His hand on the light switch, he hears a scrabbling sound that nearly sends him running. In his heart miniature boxes of cereal are falling like hail and a pick-pocket's hand is snatching them up.

And then he hears the twitter of starlings in the eaves and relief floods him. I must call an exterminator to get rid of them, he thinks, for he has heard stories of starlings stealing lighted cigarettes from ashtrays left by open windows and sticking them into their nests. Great buildings have been brought low by such small causes.

Carefully turning off all the lights, he walks downstairs. The house is empty. And this certain knowledge floods him with a loneliness he had not expected.

Time! Time! The deacon is sitting down to dinner without him. Father Hayden hurries to take the box of puppets from his closet shelf. Is it possible he dreamed of animals this morning? He cannot remember their shapes now, only that he wanted them and looked for them in the street he saw upon waking.

And now see him. It is eleven o'clock, the faithful have arrived in their best clothes, they rustle in the pews, waiting eagerly for the service to begin. In the corridor, Father Hayden fastens his cope; its scarlet cross slopes down his back as he takes his place behind the acolytes and folds both hands over his prayer book. The acolytes lift their candles. Now he is standing at the borders of the forest of lights. He hears the opening measure of the processional hymn. And as the door opens and they move into the sanctuary, his heart too is lifted. For among the faithful, perhaps the madman has come back and is even now sitting on the bench behind the last row of pews like a stray animal that has slunk out of the cold, caring nothing for the Word but wanting only to warm its paws at these mysterious fires.

∽ 3 ∽

The Doctrine of the Leather-Stocking Jesus

───────On the day before Easter, in my father's garage, just before supper, I drew a chalk circle around Galen Malory, and said, "Now I am going to change you into a donkey."

"Don't," pleaded Galen.

He was five, three years younger than I, and the second youngest of eight children. His father had worked for forty years on the assembly line of the biggest furniture factory in Grand Rapids and was given, on retiring, a large dining-room table with two unmatching chairs. On holidays Mr. Malory sat at one end and Mrs. Malory sat at the other, and in between stood the children on either side, holding their plates to their mouths. The rest of the time, they ate on TV tables all over the house.

"Now you will turn all furry and grow terrible ears," I said, smoothing my skirt. "Heehaw."

"If I turn into a donkey," shouted Galen, "my mother won't ever let me come here again."

"Too late," I howled, rolling my eyes up into my head. "I don't know how to undo it."

Suddenly Mrs. Malory rang her cowbell, and all over the block children leaped over hedges and fences and fell out of trees.

"I have to go," said Galen. "See you."

As he ran out of the garage he bumped his big furry nose on the rake leaning against the door. He stopped, reached up and touched his floppy ears, and burst into tears.

Out of sight of God-fearing folk, we sat together on the compost pile where three garages met, and we wept together. I stared at Galen's ears, large as telephone receivers, and at his big hairy lips and his small hands browsing over all this in bewilderment.

His hands. His hands?

I looked again. I had not turned him into a donkey. I had only given him a donkey's head.

And I thought briefly and sorrowfully of all the false gifts I'd given him. The candy canes I hung on his mother's peonies, left there, I told him, by angels.

"Dear God," I bellowed, addressing the one power I did believe in, "Please change Galen back."

"Somebody's coming," whispered Galen, terrified. "I think it's my father."

An old man in a brown overcoat and curled-up shoes was crossing the snow-patched field, poking the ground with a pointed stick. He was spearing bunches of dead leaves and tucking them into a white laundrybag.

"That's not your father," I said, "and he doesn't even see us."

But who could fail to see us? The old man skinned the leaves off his stick like a shish kebab, put them in his pack, and sat down half a yard from us, nearly on top of the hole where a little green snake once stuck her tongue out at me. He pulled a sandwich out of his pocket and ate it slowly, and I saw he had dozens of pockets, all bulging, and sometimes the bulges twitched. We watched him wipe his hands on his coat, stand up, and turn toward us.

"Once a thing is created," said the old man, "it cannot be destroyed. You cannot, therefore, get rid of the donkey's head. You must give it to somebody else."

"Who?" asked Galen.

"Me," said the old man.

"I asked God to get rid of it," I said.

"I *am* God," said the old man. "See if you can change me into a donkey."

The smell of crushed apples and incense filled the garage when God stood in the center of the chalk circle and my voice weasled forth, small and nervous.

"Now I am going to change You into a donkey."

And because it was God and not Galen, I sang the rhyme that expert skip-ropers save for jumping fifty times without tripping:

> *Now we go round the sun,*
> *now we go round the stars.*
> *Every Sunday afternoon:*
> > *one, two, three—*

Then I saw God stroking the tip of His velvet nose with one hand. His eyes, on either side of His long head, smiled at Galen's freckled face.

"After all, it is not so dreadful to be mistaken for an ass. Didn't Balaam's ass see My angel before his master did? Wasn't it the ass who sang in the stable the night My son was born? And what man has ever looked upon My face?"

"We have," said Galen.

"You looked upon my God-mask," said God. "Only the eyes are real."

He stepped out of the circle, opened His bag of leaves, and peeped inside.

"What are you going to do with all those leaves?" I asked him.

"I save them," said God. "I never throw anything away."

The leaves whirled around as if a cyclone carried them, as God pulled the drawstring tight.

And suddenly He was gone.

And now I smelled the reek of oil where my father parked his Buick each night, and an airplane rumbled overhead, and Galen was jumping the hedge into the Malorys' yard, and Etta called me for dinner.

And, conscious of some great loss which I did not understand, I went.

My mother and my sister Kirsten had already left for church to fix the flowers for tomorrow's service. Etta the babysitter and I ate macaroni and cheese at the kitchen table, out of the way of the apples waiting to be peeled, the yams and the onions, the cranberries and avocados, and the ham which Etta had studded with cloves.

I wanted to tell Etta all that had happened, but when

the words finally came, they were not the words I intended.

"Do you know what Reverend Peel's collar is made of?"

"Linen," said Etta.

"Indian scalps," I told her. "Do you know what chocolate is made of?"

"It comes from a tree," said Etta.

"It's dried blood," I said.

"Who told you that rubbish?" she demanded.

"Timothy Bean."

"A nine-year-old boy who would shave off his own eyebrows don't know nothing worth knowing," snorted Etta.

Etta gathered up our dishes and rinsed them in the sink.

"Can we go over and see the Malorys' new baby? I asked.

When we arrived, Mrs. Malory and five of her daughters had already gone to church to make bread for the Easter breakfast. The Malory kitchen smelled of gingerbread, but nobody offered me any. It was so warm the windows were weeping steam. The corrugated legs of a chicken peeked out over the rim of a discreetly covered pot. Etta comfied herself in the Morris chair by the stove, mopping her face with her apron as she crocheted enormous snowflakes which would someday be a bedspread. Helen Malory, who was nineteen, plump, lightly mustached, and frizzy-haired, sat in the rocker nestling her baby brother in her arms. She was newly engaged to a mailman. Thank God! said my mother when she heard it. Helen's got so many towels and sheets in that hope chest down cellar, she can't even close it.

Today Helen had given Galen a whole roll of shelf

paper and some crayons and now he and I were lying under the table, drawing. Because tomorrow was Easter, I drew the church: the carved angels that blossomed on the ends of the rafters, the processional banners on either side of the altar, the candles everywhere.

Galen drew Nuisance, the golden retriever who at that moment slept beside the warm stove. The dog's head would not come out right, nor the legs either, so he drew Nuisance wearing a bucket and walking behind a little hill.

Tenderly Helen tested the baby's bottle on her wrist and touched the nipple to its mouth. The baby squinted and pawed the air and milk sprayed down its cheeks. The lace gown it would wear tomorrow for its baptism at the eleven-o'clock service shimmered in a box on the kitchen table. Etta was allowed to touch it before Helen put it safely away on top of the china cabinet.

"What are you giving him?" inquired Etta.

"Scalded calves' milk," said Helen.

"You could add a little honey. That won't hurt none. John the Baptist ate honey in the desert and he grew up strong as an ox." As Etta spoke, she peered at the baby knowingly over her glasses. "Is that a scratch on his nose?"

"He scratched himself in the night. His nails are so small I don't dare cut 'em," explained Helen.

"If it was mine," said Etta, "I'd bite 'em off. 'Course I'd never bite anyone else's baby," she added quickly.

A white star gathered slowly at the end of Etta's crochet hook. Comfort and mercy dropped upon me in good smells that filled the ktichen. I was in heaven. I was lying in a giant cookie jar. Cuckoo, cuckoo, shouted the bird in the living-room clock. On its fifth cry, the grand-father clock in the hall started bonging away, nine times.

"Galen, take your thumb out of your mouth," said Helen sharply.

Galen took it out and examined the yellow blister on the joint.

"I had a niece who sucked her thumb," observed Etta. "Her mother tried everything. When she got married, her husband said, 'I'll break her of it.' She finally quit when she lost her teeth."

"Better to suck your thumb than smoke," said Etta.

"Why?" I asked.

"It's wicked," said Helen.

"It'll stunt your growth," said Etta. "I had an uncle who smoked young. He never grew more'n three feet tall."

Deep in a shaggy dream, Nuisance growled and thumped his stubby tail.

"I think I'll latch the screen," said Helen, and she stood up fast. "Caleb Suarez told Penny if she wouldn't go out with him tonight, he'd come and break down the door. But I do love the fresh air."

"You want to go upstairs and see Penny's stuff?" whispered Galen.

"Sure," I whispered back.

I was more comfortable in the same room with Penny's stuff than with Penny. Penny was sixteen and religious, but like every other girl in the high school, including my sister Kirsten, she dreamed of Caleb and would dream of him long after she was married to someone else. Whenever she looked at her mother, she would burst into tears, and her mother would shout, "So sleep with him! Go ahead! But let me tell you, you can't get away from your upbringing. You'll feel guilty all your life. It's a sacred act, you don't just do it with any boy that comes along."

Caleb had black hair, all ducktailed and pompa-
doured, blue eyes, a handsome face, and a withered arm—
the scar of infantile paralysis, my mother explained. His
father was one-quarter American Indian and owned the
Golden Cue Pool Parlor and came, when Caleb was six,
from Sioux City to find his relatives in Northville. There
were no relatives, and as far as anyone could see, there was
no wife.

Caleb spent his days at the fire department, reading
and waiting for fires, and his nights drinking at the Paradise
Bar.

"He's read all the books in the library; now he's starting the second time around," said Mr. Malory, shaking his
head at such folly. "I will say one thing for him, though.
I've never seen him drunk."

Galen turned on the light in the room Penny shared
with Helen. Over a dressing table littered with bottles hung
a big framed picture of Jesus, surrounded by photographs
of brides clipped from the newspapers.

"That's Penny's," said Galen bravely, pointing to the
picture. His voice was too loud for the room, as if he were
shouting before a shrine. "We gotta go now."

"Did you tell anyone about God?" I asked.

"I wanted to, but I couldn't," said Galen.

"Me neither."

Down the hall, Helen was putting the baby to bed.
Suddenly it cried furiously, and Galen and I hurried back to
the kitchen. Seeing us, Nuisance lifted his head, and his
rabies tags jingled like harness bells.

"Here, Nuisance," I called.

"His real name is Winthrop," said Galen. "He has a

pedigree. If he had the rest of his tail, he'd be worth a lot of money."

Nuisance loped after me into the dark dining room, his nails clicking on the bare floor. China gleamed on the sideboard like the eyes of mice.

"Galen, get me a piece of chalk."

"If you change Nuisance into a donkey," said Galen weakly, "my mother will never let me play with you again. That's my dad's best hunting dog."

But he brought the chalk.

"Sit, Nuisance," I commanded.

Nuisance rolled over. I drew the circle around him and stepped back.

"Out of my way, Galen."

Galen did not need to be told twice. I fixed my eye on the golden shape of Nuisance, motionless, save for the stump of tail which wagged.

"Now I am going to change you into a donkey," I whispered.

And because it was Nuisance and not Galen, I sang to him:

> Nuisance go round the sun,
> Nuisance go round the stars.
> Every Sunday afternoon:
>   one, two, three—

The sweetness of apples and incense hovered around us again. But nothing happened.

Then suddenly Nuisance jumped three feet into the air and, barking wildly, charged across the kitchen and crashed through the screen door. Etta shrieked and Helen came running.

"Is it Caleb?" she yelled.

"Nuisance broke down the door," shouted Etta. "You better lock him up good."

Galen burst into tears, and Helen sank to her knees beside him.

"There, there, honey lamb. No one's going to hurt you. Helen will lock the doors and windows." She held his head against her neck. "And I'll let you play with my Old Maid cards." Galen's shoulders stopped shaking. "And I'll even let you touch my new lampshade."

"Can I go down cellar and see your chest?" Galen said in a sodden voice.

Flicking the switch by the cellar door and taking each of us by the hand, Helen led us down the steps, dimly lit, past a clothesline sagging with diapers, to a big brassbound chest.

"Can I open it?" snuffled Galen.

"Go ahead," said Helen.

So Galen lifted the lid very slowly. It was like a thing from dreams, this box, big as a coffin, full of bedspreads and blankets and dishes. This is the way I would like to keep my whole past, I thought, folded away where I could take out last year's Christmas or my first birthday and play dress-up whenever I liked. Resting carefully on top of a platter painted with turkeys, the lampshade waited. It needed a light to show clearly the man and woman walking in a garden painted on the front.

"I got it for seventy-five cents at a rummage sale," Helen announced proudly. "It's not paper, either. It's real satin, and all clean."

"Too bad it's purple," I said thoughtlessly, and then, seeing I'd hurt her, I added, "but I like the two people in the garden."

"What comes after the garden?" asked Galen, pointing to the edge of the picture.

"Nothing. Don't poke at it," said Helen crossly.

And she herded us upstairs.

Etta had gotten control of herself and was crocheting as if nothing had happened, but her face looked like bleached flour. The lower half of the screen door was hanging out, torn in two—I touched it, awestruck. Helen went to the sink and started snapping the stems off the beans heaped on the drainboard.

"Etta," I said, and I felt my tongue thicken in my mouth, "Did you ever see God's face?"

"Nobody has ever seen God's face," said Etta. "Only His hinder parts."

Helen touched her buttocks absentmindedly.

"His what?" said Galen.

"His hinderparts," repeated Etta. "Nobody will ever see His face till the last day."

Etta knew the Bible better than any of us, but she didn't know I gave God the head of an ass.

"How do you know which day is the last day?" asked Galen.

"When all the signs have come to pass, that will be the last day," said Etta mysteriously. "Oh, they won't all come at once. They'll be spread out over the centuries, for a thousand years in the Lord's sight are but as yesterday when they are past."

"Something's burning," exclaimed Helen. She peeked into the soup pot, pushed the chicken legs down, clapped on the lid like a jailer, and turned off the stove. Then she said to Etta, a little sadly, "All those things are mighty hard to understand——"

A crash outside cut her off. For an instant none of us moved.

"The raccoon is rummaging through the garbage pail again," Helen squeaked. "He comes pretty near every night."

We all exhaled.

"Go on about the signs," I urged Etta.

Etta smoothed a finished snowflake across the back of her hand.

"When my grandfather was a little boy, he saw the darkening of the sky. That's one of the signs. The cows came home and the chickens went to roost just like it was night. And stars fell out of the sky. People thought they would get burnt up, and some folks killed theirselves."

"Is this a ghost story?" asked Galen nervously.

Etta scowled at him over the top of her glasses.

"I'm telling you what's in the Bible."

She opened her purse and pulled out a small book bound in white paper. "It's the new translation, and it only costs twenty-three cents. You could own three of 'em if you wanted to. And it's got pictures. See——"

"Who's that wild man?" demanded Galen.

"Where? Where?" cried Helen.

"There."

He pointed to the picture of a hairy man dressed in skins waving a big stick.

"That's John the Baptist," explained Etta. "But I believe this one is my favorite. It's from Revelations."

Over a crested wave, the red sun and the black moon bobbed like apples, and fish floated belly up among the spars of sunken ships.

"And every living soul in the sea shall die," said Etta.

"Fish don't have souls," said Helen.

Etta frowned.

"But that was the title of our lesson last week! What could it mean, then?"

"Don't fish have souls?" I asked, surprised.

"Of course not," answered Helen. "Only people go to heaven."

"What happens to the animals?" I hardly dared ask her.

"They turn back into earth."

"All of them?"

"All of them."

And my lovely spotted cat who loved nothing better than to nap by the stove in winter, would she too lie down in darkness? But I knew there was no point in asking about special cases if the rule applied to all. No doubt God didn't want puppies chewing up His golden slippers and peeing on His marble floors. I felt like crying, I could not imagine a world without animals. Even if I had none around me by day, I would need them at night. For whenever I could not sleep my mother would say, count sheep. I counted, one, two, three, four, and waited for the sheep to appear. But it was always buffalo that came to be counted, shaggy yet delicate, as if sketched on the walls of a cave. They floated out of the wall by my bed, crossed the dark without looking back at me, and passed silently into the mirror over my dressing table.

Suddenly I thought: if God does not mind wearing an ass's head, then why doesn't He let the whole animal into heaven?

"Not a one will get there, because they have no souls," said Helen.

"Do you think Nuisance will come back?" asked Galen.

Helen sighed.

"Dogs always come back."

"Tell some more signs," I said.

"In the last days," continued Etta, "God will send His star, just like He did when Christ was born. It will look like a big hand coming closer and closer. And then God will appear, not just to a few people in Sweden or Japan, but to everybody at once, like lightning."

Somebody tapped on the window over the sink, and a man's face lurched past, like a cracked moon.

"It's Caleb!" screeched Helen. "Don't let him in!"

We all rushed to close the kitchen door, but Helen rubbed the latch on the screen the wrong way, and in walked Caleb with his hands up, empty whiskey bottles on all his fingers.

"I've come to pick up Penny."

"Penny is at church," said Helen, her voice shaking.

"Church? Well, I'll wait for her."

"Suit yourself," sniffed Helen. "When my father comes home, you'll get it."

"Me and your old man are going hunting together next Sunday. Doves are thick this year."

"You shoot doves!" cried Etta. "Dreadful!"

Caleb shook the bottles off his fingers, one by one, and lined them up against the stove. Then he pulled off his sheepskin coat and threw it on the floor. Then he kicked off his boots. I could see skin peeking through his black socks like stars.

"Tell your dad to keep his bottles at home," said Caleb. "Tell him I saw ten empties running up Mulberry Street like a pack of dogs."

He drew up a kitchen stool and sat down.

"You can wait here till doomsday," snorted Helen. "No girl will look at a man who can't make a decent wage for himself."

Caleb smiled. He'd seen plenty of girls looking.

"I make a decent wage. I got my own place now too. A little cabin behind Mount Holly. No water except for a stream. No electricity. No cops." And then he added as if it had just occurred to him, "Why doesn't Penny want to go out with me?"

"Because you're no good," Helen said vehemently. "What woman wants to sit up with a man on Mount Holly? A woman likes to be comfortable."

"Penny said that?" asked Caleb, surprised.

"Mother said it," admitted Helen.

I knew it was all over now with Mrs. Malory. Caleb's revenges were swift. When a Mercedes nosed his old Ford out of a parking place, Caleb came back to let all of the air out of the tires and stole the hubcaps. He sent snakes to those who spoke ill of him; Reverend Peel's wife received one in a teakettle, sent anonymously, which slithered out of the spout the first time she filled it with water.

"What do you do on Mount Holly?" I asked him.

"I watch for forest fires and make shoes."

"Shoes?" exclaimed Etta. "Who taught you how?"

"I taught me. When I've learned everything there is to

know about leather, I'm going out to the West Coast to make me a fortune."

A thin wail brought Helen to her feet.

"The baby wants his bottle," she said brusquely, and hurried out.

"If you ever need a sitter," Caleb called after her, "I'm available."

Etta snorted, but Caleb paid no attention and turned instead to Galen.

"I've got a little present here for Penny."

And he bent down and began searching through the pockets of the coat he'd thrown on the floor. A couple of quarters spun out on the linoleum. A key ring with a medal on it plunked at his feet.

"What's that?" I asked.

"That's Jude, Saint of the Impossible," he answered, pocketing it and still searching.

"But you ain't Catholic, are you?" said Etta.

"No, I'm not Catholic. I got it from a buddy in the army."

"Do you believe in God?" persisted Etta.

Caleb shrugged. "When I was an altar boy in Sioux City, I wanted to be a preacher."

"You! A preacher!" shouted Etta, turning red. "The way you drink!"

"Christ drank," said Caleb quietly.

"And running around with women!"

"Christ ran around with a lot of women."

Etta was speechless. She wanted to walk out on him, but she could not take her eyes off what looked like a couple of leather bandages he was unrolling across his knees. Black leather, painted with flowers, the toes tooled with leaves, the cuffs studded with nails and, unmistakably, silver garters at the top.

"What beautiful boots," I told him.

"These are stockings," he corrected me.

"Leather stockings?" exclaimed Etta, astonished. "I never heard of leather stockings."

"Well, now you have," smiled Caleb.

He picked one up and stroked it like a cat, then laid it across the kitchen table. For the first time I noticed he used only one arm. I nudged Galen and whispered: see, one arm.

"How did you hurt your arm?" asked Galen loudly.

I saw Etta close her eyes.

"Jumping down Niagara Falls when I was young."

Etta opened them again.

"How old are you?" I asked.

"Twenty-three."

This saddened me. Anybody over nineteen was, in my mind, old enough to be my grandmother. As Caleb was leaving, we heard Helen tiptoeing down the stairs. Waving to us, he called over his shoulder.

"I'm going to church, ladies. And if Penny is with anybody else except her mother and her sisters, I'll cut him in two."

The privet hedge was wet with dew. I hoped no slugs would drop on us as Etta pushed our way through.

My mother, barefoot, in her bathrobe, let us in.

"It's nearly midnight! Where have you been?" she hissed.

But instead of scolding Etta, she scolded me. "If you want to get up for the sunrise service," said Mother, "you'd better go to bed instantly. You and Kirsten are sleeping on cots in the kitchen. Your aunt and uncle are here. Etta, I made up the sofa bed for you. It's too late for a cab."

"My nightgown is in my room," I whispered.

"Never mind your nightgown," said my mother. "Uncle Oskar's asleep in there. You can sleep in your underpants. And if you smell the ham burning, wake me up. I've got it on low."

Kirsten was sleeping in the middle of the room with a pillowslip over her head, which she started wearing the night a bee crawled into her hair. Though I lay perfectly still, I could not fall asleep. The buffalo did not come to be counted, and the enamel pots hanging on the walls watched me like a dozen moons.

I heard my cat scratching faintly at the front door.

I got up and opened it, and somebody pulled me outside. But outside was inside; all around me, torches sputtered and popped, clothes smelt of pitch, and my spotted cat was no cat at all, but a girl in a pied gown who scampered away down the aisle that opened at my feet.

The church looked fuller than I'd ever seen it. In front of the altar, Reverend Peel, by the light of the acolyte's torch, was censing the people with a sausage in his left hand and a pot of smoking shoes in his right. He had wreathed his bald head in poppies, turned his vestments wrong side out, and thrown away his glasses.

Kyrie eleison kyrie eleison

shouted the choir from the balcony over my head. And the people shouted back,

Heehaw! Heehaw! Heehaw!

Helen was walking, with measured tread, down the center aisle, holding the baby wrapped in a rabbit skin. Diamonds blazed on her hair and on her eyelashes and on her white gown.

The King is coming, whispered Mother into my ear. The King is coming from a far country to bless the baby.

Everyone turned.

A donkey was walking down the aisle, its ears crowned with ivy, its legs sleek in black leather stockings, a scepter locked between enormous teeth. The moon sprang out of its left ear, the sun out of its right.

Riding before it on a black goat, Caleb, splendid in white buckskins, strewed grapes for the donkey's hooves to crush into wine. And loping along behind came Nuisance, ribboned with penny whistles piping by themselves.

Now a shout went up from every throat. And in that instant I knew this was no donkey, but a magician disguised as a donkey, and one far more powerful than I. Slowly the beast turned around, showing its handsome black stockings. It stepped up to the altar and laid aside the scepter. Helen held up the baby and it touched the holy water to eyes, lips, and ears.

When it finally spoke I knew the King had always been speaking, only I had not had the ears to hear. It did not ask Helen to abjure the devil and all his works, yet I knew it was not the devil. It did not promise salvation, yet I was sure it had come to save us.

"And some there be," said the donkey, speaking very quietly, "who have no memorial; who are perished, as though they had never been."

Over our heads, the carved rafters remembered their names: oak, ash, maple, and pine. They put out bark and leaves, and the angels carved there were no more. The scepter shrank to a hazel wand, but the beast did not notice.

"But these were merciful men," it continued, "whose righteousness has not been forgotten."

The glass in the windows blew away, sparkling like a million grains of sand. The pews rolled up into logs, grass grew between my toes, I could not see who stood beside me and I could no longer remember my own name.

But the donkey's voice breathed over me like wind across a field: "Their seed shall remain forever. Their bodies are buried in peace, but their names live forevermore."

Then, not three feet away from me, Etta turned over on the sofa bed and sighed deeply.

The morning air raised gooseflesh all over me as I awakened, and I knew it would be cold on Steeple Hill when we gathered at the cemetery for the sunrise service.

Up on Steeple Hill, where all our people lay buried, a wind bowed the bare trees and sent the clouds scudding like foam as we waited for Reverend Peel to open the gates to the cemetery.

Most of the fathers, including mine, were home in bed.

Over the heads of the women and children, the gold cross swayed in the pastor's hands. The acolyte lifted the Easter banner high as a sail; its embroidered lamb sank and swelled, all heartbeat and pulse in the wind.

"Where is the sun?" I asked my mother.

"Behind the clouds."

"But how do you know, if you can't see it?"

"Because it's light outside."

Kirsten fiddled with the little silver cross she wore only

on Sundays. She had a new pink coat, and I caught myself wondering how long before she'd outgrow it and I could have it.

His vestments blowing like laundry, Reverend Peel threw open the gates at last, and we marched in singing:

Holy, holy, holy! Lord God Almighty!
Early in the morning our song shall rise to Thee!

Are the dead surprised? Do they look at us, do they look at me? Does an old woman see her features in mine, does an old man see in Kirsten his young wife who died so long before he did? Do they sit in their graves as we sit in our pews, are we the service they wait for?

We walked two by two, singing bravely against the wind:

Though the darkness hide Thee

How lovely it was there in the morning! Patches of snow gleamed in the shade of the headstones, but everywhere else the grass showed damp and green, though it had lain there the whole winter.

4

The Tailor Who Told the Truth

————————In Germantown, New York, on Cherry Street, there lived a tailor named Morgon Axel who, out of long habit, could not tell the truth. As a child he told small lies to put a bright surface on a drab life; as a young man he told bigger lies to get what he wanted. He got what he wanted and went on lying until now when he talked about himself, he did not know the truth from what he wanted the truth to be. The stories he told were often more plausible to him than his own life.

What was the first lie?

That his father was rich. The richest man in Germany.

Told to whom?

Ingeborg Schonberg, the parson's daughter he loved in Potsdam, where he grew up. Yes, a lie, because his father was not rich. Karl Axel owned a secondhand shop in one of the shabbier quarters of the city. The family lived behind the shop: Hans the oldest brother and after him Heinrich, who were tall and blond and loved practical jokes and wanted to go to sea. Johanna Axel, née Schweber, daughter of the widow Schweber, who cooked for a doctor and his family in Potsdam. Johanna Schweber made good money till she married Karl. Morgon Axel, born in 1896, when Hans was seven and Heinrich was six. Yes, that's the one: Morgon, who from the beginning was dark-haired and short like his father. He was five years old when he told his first lie. No, not his first lie. Let us call five the age of discretion here: therefore, the first lie on record. Told to the parson's daughter, age five and a half. The second lie does not concern us. Because then we would have to deal with the third and fourth also.

Look at him now, seven going on eight, a pack of lies behind him, reading at a cherrywood table in his father's shop, among busts of Kaiser Wilhelm II and Frederick the Great, who lour at him like schoolmasters. Morgon has made himself a little place for his books behind a barrier of cut-glass bowls, stags' heads, stuffed owls, and nutcrackers carved like the heads of dogs. And don't forget the cuckoo clocks and the shields and visors and guns of the hunters who have gone down at last with the stags and the owls they killed. Morgon has befriended the guns and named them: Ernst, Dieter, Barbarossa.

Sometimes Saturday and always Sunday (on Sunday Johanna Axel is singing in church), Karl takes his three sons hunting in the forest beyond the city. In the forest live woodcocks, partridges, wild boars, and deer with antlers that branch out like coral. Morgon's brothers knock partridges out of the air as easily as winking. His father shoots hares and saves the paws for luck. He has hundreds of paws stacked away in a cupboard. Morgon hits nothing, but that's because he's so new at it. In his sleep he dreams of shooting so straight and so far that he knocks the sun out of the sky.

Is there anything more monotonous than shooting partridges and hares every Sunday of your life? It is the fourth Sunday of his tenth year, and he's been hunting with his father ever since he told his first lie at the age of five. The creatures they've shot, he says to himself, would fill the Nymphenburg Palace. Has Morgon seen the Nymphenburg Palace? Never in his life. But he has read about it. He has tried to read every book in his father's shop and all the books in his father's house, though he understands very little of them: *The Memoirs of the Margrave of Augsburg, History of the Imperial Army, The Court of Karl-Eugen, Prince of Württemburg*. Morgon has told himself that if he can read them all, his brothers will come back.

They come back before he has accomplished this. One clear July afternoon there they are, standing in the middle of Johanna Axel's kitchen, both of them shining like the family silver. Trim blue jackets buttoned high at the throat, gold epaulettes, gold buttons where eagles sleep, a spiked helmet where an eagle is spreading its wings. The iron cross nestled in ropes of gold braid that glitter like icicles across their chests. Boots so tall their legs look slim and graceful as a girl's. Johanna Axel nearly goes out of her mind with joy.

"I have a son in the academy at Kiel and another doing us proud in Berlin: I couldn't possibly ask for more."

It is Saturday. Have they forgotten?

"Tomorrow we'll go hunting," says Hans, slapping Morgon on the back. "It'll be like old times."

That afternoon they all go visiting, all except Morgon who stays home to mind the shop. That's how he happened to be there when the bell tinkled and in hobbled a wild boar which lifted its head over the counter.

Morgon jumped: the cut-glass bowls and nutcrackers jumped with him. The boar's face slipped away and he saw an old white-bearded Jew in a skullcap and black coat.

"I wonder," said the Jew, "if you'd be interested in buying a few items I have here."

Morgon eyed him suspiciously, for hairs stuck out of his nose like tusks. From the box he had set on the floor, the man brought up a clock case, carved to resemble a country church.

"A few repairs, and you can sell it for a fortune. It belonged to the fourth Duke of Württemburg. When the clock strikes, twelve angels rush out to beat the hours. The Crucifixion takes place in the upper window, and the twelve apostles come out of the lower door two by two, bow to the Savior, and return. All the while it plays *Ein' feste Burg ist unser Gott.*"

"But it doesn't keep time," said Morgon, staring at the motionless hands.

"No. But if it did, you could sell it for a fortune."

"Then my father won't want to buy it. What else have you got?"

The Jew sighed.

"I have here a fine collection of masks, at least two hundred years old. They come from the castle of Grafeneck. The duke's guests wore them at a masked ball. Here you see the mask that the archbishop was forced to wear in order to have an audience with the duke——"

He pulled out the face of the boar, carved in wood and

79

painted bright blue. Gold rings hung in its ears. The old man laid it on the counter.

"And here's the mask ordered by Baron Wimpffen. A great joker, I've heard."

A red hyena with pearls in its snout joined the boar.

"And of course, for the Baroness d'Oberkirch, this lovely brown doe wearing a tiny crucifix in a golden crown. The others, well, I'm not sure who wore them——"

He laid them out in a row across the counter for Morgon's approval. An emerald green dog with roses curled on its cheeks. A black bear wearing a mitre, and an animal that looked rather like a goat, though Morgon couldn't be sure. Under the jeweled eyes of each face were slits for the wearer to see out.

"Six masks in all, young sir. They're absolutely priceless."

Morgon lifted the bear to his face, the Jew lifted the dog, and they looked at each other, then each set his mask aside.

"Well, I don't know," said Morgon. "Can you come back Monday? My father does all the buying. I only wait on people."

The Jew's expression passed from polite reserve to polite terror.

"Can't you give me something toward them now? They're worth at least four hundred marks."

"I'm sorry, I can't. You'll have to come back."

When Karl Axel returned and saw the masks, he was delighted.

"They're superb," he exclaimed. He was in excellent spirits: they had gone to see his brother Ernst who ran a butcher shop and whose wife had given him nothing but

THE TAILOR WHO TOLD THE TRUTH

daughters. Business would never be better than in the next few days: Rabbi Mendel's grandmother had gone mad, fled out of her house, and plunged a knife into Ander Krüller's only son. Yes, that same Krüller who sat on the city council, and all the cousins of Rabbi Mendel and his wife, who numbered in the hundreds, were selling their possessions and fleeing the city.

"If he comes back, we'll give him two hundred marks. But it's likely he's on his way to Berlin by this time."

Is there anything more monotonous than hunting partridges and hares every Sunday? Is there anything more exciting than an animal who might, at the edge of enchantment, turn itself into a human being? The next morning Heinrich and Hans and Morgon packed up the masks, shouldered air guns, and traveled to the forest beyond the city. Morgon carried the masks on his back. The forester let the brothers take the horses they always rode with their father. When they reached a clearing they dismounted. Morgon threw the masks on the ground.

"The rule is," said Hans, "that whoever plays an animal will try to avoid the hunter for one hour. If he succeeds, the animal wins. If the hunter shoots him, the animal loses. Who wants to be what?"

"I'll be the bear," said Heinrich. He stopped, picked up the bear's face, and slipped it over his own. Morgon gasped. Before him stood a bear in Prussian uniform, cruelly raised to the tenth power.

"Morgon, your turn."

"The dog," said Morgon. He put on the mask. Its features pressed against his face. He felt hot inside and the eye slits did not fit him properly. He could hardly see.

"Go and hide yourself," said Hans.

"But the animals should be allowed to take their guns," exclaimed Heinrich. "In case we meet the boars and bears who do not turn into humans."

Hans played the hunter, and Morgon had never known such excitement. To lie in the bushes and hear his brother stalking him, to hear him cocking his gun, that was much better than watching woodcocks drop out of the sky. Furthermore, in the role of the animal Morgon excelled both his brothers, because he was smaller, and as he was unhampered by a uniform he could move faster.

"The hunter has the worst of it," said Hans. "He knows it's just a game and there's not a chance of hurting anybody when you're protected by a mask. We ought to play without masks."

"Without masks?" repeated Morgon.

"Why not? Once you've played the animal, you don't need a mask to turn you into a dog. Then you're as vulnerable as an animal really is. It makes you play harder."

That's how Morgon Axel, at the age of ten, crawled out of a bush in the forest outside Potsdam and lost his right eye to the gun of his brother. The hunting came to an end, the brothers went back to their regiments, and Morgon Axel got fitted with a blue-glass eyeball.

"Don't be bitter," his mother told him. "It was a game that turned out badly."

On his eighteenth birthday, he went to enlist in the Imperial Army, but no lie was big enough to cover the blue-glass eyeball he wore in his head. So he went to Berlin and applied as assistant to Otto Strauss, a tailor who specialized in uniforms, on whose door you could read in bold Gothic script:

O. Strauss, kgl. preuss. Hoflieferant

Inside you could find all those decorations which so warm the heart of your Prussian officers. Drawers of epaulettes, gloves, and buttons for every rank. Yes, and the shelves of spiked helmets embossed with shining eagles, like the blessed instruments of a holy sacrifice. Yes, and the bolts of blue wool and spools of gold braid; tasseled swords and riding whips and slim black boots. On the walls, O. Strauss had kept several large photographs of the Kaiser and his family and many smaller ones of high-ranking officers wearing the uniforms he had made for them. And look, over here's the most recent one: a fine photograph of General von Kluck's First Army entering Brussels, with horses and caissons. (Did Otto Strauss know General von Kluck? No.) It was August 1914, and uniforms were greatly in demand. O. Strauss marched up and down the shop and surveyed his prospective assistant.

"What I need," he said, "is somebody who knows as much about the military as he knows about fitting and altering clothes. Tell me: how many centimeters should you leave between the cuff buttons on the uniform of a captain in the reserves?"

"Herr Strauss, you insult me," exclaimed Morgon Axel, waving his hand grandly. "I come from a long line of tailors. My ancestors were the royal tailors to Frederick the Great. A dressmaker on my mother's side designed the wedding gown of Wilhelmina von Grävenitz."

O. Strauss leaned against his counter and stared, but Morgon Axel continued unabashed.

"And as for the military! I have two brothers. The

oldest is a lieutenant in the Imperial Navy. The other is the captain of the division of the Prussian Guard recently cited by General Ludendorff. I am related by marriage to Colonel von Lettow-Vorbeck and my oldest brother has the ear of Admiral von Holtzendorf."

O. Strauss touched his ear nervously.

"My father won the *Pour le mérite* in the last war." And as he spoke, Morgon saw his father dashing through Ypres on a black horse, shouting to the soldiers lounging in the courtyard: *Attack! We are being attacked from the west!*

"Why, may I ask——"

"I had the misfortune to lose my right eye in a hunting accident. But my left one is as sound as yours."

"Well, well," murmured O. Strauss. "I'll be glad to try you out. We have all sorts of men coming in here. You'll find most of them are hard to please."

From that lie forward, Morgon Axel acted as O. Strauss's assistant. By day he helped him lay the patterns for cloaks and jackets on long fields of blue wool, and he pinned sleeves and collars on the stocky bodies of officers who made appointments to be fitted. After work he hurried to his room high up in Frau Nolke's house at the other end of town, lugging the shop's manuals on the regulations for military dress which he read far into the night. When he had memorized the fundamentals, he began borrowing uniforms, every night a different rank, so that he could examine how they were made.

In the house next door, the West Bavarian Singing Society met twice a week, and on those evenings Morgon Axel could not study. Rich joyful voices flooded his silence, and he opened his window to hear them.

Über's Jahr, über's Jahr, wenn me Traübele schneid't,
Stell' i hier mi wied'rum ein;
Bin i dann, bin i dann dein schätzele noch,
So soll die Hochzeit sein.

He leaned on the sill and looked out. Across the street on the sixth floor of a tottering building, an aged dancing master was teaching young women in bloomers and tights the intricacies of the pirouette and the entrechat. From his window, Morgon Axel could plainly see into theirs. A war is going on, he thought, and people are still dancing as if Germany meant nothing to them.

Sitting down at his table once more, he tried to consider the width of the collar on Captain Hess's uniform but found himself staring vacantly at his own face on the mirror of the wardrobe. It was a warm September night. Under the linden trees, the officers were walking, yes, those officers over whose flesh his fingers had walked miles and miles, gathering pleats and folds on the way. He got up and slipped into the uniform of Captain Hess. Slipped into the sleek trousers and longed-for boots. Buttoned the blue jacket across his chest, fastened the belt, and stood barefoot in front of the mirror. And then stepping out of the bar reserved exclusively for commissioned officers, he leaned on the windowsill and looked up at the figure of a single girl dancing by herself. Perhaps she knew that Morgon Axel was watching. What was the good of military regulations, of drills and marches, if it couldn't protect you against longing to be free? Captain Morgon Axel would send someone to fetch her, but that wasn't the way. The next night, another would take her place.

One evening Morgon noticed the studio was dark; no

one ever danced there again, and shortly afterwards the singers, too, disappeared. For the next three years he lived on Frau Nolke's turnips and O. Strauss's chocolates (courtesy of his customers), which the old gentleman hoarded shamefully. A young lieutenant, being fitted for a cloak, told Morgon that he had bought all his Christmas and birthday presents for the next year, though it was only March, so that if he were killed in action, his family and friends would know he hadn't forgotten them. A captain from Bremen, who lisped in honor of the Kaiser and wore a monocle, ordered six pairs of Hessian boots, because, he explained, a soldier should live at all times in his boots. He was modeling his conduct on Frederick the Great who kept his hat and his boots on even when he was ill, rose at four every morning, and in the evening played the flute for recreation. Both the captain and the lieutenant left their photographs for O. Strauss to hang on his wall and both were killed at Soissons.

But one clear night in November, Kaiser Wilhelm fled into Holland. What was to be done? The Imperial Army marched grimly back to Berlin, passing through the Brandenburger Tor. Wreaths crowned their helmets, and they carried a new banner: "Peace and Freedom." Morgon Axel wept and applied for passage to America, taking with him one fur-lined cape (Army surplus), one suit (much worn), and seven animal masks which his father had willed him; there was nothing else left, and Morgon Axel was the sole heir.

Now look at him, middle-aged, still short and rather stocky, a square figure, in a tweed hunting jacket with absurd shoulder pads, standing in the doorway of his tailor shop on Cherry Street, Germantown, New York.

Wait. You must give an account of the years in between.

The evidence for those years has been lost, except for some brief scenes, undated, by which we may only surmise that he worked as a tailor in New York City and married Ursula Rincetti, daughter of an Italian cabinetmaker and restorer of styles past.

Now Morgon is sitting in the tiny apartment where he lives with his wife and his son, Amyas, aged twelve. Christened Hans Federico but nicknamed Amyas by a young English girl who worked in the Germantown bank auditing accounts and occasionally babysat with Amyas and held him in her arms and sang him to sleep with an old song:

> *You and I and Amyas*
> *Amyas and you and I.*
> *To the greenwood must we go, alas!*
> *You and I, my life and Amyas.*

It is spring. Or summer. Or any season. What you will. Morgon is sitting in front of the television set, watching the "Ed Sullivan Show." Morgon Axel has the only color television on the block. He is admiring the red sequined suits of the dancing couple, "who have recently played at the Copacabana." There is a Copacabana in Los Angeles—but it is another Copacabana which concerns us here, just as it is another Sunset Strip, another Hollywood, another Las Vegas and Broadway that we are speaking of, rather than the ones generally known. Long hours of watching television and films have rebuilt these streets in Morgon Axel's head like a stage setting, deficient in details but peopled with a cast of thousands. Captain Hess and General Ludendorff and Colonel von Lettow-Vorbeck have given way to Roy Rogers and Gene Autrey and Fred Astaire. Sometimes Morgon watches the talent show on the Albany station, "Stairway to the Stars," and as the young people sing, tap-dance, and play the piano, it is Amyas he imagines, leaping on a trampoline and being discovered.

For Amyas is talented that way, no doubt about it. He has that grace which Morgon so marveled at when he shouldered the weight of Captain Hess's uniform one night in Berlin and saw, in the opposite window, a young girl dancing. Once a week Amyas studies gymnastics and trapeze acrobatics with Taft Toshiho in Yonkers, who also teaches judo to secretaries and housewives. Amyas and the six other boys in his class have already performed in high schools and Kiwanis clubs around the state and at the Ulster County Fair. It's only a matter of months, says Morgon to his friends, till you'll be seeing Amyas on television. On Broadway.

"Tell me about how it was when you worked in the theater," says Amyas. He is five years old and his father sits on the edge of his bed, waiting for his son to go to sleep.

"Well," says Morgon Axel, "the shows are not worth mentioning compared to the fêtes. Before the war, such fêtes! I remember one fête I designed for the Count of Ansbach-Schwedt."

And as he speaks, he sees himself very clearly standing on a balcony in the castle of the count, surveying the garden and the woods beyond, brilliant with thousands of lanterns.

"All the guests came in hunting costumes. I designed over a hundred masks like the faces of animals, no two exactly alike. The women put on the masks and the men had to hunt for their partners in the forest."

The next morning there is no forest, only the shop, which is small and untidy. The front room contains two mirrors, a few chairs, bolts of wool and gabardine, catalogs and swatches spread open on a table, and a rack of finished garments which barely hides a dressmaker's dummy. In the window Morgon drapes remnants of silk over a truncated plaster column. On the walls hang his masks and his guns. That's the front room, where the tailor receives his customers.

But there's another room behind it, separated from the first by a red curtain. Sybil, the tailor's golden retriever, lopes back and forth between them like a messenger. Customers waiting for their packages can hear the tailor's wife stitching and sighing behind the curtain. Also, the clicking of Sybil's toenails against the bare floor; they have grown long from lack of exercise, for though the tailor dreams of hunting and has his dog and his guns all ready, he seldom finds the time.

Why do you say nothing of Ursula, the tailor's wife?

Searching the tailor's memory, we find that up till now she passed through it as through water, leaving no footprints. A dead civilization which shapes what we are though we will never know what it is.

Nevertheless, give us a picture of the tailor's wife.

Why, when the customers slipped through the curtains for their fittings—the tailor had built a tiny dressing room here—they saw sitting under the naked bulb that dangled from the ceiling a slender woman with dark hair clouded around her face as if she wanted to hide herself. She was always bending over a piece of work and treading the sewing machine with her heel. In front of her on the pegboard wall, which was no more than a foot from her nose, hung spools of thread in every size and color, and this was her horizon from eight in the morning till six at night.

Behind her the table was heaped with dresses to be mended, zippers to be put in, skirts to be hemmed, trousers with ill-fitting cuffs, and suits cut and basted, which had to be finished. The tailor's wife never looked back for fear she couldn't go on. She had told this to the priest one Sunday when she went to confession, for she was a devout Catholic, though her husband, raised Lutheran, attended no church now.

"Sometimes I think I'll die of despair, Father. I look back and see that the pile never runs out, for just when I think I'm near the end, Morgon heaps on more work. What's the use, I say to myself, of working my way through a pile that's got no bottom? And then my fingers just stop, Father, they won't turn the wheel one more time."

"Then you mustn't look back, my daughter," whispers the voice behind the grille. "Reach behind you and pick up one piece at a time. One at a time. Then you'll be able to get through the day. Not to finish the pile; that's not a thing any of us could do in a lifetime. But to get yourself safely across to the next day. God Himself doesn't ask more of you."

"If only He'd give me a vision to help me through the bad times, Father. Just a small one, so I don't forget what's under the pile." *An angel dancing on the point of her needle. A wheel within the wheel of her machine.*

Having no visions, she settled her love on her son. If

he was not an angel, he at least came close to flying like one. When she sewed costumes for Amyas and the six boys in his troupe, the needle leaped for joy like a dolphin in the sea of nylon and satin, and the stitches unwound themselves in love. And all the while Morgon Axel walked up and down in the front room and graciously accepted an order for yellow jodhpurs from William Harris, the fiery-haired riding master of High Stepping Stables outside of town.

"Can I make jodhpurs? My dear Mr. Harris, I can make anything. You should have seen the silver jodhpurs I made for Gene Autrey when I worked in the city. Why, I could make jodhpurs to fit a spider! I remember the first riding outfit I ever made—it was for the Duke of Augsburg who was giving a ball at his castle in Westphalia." (A self-indulgent laugh.) "All the guests came in hunting costume. Well, I made the Duke a splendid habit in russet velvet, and when it was done, what do you think? I'd cut the trousers with the nap going up one leg and down the other and when the light struck him he seemed to divide himself like a pair of scissors. But he was very kind about it. 'I've invited so many beautiful women,' he said, 'that no one will notice.'"

Mr. Harris pulled off his gloves, a finger at a time, hung his camel's hair overcoat on the rack, and stood stiffly in the middle of the room while the tailor crawled around him on the floor, puffing a little as he took the measurements of the riding master's trim figure.

"Ah, the life I've seen," sighed Morgon Axel, pulling pins out of the cushion that dangled next to his heart. "When I worked in the city, I had my own place right over the Stork Club. Kitchen, bathroom, shower. I had the whole floor to myself, just for work space. Did I ever tell you about the time I had dinner with Jimmy Durante and an English housewife who was flown over because she'd won something in a soap contest? The company gave me a Lincoln—turn, Mr. Harris."

Mr. Harris turns and looks straight ahead at the curtain. Behind the tailor's story, he hears the chugging accompaniment of a sewing machine.

"You ought to give your wife a vacation," he says suddenly. "Every time I come in here——"

The tailor hears and does not hear.

"A Lincoln, Mr. Harris. It had a built-in bar where most cars have the back seat. But I'm glad to leave it all behind. Here in the country, I'm happy. I go hunting when I want to, I take off a week here and there when the weather's nice. I'm nobody's slave."

A sigh floats out from behind the curtain, as from a dark well. The tailor has unwittingly spoken the truth.

What did Mrs. Shore, the banker's wife, size eighteen, coming to have her new coat lengthened, tell the tailor?

"I've been hearing so much about that boy of yours! My husband saw him and his group at the county fair."

"Oh, you'll be hearing from him one of these days, Mrs. Shore. Any day now, you'll be seeing him on television."

One day the letter from Albany arrives. Now the boast has come true, Morgon is as nervous as a flea, and he appraises the most casual movements of his son.

What does the tailor see when he looks at his son?

Himself. Younger. Morgon, yes, but he has lost all the heaviness of a Prussian upbringing. Amyas ambles into the shop after school and throws his books on the chair. He is fourteen.

"Did you practice today?" asks the tailor.

"Yes," says Amyas, pulling a candy bar out of his pocket. He is tall, nearly six feet already, and has an enormous appetite which worries his father.

"Don't eat that," says the tailor, slapping it out of his son's hand. "You don't want to get fat."

"I burn it up fast enough, don't I?"

On the television screen, he moves like a flame. Morgon Axel has called all his friends. He brings the portable TV down to the shop, and Tuesday morning they come by to watch. His wife wanted to go to the studio and watch it live but then they would never know how it looked to everyone else. Here they are, the butcher who works in the grocery shop next door, the fellow from the gas station across the street, Amyas's classmates and teachers, and Knute Kristofferson, the old violinist who lives upstairs and doesn't have a color TV. They stand around the set, which Morgon has perched on one of the shelves, having removed the heavy bolts of cloth in honor of the occasion. After a tap-dancing girl and two young boys who play an accordion duet, the master of ceremonies appears on a corrugated pedestal studded with stars. He says something which the tailor barely hears, about the seven members of an acrobatic troupe, led by Amyas Axel. And then suddenly it is he, the fulfillment of all Morgon's dreams, flying like an angel, like an eagle, from intricate trapezes, hanging from the ankles of one boy, jackknifing to another, like a squirrel jumping from tree to tree.

Without fear.

Then all at once the screen goes black.

"Oh!" cries the tailor's wife.

Across the darkened screen appears the words:

Power failure. Please stay tuned.

But though they hover around the set for a quarter of an hour, Amyas does not return, and when the image flashes on, a young girl in a tutu is spinning around on her toes.

In the evening when he's watching television, the tailor sees out of the corner of his eye another performance going on, less important than the one he's watching only because he's not a part of it and it goes on all the time. Amyas on a stool, his legs crooked around the rungs; his mother shelling peas, nodding, listening; the window open, the warm spring air coming through—

You have told us about the tailor and the tailor's wife but very little about Amyas. Who is he?

It is impossible to say for certain, because he's always moving, and his mother's testimony is so different from his father's memories that they might well be describing two different people. Parents seize an image of what they want their children to be, behind which the child moves, trying to fit his body to the shadow-child or hold it up as a shield which lets him grow in secret.

But when Amyas was sixteen, he had nothing in common with this shadow-child. He became a new person. And that is always terrible for the parents, who have chosen someone else.

That is to say, having grown tall he began to grow wide. Enormous. From slim acrobat to a man pregnant with the acrobat that had been himself, for you could see the old Amyas still, in his eyes, in his gestures, and you could hear it in his speech. At the age of sixteen he weighed four hundred pounds, through some imbalance of his body which had been waiting all those years to take away his grace.

The tailor knew nothing of glands and imbalances. He began to loathe the very sight of his son, who seemed to give himself up to the slovenly spirit that had gotten hold of him. Amyas grew a scraggy beard and let his mother trim his hair only around his ears.

It was his mother who made his clothes now—acres of tweed, of gabardine, which heaped the pile behind her like a mountain. The sick child cries out for love. At dinner she saved the best pieces of meat for Amyas, the extra piece of pie. These acts of favoritism enraged the tailor.

"Amyas, you look like a pig. Don't eat like one."

(Amyas has just dragged his sleeves into his soup. He is not used to his new body.)

"You just want the rest of the blueberry pie for yourself. Be glad you don't have a big belly to fill," snapped his mother.

She set the piece of pie in front of Amyas. But shame overcame him. He pushed it toward his father. The tailor found that he did not want it either, yet having asked for it, he pretended to eat it with relish.

He knows Amyas is always hungry, and he takes great delight in keeping him that way. Didn't he bring Amyas up in the paths of righteousness and didn't Amyas fail to bloom? In the back of the tailor's mind is a lurking suspicion that his son *could* turn into the old Amyas if he really wanted to, that he's done this to humiliate his father in front of his friends and customers, to whom he has boasted over and over, "One day you'll be seeing him on Broadway."

You can't spank a child for taking this way to get back at you but you can humiliate him back to his senses. Amyas sits in back of the shop with his mother, helping her ease the weight of that unfinished pile on her soul. The tailor struts around in the front room—yes, he is prouder than ever now—joking with his customers.

"Well, if I can't have an acrobat for a son, I'll have the male Mae West. Sometimes I feel like I'm running a side-show in here!"

He whispers it into Mrs. Shore's ear, or into Mr. Harris's ear, or into the ears of the young girls who come to have their skirts shortened, and they giggle, for they don't know that it has gone into Amyas's ear also.

There is another voice that only Amyas hears. It tells him to go away, it marshals his father's words and looks together. His mother worries about him, of course, but when she sees he is determined to go, she gives him the names of relatives in the city and a few old friends.

"I'll write," promises Amyas.

But he never does. And when, after two weeks, his mother writes her friends and her relatives, she finds that Amyas has never stopped there at all. And that's awkward to the tailor, almost as awkward as having his son home, because people are always asking, "How's Amyas doing in the big city?"

"Oh, you can't imagine the tales he writes us. He's doing impersonations now. He has a huge apartment over the club where he works—the Cobra, I think it's called. People come up to his place all hours of the day and night. He told us that one night all the Rockettes showed up in his room with a case of champagne."

It gave Morgon the fright that comes over a man who discovers he's a prophet, when nearly a year after Amyas left home, Mr. Harris came in one morning to order a tuxedo and remarked to Morgon, who was fitting a sleeve, "I think I saw your son yesterday."

"Amyas?" squeaked the tailor. "Where?"

The sewing machine in the back room came to a dead halt.

"In a little restaurant on MacDougal Street. I don't remember the name of it—I'd gone there with some friends, and we were having dinner, when suddenly a man came out and announced there would be a floor show. And the act he introduced—well, there was this very large man" (he avoided the word fat) "who came out in pink rompers and played a mandolin and sang. I don't remember what he sang. But he was awfully funny."

"Amyas doesn't play a mandolin," said the tailor, trying to calm himself.

"Well, perhaps it wasn't Amyas. But it looked like him. I asked the waiter to tell me the name of the man we were watching. 'Pretty Baby,' said the waiter, 'he doesn't call himself anything else. The manager makes his check out to Pretty Baby.' I asked if he played here often, and the waiter shrugged. 'He comes and goes like the wind. We have people who drop by every night, hoping he'll show up. Sometimes he'll stay away for months.' They say he's turned down a couple of movie contracts."

When Mr. Harris left, the tailor hurried into the back room. His wife sat at her machine and looked past her husband as if she were trying to focus on a point just short of infinity.

"You think I don't feel it, too, Ursula? You think you're the only one who feels it?"

But inside he was afraid. How could the news of Amyas so change the shape and color of his wife's face?

"Why don't you go upstairs and lie down? I'll take care of the shop."

She went without a word. By the machine lay the little date book where he noted the work to be done; Morgon picked it up. At ten o'clock the Fitz girls were coming to pick up the skirts they had left to be shortened and that Miss Johnson who handled trouble calls for the telephone company wanted three zippers repaired in the dresses she'd brought in last week.

At eight o'clock, Morgon stood in the back room and surveyed the pile. Dresses. Trousers. Jackets. Skirts. Seams to be let out, hems to be taken up, buttonholes to be moved over; he had counted on Ursula finishing them today. He sat down and picked up the first skirt, which was already pinned, and started slowly around the hem. Yellow flowered cotton. Like stitching bees into a meadow. When Mrs. Shore came at a quarter of nine to call for her coat, he had hardly fenced in half the pasture.

"I don't hear the machine," said Mrs. Shore as she tried on the coat before the mirror.

"Ah, my wife's not well. I think she's got a little attack of sinus."

Saying it almost took away the dull fear in his stomach. Nobody he knew had ever stayed in bed with a sinus infection for more than a few days. After Mrs. Shore left, he hurried back to finish the skirt. But every time he looked at the pile to be done, a panic came over him. He locked the front door, hung out his sign: *closed*, and worked all morning in silence. At noon his eyes ached and he went upstairs to find his wife.

He found her in bed. Her face over the top of the bedclothes looked pinched and craven. The old fairy tale:

the wolf grinning in grandmother's nightgown. Morgon stood at the foot of the bed and stared at her helplessly.

"You should drink something. Shall I make you some tea?"

Silence.

"What can I do for you? Does anything hurt?"

"Here."

She pointed to her heart.

All afternoon they sat in the waiting room of the emergency clinic, among crying children and a few old women bent nearly double with age. When the receptionist finally called *Mrs. Axel,* she rose from her chair and trudged into the doctor's office without looking back. It hurt Morgon that she had nothing to say to him.

Morgon waited. He picked up the *Reader's Digest.* The elevator to the right of him opened and closed; flocks of young doctors hurried in and out, white-coated like geese. Presently he heard his name. Everyone in the room watched him go.

The doctor's office with its certificates and abstract paintings and cabinets of instruments made Morgon feel shoddy and stupid. The doctor was younger and taller than Morgon. Wearing his white coat and the casual emblems of his profession, the stethoscope and head mirror, he introduced himself and peered over his glasses at the tailor.

"You're Mr. Axel? Please sit down."

Morgon pulled up a chair and faced the doctor at his desk like a student waiting for a reprimand.

"I'm sending your wife to St. Joseph's for a rest. You are familiar with St. Joseph's, I presume?"

"I thought," stammered the tailor, "that St. Joseph's was for people who—"

He stopped. Waited. He didn't want to give the wrong answer.

"Your wife hasn't had a heart attack, as you both feared. Rather, it's a case of severe depression. A mild nervous breakdown, you could call it. I think that with a month of rest she'll be able to come home."

What did the tailor do on his first night alone?

He rambled aimlessly from one room to the next, feeling as if a burden had been lifted from him: *the moment before you savor your freedom.* He fed the dog, washed a few dirty dishes, and put them away. He had no desire to cook anything for himself and decided to eat at a Hungarian restaurant on the other side of town which had always intrigued him. Mr. Harris told him that a family ran the restaurant in an old house and he praised it for "local color."

When he entered the front hall of Czerny's and hung his jacket on the rack, he felt as if he were coming to visit an old friend. The first room he saw contained nothing but a pool table where several young men in leather shorts were shooting a game. Morgon passed quickly into the spacious dining room; it was completely deserted though each table was elaborately set, as if for a banquet of ghosts. Fifty napkins, folded like mitres, perched between the knives and forks and water glasses; a nesting ground of strange birds.

The tailor found a seat in the corner. To his distress he found that he could look right into the kitchen, where three women were eating at a little table. It would be awkward to move now, he decided. After all, they were paying no attention to him. A baby crawled over to the largest woman, dragging a long rope behind it, which seemed to be tied to one of the table legs.

But an old man in a white apron was standing in front of him, his pencil poised on his pad.

"Will you have wine?"

Morgon nodded and looked around for the wine list; there was none.

"For dinner we're having skewered meat and noodles stuffed with red cabbage."

It was an announcement rather than a menu, for the old man whisked out of sight and reappeared a moment later with a bottle of wine: *Schwartze Katz*. Morgon felt he ought to say something.

"Is it good?"

"Everyone likes it," said the old man, shrugging as he yanked out the cork and poured the tailor a glass.

In the tiny kitchen, the youngest of the three women got up and hurried to the stove. His order had set them all in motion. He avoided glancing at them, but he could hear them chattering in their own tongue as they stirred and scraped and shifted the dishes about. They had interrupted their dinner to serve his.

The tailor ate slowly, aware that at last the women had sat down again and were eating exactly what he was eating, only without the amenities of clean linen and good service. Suddenly he imagined that they saw him as an eccentric, a crank, and he longed to go and sit down with them. The light outside was falling away; the woman with the child rose from the table and stood at the window, and suddenly everything flared up gold under the last look of the sun. Then the darkness dropped; the old man turned on the lights in the dining room, and the oldest woman began scrubbing a large kettle at the sink.

When did the tailor first miss his wife?

Not until he saw a strange woman washing dishes in a strange kitchen. So it had always been, so it would always be. The man out in front, the woman in the kitchen with the child—ah, that was where the real life started. Amyas, ten years old, sits on a stool in the kitchen and talks to his mother, who is shelling peas, nodding, and listening; the window open, the warm spring air blowing through.

Morgon paid his bill and left. He did not want to go home. He walked over to Main Street and peered in the windows of the shops. It was Saturday night, it was summer, and the young people parading up and down the street gave it the air of a carnival. Standing in front of Pearlmutter's pawnshop, Morgon examined, with great interest, guns, suitcases, rings, boots, electric fans, cameras, and hair dryers. By the time his bus arrived, he felt sated. Pressing his face to the window he tried in vain to separate his own image from the passing world outside. He got off the bus and felt the first drops of a warm rain and hurried toward his building. As he passed the butcher's door he saw a little boy, barefoot, hugging himself on the stoop, smiling at him. The tailor hardly realized what he had seen until he was inside his own door and it was too late to smile back.

What were the tailor's thoughts as he lay in bed?

The room is still and nothing is lonelier than the dark.

What did the tailor see when he entered his shop on Monday?

A pile of unfinished garments in the back room. How was he going to finish everything? No kindly priest had told him the trick of reaching behind and taking one at a time, the trick of not looking back. Furthermore, he couldn't very well sit and sew while customers were knocking at the door, demanding to be fitted or to pick up their packages, or simply wanting to pass the time of day. The front room faced the world, resounded with courtesy and opinion; light flooded it from the outside and everything appeared to be under control. But now the tailor found that all this depended on the state of things in the back room, where a deep paralysis had set in. Overcome with anxiety, he closed shop on Thursday and Friday to catch up on back work. He sat in his wife's chair and lost himself in the tedious tasks that banded her life like a ring.

And what did the tailor say on Sunday when he visited his wife?

He stood at the foot of her bed, clutching his hat, staring at this woman who was almost a stranger to him. Her hospital gown gave her an antiseptic air. She seemed to have lost so much of her coarse dark hair that Morgon could almost see the outline of her skull. For the first time, he heard himself lie.

"You look pretty good, Ursula."

Silence. She gazed at him curiously, as if she had forgotten his name. To Morgon's relief, the patients whose medicine bottles cluttered the other three night stands were gone.

"Are you comfortable here?" he asked.

"It's all right."

"You got nice neighbors?" He jerked his head toward the next bed.

"Margery Wilkes and Norma Tiedelbaum are nice. They're downstairs with their visitors. But Mrs. Shingleton —agh, she's disgusting. Saves all her toilet paper, keeps it in her pillowcase. She's supposed to move up to the sixth floor next week."

"Terrible," said Morgon. Then, hesitantly. "Have you

seen the doctor? Has he told you when you'll be ready to come home?"

"I will come home," said Ursula slowly and distinctly, "when I can find someone to take my place here."

"What!" exclaimed Morgon. "Why, there are plenty of people waiting for hospital beds."

"Yes. But nobody willing to take my place."

The tailor felt a little frightened, for it dawned on him that his wife was really losing her mind.

"Do you mean to say that when you're well, you can't leave the hospital? Did the doctor tell you that?"

"No," said Ursula. She closed her eyes. "Amyas told me."

"Amyas!" cried the tailor.

"Every night he comes and stands at the foot of the bed. 'Amyas,' I say, 'when will you come home?' I plead with him, Morgon. I plead with him. 'It would take a thousand years of weeping,' he says, 'to pay a fraction of the grief I've had to bear since my father turned me out.' "

"That's not true!" shouted the tailor. "I never turned him out. He left of his own free will."

Ursula opened her eyes, as empty of feeling as those of fish.

What was the vision of Amyas's mother?

Amyas, dressed in a doublet of green taffeta cut like oak leaves, on a cloth of gold. He hangs like a lantern on the trees outside, his white face shining through the window.

A full moon tonight, says Margery Wilkes in the next bed.

Amyas, whispers his mother, when are you coming home?

What was the vision of Amyas's father?

Gabardine in a heap; bills to be paid; a dress form with a hole in its belly and no head or arms or legs; the orders streaming in; his wife's face. Himself dancing on a treadmill, fed by days pointed like spikes. Without undressing he lies down on his bed, closes his eyes, and sees, brilliant and strange, the mask of sickness that has come over his wife's face.

"The animal always tries to avoid the hunter. If the hunter shoots you, you lose. If you avoid him, you win."

Ursula shakes her head but already Morgon is counting for her to hide.

"Eight! nine! ten!"

Shouldering his gun, he sets out. Trim blue jacket buttoned high at the throat, gold epaulettes, gold buttons where eagles sleep, the iron cross nestled in ropes of gold braid. Every bush shelters a victim. Far ahead of him, Amyas is running for his life, and Ursula hobbles through the underbrush after him, dragging a trap on her foot.

"Ursula, wait! The game is over!"

But the gun springs back into his hand. He pulls off the epaulettes and the iron cross, he throws his jacket to the ground. His wife does not stop running; she knows he is the hunter who will never take her alive till he runs beside her as a creature of prey.

Darkness is rolling in; at the end of Market Street you may see Pearlmutter's pawnshop. Inside, Solomon Pearlmutter in pinstriped pants and a Hawaiian shirt, is standing at the till, counting his coins into a deerskin pouch.

Suddenly the shop bell tinkles and in limps a stocky man carrying a huge knapsack on his shoulder and a rifle in his hand. Solomon touches the pistol he keeps under the counter.

"I have here a number of things I'd like to get rid of," says the man.

And he begins to empty the bag on the counter with ritual precision. Masks carved like fabulous animals, photographs of acrobats, broken trophies, a box of military decorations. Solomon keeps his left hand on the pistol and shakes his head.

"If I can't sell 'em, I don't want 'em. You see the kind of things I got here. Watches, rings, guns."

His right hand waves toward a wall studded with electric guitars. Everything in Solomon's shop knows its place; the guitars stay on the wall, the pocket watches and diamond rings lie in a glass case by the cash register, the accordions huddle together in the front row, the guns hang high over the desk at the back of the store where he figures his earnings at night.

"You won't take any of them?"

The wild look that comes over the man's face makes Solomon uneasy.

"No. Sorry."

"What will you give me for this rifle?"

"Let's have a look," says Solomon and reaches for it.

Quick as a snake the tailor takes aim, but he does not shoot.

Long afterward, when the tailor's body had crumpled across his mind a thousand times, Solomon Pearlmutter wondered why his attacker had not taken the first shot.

When Morgon Axel awoke, he was lying in a strange

bed. He tried to prop himself up on his elbows and felt as if a knife had cut and salted a deep crevice between his shoulders. Letting his head sink back to the pillow, he turned it slowly to the right and the left. An endless row of beds echoed each other in both directions, yes, and across the aisle as well, though someone had dimmed the light in this room and drawn the window shades. The only light that let him see all this came from the hall.

Those who cannot walk must fly. So Morgon Axel raised himself up until he saw his own body tucked under a blanket on the bed beneath him. But the real Morgon Axel was floating horizontally out of the ward and down the corridor, like a dandelion seed. Past closed doors, Past a green oxygen tank next to one of them. Past the vases of flowers which the nurses set outside the rooms every night.

Far ahead of him, he heard voices. A buzz, a confusion as of owls' wings, crickets' cries, pigs rooting for truffles in the woods, squirrels rolling acorns in attics. A murmur and cry of doves. Hovering six feet above the floor, Morgon grabbed the door—*Doctor's Lounge*, said the letters under his hand—and pushed himself through.

A forest was growing in the doctor's lounge. Yes, and there was a judge's bench where an old Jew sat, pounding a gavel and calling the quails to order, and a skeleton stood at one end of the bench and at the other end Amyas Axel, in green doublet and white stockings, was walking on his hands back and forth under the nose of the owlish clerk, who perched on the Jew's shoulder and saw everything. The woods were packed with spectators, rabbits and bears and deer, who lifted their heads behind the witnesses in the front row, blond Ingeborg the parson's daughter and Hans who died years ago and Heinrich who died with him; only their spiked helmets survived. And here's Otto Strauss, and next to him Frau Nolke, peeling a lapful of turnips.

When the last leaf stopped rustling, the Jew began to speak. At his first words, Morgon sank to the ground like a dead balloon.

Members of the jury, we are entering upon the last stages of this trial. You know that we have been trying to administer justice in accord with the law. What is the administration of justice but this, that a guilty man be found guilty and an innocent man be acquitted?

Let me remind you, members of the jury, that your role is very different from mine. I sit here to see that this trial is conducted in accord with the law and to clarify to you what the law is. You have heard half a century of evidence and it is the task of each of you to decide whether the facts presented to you support the charge against this man: the failure to love. The punishment, if he is convicted, is death by loneliness.

And now let me deal briefly with the evidence of the case. You have heard the testimony of the prosecution—

(The skeleton bows; like a cardsharp, a bookie, a flim-flam man, his skull is always smiling.)

—who has argued that Morgon Axel never knew what he saw and never touched what he knew but hid it in lies and loved his lies more than the naked face of truth. The face of truth is neither steady nor kind. That is why we cannot subpoena the key witness at this trial: we should have to summon everybody on earth.

(Amyas, in hobo clothes, is walking on a single strand of hair that extends over the judge's head. From an inside pocket he pulls a pair of white doves and sends them circling over the courtroom.)

The case rests on the testimony of Solomon Pearlmutter—

(Solomon Pearlmutter, subpoenaed during sleep, stands up in the front row and bows. When his wife wakes him tomorrow, he will tell her he dreamed an extraordinary dream. She will ask him what it was, but he won't remember; already herds of rabbits and quails are arming on the borders of his sleep, ready to drive his broken dream into the pit.)

—who concedes that before he shot the accused, there was enough time for the accused to take aim and fire. What you must decide, creatures of the jury, is whether Morgon Axel did indeed wish to shoot Solomon Pearlmutter or whether the accused wished Solomon Pearlmutter to shoot him, so that he might take his wife's place and put on the terrible eyesight of truth.

You have heard the defense, Amyas Axel, plead most eloquently on behalf of his father. Over the objections of the prosecution, I am admitting into this court a kind of testimony never before, I think, admitted into any court.

(Amyas, balancing on the strand of hair, takes an invisible loaf of bread from an invisible oven and slices it into baskets.

The birds take the baskets in their beaks and fly down with them to the jury and to the spectators.

Morgon Axel reaches for an imaginary slice and pulls out a real one.)

Creatures of the jury, I have nothing more to say to you. I ask you to go out and consider your verdict and tell me whether you see before you (a rustle of leaves and collars; a thousand heads turn to look at Morgon Axel leaning against the door to the forest) a man who is guilty of loving nothing but his own lies or whether you see a man who has tried to patch himself together a good life out of a bad one, and who is capable not only of love but of change. Of giving himself up to put on another man's truth.

Morgon Axel sits up in bed. A young nurse is speaking to him, smiling pleasantly.

"You may go this morning, Mr. Axel. The X-rays of your shoulder show that the wound is superficial. If you take the elevator at the end of the hall down to the ground floor, you'll find yourself directly across from the front entrance. There's a taxi stand outside."

Morgon Axel climbs unsteadily out of bed. Someone has laid his clothes on a chair. He dresses and rides downstairs in a crowd of doctors and wheelchairs, and chooses a taxi. A nice green checkered one. When he leaves the cab, he hands the driver all the change in his pockets, which isn't a great deal. He travels lightly, this Morgon Axel, without any baggage to hold him down. The sky is clear, the air as sweet as forgiveness. He unlocks his shop, and bending over, he props the door open with an empty spool. The room smells stale and musty. Morgon Axel pulls a chair outside, sits down in the sunlight that dapples the front of his shop, closes his eyes, and waits for his wife to come home.

5

Amyas Axel, His Care and Keep

I

As Nicholas Mardachek turned up Hester Street, he felt his anger lift a little, and when he passed a restaurant full of people, he pushed open the door and walked in.

A wave of warm air and the fragrance of food greeted him. Under posters of ruined Greek temples and photographs of President Kennedy, people were chattering and eating: a few glanced up. Looking about him, he spotted one empty seat in the back, at a table already occupied by an elderly man and woman, who sat opposite one another like strangers, and a girl who sat opposite no one but kept glancing behind her toward the kitchen. Nicholas followed her gaze but saw nothing remarkable. The cook was standing at a counter chopping vegetables, and another fellow in a scruffy hat was pouring wine from fancy jugs into plain bottles. The clatter of dishes rose over a hundred conversations. Nicholas pushed his way down the aisle past the long rows of people eating, sank into the empty seat, and hung his knapsack on the back of the chair. The girl frowned at him. She had a thin, pretty face, and although she wore a velvet headband to hold her long red hair in place, she kept brushing her bangs out of her eyes. She looked close to his own age, or at least no more than twenty. Presently she leaned forward and hissed into his ear.

"That seat belongs to Amyas."

Nicholas pretended not to hear. He picked up the menu and made a great show of studying it, all the while reaching back to feel for his knapsack, once, twice, three, four times. It contained everything he owned, which was not a great deal—a few books, his razor, toothbrush, twenty-five dollars, and his harmonica, which he made himself play whenever he wanted a cigarette. He had started carrying the knapsack on his back, even in his own house, when he discovered his wife was stealing from him. Or if not stealing, then misplacing things—his comb, his razor, the book he had put away so as to have it when he wanted to read it—believing perhaps that if she tormented him enough, he would rather work than sit around at home.

She was wrong. All those days at his father's filling station in Akron, all those hours of cleaning windshields and pumping gasoline into more cars than he cared to remember, he dreamed of servants, of electric guitars, of a movie projector that he would set up in his bedroom and watch whatever he liked the whole night long. "If you can't make it, you got to marry it," his mother had told him whenever she caught him lazing around. So he had gone east and worked even harder and married a buxom girl from Long Island who turned out to be even poorer than himself and batty as well. He had ended up waiting on her and carrying his meager goods around in a knapsack.

Suddenly everyone in the room burst into applause. Out of the kitchen marched a dwarf lugging a guitar and after him waddled a man so large that the diners had to push their tables sideways to let him pass. Under his arm he carried a mandolin.

"Gunther! Amyas!"

"Amyas! Amyas!"

The dwarf waved to the two girls who had called out "Gunther." But the larger man, who seemed much more in demand, smiled over their heads.

"Amyas!"

Amyas was huge. At least four hundred pounds, Nicholas decided. He could not take his eyes off the man; next to the dwarf, Amyas was overwhelming. Where the dwarf was nearly bald, Amyas's brown wavy hair thatched his ears. Where the dwarf was cleanshaven, Amyas had a beard that curled halfway down his chest and forked out like a serpent's tongue. Where the dwarf slouched under the sagging shoulders of his huge tweed jacket, Amyas wore a white shirt and tie and a tiny black vest embroidered with flowers. It hung like a bauble on a Christmas tree.

Behind them came a waiter, carrying a chair which he set up against the jukebox on the other side of the room, directly opposite Nicholas's table. The dwarf began to tune his guitar, holding it high against his cheek as if he were sighting through a gun. Amyas seated himself and rested his mandolin against his belly. Looking at each other, they thumped out several measures of a fast tune in a minor key.

Then the dwarf opened his mouth and shouted a refrain, which Amyas punctuated with hoots and cries:

> *You and I and Amyas,*
> *Amyas and you and I,*
> *To the greenwood must we go, alas!*
> *You and I, my life and Amyas.*

The elderly couple had stopped eating to listen. The girl sat rapt, her mouth repeating the words ever so lightly as she rested her chin in her hands. But now they were playing the verses, which told at great length of a faithless wench whose lover caught her at her tricks and threw her out of the house. There were a few titters from those who knew the song and looked forward to the last words of the angry lover.

> *Who's gonna shoe your pretty little foot*
> *with boots of Spanish leather?*

The dwarf, singing at the top of his voice, was making as many gestures as his music would let him. Nothing of Amyas moved but his fingers, plinking the strings.

> *I'll go no more to her bedside*
> *so let the devil take her!*

Let the devil take her! roared the audience, stamping its feet.

Then the dwarf lifted his hands from the strings, Amyas stroked a final chord, and everyone applauded. All over the room, purses snapped open and silver rang on the tables. The dwarf skipped nimbly about, thrusting a bread-basket decked with paper flowers into the midst of the crowd, and the money rang in. Amyas laid the mandolin on his chair and hailed the waiter, who at once slid an extra chair between Nicholas and the girl.

"Move over," she said, tapping his arm. "If Amyas sits in the aisle, the waiters can't get by with the food."

Grabbing his knapsack, Nicholas eased his way out and let Amyas through. The great belly brushed him, the brown eyes peered at him over the forked beard, and Nicholas shuddered. Amyas's gestures were grander than anyone else's in the room, his smile wiser as he drew up the chair and sat down, and his courtesy to the girl and to Nicholas seemed to overflow from some kingly largesse. As if summoned by mutual understanding, the waiter laid out before him a basket of bread, a bottle of wine and two glasses, a bowl of clear soup, and half a sheep's head cut lengthwise, its eyeball shining, on a bed of cooked cabbage leaves. Amyas rubbed his fleshy palms together and smacked his lips.

"My little dove," he exclaimed, pinching the girl's cheek as he poured two glasses from the anonymous bottle of wine. Then he noticed Nicholas's empty place and shouted, "George! Another glass here!"

"Thank you," said Nicholas.

"Has the waiter taken your order, sir?"

"No," said Nicholas.

"May I recommend the specialty of the house? Clear soup for an appetizer, then a plate of roast kid or—" he pointed to the dish in front of him—"baked head of lamb."

"I think I'd just like the soup," said Nicholas. "I'm a vegetarian."

Amyas's beard twitched into a smile.

"Soup and a plate of spaghetti," he murmured into the ear of the waiter, who flashed away like a bird.

Then Amyas gave himself over to eating his dinner. Nicholas stared at him appalled. His sleeves glided into the soup like sops of bread. He slurped it away in a twinkling and, giving a satisfied grunt, he pushed the empty bowl aside; then, picking up the lamb's head, he began to scoop it out with his fingers, stuffing his cheeks full and popping the eyeball into his mouth like an olive. At the same time he held out tidbits to the girl, who nibbled from his fingers like a sparrow. When he had scraped the skull bare, he set it on the table, seized the plate, and licked it till it shone. His tongue was as pink and elastic as a cat's. Then he replaced the skull, belched a little, and turned to Nicholas.

"Have you a handkerchief, sir? I seem to have lost my napkin."

Nicholas unbuckled the knapsack, rummaged through it, and brought out a toothbrush and a battered copy of *Moby Dick*. Amyas smiled.

"Do you always carry so much?"

"It's all I have," said Nicholas and giggled, for the wine had gone to his head. "I've just left my wife. So I've no place to go."

"And making up again is so pleasant, isn't it?" said Amyas.

"You don't understand," said Nicholas, and he suddenly felt himself growing very agitated. "I've left her for good. She just got out of Bellevue last week. A whole month she stayed there, and she's worse now than when she went in. Spying on me, nagging at me, telling me she hears voices that say I'm no good. 'Nicholas Mardachek is the scum of the earth!' 'May his teeth break in his head!' 'May a black dog devour Nicholas Mardachek!' "

His own voice choked him. He wanted to lay his head on Amyas's huge shoulder and burst into tears.

"How old are you?" asked Amyas.

"Nineteen," said Nicholas, and he opened his blue eyes very wide.

Amyas shook his head and looked up at the ceiling as if he were praying.

"I know nothing about you. You might be a thief, for all I know. A thief and a cutthroat. And indeed, I have made such mistakes before. I once gave shelter to a man who stole one of my boots. Now that was odd, wasn't it? For of course he couldn't wear one boot. He might have taken my mandolin. Or my wallet. But he stole only one boot. I never found another pair to fit me. And we had talked and sung the whole night together too. He was a fighter pilot during the war and flew a record number of missions over Germany. He showed me his medals in a little box. You, sir, do not look like a cutthroat. But I might be mistaken. Nevertheless, I can offer you my chambers if you are without a bed and without means."

When they rose to go, Amyas pulled an elegant cane down from the coatrack and gave it to the girl. Only then did Nicholas observe that her left foot was several inches shorter than the other. She wore a shoe with a built-up sole.

"Janet, my little dove," said Amyas, and handed her his jacket.

He planted himself in the aisle while she hung it over his shoulders, as if she had long since abandoned the task of easing his arms into the sleeves. My God, thought Nicholas, the smallest things are impossible for him. The girl leaned on her cane and Amyas leaned on her arm, and together they made their way to the door. Clutching his knapsack, Nicholas followed. The waiter handed him the mandolin at the door.

In the taxi Nicholas sat next to the driver, for Amyas filled the entire back seat. Janet perched herself on his huge thighs and whispered like a running brook into his ear, so that Nicholas only caught a few words now and then. Her voice was as high pitched as a child's.

"So I got the green one. That was right, wasn't it, Amyas? Green was the color you wanted?"

"Green was exactly right," whispered Amyas, and nibbled her ear.

"And then I didn't know whether I should buy one or two. It's so hard to find them that I thought I should buy several. On the other hand, it's not very economical, because they don't wear out very fast. Was it right of me to buy two?"

"It was very wise of you to buy two," said Amyas.

"Good," said Janet, and turned to look out the window.

When the taxi drew to a stop, she pulled a little leather coin purse out of Amyas's coat pocket and counted out the fare. A wave of sleep pulled Nicholas down; he could hardly find the energy to open the door, and he shivered in the night air. But how much more difficult it was for Amyas! His grunting and wheezing shook the entire cab. Slowly, as if he were being born, Amyas emerged feet first from the darkness. Then he turned and offered his arm to Janet, who glided out like a feather and, leaning ever so lightly on her cane, tucked the purse back into his pocket again.

"My place is up there, sir," said Amyas.

And he pointed to the top floor of the building in front of them.

"Where are we?" asked Nicholas.

For he saw no sign of life except themselves, no apartment windows with bars and curtains, no stairway leading up to the front door, and no cars lining the curb. Some papers blew down the sidewalk and swirled over their heads. It was one of those empty streets given over to printing companies, warehouses, and wholesalers.

"Prince Street," said Amyas.

Janet took a key ring from her own pocket and unlocked the door. In the vestibule hung an outdated poster for an art show, four small mailboxes, and one large one lettered with two names: AMYAS AXEL, JANET WEST. Beyond them an elevator door stood open. They entered, closed the gate, and rode up slowly. Nicholas watched the layers of plaster fall away under them as they ascended.

"Do you know the Akton Photographic Company?" asked Amyas suddenly.

"No," said Nicholas.

"They have their main darkroom on the second floor. I'm on the sixth. It isn't so bad when you ride up. I knew a man on Spring Street who had a loft on the ninth floor, and there was no elevator. He was always tired. I believe he's dead now."

Amyas's face was flushed, and he was breathing heavily; the walk from the taxi had exhausted him. Nicholas found himself admiring the man. Amyas was really beautiful, the way a brawling merchant in an old Dutch painting is beautiful. His face was vivid rather than gross, and his weight glorified rather than shamed him.

"Who else lives in this building?"

"Let me see." Amyas closed his eyes for several minutes. "A lady welder just moved into the place below mine last week. On the other floors you find mostly private clubs and businesses of various sorts. I rarely meet anyone from those places. But on the fourth floor the Apple Town Players have their loft. Have you ever heard of the Apple Town Players?"

"No," said Nicholas.

"We'll go to one of their plays some evening. Janet acts in them quite often. You'll recommend a good one, won't you Janet?"

But Janet was falling asleep on his arm. When the elevator jolted to a stop, she straightened up and unlocked a heavy bolt on the door in front of them. It sprang open with a sigh, and Nicholas stepped into a spacious room. Half the floor was carpeted in green, the other half was painted a dull gray, and the door marked the boundary between them. The green half looked by far the more comfortable. It had a window, curtained in yellow silk, which ran nearly the length of the wall. In front of it stood a wardrobe, a bookcase, and a huge bed. The bedposts and legs were carved to resemble hundreds of spools strung together, and on the top lay a bedspread solidly embroidered with tiny green and gold dragons.

In the gray half of the room he saw an icebox, painted bright blue, and a sink under which someone had stacked several fifty-pound bags of cracked corn. There were also a small stove, a cupboard, and a kitchen table, and against the wall to his left were a sofa and a vanity table. But what struck him most were two singular objects in the middle of the room. Placed so as to obstruct rather than save space was a large cupboard with two swinging doors. On an inside hook hung a nightgown; inside was a neatly made bed. Behind the cupboard a huge winged machine crouched as if about to devour the sleeper.

"That's a glider you're looking at," said Amyas, taking the mandolin from Nicholas and leaning it against the wall. "Have you ever flown one?"

"No," said Nicholas. In another moment he would be asleep on his feet. To his dismay, Amyas was growing lively. Janet dropped her coat on the floor and curled up on the sofa.

"It's one of the few flying machines that doesn't require a motor. It glides on air currents, the way a bird does. "You buy the parts in a kit. Janet!"

Janet raised her head.

"What?"

When she saw Amyas roll his eyes toward the ceiling and shrug helplessly, she blinked and curled herself up again, like a cat.

"I could teach her so many things, but she falls asleep," said Amyas. "I hope you'll have some coffee with me, sir. I can't bear going straight to bed. That's her one great failing," he went on, pointing to Janet. "She can't stay awake. I could teach her so much, yes, and all the players in her troupe. Nobody listens to me. Nobody cares about discipline any more."

While he was talking he filled a saucepan with water,

set it on the stove, and measured out coffee into two cups.

"That's what it takes to fly," he said, and shook his finger at Nicholas. "Discipline. Do you ski?"

"No," said Nicholas. And now it seemed to him that Amyas was flying with amazing grace, though pots, pans, and dishes rattled and the floor creaked when he walked.

"A pity. You've probably never known the freedom of flight. But you can't fly without discipline. I learned that when I was a dancer. Don't laugh! Would you guess that when I was your age, I was a superb acrobat? I was the director of the Blue Angels. We did a spectacular trampoline act on television and in nightclubs. I demanded absolute obedience of my performers and of my own body. Every night we flew into each other's arms. And we never fell."

He handed Nicholas a cup of coffee and motioned him to sit at the table; then he disappeared behind the wardrobe at the other end of the loft. Presently he returned wearing a green silk caftan.

"It's from Morocco," he said, holding it out for Nicholas to feel.

Nicholas felt it.

"Very nice," he said. He could hardly keep his eyes open, but he did not want Amyas to accuse him of falling asleep on the threshold of instruction. Amyas pulled up a chair opposite him, brought out a small phial and a silver box, flicked the lid of the box open, and lifted from its velvet lining a hypodermic needle. He filled it from the phial, studied the inner side of his arm for a moment, then plunged the needle in.

"I hope this doesn't bother you, sir," he said. "I've done it so often I hardly feel a thing."

Nicholas tried to appear casual.

"I don't use the stuff myself."

"No, of course not! Do you know what this is?"

Amyas leaned forward, as if imparting a great secret. *The urine of pregnant women.*"

"Ah," said Nicholas.

"Don't try to pretend you aren't curious. How many people do you know who inject themselves with the urine of pregnant women? It's said to contain a hormone that controls excessive weight. Excessive bodily weight," he repeated, as if distinguishing it from some other kind, "due to glandular imbalance."

"Glandular imbalance," nodded Nicholas.

"Be thankful you passed through adolescence without it."

He wiped the needle on his sleeve and laid it tenderly into its case. A loud snore startled them both. Nicholas turned around. Janet was sleeping with her arm stretched out over the edge of the sofa.

"If only I could keep her awake! I'd teach her everything I know. And I know so much. Look at that body—light as silk. I could teach her to fly if only she didn't fall asleep. My little pigeon," he cooed as he bustled over to her. Bending down he tried to lift her. Nicholas ran to help.

"Just set her down in bed. She gets very cross when she's wakened. But if you leave her alone she'll wake up of her own accord and put on her nightgown without a fuss."

"Does she like the doors closed?" asked Nicholas.

"No. She likes to close them herself. It's a Dutch bed. I had a terrible time finding one for her. And now she wants a bedspread like mine embroidered with a thousand dragons. You can sleep on the sofa, sir. It unfolds into quite a comfortable bed. There's toothpaste by the sink. The toilet doesn't flush. Fill that yellow bucket by the door before you go in, or there'll be a great stink by morning."

Amyas trotted down to his end of the loft, then stopped and called, "I've forgotten your name."

"Nicholas Mardachek." He did not remember having given it before.

"Shall I turn off the light, Nicholas? There's only one switch."

"Yes," said Nicholas, for he was too sleepy to take off anything but his shoes. No bed ever felt better. The blanket was very thin. He pulled Janet's coat over him, let his knapsack slide to the floor, and stretched himself out. In the darkness he could hear Janet moving around. The door slammed shut. Now she was singing in a high scratchy voice. A thin streak of light from outside touched the door, like someone listening to an old-fashioned radio. The last thing Nicholas saw was Amyas's belly, under the skins of one thousand dragons, silhouetted against the window like a hill, waiting for the crest of morning.

II

When Nicholas woke up, he heard Amyas singing over a commotion of cooing and a flutter of wings.

"My little pigeon! My honey dove!"

And then a snatch of song:

> *Who's gonna shoe your pretty little foot*
> *with boots of Spanish leather?*

Nicholas stumbled to his feet. His throat was raw and his head felt stuffed with cotton; had he drunk that much? The loft was so hot he felt cooked dry, and his own flesh weighed him down. Behind his bed sunlight streamed in through a door he had not noticed before. He padded out on the fire escape in his stocking feet and found Amyas, in a tweed hunting jacket, walking on the adjacent roof among cages and cages of pigeons. Out of the corner of his eye, Amyas saw him coming. One by one he opened the cages. With a beating of feathers and much clucking and crying, the birds soared out so eagerly that Nicholas ducked and covered his head.

"Watch," said Amyas.

He drew up a chair and sat down. For several minutes the birds twittered about him at random, then settled into an enormous circle around his head. Wider and wider the circle grew, like the rings that flow out from a stone tossed into water, till Nicholas would not have known it as a circle if he had not seen it from the beginning. To see all of it, he had to tip back his head and stare up into a bright sky. And then a strange thing happened. A flock of unknown birds, flying north after the winter, cut through the circle and passed on. But Amyas's birds did not swerve; only gradually the circle grew smaller until they lighted on the tops of their cages. Amyas positively glowed as he opened the doors and lifted the birds in.

"You know, when I was six, I asked the elementary school librarian for a book on flying. She took me over to the section on airplanes. 'No,' I said, 'I want to fly with wings.' Well, she was a resourceful woman, and she gave me a book about Icarus. I sat down and read it through twice, to make sure I hadn't missed a word of the instructions. But it didn't give many details. And even if I'd had the wax, I couldn't have gotten the feathers. My father was fastidious, a real Prussian. When the army rejected him, he turned to making uniforms. The only outrageous thing he ever did was to marry my mother."

Inside the loft a door slammed. Both Amyas and Nicholas hurried inside. Janet was setting a bag of groceries on the table.

"I found everything except the pickled udders. You'll have to do without them."

"But the recipe calls for udders," exclaimed Amyas.

Janet gave a little shrug.

"Do you want me to try somewhere else?"

"No, no, I'll make do with pickled tripe."

"Well, I've got to go back out again to get some white makeup for the play tonight."

"Why didn't you get it just now?"

"I couldn't carry any more."

"What is the play?" asked Nicholas.

"Tonight we're having a pantomime workshop. If you want to come with me now, I'll wait for you. Prince Street doesn't look like much at night."

She and Amyas retreated to the far end of the loft. As Nicholas pulled on his shoes, he heard them talking in loud voices, pitched at the edge of anger.

"What's the good of cooking sea urchins if they taste bad?"

"My little dove, how do you know they taste bad? You've never eaten any. The Romans ate them."

"That's because they didn't have anything else."

"Of course they did. The average Roman citizen had a

far more sensitive palate than you or I. No eat-and-run places in ancient Rome. No waiting at counters."

"And I can't stand five courses of soup."

"I wish you'd let me teach you about these matters. There are soups and there are soups. Joan of Arc ate nothing but soup five times a day."

"I'm ready," called Nicholas rather awkwardly. He stuffed his harmonica into his back pocket, closed the knapsack, and pushed it under the sofa.

"Good," said Janet.

They rode the elevator down in silence. Nicholas stared at the ceiling, Janet looked down at her cane, at her white stockings and white gloves, and picked a spot off her navy blue coat.

"Nice coat," said Nicholas.

"It's new. Amyas got it for me last week."

She offered him her arm, and they stepped out onto the street. He had been right about the neighborhood. The doors and windows were inscribed with the neat gold lettering of an earlier time: *Doll Manufacturing Company; Bolts and Parts*. They walked to the end of the block in silence and came to a newspaper store. A small sign in the window advertised egg creams.

"You want one?" asked Janet.

"I don't have any money with me."

"I have some. Amyas usually buys me one. We'll get one on the way back."

In the handball court on the other side of the street, a pack of young boys was starting a game.

"Let's watch," said Janet.

They crossed the street and stood with their faces

pressed against the wire. If I were alone, thought Nicholas, I'd join them. But the heat in Amyas's loft had made him lethargic.

"How old is Amyas?" he asked.

"I don't know. About forty, wouldn't you think? Or maybe thirty-five."

"Where is he from?"

"Why, I guess he's lived in lots of places," said Janet vaguely. "His parents used to live in the city but they moved up the river a few years ago. I forget where."

"How old are you?"

"Nineteen."

"Nineteen!" Nicholas pretended to be greatly surprised. "I thought you were younger. Maybe sixteen. Or fifteen. It's the way you dress. And that headband you wear."

"Amyas likes me to wear it."

He wanted to ask her how she had met Amyas, but that seemed rude. Instead he asked, "Where are you from?"

"Buffalo."

"And you left home and came to the city."

"Yes," answered Janet, and she fixed her eyes on the boys who were now shouting and scrambling all over the court. "I left home and came to the city. With friends. You'll meet some of them tonight."

He very much wanted a cigarette. He felt for his harmonica and sucked out a blur of chords. It was a spring day and he was much younger, loitering around the playground after school. The sound wailed up and down; it was almost summer.

"Tell me," said Janet. "What is your wife's name?"

"Norma. Norma Mardachek." It sounded unreal to his ears.

"Is she pretty?"

"Not as pretty as you are," said Nicholas. The truth was, he suddenly couldn't remember what she looked like. Her features swirled away when he tried to pinpoint them: a nose. Take that first. What did it look like? Her eyes. What color were they?

"What does she look like?"

"Dark-haired, and a little on the fat side."

Jostling each other and shouting, the boys ran off the court, past Janet and Nicholas, and headed up the street.

"Let's go," sighed Janet.

They passed the courts and stopped at a dingy little shop that had a large piece of cardboard taped into the empty window. Glass lay scattered on the pavement below. On the cardboard someone had written in a huge black scrawl:

THEATRE MAKEUP. NO MINORS ALLOWED.

Janet led the way inside. A large, frowsy woman in a housedress and cardigan rushed out from the back of the shop. She had painted her eyebrows and eyelids so that the outside corners turned up. Behind her hung a rack of gorilla and skull masks, hats, trumpets, paper snakes, spangled vests, and tambourines. On a shelf over her head were round tins of greasepaint and a few wigs and beards.

"What can I do for you?" she asked, and rested her arms on the counter. They were heavily bandaged to the elbow.

"A can of Max Factor white—why!" cried Janet, "what happened to you?"

The woman shook her head mournfully.

"Kids came by here and broke my window. They broke it so bad I cut myself when I tried to fix it. Can you reach that can up there, mister? I'm so clumsy I don't dare."

Nicholas slid behind the counter after her.

"That one," she said, pointing her arm up like a primitive wing. "Thank you, sweetheart. I ask myself, why do those kids want to come in and beat me up? Why me? So I put up a sign to keep them out. It don't help though. They come around just the same."

One night in Amyas's loft had passed like a thousand years in the sight of God. Was this 1963? Not until he found himself beside this old woman, heavily rouged and lined as if for the drama of staying alive, did he feel again the terrible urgency of the streets.

When they returned, Amyas was stirring a large kettle at the stove.

"There's a little prune butter on the table and some Russian pumpernickel if you're famished," he called out gaily.

"That's all right," said Nicholas. "We had egg creams."

"Did you! Don't spoil your appetite for dinner."

"Are you cooking dinner?" exclaimed Nicholas, very much surprised. "Why, it's hardly noon."

"There's more to a good dinner than meets the tongue. Come and look."

He threw open the top door of the cupboard beside the stove. Neatly stacked on the top shelves were various hooks, pitchers, poachers, scoopers, pepper mills, racks, and broilers of every shape and description. There were more kinds of strainers, forks, parers, grinders, and graters than Nicholas had ever imagined existed; there were pressers and cheese bells and cruets, there were four coffee pots and a mortar and pestle and half a dozen sets of pots, pans, and casserole dishes.

"Very nice," said Nicholas.

"And over here—"

Amyas opened the bottom door to reveal stacks of tins, jars, and fancy little crocks. Nicholas bent down and examined the labels: lambs' tongues, mushroom nibbles, quiche Lorraine, tender young cactus, tripe à la mode de Caen.

"What are we having tonight?" he inquired.

"Smell it!" Amyas lifted the spoon. Nicholas bent over and sniffed. "Not bad. What is it?"

"An early Roman recipe: sow's udder stuffed with salted sea urchins. Janet couldn't lay her hands on an udder, so I've had to substitute tripe. Oh, I know you're a vegetarian, Nicholas. You may beg off from the main dish if you like, but I hope you're not allergic to dandelion wine. I made it myself with dandelion blossoms from—where did we get those blossoms, Janet?"

"From the Chinese grocery store," said Janet. She was standing in the doorway, looking out at the dovecote.

"Janet shops and I cook," said Amyas, stirring briskly. "I feel that taste and smell are neglected in our culture, Nicholas. Don't you think that each person has his own smell?"

"Why, I suppose so," said Nicholas. The stirring of the spoon was beginning to hypnotize him; he turned away quickly and began to walk restlessly around the loft.

"I believe that when a man falls in love, he is attracted by some subtle scent of which he is hardly aware," Amyas went on. "I don't mean perfume. I mean the scent of—of the soul."

And then suddenly, out of nowhere:

"I've arranged a job for you."

Nicholas thought he had misheard. He stopped walking.

"What kind of a job?"

"In Akton's darkroom on the second floor. Have you ever worked in a darkroom?"

"I worked in a camera shop for five months. But never in a darkroom."

"You'll learn. And it's so terribly convenient. You won't have to go out of the building at all."

"I don't mind going out of the building," said Nicholas.

"In the winter, the wind is excruciating."

"But it's only April! We've the whole summer before us."

"Oh, dear!" Amyas dropped the spoon in the kettle, and seized both of Nicholas's hands in his own. "I just thought you'd be happier if you had something to do."

"It's all right," said Nicholas. "I've always wanted to work in a darkroom."

"Have you really? You can start any time."

He hurried back to fish out his spoon. Nicholas edged his way over to the elevator.

"Are you going to sing with the dwarf tonight?" he asked.

"No. I promised the players I'd sing for them. My dear fellow, where are you going?"

"Outside," said Nicholas, "if I can get the door open."

"We're boring you," cried Amyas. "How dreadful."

"No. I need—I need exercise."

Amyas sighed deeply.

"Janet, unlock the door for him. Or would you prefer to try the stairs? The other door is by the wardrobe. One thing before you leave—please be back in plenty of time for dinner. It's going to be an occasion you don't want to miss."

Outside on the landing Nicholas felt blissfully alone. He hurried down the stairs past a precipitous landing and arguing voices behind a closed door. Across the next landing someone had set up a picket fence to prevent accidents. Nicholas quickened his pace but paused at the third landing to read messages scrawled on the doors that seemed to challenge each other from opposite ends of the corridor: CHINESE MEN'S CLUB—PRIVATE. KEEP OUT! LEATHER AND FURS. Presently the corridor grew light, and he plunged out into the street.

It was a spring day.

He pulled out his harmonica and tried to recapture the feeling: it was a spring day and he was much younger. He walked slowly up Prince Street, sucking at a tune. Twenty blocks away his wife was eating her lunch alone, or washing her hair, or sleeping. Would she call the police to find him? Would she call up her old lovers? The first week of their marriage all sorts of strange people had shown up at all hours of the day and night, and he had thrown them downstairs. Like a test of strength in a carnival booth. Pizza makers, salesmen, even a piano teacher.

Who's gonna shoe your pretty little foot?

He came to the end of the block. A group of older boys were playing handball on the court. If this were yesterday he would have gone over and joined them, but today he could not make himself do it. He was not tired but shy. Blowing a tune to himself, he turned and walked slowly back to the loft.

All afternoon he hung around on the roof and listened to the murmur and crying of the doves, still calling to themselves in the forest that years of breeding had not dislodged from their memory. Janet had gone off to rehearse and Amyas was napping. Nicholas settled himself so close to the cages that he could see the brown rings on the throats of the white birds and the irridescent sheen on the breasts of the slate-colored ones and the pale rings around the eyes of all the birds, as black and blind-looking as shoe buttons. He watched until he heard Amyas moving about, then he stumbled inside.

Dinner was a slow and elaborate affair, punctuated by shouts and crashes from the loft below. On a silver platter in the middle of the table sat the stuffed tripe, like a baked volley ball. The sink held a tower of dirty pots, dishes, strainers, and knives. The five soups, variously made of chicken and crayfish and snails, left Nicholas feeling bloated. He sat solemnly opposite Janet while Amyas served them and kept up a running chatter.

"I hope you won't let our neighbors downstairs spoil a good meal. They have the most dreadful arguments. She's a welder. I don't know what he does. But I assure you, it's far worse to be out on the street. Sometimes they throw all their furniture out of the window. Once Janet caught a bottle of olives. We ate them in a salad the next day. Didn't we, Janet?"

Janet was sawing a sea urchin with her knife and making terrible faces. Amyas watched her as he beat whipped cream.

"The meal would have been much tastier if we could have found an udder, I assure you. A meal fit for Caesar, if I hadn't had to substitute tripe and if Janet hadn't insisted on serving string beans. Caesar had an aversion to string beans. He said eating string beans was like eating hairs. And we ought to have worn togas. Meals taste better when you dress for them."

Crash! Something fell over in the room below and the table gave a violent twitch. Nicholas filled his mouth with rubbery pieces of tripe and washed them down with great gulps of wine.

"Tomorrow I want to try carp à la Napoleon. Only think how you would feel having to eat with a peruke on your head. Once Monsieur de Souze, the Portuguese ambassador to Paris, was dining at the house of Talleyrand, prince of Benevento, and as the servant placed the soup before him, he caught the gentleman's wig in his cuff button. Whisk! The ambassador was completely bald. Do you know that story?"

He turned his eager eyes on Janet, who was staring off into space and chewing as if to a secret tune.

"I could teach you so much, but you fall asleep," he whispered into her ear, pinching her lightly. "What an actress I could make of you, my little dove!"

"Amyas, sit down with us," exclaimed Nicholas. "You've cooked a big dinner and you don't sit down to help us eat it."

"I eat as I go," said Amyas, and he began to clear the plates. "You may well imagine, Nicholas, when I sit down,

I don't do it lightly. It involves making a sort of commitment to the chair."

Raucous singing came up from the corridor below, then died away.

"What time is the play?" asked Nicholas.

"Eight o'clock," said Janet. "It's seven now."

"Seven! That leaves us barely an hour to dress and get there," cried Amyas. With a grand sweep of his hand he pushed all the dishes into the sink. "We'll do them tomorrow morning. I hope you'll excuse me. We haven't the advantage of an elevator when we visit others in this building."

And he hurried back to his end of the loft. Janet followed him in silence, leaving Nicholas alone at the table. His stomach sighed loudly. He got up and lay down on the sofa to wait for the others.

"The only inconvenience of this loft is not having bathing facilities," called Amyas's voice from the wardrobe. The words sounded curiously muffled, as if he had clothed them in one of his tweeds or caftans. "It's a nuisance having to bathe at the houses of friends or drawing tubs of water. I should like to get something installed."

When he finally appeared he was wearing the white shirt and flowered vest he had worn in the restaurant the evening before. But now he had added a kelly green ascot and red suspenders. For a few moments he studied Nicholas appraisingly.

"Have you nothing else to put on?"

"No," said Nicholas. His old chinos and sweat shirt and his ragged windbreaker suddenly embarrassed him.

"We must buy you some clothes. The man who runs the fur and leather shop downstairs sells suits. I've asked him to stop by tomorrow."

Janet emerged from behind her bed looking very demure in a high-waisted print dress with full sleeves and a high collar. Amyas beamed approval.

"My little dove," he whispered, and stroked her hair. "Go and fetch my mandolin."

They set out down the stairs. It was certainly easier for so large a man to go down rather than up, thought Nicholas. But two flights in any direction were too much for Amyas. He huffed and groaned and leaned first on Nicholas and then on Janet, not because he couldn't manage the stairs but because he was afraid of losing his balance. He trembled and gasped but never broke off his shrill chatter.

"One can't be too careful—there's no light and nothing to take hold of," he panted. "This is where the lady welder lives. A club for Lithuanian refugees used to meet there. And do you know, whenever a Lithuanian met a Chinese from the club downstairs, they passed without speaking. Ah, if I could only fly!"

A sense of deep injustice filled his voice, as if he alone of all men had been born with the defect of gravity. Breathing heavily, he held Janet's arm and clutched at Nicholas's shoulder, and soon they heard voices and saw a light that fell on the railing of the fourth floor landing. A man was leaning over and looking up at them.

"Amyas!"

As they reached the bottom of the stairs they heard singing:

> *You and I and Amyas*
> *Amyas and you and I,*
> *To the greenwood must we go, alas!*
> *You and I, my life and Amyas.*

Puffing and limping, Amyas entered the loft with his two faithful servants. Several dozen people were sprawled on both sides of the doorway, leaving a center aisle free. Down the aisle walked Amyas, so joyfully he might have been walking in his own wedding. Nicholas felt a brief surge of pleasure that he was part of this procession, though even before he could name it as pleasure, it turned to quiet anger.

"Amyas!"

There was a round of applause. Bearded and costumed, Amyas waved. He was a play unto himself; what need have we of players? thought Nicholas. Amyas smiled his kingly smile and shook the hand that reached out to him. A boy in a striped poncho hurried up to Nicholas.

"I'm Homer Sax. Welcome to the city of strangers and dreamers. Mike, bring Amyas his chair."

As if by magic, an upholstered armchair appeared in the front row. It was the only chair in the room. Amyas sank into it graciously. Nicholas sat on the floor to his left, feeling embarrassed. He looked around for Janet but she was nowhere to be seen.

Suddenly Homer Sax stepped out in front of them and clapped his hands for order. Gradually the voices stopped and everyone fell quiet. Three men and three girls sat down in a line to the right of him. Nicholas was startled to see Janet at the far end.

"This is our workshop of dreams," said Homer Sax, shifting nervously from one foot to the other. "Anyone from the audience can come up and tell his dream. Afterwards we'll have music and dancing—" he turned toward Amyas—"and wine. Did someone bring the wine?"

A few snickers from the back.

"Yaaas!" shouted a voice.

Everyone laughed. Homer Sax took off his beads and threw them on the ground.

"Well, who wants to go first?"

No one moved. At last a shuffling sound in the back row broke the silence, and a pimply blond boy lumbered up to the front, hopped up on a little wooden box at the back of the stage, and cleared his throat.

"I dreamed I was looking out of the window. Looking down at Prince Street. It was early in the morning."

A black boy in jeans and a sheepskin vest leaped up from the line of actors, picked up the beads and hung them around his neck, and stared over the heads of the audience, keeping his hands behind his back.

"It was cold. Down in the street people were beating each other up."

The boy wrapped his arms around himself and shivered. Janet got up and limped out of the line, leaning on her cane. A red-haired boy in black pants and a black sweater seized the cane and pretended to beat her with it. She cowered and sank to the ground. Amyas made a strange noise in his throat. Nicholas looked at him. His enormous hands were gripping the arms of the chair.

"Then I heard the humming of many bees. I looked up the street and saw a procession of animals, all holding each other's paws and dancing the hora down the street."

The rest of the players scrambled to their feet and began to bow and skip.

"And it stopped being cold. And people stopped beating each other. And I woke up."

Janet rose and shook hands with her assailant. Leaning on her cane like an old woman, she hobbled across the stage. Janet the old woman, Janet without Amyas, living out her days alone, turning into Norma Mardachek. Nicholas tried to shake her from his mind, but she hung with sharp claws like a fierce bird.

Now everyone was clapping. The dream teller plumped down on the other side of Amyas.

"A splendid dream, sir. A splendid dream."

Slowly the players returned to their line.

"Amyas," shouted Homer Sax, coming to the front of the stage. "You tell us a dream. Yours must be extraordinary."

Amyas glanced at Janet who was sitting on the floor among the players. She was drawing circles on the floor with her cane.

"Nicholas," he whispered, "help me up."

Nicholas jumped up and offered his hand.

"Steady the chair," whispered Amyas.

Nicholas held the back of the chair. Amyas rocked to and fro several times; then giving a great heave, he threw himself on his feet and thudded across the stage. Somewhere behind him empty wine bottles clinked their heads together. He mounted the box and faced the audience like an elephant on a barrel. There was a sharp splintering sound. Nobody laughed. Amyas stepped off without embarrassment. He closed his eyes, opened them again, and began to shout as if he were delivering a sermon into the wind.

"I dreamed I was a shepherd, leading a flock of sheep across the red desert."

The black boy in the sheepskin vest threw down the beads and walked slowly across the stage, leaning on an imaginary staff. Janet and three other girls crawled on all fours after him.

"Then I saw an old woman and a little boy whom I knew to be very evil."

A tall, skinny girl led the red-haired boy to a place in front of the shepherd. Crouching on the floor, they grimaced and pointed to him.

"To prevent them from destroying us, I changed my entire flock into stones."

The sheep curled up into four limp mounds.

"Yes, I even changed myself into a stone, except for my right ear, which I left unchanged so that I could hear if any evil was being plotted against us."

The shepherd hunched himself up like a beetle but laid his hand against the side of his head.

"Then I heard one of my sheep escaping." Amyas's voice trembled a little. "Yes, indeed, I heard one of my sheep escaping. And I thought, have I not changed them all into stones?"

No one moved on stage. Amyas's eyes glittered and seemed to bulge from his head. Not a sound could be heard but Amyas's heavy breathing and the *clump clump* of Janet's shoes, like an animal dragging a trap. When Amyas spoke his words hissed out like steam.

"Then I said to myself, though I am stone, yet I will fly!"

He let out a yell and lunged toward the door. Nicholas flew after him, sprang on his back, and hung on. They tumbled through the doorway together in time to see Janet running down the stairs. Amyas heaved himself this way and that but Nicholas locked his arm around the other man's neck and pinned him against the railing.

"Janet, run!" he shouted.

A terrible cracking followed. The railing snapped and

split and Amyas dropped to the stairs below, with Nicholas riding him like a boy on a dolphin. It felt stranger than any dream, this sudden loss of weight and support, this falling through space, this turning into a pair of struggling swimmers who suddenly hit rock at the bottom of the air. Then Nicholas saw only Amyas's eyes staring past him and a gush of blood from his head spreading over the floor.

Far away he heard cries.

"Call an ambulance!"

"Don't move him! For God's sake, don't move him!"

Hands lifted Nicholas to his feet. He ached in a hundred places but he knew he was not hurt. Amyas had cushioned the fall, and now he lay with bloody head and twisted limbs like a drowned man, bloated and washed up on a strange shore. Janet was wailing like a child. Homer Sax's voice rose over them all.

"Give him air. Clear out, all of you!"

Nicholas staggered upstairs. The tall, skinny girl took him by the arm and tried to wipe away a thin trickle of blood that flowed from a cut over his left eye. Something unpleasant was thumping inside his skull. He sat on the floor where the players had been but a moment before, and obstinately refused to move. But a little while later when Homer Sax came to help him back up to the sixth floor loft, he took his arm meekly enough. The stairway was littered with broken pickets like toy swords. Amyas and Janet had disappeared.

—————— III ——————

Nicholas woke up suddenly. Someone was pounding on the door.

"Coming!" he shouted. As he eased himself painfully out of bed, he heard a discreet cough. By the elevator door stood a small, dark-haired man with large teeth. He was leaning on a rack of trench coats, slacks, and jackets.

"Excuse me. Your door was open. I assumed that Mr. Axel left it open so that I could deliver the suits."

"What suits?" said Nicholas. The man was staring at his sweat shirt and chinos, torn from the struggle on the stairs and wrinkled from last night's fitful sleep.

"You're supposed to pick out whatever you like. I got some nice Harris tweeds here and some good slacks if you don't like anything so fancy as a suit."

"Not now," said Nicholas. "Come back tomorrow."

"Oh, I can't do that," cried the man nervously. "I have no idea what we'll come across tomorrow. These may be gone. And we might not get any more tweed in for a week. You don't find so many in the spring."

"Please go," said Nicholas.

"Listen," persisted the man. "I can't go unless you pick one. Mr. Axel has paid for two suits, and he wanted them brought up right away. He's very fussy about his orders. Do you mind if I pick some things for you?"

The man pulled a corduroy jacket and a pair of slacks off the rack and hung them on the open doors of Janet's bed. Then he pushed the rack into the elevator, closed the door, and disappeared as mysteriously as he had arrived.

There was no point in going back to bed. Nicholas put

on the jacket and noticed a cigarette hole in the left sleeve. He felt he should return it at once, but to whom? Furthermore, the loft had grown chilly without Amyas. Nicholas opened the door to the roof and heard the chimes from the church on Sullivan Street, like the twelve clocks of God that his wife once told him would ring the elect into paradise. A man at Bellevue heard it three times a day: the passing of time depends, he said, on the three golden bells that turn slowly inside. Nicholas started to open the first cage, then decided it was too risky. He went back inside and scooped a bowlful of cracked corn from one of the bags under the sink. He was on his way out to feed the doves when he heard voices ascending the elevator.

"My little bird, you mustn't worry so much. If he's not there, we'll wait till he comes back."

Then the door opened and Janet, looking very pale, walked in pushing a wheelchair. Amyas overflowed it on all sides. Seeing Nicholas he gave a yelp of joy.

"See, Janet, didn't I tell you he'd still be here?"

It was the same voice, the same fat belly, the same forked beard. But his face was badly swollen and his thick hair had been cut shorter and the back of his head was heavily bandaged. His right leg ballooned out in a heavy cast, like a piece of artillery.

"They wanted me to stay, but I told them I had important matters at home. A family to look after. I see you've been feeding my doves."

Then he noticed the new jacket.

"Richie came, did he?"

"My God, Amyas, I'm so glad to see you," cried Nicholas. He wanted to embrace him but instead shook both his hands.

"Are you glad, Nicholas? Are you glad? Wasn't it silly of me to think you would go away?"

"Where should I go?"

It startled Nicholas as he said it, because for the first time he realized it was true. This knowledge made it easy for him to settle into the slow timelessness of Amyas's recuperation. From that hour on, the past did not exist. None of them mentioned the accident except as a way of marking the end of one life and the beginning of another: the day Amyas broke his leg. In Nicholas's mind the mornings that followed blurred into one continuous morning without end. Even after Amyas got his crutches, Janet would wheel him out to feed his birds—for he hated to leave his chair—and let them out to circle around the roof.

"I've never lost one, Janet. Not one!"

As morning slid imperceptibly into afternoon, Amyas puttered with his glider, Janet went down to rehearse with her players, and Nicholas, following Amyas's wishes, took a job in the Akton darkroom on the second floor. He arrived knowing nothing at all and wondering if perhaps Amyas hadn't bribed Mr. March, the manager, to take him on. The first morning he watched half a dozen men and women wash the shining rolls of film in huge tanks while others ran off masses of prints under the red glow of the safelights. The second morning he cleaned trays, numbered film envelopes, and sorted prints. The third morning he was given his own rolls to wash and another set to print.

It wasn't a bad place to work, he told himself. But when he walked out of the darkroom, the sight of ten old women sitting at a long table and stapling envelopes of photographs depressed him. The packaging room was unimaginably drab, like an airplane hangar. The darkroom, on the other hand, seemed always about to explode. The soft red light which infused all their work whetted and roused strange passions. The women were large and buxom, the men small and hairless, and they worked side by side in a room so tiny that they couldn't help rubbing against each other. The men sidled up behind the women and pinched them, and the women brushed the men with their enormous breasts, and the air grew hot with sweat and promises. The smallest and most brazen among them all, a retired jockey named Jon Spalding, would sometimes whisper in Nicholas's ear, "You'll never have a better chance."

Nicholas felt at ease only with the two women who worked on either side of him, Charlene Schwartz, a divorcée who had two children and lived in the Bronx, and Barbara Wiggins, a plump girl who had recently quit her job as a waitress and was constantly regretting it. A week after he arrived she began to wear such strong perfume that one of the other women threatened to complain to Mr. March.

"She's sweet on you, she is," grinned Jon Spalding, nudging Nicholas significantly as they passed one another in the red light.

But Nicholas had lost his taste for large buxom women. Skinny women, with some defect, these were the kind he loved now. No such women surrounded him here, and not wishing to have his taste challenged, he tried to lose himself in his work. He told himself that nothing pleased him more than seeing the images find themselves in the developing fluid. Slowly filling the blank paper, they would arrive, lined up in their Easter clothes on hundreds of doorsteps all over New York. Children blowing out candles, families crowded and smiling on low sofas. And occasionally an attempt at something serious—a landscape, badly out of focus, from a kid's cheap camera.

He arrived at one and left at four, well pleased. He knew that if he quit tomorrow the loss of his small income would hardly ripple their lives. Amyas took care of them but knew the value of keeping up certain illusions about independence, and Nicholas was happy to let Amyas think he accepted the illusions as truth. The truth was, Nicholas enjoyed being comfortable.

With Amyas confined to his chair, the great feasts and exotic dinners came to an end. Amyas did not complain, but when Janet put a plate of peas and hamburgers before him, he sighed deeply.

"How much I could teach you, my little dove."

And afterwards, plucking the stray peas from his beard, he wheeled himself over to inspect his glider.

"Janet, do you think you could get me a pair of wheels?"

Janet was washing the dishes and handing them to Nicholas, who dried them and stacked them in the cupboard.

"How would I get you a pair of wheels?" she asked.

"You could find a pair. You could have them delivered."

Nicholas stepped behind Janet's bed to have a look. Amyas had recently installed a cockpit, and the glider looked less like a dream of Leonardo da Vinci's and more like a working machine.

"Isn't my blue angel handsome?" exclaimed Amyas, fingering the tip of one wing.

On an afternoon that started out as no more than a brilliant chip off the long dream of their life together, Nicholas entered the loft after work and heard Amyas and Janet arguing. Sitting alone beside the table, which was already set for dinner, Janet was darning a huge black stocking. It belonged, Nicholas knew, to Amyas. She broke the thread and threw the stocking across the room.

"I don't know why I can't go with them. You have Nicholas."

"My little dove," rumbled Amyas's voice from the bathoom, "Nicholas isn't you. I would worry about you terribly."

She pulled a pale nylon stocking from the pile on the floor beside her, yanked a single strand of hair out of her head, threaded the needle and began to mend a long run.

"And why do we have to eat dinner so close to the bathroom where a person can smell and hear everything that goes on in there?" she called to him.

"I'll ask Nicholas to move the table," said Amyas.

Catching sight of Nicholas, she raised her voice.

"Isn't it odd that the only person who has carpeting around his bed is Amyas? Nice green carpeting. You know why, Nicholas? Green is the color of life, it scares away the rats. On a gray floor they feel right at home. But gray is good enough for you and me."

From the bathroom came an inarticulate moan.

"And why should Amyas get half the room to himself while you and I share the other half with the kitchen and the bathroom and the glider?"

Suddenly she burst into tears, dropped her sewing, and flew over to her bed. Its doors slammed shut. Amyas burst out of the bathroom and wheeled himself after her.

"My pigeon, what is it? Nobody's making you work if you don't want to. I've plenty of money to hire someone to clean the loft and fix our meals."

From behind the doors came a drawn-out snuffle. Amyas turned to Nicholas who stood rooted in the doorway.

"Ah, Nicholas, what to do! The Apple Town Players are going on the road and she wants to go with them. The whole venture is terribly impractical. They've borrowed an old truck—I'm sure it will break down—and they'll earn their keep by passing the hat at performances. Who will look after her there?"

He wheeled himself up to the doors and pressed his ear against them.

"Are you ill? Do you want me to fetch a doctor?"

No response.

"Nicholas, sit down and eat before everything gets cold. I hope you like macaroni and cheese."

"I'm not going to sit down alone," said Nicholas.

"Did you hear that?" cried Amyas, drumming his fists on the doors. "Nobody can do anything. We're completely prostrate. How can we eat dinner when you've locked yourself up?"

Still no reply. Amyas sighed.

"Leave a dish of macaroni by the doors. I don't want her starving to death in there."

Amyas watched every move as Nicholas spooned it into a bowl.

"Don't forget the napkin and the fork."

Nicholas placed it on a chair outside the bed, like an offering to some petulant sybil. Then Amyas motioned him to sit down and fell upon the meal with both hands. He seemed to have forgotten the use of a fork. After dinner they worked on the glider together and conversed without pleasure. Both went to bed early. Janet brooding in her dark nest did not utter a sound.

——————————— IV ———————————

The first thing Nicholas saw when he woke up the next morning was the doors swinging wide and beyond them the rumpled empty bed. He rushed over to Amyas and shook him awake.

"She's gone! Flown away! The bed is empty!" he cried.

Amyas, in a peacock blue Nehru nightshirt, opened his eyes and turned deadly pale.

"My chair, Nicholas," he said.

Nicholas steadied the chair, eased him into it, and settled the heavy leg in its cast.

"Go and put on some clothes," snapped Amyas. "It's chilly. Do you want two invalids up here instead of one?"

Then he wheeled himself over to Janet's bed, peered inside, closed the doors, and backed over the empty dish on the floor, smashing it. Under Nicholas's gaze, he rolled around the room, pausing to look into the wardrobe, the sink, the cupboards, until he had examined everything.

"At least she had the sense to take enough clothes," he said. "She also took a new loaf of pumpernickel she got for my breakfast this morning. We shall have to make do. Nicholas, put on the coffee."

Slightly annoyed at being ordered about, Nicholas filled the coffeepot and plugged it in.

"Move the table please. It is really too unpleasant sitting so close to the bathroom where the most offensive smells mingle with the odor of the food. I suppose she took the pecan roll as well."

Nicholas peered into the cupboard and into the icebox.

"I don't see any roll."

"Get out the toaster, then. We'll have toast. Assuming that she didn't take the last slice of white bread."

They sat opposite each other in silence like a quarreling couple until the first slice of toast popped up. Amyas gulped down six slices as if they were crackers. Nicholas managed to save one for himself. He shook the bread bag for the last slice, but it was empty.

"Well," said Amyas, pushing himself away from the table, "what do you think of carpeting the whole floor, Nicholas?"

"Why, I'd like it, I guess," said Nicholas. Amyas's reaction made him uneasy; he was taking Janet's flight too lightly.

"So would Janet. But one mustn't give in too fast. It's not worth compromising one's character to settle an argument. The most important thing to remember is that she'll come back." A glazed, dreamy look passed like a film over his eyes. "She always comes back."

"Oh," said Nicholas, greatly relieved. "Then she's done this before."

Amyas nodded.

"She goes away sometimes to test me. And when she comes back, the bond is even stronger. Don't think she's left me behind, Nicholas. When she first arrived, I sewed my gold Saint Christopher medal into the lining of her jacket."

"Are you Catholic?" exclaimed Nicholas, very much surprised.

"No. My mother was a convert. I don't know whether Saint Christopher will do much for Janet; he never helped my mother. What matters is that she hasn't really lost me. Whenever she goes out, she carries some part of me, some small token of myself. And one day she'll be feeling in her jacket for some change and she'll feel a coin buried deep in the lining. She'll be curious. She'll fetch scissors and open the lining. And out will fall my medal, engraved with my name, Amyas Axel. Then she'll remember where she lives and come home."

Nicholas got up and started toward the door.

"Are you going to the darkroom?"

"Yes, I thought I'd work a little today."

"You don't have to work, you know, if you'd rather not."

"I know," said Nicholas. He wanted to get away. "But it gives me something to do."

To enter the darkroom, to plunge his hands into its mysterious baths and bring out the faces of the past comforted him. He hurried past the gray ladies packaging prints to his place in the darkness between plump Barbara and boisterous Charlene.

"Oh, God. One more picture of kids in Easter bonnets and I'm quitting," cried Charlene.

But Nicholas was leaning over his tray of fluids, transfixed. A bride and groom were slowly coming alive on the paper, figures torn from the past, looking a little bewildered until their features clarified and they recognized one another, and now they were smiling forever. Where are you now, thought Nicholas as he dropped them into the fixative bath. For the bride wore the graceless style and curled pageboy of an earlier time. Once it pleased Nicholas to mediate between the past and the present, to remember again the centuries of lives and cities that stretched in all directions away from Amyas's loft. To remember and touch nothing.

"She's testing me," said Amyas every morning. "She'll drop us a line in a day or two."

He quit work on the glider and began reading cookbooks and planning the menus he would prepare when she returned: stuffed dormice, snails fattened in milk, violet wine. To Nicholas he gave the task of ordering groceries from the Chinese grocery store once a week. Monday night a young boy deposited them in the elevator and Nicholas accompanied them up to the loft, where Amyas ordered him to put everything away while instructing him in matters of the palate.

"The paper belongs on the top shelf—that's right. Now where was I?"

"The Frankish dishes," said Nicholas wearily.

"Yes. I'm glad to see you're really listening. The Frankish dishes bring to the meal a—how shall I describe it?—a primitive flavor. Oh, Nicholas, do remember to order me some snails. Janet will adore them."

But when two weeks had passed without a word from her, Amyas's calm began to crack. Before she left, the days flowed around them as indivisibly as a river. Now they counted not only the days but the hours. On the fourteenth day after her flight, Amyas took action.

"Nicholas," he said, when the noon mail had brought him nothing, "why don't you go down to the dead letter office and see if there's a message from Janet?"

"Why, she knows how to reach us if she wants to."

"Oh, but she might have misaddressed the letter. Or it might have got lost. Thousands of letters disappear every year."

"I don't know," said Nicholas doubtfully. "If it's lost, how are they going to find it?"

But Amyas persisted until Nicholas finally gave in. Five days later, on a Friday morning, he took the subway to the main post office on Eighth Avenue. It seemed to him that never in his life had he been jostled by so many people and touched by so many different shades of frustration. Watching the faces of humanity blossom and ripen in the darkroom, he felt he had detached himself from them. Now he sat in the crowded car and tried to gather himself together while thighs, coats, behinds, and packages pressed upon him. The names of streets flashed by on the wall outside like milestones, as if all the passengers were hurtling on a timeline and would step out in an unknown century.

A hefty black woman at the other end of the car let out a cry.

"I left it on the *platform*. On the *platform*. No use goin' back. Somebody's got it by now."

The white girl in front of Nicholas gripped her purse and felt for the shopping bag wedged between her feet.

"No use goin' back," chanted the other, swaying on her feet as if she were crooning to herself.

> *No use goin' back.*
> *No use goin' back.*
> *No use goin' back.*
> *Somebody's got you by now.*

Nicholas walked into the lobby of the post office, huge, austere, and empty. In such a room the unbaptized and the unforgiven could wait in vain for a glimpse of the mercy of God. Only one window was open for service. Nicholas walked over to a face as closed and hostile as a fist. The old man on the other side of the grille heard the resonant boom of footsteps and glanced up.

"Excuse me," said Nicholas. "I'm expecting a letter from someone, and I think it might have gotten lost. Is there any way of checking the dead letter office to see whether—"

He could not finish; the old man's eyes were widening with disbelief. Presently he answered, so slowly and deliberately that Nicholas had the curious feeling he was watching a dubbed-in performance.

"Do you know how many dead letters we get each year?"

"No," said Nicholas.

"Hundreds. Thousands. We have rooms full of letters that we can't deliver. The writers are dead, the people they're addressed to are dead. Every Christmas we're flooded with cards to people who've been dead for years."

He was warming to his subject; he slapped the counter with the side of his hand.

"And the worst of it is, not one of those letters has a return address. Then it would be simple; we'd stamp it 'deceased,' and send it back."

"I just thought—that is, this letter would be very recent——" Nicholas stammered.

"You don't understand! Once a letter goes into the dead letter office, it disappears like a snowflake in a blizzard. The pile is always shifting, so you can't count on finding the recent ones. In warm weather they may work their way clear down to the middle of the pile."

"Then I guess there's no hope, is there?" said Nicholas.

The man shook his head.

"None."

Amyas took the news bravely.

"She's testing me," he repeated over and over. "She'll come back."

But already Nicholas found himself making those subtle adjustments of thought and feeling that people discover to help them accept loss. Already Janet had crystallized into a series of snapshots which his mind brought forth whenever he saw a girl wearing a velvet headband over straight hair, or when he passed the theatrical makeup store, which because of fire was now closed indefinitely. When she finally did return, she seemed to have passed through layers of experience so far beyond his understanding that she was hardly the same person.

------------------------------ V ------------------------------

Nothing could have been simpler than her return. It happened on a May evening after a light rain when the smell of clean air blew through the loft from the roof outside, like a friendly guest. Amyas and Nicholas were puttering with the glider when both heard the elevator climbing to their room. It jolted to a stop and somebody fumbled at the lock on the door. Nicholas felt himself go cold. But Amyas, turning as pale as the cast on his leg, wheeled himself to the door just as it sprang open. In walked Janet. When he saw her, he let out a cry.

"My God, what has happened to you?"

Only her heavy shoe and her cane told Nicholas here was the old Janet. In every other way she seemed a changed creature. She had cut her hair short and she wore a man's pinstripe suit, taken in at the shoulders and waist; everywhere else it bagged outrageously. Yet she was not a comic figure but as sly and cautious as a stray cat.

"Evening," she said, nodding to Nicholas.

Then she opened her mouth to say something to Amyas, but no one ever heard what it was, for when he lifted his arms, she rushed to him and buried her face in his beard, and they clung together like wrestlers engaged in some bizarre test of endurance. Then her body relaxed and she raised her face and smiled first at Nicholas, then at Amyas, who stroked her hair.

"We'll celebrate," whispered Amyas. "We'll go someplace together and celebrate. My little dove," he exclaimed, "you don't have to tell me anything. We'll go to Tony's. Nicholas, go fetch my mandolin. This evening I'll initiate my new crutches."

In the taxi, Janet perched on Amyas's good knee and laid her arm around his shoulders. The hair shaved from the cut at the back of his head after the accident had not quite grown back. Janet rubbed her fingers over the stubble, and Nicholas, sitting in front, tried to focus on the meter.

"Are you glad to see me, Nicholas?" she asked.

"Very glad," said Nicholas.

"We're here," exclaimed Amyas. "Nicholas, do you have the fare? I find it difficult to get at my purse just now."

When the taxi stopped, Janet leaped to the sidewalk and offered Amyas her arm. He spilled out of the cab, puffing and groaning, and teetered unsteadily on his crutches. Like two maimed derelicts, they entered the restaurant together, leaving Nicholas to search his wallet for something smaller than a twenty-dollar bill. He could hardly hide his impatience as the driver slowly counted out the change.

"Five, fifteen, sixteen, seventeen dollars. Thank you, mister."

Stuffing the bills into his jacket, he hurried inside. How many years had passed since he last walked through this door, in some other life, his life before Amyas? Looking about, he spotted one vacant seat in the back at a table occupied by two young men and a girl in a pinstripe suit who sat opposite the empty place and kept glancing behind her toward the kitchen. A waiter, seeing him, took the mandolin out of his arms and hurried away. There was no sign of Amyas in the kitchen. The cook was standing at a counter chopping vegetables. Nicholas pushed his way down the aisle past the long rows of people eating and sat down opposite Janet.

Suddenly everyone in the room burst into applause. Out of the kitchen marched Gunther the dwarf lugging his guitar. Amyas the giant limped after him, swinging his elephantine leg as he leaned on his crutches. When Nicholas saw again the black vest embroidered with flowers, he could almost believe that Amyas had never taken it off.

"Gunther! Amyas!"

"Amyas!"

Gunther waved to the girl who had called out his name. But Amyas smiled only at Janet. Behind them, the waiter carried the mandolin and a chair, which he set directly opposite Janet's table. The dwarf tuned his guitar, holding it high against his cheek. Amyas leaned his crutches against the wall, seated himself, and laid his fingers on the fretboard of the mandolin. Looking at each other, they thumped out a few measures. Then the dwarf opened his mouth and shouted the refrain, which Amyas punctuated with cries of joy:

> *You and I and Amyas,*
> *Amyas and you and I*
> *To the greenwood must we go, alas!*
> *You and I, my life and Amyas.*

The two young men stopped eating to listen. Janet rested her chin in her hands and Nicholas felt her eyes upon him. He gave her a quick smile. She did not smile back, nor did she take her eyes from him. Now the dwarf was bobbing up and down as he cantered toward the last verse.

> *Who's gonna shoe your pretty little foot*
> *with boots of Spanish leather?*
> *I'll go no more to her bedside,*
> *so let the devil take her.*

Let the devil take her! roared the audience, stamping its feet.

The dwarf lifted his hands from the strings, and everyone applauded. Nicholas rose automatically as the waiter slid an extra chair between Janet and himself. When Amyas sat down, a feast appeared as if by silent command. Where there was nothing, now there was bread, wine, soup, half a sheep's head, and a plate of spaghetti. Amyas's eyes followed the waiter's hands with pleasure, till the last dish appeared on the table.

"*Meine Kinder,*" he said. He looked from Janet to Nicholas, reached across the table, and took their hands. "My little doves."

Then he gave himself over to his dinner. Janet twirled the spaghetti around her fork and when Amyas lifted a tidbit for her to take from his fingers, she shook her head. But neither Nicholas's silence nor Janet's reticence could dim the luster of his joy. As Nicholas drank, he felt some part of himself drift away in sleep while another part of him entered an elaborate and familiar dream. Of Amyas reaching for Janet's cane. Of Janet draping Amyas's coat around his shoulders. Of himself following them outside, into the taxi, into the elevator. Cautiously he stepped into the spacious room and entered his own life as a stranger.

In the darkness he heard Janet tossing and singing to herself behind the closed doors of her bed. Under the embroidered skins of one thousand dragons lay Amyas, his immense belly shaken with snores. Nicholas closed his eyes and drifted back to sleep. All at once someone touched his cheek.

"Be quiet," whispered Janet. "It's just me."

She was sitting on the floor beside him, wrapped in Amyas's peacock blue nightshirt, barely visible in the weak light from the street.

"What's the matter?"

"Nothing's the matter. I want to talk to someone."

"Oh." Nicholas relaxed a little. "What do you want to talk about?"

"Don't, Nicholas. I couldn't fall asleep."

The silence between them rippled with Amyas's snorts and sighs.

"Nicholas, do you ever miss your wife?"

"No," said Nicholas.

"You don't? I just don't see how you could love her and go away and not think of her afterward."

Nicholas considered this carefully.

"You did love her, didn't you?"

"I don't think so. I was lonely and she came along at the right time."

"I wish you'd met me then."

"Then I would have married you."

Suddenly she put her lips close to his ear and whispered, "Nicholas, I've got us a place to live. Will you come with me?"

"What did you say?" cried Nicholas.

"Not so loud! I've got us a place to live."

Nicholas stared at her in astonishment.

"Do you want me to marry you?"

Her shoulders shrugged under the peacock folds.

"I want to go away for good. I feel like I'm rotting here. Don't you feel like that? Day after day, always the same thing, the same room. Except to do the shopping. Amyas never wants me to go outside at all."

"Why did you come back?"

"I don't want to live alone."

"I thought," said Nicholas very slowly, "that you were in love with Amyas. And I don't think you're in love with me."

Janet twisted a corner of the nightshirt.

"You start depending on a person to tell you what to do, and pretty soon you can't leave."

Nicholas was silent. He tried to imagine himself not feeding Amyas's birds, cooking his meals, or working on his glider, and in turn not eating at his table, and sleeping under his roof, and not wearing the clothes that Amyas bought for him. The four walls of the loft seemed to cave in around him, and the winds of freedom blew fear into his heart.

"When are you planning to leave?"

"I want to leave right now."

"You can't leave in the middle of the night."

"Don't be silly, Nicholas. It's almost morning. Get up and pack."

"I can't pack in the dark."

"Why not? All you have is your knapsack. It's under the sofa. Everything else belongs to Amyas."

She reached down and pulled it out for him.

"There's no need to sneak off like this," protested Nicholas. "It's stupid and ungrateful. I really don't see why we can't tell him tomorrow morning that we want to leave and walk out the door."

"You know he won't let us go," said Janet softly. "You know if we ask him and he says yes, we'll have to come back sometime. Ten years later maybe, but we'll still have to come back."

Far away, the huge figure on the bed by the window sighed deeply. Amyas lay with his arm thrown over his face. When they left, he looked like a drowned man saying good-bye.

There was almost nobody on Prince Street. Somewhere out of sight the sun rose. A heavy fog bandaged all the buildings and a warm rain began to fall.

"Smell," said Janet, drawing in her breath. "It smells like summer."

That afternoon they moved into a small, shabbily furnished apartment on Ninth Street. It belonged to Homer

Sax's brother, Paul, who had left a month earlier to study painting in southern France. Every wall in the living room was painted a different shade of red; the kitchen and bedroom were Prussian blue. Paul Sax left them all his furniture, some of his books, and a box of Graham crackers on the kitchen counter. That evening Janet bought a book on cockroaches, explaining to Nicholas that you had to know your enemy in order to fight it. She put their names on the mailbox as Janet and Nicholas Mardachek, and after a week Nicholas felt as if he'd been married forever. The six months he'd spent with his wife seemed but a trial to be passed through before he could enter the life he had always imagined. The two months with Amyas were an intermittent season, a time of healing.

It was a spring day and he was much younger.

He did not return to the darkroom. All those days at his father's filling station in Akron and then the days after that when his wife nagged him to find a job, he had dreamed of someone to wait on him. Of someone with money who wouldn't make him work. He would buy a movie projector and set it up in the bedroom and they would watch old westerns all night long. Janet was delighted. She did not want to be alone and she was eager to please. They rose at noon and spent the rest of the day browsing in the camera shops around Harold Square.

At Olden's, the clerk offered them a secondhand projector for seventy-five dollars. Janet took Nicholas aside.

"How much does a new one cost?"

"A couple hundred."

"Well, we can afford that."

"We can?"

He was amazed. He knew she had some money, as she never asked him for any, but not so much that she could afford to spend it freely.

"How much have you got saved?"

"Enough," said Janet.

"You didn't earn very much with the Apple Town Players."

"No," she agreed. "I took money from Amyas."

Nicholas looked so shocked that Janet tried to make light of it.

"But, Nicholas, he's very rich. You mustn't feel bad. He has all sorts of connections and more money than he knows what to do with. Why, Nicholas, he'd *want* me to have it. He always bought me whatever I asked for. He kept all his money in an envelope under his cookbooks. I'd tell him, 'Why don't you get yourself a bigger place?' But he has this notion of discipline. Even when you've got money, you don't spend it."

The clerk was smiling at them.

"Will you take this one, or would you rather wait for a new one?"

"I'll wait, thanks," said Nicholas. Janet took his arm. They rode the subway home in silence.

Though they did not speak of it again, the source of Janet's money lay between them like ill-feeling. For it seemed to Nicholas that they had escaped nothing; they were living in one of the many annexes of Amyas's love. At night, the faces of those he had cast away, Norma Mardachek and Amyas Axel, formed themselves over and over in the darkroom of his mind, and though he could not see them so clearly when he was awake, they fettered his joy.

Every afternoon he took long walks alone. Janet saw him to
the door with a smile.

"You see?" she said. "I'm not going to keep you locked
up like a tame bird."

She never asked him where he went and he never told
her. Sometimes he would describe what he had seen.

"I saw a man walking two goats, a black goat and a
white one."

"Did you? Where?"

"I don't remember exactly."

He never told her that he had gone to his old place off
Hester to see if his wife still lived there. It would be no use
explaining that he didn't really want to see his wife, that in
fact he hoped he wouldn't meet her. He simply wanted to
put his past in order. Yet when he approached the house he
could hardly breathe for excitement. Cautiously he climbed
the front stairs, entered the vestibule, and peered at the
names on the mailboxes. A pang of disappointment shot
through him. Hers was not there. He had no hope of locat-
ing her now. As he walked away, he tried to call up the
dreadful scenes they had played out together.

"I saw a little boy trying to push another little boy into
a mailbox."

"Did you really? Where?"

"Downtown."

He did not tell her that it was Prince Street and he had
gone to see Amyas. No, not Amyas himself, but the residence of Amyas, as one makes a pilgrimage to see
Beethoven's house or Grace Kelly's swimming pool, com-
fortably assured of not meeting the real object of one's
worship. That Sunday morning everything felt as still and

changeless as a prayer lettered in gold and touched with peace. *Doll Manufacturing Company. Bolts and Parts.* The make-up shop, its windows boarded over. The vacant handball court. The newspaper store.

Nicholas went in, brushing past layers of magazines clipped on wires like an elaborate quilt. An old man who was reading and stroking his gray moustache stood up behind the counter.

"One egg cream," said Nicholas.

It was a spring day and he was much younger, loitering around the playground after school.

"Nice day," said the old man, smiling as he watched Nicholas drink till the air in the empty straw made a loud noise. Nicholas pushed the paper cup away.

"I'm trying to find a fellow named Amyas Axel," he said. "Do you ever see him much?"

"The big fat fella? I knew who he was, but I never run into him myself. Did you say you're trying to find him?"

"Yes," said Nicholas.

"Well, he's dead."

"I—"

He could not bring out the words; he did not know what the right words were.

"I didn't see it happen. Some kids who live in the building told me he tried to fly out the window. He had some kind of flying machine and he stuck a pair of wings on himself and just took off. Jumped clean out the window."

Nicholas said nothing but felt himself turning to stone.

"He didn't have no family. There wasn't nobody to tell about it. The police carted him away like a dead horse."

The man allowed a few minutes' respectful silence before he said, "That'll be fifteen cents for the egg cream."

Fumbling in his pocket for the change, Nicholas touched the shape of a coin caught in the lining. A coin? A medal, wishing him a safe journey, a medal from Amyas? Wasn't the jacket a gift from Amyas, too? He tore the jacket off his back, threw it on the counter, and fled.

Although he did not speak of Amyas's death to Janet, the weight of his new knowledge bowed him. During dinner, he could not concentrate on her plans for repainting the living room white and buying a formica table for the kitchen. That night she showed him a new nightgown she had bought, a high-waisted cotton print with full sleeves and a velvet sash, and when she crawled into bed beside him, smelling of perfume and new flannel, he could not restrain himself.

"Did you buy it for Amyas?"

Janet shrugged. Then she said, "You went to visit Amyas today, didn't you?"

"Yes," said Nicholas.

"How is he?"

"Dead."

She gave a sudden jerk.

"He jumped out the window last week."

Silence, broken only with difficulty.

"Oh, Nicholas, even when he's dead, he's still got us in the palm of his hand," whispered Janet, and started to cry.

Nicholas couldn't bear that; he shook her and pulled her face against him.

"Cut it out. Listen, Janet, can't you just think of him as someone who brought us together?"

She sniffled a little, then allowed herself to curl up against him, and each knew who the other was thinking of and Nicholas knew it was best to say nothing because he felt that they were lying under one huge shadow, like two creatures curled together in one womb that carried them still. He would not let himself cry until Janet fell asleep. But when his heart showed him that huge man bedded down in the sticks and stones of Potter's Field, he thought his whole body would burst with grief.

8 Essays

∽6∾ ————————————

The One Who Goes Out at the Cry of Dawn: The Secret Process of Stories

——————————— I wonder how many writers can re-member the person or the experience that called them to their craft. If you ask a dozen writers why they started writing, their answers will be as various as their work. One might name a parent who encouraged him, another would name a teacher who loaned her books. Several might mention a creative writing class they took in college. Somebody might say, "I wrote my first sonnet when I fell in love." Falling in love has made poets out of many who abandoned the calling when they fell out of it.

It was neither a teacher nor a parent that called me. It was a dream. I was three years old and not yet going to school. As I could not write, I was forced to remember my dreams in greater detail than I do now. I dreamed I was lying awake in the early morning, listening. Or perhaps I was half asleep and half awake. There is a brief span of time when we cross over from one kingdom to another, with darkness on our left hand and morning on our right. The dreams we dream at that hour we often remember, perhaps because we do not have to carry them so long and so far.

So at that hour when we who live in both places belong to neither, I listened. Someone was calling my name. In my dream I climbed up on the window sill and looked past the broad copper roof that slanted over our sun porch. The patches newly laid on shone like my mother's brightest teakettle, which stayed bright because she never used it. Over the eaves above my window, the vine that my father said bloomed once every hundred years, and whose flowers I had never seen, wore clusters of orchids, heavy as grapes. Our neighbors' chimneys, our garage, our forsythia bushes, even our clothesline, had all disappeared. The land had gone back to oak and hickory and beech, the way it must have looked before white men built their homes on it.

Through that ancient forest marched animals: elk, moose, possum, bobcat, deer. No lions, no tigers, no elephants, only the animals that had played in my yard long before I did. They moved in a silent circle around the house. I knew from the cricle that they came as friends, because the circle was the shape of the games I played with my friends. It was the shape of our kindly kitchen table, where nobody got poked by sharp corners and no one sat higher or lower than anyone else.

So I did what any of you would have done. I climbed down the vine, clambered up on the back of the red-tailed deer who knelt to receive me, and I rode away with my new family into the forest.

My story does not end happily. Before I could find out

what lay in the forest, my mother called me and I woke up. I have always felt sympathy for Coleridge at the moment he woke from his dream of Kubla Kahn's stately pleasure dome and was writing at white heat to catch it when the grocery boy arrived and the poem fled, ending itself with these lines:

> Weave a circle round him thrice,
> And close your eyes with holy dread,
> For he on honey-dew hath fed,
> And drunk the milk of Paradise.

We will never know how the milk of paradise tasted, and I will never find out where my magic animals wanted to take me. The lives of writers are one long tale of mothers calling at inopportune moments, children coming home from school in the middle of a chapter nearly finished, salesmen and grocery boys breaking into our solitude with armloads of lemons and ice cream.

A few years later, when I learned to write, I set down my dream, feeling greatly relieved that I did not have to carry it around in my head any longer. And since that dream was the first story I ever wanted to write, I have always respected the strong connection between the process of dreaming and the process of writing.

As a child I did not know where dreams came from. Innocent of Freud, I supposed they came from someone outside myself. To this unknown benefactor I gave the name Giver of Dreams, but by the time I was old enough to name him, he had got mixed up in my mind with the Sandman and with my mother, who also brought dreams, or so I was told in the lullabies my mother sang to me at night:

*Your mother shakes the dreamland tree
and down fall little dreams on thee.*

Mothers are always trying to convince us they are indispensable. I knew it wasn't she who brought dreams. They happened, somehow, inside my head, and I had a clear image of what I would find if I could lift off the top of people's heads, like a coffeepot lid, and peer into their minds. My father's mind would look like his laboratory. The shelves of crystals and beakers and bright fluids would stretch off into infinity. My mother's mind was an enormous sugar bowl full of receipts and torn snapshots.

My mind, of course, did not look like either of theirs. Mine was an office, a round, secret room, located inside the dreamland tree. The walls of the office were lined with shelves, and the shelves were stacked with papers, and the desk was stacked with papers too, but anyone could tell at a glance that the papers were all sham and show. They had lain there undisturbed for years. The yellowed edges rose when the wind fluttered those on top, showing the brighter color of those underneath.

The only cause of wind in that still place was the man who ran the office. The only really useful thing in the office was the old water pump, out of which ran words, dreams, memories broken off from events too dim and distant to see them whole. Lest anyone think it odd that I placed such value on a pump, I should explain that every summer till I was sixteen, I lived in a house that had lots of charm, lots of land, and no plumbing. It was my job to take the bucket from the top of the oven every morning, walk a block down the road to the well, and bring back water for the day. The first person at the well had to wake the water; it was always sluggish before breakfast and took its time coming up.

So in the office of my mind stood a magical pump. Sometimes you had to wake it. Sometimes it woke by itself. Writing is like that too, and we are all trying to find ways of making our words flow and of letting our ideas for stories come to us abundantly, one after another.

Education has not erased this image of the office and the pump and the old papers and the middle-aged man that runs the place. I wonder what image each of you has of the way your imagination works. For a writer, this is no frivolous matter. It is useful to have some acquaintance with the one in whose service you are employed.

Sometimes when a story is not going well, I have a strong desire to visit that office, to see that pump, and to meet that man. In this waking dream, I find myself standing at one side of his desk like a supplicant, facing a man who looks like a harassed journalist. You know the type—shirt-sleeves and waistcoat, slacks, green eyeshade. I introduce myself. I am the writer. He introduces himself. He is the Guardian of the Well.

"I beg your pardon," I say, "but I thought you were the Giver of Dreams."

The Guardian shakes his head.

"She's tricky, that one. She's not reliable like me. I'm here right on time. I keep the place tidy. I do my job. You should see the stuff she sends me. She's outrageous. Not the faintest notion of good taste. But I take what she sends, I stick it together, I untangle it and shape it, and I send you the results. I hope you're satisfied?"

When I assure him that I have not come to register a complaint, he pulls up two swivel chairs. I get out my notebook and pencil.

"You've come to interview me," he says. He examines my fifty-cent spiral notebook from Kresge's with great interest.

"Are you addicted to notebooks?" he asks, almost tenderly.

I admit that I am.

"And what use do you make of your notebooks?" asks the Guardian.

"I write down the things I want to remember," I answer.

"And do you go back and read what you have written?"

Not until he asks does it occur to me that I almost never reread my notebooks, and suddenly I wonder why on earth I am keeping them. The Guardian does not wait for my answer.

"Some writers go back to their notebooks, some do not. I used to work for a woman who carried notebooks in her purse. She jotted down ideas for stories, conversations, memories, dreams. She was very scrupulous about jotting things down. But the notebooks, being small, were easily misplaced. The memories and conversations got mixed up with the grocery lists and bus schedules."

"She was careless to lose them," I said.

"She lost them because she didn't really need them," said the Guardian. "That is true of a good many things we lose. Writing an observation in her notebook fixed it in her mind. What she wrote came back to her when she needed it. She did not have to refer to her notebooks when she started a story."

"So she threw them all out?" I asked.

The Guardian smiled and shook his head.

"There came a day when she found herself in the middle of a story, ready to write a description of a cave. Six months before, she had visited a cave. She had described it minutely in one of her notebooks—but where was the notebook? She wrote very well about her cave from memory and finished the story, but the sense of loss continued to haunt her. So she gave up all her small notebooks and left several large notebooks in strategic places around the house. By the telephone; she was fond of dialogue. In the bedroom; she enjoyed her dreams. It is difficult to misplace a notebook bound in leather that one has paid five dollars for."

"But she didn't need her notebook to write about the cave. Why should she bother to keep them?"

The Guardian leaned forward.

"You are a great admirer of Katherine Anne Porter's stories, are you not? She too faced this question. Fortunately for us, she recorded her answer in her journal:

I keep notes and journals only because I write a great deal, and the habit of writing helps me to arrange, annotate, stow away conveniently the references I may need later. Yet when I begin a story, I can never work in any of those promising paragraphs, those apt phrases, those small turns of anecdote I had believed would be so valuable. I must know a story "by heart" and I must write from memory. Certain writing friends whose judgments I admire have told me I lack detail, exact observation of the physical world, my people hardly ever have features, or not enough—that they live in empty houses, et cetera. At one time, I was so impressed by this criticism, I used to sit on a camp stool before a landscape and note down literally every object, every color, form, stick and stone before my eyes. But when I remembered that landscape, it was quite simply not in those terms that I remembered it, and it was no good pretending I did, and it was no good attempting to describe it because it got in the way of what I was really trying to tell. I was brought up with horses, I have harnessed, saddled, driven and ridden many a horse, but to this day I do not know the names for the different parts of a harness. I have often thought I would learn them and write them down in a notebook. But to what end? I have two large cabinets full of notes already.[1]

"The real danger of relying on a notebook," added the Guardian, "is that you may feel compelled to use everything you've written. Writing too much can be as troublesome as writing too little. Thomas Wolfe might have finished *Of Time and the River* a good deal sooner if he had known when he started his book what he knew when he ended it. 'The whole effect of those five years of incessant writing,' he told me, 'had been to make me feel not only that everything had to be used, but that everything had to be told, that nothing could be implied.' "

Suddenly the Guardian looked at me severely.

"Put down your pencil. Listen first, write later."

I laid aside my pencil, but the Guardian would not continue until I had laid aside my notebook also.

"If you reach an impasse in your story," he went on, "put your story away. This is easier said than done, for many writers feel guilty if they are not writing. Nevertheless, you must put your story to sleep, you must forget about it, let it get dreamed over, out of your reach, and then wait for it to return."

"How long do I have to wait?" I asked.

"I can't answer that question," said the Guardian. "All I can tell you is how to keep the door open. Tell me, at what time of day do you write? Or at what hour of the night?"

"I write whenever I can get a babysitter," I answered.

The Guardian laughed. He is untroubled by economics, editors, or housework.

"Tomorrow morning, get up an hour earlier than usual. Don't speak to anyone, don't brush your teeth, don't read the newspaper. Take up your pen, take up your paper, and write. Write whatever comes into your head. Write until you are tired of writing or until you are interrupted. Do this for two weeks."

"And what will happen then?" I asked.

"First, you will find that the act of writing becomes easier for you. Second, you will discover that not everything you write is worth keeping, and you will learn to throw away. Third, you will be able to write with no interference from me."

"But I thought you were helping me," I said, astonished.

The Guardian took out a nail file and applied it deftly to the nails of his left hand.

"The time has come for me to make an embarrassing confession. As I greatly enjoy your company, it pains me to tell you that I can be a dangerous influence on you. When you are listening to the Giver of Dreams, take great care that you do not listen to me. When she wants to sing, I want to judge. When she wants to dance, I want to criticize.

And like the big child that she is, the Giver of Dreams doesn't care to be judged and criticized when she is giving her gifts. Her ways are not my ways, and she will never speak if she feels I am near. You, the writer, are the real guardian of the well. I am only the shaper, I work on what I am given. Only when the Giver of Dreams has finished speaking is it safe to send for me. When she teaches you to believe in your characters, I teach you to manipulate them. Oh, when I was working for Theodore Dreiser, we had many a lively argument over my job, particularly if I came before he called me. I love to make a neat plot and to stick characters into it. I love to take away their freedom. 'In the great novels,' Dreiser snapped at me one morning, 'the plot is negligible. The reason for the absence of plot in a great novel is that it interferes with the logical working out of the destinies of the characters.' "

"If I'm to put all my trust in the Giver of Dreams," I said, "I'd like to know how she works."

"Do you know the tale of the elves and the shoe-maker?" asked the Guardian. "Every night the shoemaker leaves his leather and his tools out on his workbench, and every morning he finds his leather stitched into shoes finer than he himself could ever make. Do you remember how his good fortune came to an end?"

"He stayed up one night to see who was doing him this kindness," I said. "He hid in the closet and peeked at the elves who came to work for him in secret."

"Exactly," said the Guardian. "Writers too have a helper who works for them at night. Anyone who has gone to bed with a problem and awakened with the solution has enjoyed the gift, though he may never have met the giver. Do not ask who the Giver of Dreams is; she does not like to show her face. But observe the conditions under which she comes. When and where do your ideas for stories come to you? Can you remember?"

"Mostly when I'm walking or riding a train."

The Guardian smiled.

"Robert Burns composed at the plough, W. B. Yeats on the Dublin bus, Sherwood Anderson on foot or in bed. 'Very little of the work of the writer is done at his desk or at the typewriter,' Anderson told me once. 'It is done as he walks about, as he sits in the room with people, and perhaps most of all as he lies in bed at night.' Those are my nights off. It's the Giver of Dreams they're listening for, not me. And what arrives in those diverse places is often no more than a mood, a phrase, what Henry James calls 'the mere floating particle in the stream of talk.' You have got hold of the tip of the iceberg, and seeing the part, you believe in the whole. I remember overhearing Mark Twain tell his mother, 'I am trying to think out a short story. I've got the closing sentence of it all arranged, and it is good and strong, but I haven't got any of the rest of the story yet.' The important thing is to be ready. To keep the door open. Tea?"

"What?" I said, startled.

"I've an old samovar back here, and I keep a pot of tea going all the time. If you don't mind a cracked cup——"

"No, indeed," I said.

He vanished behind a stack of papers and reappeared holding a little flowered cup, which he handed to me.

"That cup looks familiar," I said.

"It used to be a great favorite of yours," said the Guardian. "You got it for your fourth birthday and you broke it the same day. Your mother threw away the pieces. But I didn't. I throw nothing away that might be useful to you in a story."

We sipped our tea in silence for a few moments.

"I once worked for a man who wrote all sorts of things," said the Guardian. "First he published a book of poems. Everyone said 'He is a fine poet.' Then he wrote a play. Everyone said, 'He is a fine playwright.' Then he wrote a novel. As the novel was very long, not everyone read it, but those who did said, 'He is a fine novelist.' And those who hadn't read it said to the man, 'Have you given up poetry? Have you given up playwriting?' 'I don't know,' said the man. 'My head is like a hotel. I keep the door open and see what blows in.' "

"Hasn't anyone tried to be master of the Giver of Dreams?"

"Of course," answered the Guardian. "You've read the poetry of Rilke. And you remember he published a collection called *New Poems*. The poems are about animals, works of art, flowers, things he observed while he was living in Paris, where the poems were written. In Paris, Rilke had a job that many an artist would envy. He was secretary to Auguste Rodin. Every morning Rodin went into his studio to work. And Rilke, watching him, thought, Why must we writers be at the mercy of inspiration? Why can't we too go into our studios every morning and work? He resolved to see if writing under these conditions was possible. He drew up a list of more than a hundred subjects for poems, and he systematically wrote his poems from that list. As he finished each one, he drew a line through the title on his list, like a woman checking off groceries in the supermarket. And then he added the date, just as a painter may date a picture.

"But the Giver of Dreams does not like to wear a harness. Rilke fell into a period of real despair. Years later when he wrote the *Duino Elegies* and the *Sonnets to Orpheus,* the way in which poems came to him had utterly changed. 'All in a few days,' he said to his friends, 'there was a nameless storm, a hurricane in my mind. . . . everything in the way of fiber and web in me split—eating was not to be thought of, God knows who fed me.' When the hurricane comes you must be ready to write. Many a story has been lost because the writer did not answer the call."

"The call is not always convenient," I said.

The Guardian nodded.

"That is true of most things in our world that get born. It is not convenient to make time for writing. For you are asked not just to make time for the Giver of Dreams but to give her the sense that she has all the time in the world. The germ of the story arrives, it ripens and grows, you are ready to harvest it. You need time without interruption. How my good friend Charles Dickens chafed at demands made on his time by those who didn't understand it wasn't quality but continuity he needed. 'It is only half an hour—it is only an afternoon—it is only an evening. . . .' he mused, adding, 'they don't know that it is impossible to command one's self sometimes to any stipulated and set disposal of five minutes —or that the mere consciousness of an engagement will sometimes worry a whole day.' "

"And sometimes you have the time but not the story," I added. "What do you do when the well runs dry?"

"The well never runs dry," said the Guardian. "It may

get blocked, but it never runs dry. Writers have various ways of making themselves remember this. I knew a man who always kept one story unwritten. He had a clear notion of the plot, the characters, and the way in which he would tell the story, but he took care never to write it down. Thus when he finished a piece of work, he could always say to himself, 'There's more where that came from. I have yet another story to tell.' That unwritten story was his savings in the bank, his reserve.

"Another writer, to keep his momentum through a long work, writes until he feels that everything is coming together for him, the words are flowing, he can write for hours, he is face to face with the Giver of Dreams, at the brink of great things—and then he rises from his desk, like a hungry man in a restaurant who waits hours to be served and leaves the table when the meal arrives. By the next day he is so eager to return to his work that he can scarcely wait to begin. Beginning—that is the difficult thing. Let me give you a trick for getting tsarted when you think you have no more stories in the well. Take any collection of stories. I have here a collection of fairy tales. Let me read you a few beginnings:

> A king had a daughter who was beautiful beyond all measure but so proud and haughty withal that no suitor was good enough for her. She sent away one after the other, and ridiculed them as well.
>
> (King Thrushbeard)

> A long time ago there were a king and queen who said every day: "Ah, if only we had a child!" but they never

had one. But it happened that once when the queen was bathing, a frog crept out of the water on to the land, and said to her: "Your wish shall be fulfilled; before a year has gone by, you shall have a daughter."

(Little Briar-Rose)

There was once upon a time a king who had a wife with golden hair, and she was so beautiful that her equal was not to be found on earth. It came to pass that she lay ill, and as she felt that she must soon die, she called the king and said: "If you wish to marry again after my death, take no one who is not quite as beautiful as I am, and who has not just such golden hair as I have: this you must promise me." And after the king had promised her this she closed her eyes and died.[2]

(Allerleirauh)

The Guardian closed his book.

"Well, which of them do you like?"

"None of them. I don't care much for kings and queens."

"Try this one, then," said the Guardian. "There was once a lass who went out at the cry of dawn to seek her fortune, and she never came home again."

"That sounds like a good one," I told him.

"It is. Now tell me the rest of the story."

"But I don't know it."

"You don't have to know it. There are a thousand different ways of telling that story. At first you will say, 'I can't tell you the story, I know nothing about the girl.' You will be afraid of failing. Then you will find yourself thinking about the girl—Why did she want to leave? And who was she leaving? A husband? A mother and father? Where did she come from? The country? The city? And where was she going? And why at dawn? And the cry of dawn—What does that sound like? When you find yourself more interested in the girl's story than what you can make of it, a great change will come over me. I will go to sleep. Like Argos, I will shut my eyes, which judge and scrutinize. Suddenly the water will wake in the well, and the Giver of Dreams will speak to you."

"What if the story turns out badly?"

"Then you will have learned something about failure. For a writer, what does failure mean? I once worked for a man who kept all his failed stories in a big box, which he labeled FAILURES. He did not throw them away. He kept them in a corner of his study, because he found himself going to that box in search of a phrase, a name, a conversation that would be useful to him in the stories he did not consider failures. One day he made a new label for the box. WRONG TURNINGS, he wrote on it, because it occurred to him that a lifetime of writing is like a journey, full of detours, alas, but a detour is not a failure. Writers take detours because they are afraid to walk on the main road. They are afraid they will not succeed. Fear is the greatest impediment to the telling of any story.

"And what overcomes fear?" I asked.

"I am not sure," said the Guardian, "but I would say that no writer taking that journey should be without a strong sense of mystery. Do you like mysteries?"

"I used to love mystery stories when I was a kid," I confessed.

"Which ones?"

"Oh, you know—Nancy Drew."

The Guardian wrinkled his nose with distaste.

"Those are not mystery stories. They are puzzles and puzzles can be solved. A real mystery cannot be solved. It can only be celebrated. Real mysteries are personal. What is mysterious to one person may be insignificant to the next. You don't believe me? Listen, I used to work for a woman who never carried a purse. She carried her house key in her shoe and she never carried money. She owned no credit cards, no driver's license. All her friends said, 'My dear, you should carry a purse. You should never be without money or identification.' Did I say all her friends? No, she had one friend who took a different point of view. He said, 'What a mystery that you can go through life without carrying a purse! Why do the rest of us need money and identification and not you?' From his interest in the minor mystery of a human habit sprang a story. Don't all stories have their dark beginnings in such mysteries? Though you speak with the tongues of angels, if you have not mystery, you have nothing. I am only telling you what you already know. Do you remember the first time you understood the word *mystery*?"

"No."

"Oh, but I do," said the Guardian, "because in this place we never throw anything away. It was Ash Wednesday, you were eight years old. The priest's voice lapped at your ears like waves. He was preaching on the Book of Job:

Thy sons and thy daughters were eating and drinking wine in the eldest brother's house:
And, behold, there came a great wind from the wilderness and smote the four corners of the house, and it fell

187

upon the young men, and they are dead; and I only am escaped to tell thee.

"The saints in the glass windows had blackened their faces, the candles had burned down to stumps. Now the priest was intoning the names of the dead. Your mother, feeling chilly, reached over and buttoned your coat. You thought it was time to leave. Suddenly a woman's voice from the darkened choir loft sang out:

Sing, O my soul, the mystery of His body.

"It woke you like a plunge into cold water. You looked at your mother's forehead, marked with a cross of ashes like a tree in the forest marked to be cut down. And everyone around was so marked, this man, that woman, all separate, all alone. And you thought, What a mystery the body is! When this man leaves the earth, the sun will not shine on exactly this body again. When that woman dies, no one will ever again see exactly that face. And the woman singing of mystery; in a hundred years who will be left to praise her voice breaking into the dark?"

The Guardian stopped speaking. His face seemed to fade, as if twilight had found even this place without windows to let in the weather.

"What time is it?" I asked.

"It's the time between morning and night. Soon you will wake up."

"Am I not awake now?"

"Now you are crossing from darkness to morning. The dreams you dream at this hour you will remember, because you do not have to carry them very far."

In the silence that followed, I heard someone calling my name. Oh, here was the window to my room and the vine over the eaves about to bloom. I climbed on the sill and looked out on oak, hickory, beech, the land as it lay when only animals lived there, elk, moose, possum, bobcat, deer. They moved in a silent circle around the house. The Giver of Dreams is shining in my doorway, the Guardian has fallen asleep.

There was once a lass who went out at the cry of dawn to seek her fortune, and she never came home again.[3] Now I see the woods that hid her, the town on the other side that welcomed her. I hear her singing as she goes, and it's her voice that will make her fortune, I know, and in a house at the edge of the woods I hear her mother and father calling her, for they don't realize she's riding the red-tailed deer at dawn, going to seek her fortune. Oh, she'll never come home again. Not that one.

I take paper and pen and I write her story.

❦ 7 ❦

Becoming a Writer

_____ I have been asked to give advice to young writers, but I can never endure advice unless it comes disguised as entertainment. So let me begin by telling you a story.

First I should explain that I grew up in Ann Arbor. My father taught chemistry at the university for forty-six years. And while I was growing up, ours was the only family I knew that did not buy its clothes in a department store. Spring and fall, an ancient lady would arrive at our house in a car nearly as weathered as herself. Her name was Ella. She came from Owosso, Michigan, and she stayed for a week. She would set up her portable sewing machine in our sun room and plug in her radio and ask us, What clothes did we want her to make us this season?

My mother and my sister prudently chose ready-made

patterns from the big pattern books at Muehlig's. My aunt
sent Ella an assortment of dresses she'd bought on sale, with
instructions to "fix them so I look like I have a little more
on top and a little less in the behind." I drew pictures of the
dresses I wanted, leaning heavily on third-rate Victorian
novels illustrated with consumptive young women in long
skirts and blouses that ballooned at the shoulder and
pinched at the wrist. To my girlfriends, who read *Seventeen*
and wore cashmere sweaters and tailored skirts, I must have
looked like the victim of a time warp. But Ella's business
was to sew, not to criticize. She would study my sketch,
draw up a pattern, and send me forth to select the material.

Velvet, wool, muslin, corduroy, heaped on tables and
folded on chairs, flooded the sun room with promises of
better things to come. One by one the fabrics, ample as
flags, submitted to Ella's shears and took shape. She snipped,
she basted.

"Try it on," she said.

Whatever I tried on was always full of pins. Whichever
way I turned, the dress hit me, needled me. I stood with
my arms straight out, as if directing the invisible traffic of
needles and thread, while Ella crept round me on her knees,
taking the measure of the hem, her tape measure dangling
around her neck like a stole, her mouth so full of pins that
she seemed to have grown whiskers. I turned, she pinned,
and her radio told us its troubles. We listened to "Portia
Faces Life," "Ma Perkins," "Stella Dallas, Backstage Wife,"
we listened to ads for Oxydol and Rinso, we heard how
many boxtops of both you needed to send for your free
recipe file and earrings. To this day when I read the story of
creation in the book of Genesis, when I hear God com-

manding the light to come out of hiding and the earth to bring forth grass and creeping things and every beast after its own kind, I see them all falling from Ella's shears, waking to life under her needle. And behind God's voice, I hear the still, small voices of Portia and Stella Dallas and Ma Perkins, who are picking up the pieces of their lives and carrying on.

On the day of Ella's departure, which was always after lunch, she would intone a long blessing over our food, in which she thanked God for my mother's cooking and implored Him to keep her car from breaking down. As she drove away, we could see her sewing machine and her radio and our half-finished garments piled high in the back seat, watching over her. Three weeks later a large box would arrive in which we found all we'd asked for and more. The dresses were folded and pressed. Attached to each were the scraps, rolled neat as a prayer rug. Years of sewing had taught Ella never to throw anything away.

One day my mother reminded me that Ella would not be around forever, and she bought me a sewing machine for Christmas and hired Ella to instruct me in its use. What Ella taught me about sewing has passed into my hands and become as automatic to me as tying my shoe. But more important than what she taught me about sewing was what she taught me about craft. An indifference to fashion. A respect for what is well designed and well made. Save all your scraps. Throw nothing away. If you don't get it right the first time, take it apart and try again. Revise. Anything well done takes patience, experience, and a lot of time. And time is not given, it is made. "Five minutes, ten minutes, can always be found," says William Carlos Williams in the foreword to his autobiography:

I had my typewriter in my office desk. All I needed to do was to pull up the leaf to which it was fastened and I was ready to go. I worked at top speed. If a patient came in at the door while I was in the middle of a sentence, bang would go the machine—I was a physician. . . . When the patient left, up would come the machine. Finally, after eleven at night, when the last patient had been put to bed, I could always find the time to bang out ten or twelve pages.[1]

And I think of Jane Austen, as one of her nieces recalled her, how she would sit quietly sewing by the fire in the library "and then would suddenly burst out laughing, jump up and run across the room to a table where pens and paper were lying, write something down, and then come back to the fire and go on quietly working as before."[2] A nephew adds that his Aunt Jane had

> no separate study to retire to, and most of the work must have been done in the general sitting-room, subject to all kinds of casual interruptions. She was careful that her occupation should not be suspected by servants, or visitors, or any persons beyond her own family party. She wrote upon small sheets of paper which could easily be put away, or covered with a piece of blotting paper. There was, between the front door and the offices, a swing door which creaked when it was opened; but she objected to having this little inconvenience remedied, because it gave her notice when anyone was coming.[3]

Learning to write, for me, is so bound up with learning to do other things that I sometimes ask myself, How do writers learn their craft? A few years ago, I was asked to judge a poetry competition. I was given forty manuscripts and told to choose the three whose authors I felt deserved a sizable sum of money. The more manuscripts I read, the more it seemed to me that all the poems had a single author. But nobody, I told myself, would go to such lengths to carry out a practical joke. Had the forty poets all studied with the same teacher? That didn't seem likely, either. But they might have all read the same books. Everypoet—as I named the single voice in these manuscripts—had read his contemporaries. He had taken from them what they had in common, a language close to speech, sometimes indistinguishable from prose. But the variety of experience and influences that resonates in the work of the best writers was absent. Reading Everypoet's work was a little like hearing Bach played on a harmonica. Yet his poems were competent and as succinct as if a good editor had gone over them, taking out and paring down. I could not put my finger on the place where they went wrong. Though his range was small, Everypoet could write.

When I was an undergraduate in Ann Arbor, I took a course called creative writing. I took it every semester. It was in this course that I first read Fitzgerald, Roethke, Bishop, Jarrell. Though the students read and discussed each other's work, we always studied something besides ourselves. Yet if you ask me what I learned, I confess that I remember no precepts and only a few poems. But I do remember the people. The boy who spent the entire semester revising a single poem. The boy who carried three-by-five cards in his shirt pocket where some men carry handkerchiefs, on which—when he had a good audience—he would take copious notes. The girl who was rumored to have written five hundred sonnets over summer vacation. I did a rough calculation and figured she must have been writing them with both hands, simultaneously. And I remember a class, just before Christmas vacation, when our teacher, expecting that only the most serious students would show up, explicated one of his own poems. To this day, I remember how much experience a single line can carry.

When a student brings his writing to a teacher, the teacher usually responds in one of two ways. On the one hand, you have Rilke's response to the young poet who sent him a manuscript and hoped that Rilke would critique it. Rilke was quick to refuse. "I cannot go into the nature of your verses," he writes, "for all critical intention is too far from me." But he was willing to give advice of another kind:

> You ask whether your verses are good. You ask me. You have asked others before. You send them to magazines. You compare them with other poems, and you are disturbed when certain editors reject your efforts. Now . . . I beg you to give up all that. You are looking outward, and that above all you should not do now. . . . This above all—ask yourself in the stillest hour of your night *must* I write? . . . then build your life according to this necessity . . .[4]

On the other hand, you have Jane Austen's advice to her niece, who I suspect was looking more for praise than criticism:

> We have been very much amused by your three books, but I have a good many criticisms to make, more

than you will like. We are not satisfied with Mrs. Forester settling herself as tenant and near neighbor to
such a man as Sir Thomas, without having some other
inducement to go there. She ought to have some friend
living thereabouts to tempt her. . . . Remember she *is*
very prudent. You must not let her act inconsistently.
. . . Sir Thomas H. you always do very well. I have only
taken the liberty of expunging one phrase of his . . .
—"Bless my heart!" It is too familiar and inelegant. . . .
your descriptions are often more minute than will be
liked. You give too many particulars of right hand and
left.[5]

Jane Austen could have run a terrific workshop. I
mention workshops a bit shyly, for though I have conducted
them, I have never in my life taken one. At their best,
they give the student who has written a good deal the careful criticism that an editor gives. At their most mediocre,
they produce poems and stories that are carbon copies of
the teacher's work. At their worst, they are destructive.
Nothing is served by telling a student his work is hopeless.
To write well demands confidence and a willingness to fail.
As my piano teacher was fond of saying, When you make a
mistake, make it good and loud.

Workshops serve another purpose for many writers,
one that I think they are scarcely aware of. They offer community. I have one student who has almost managed to
make a career for herself moving from one workshop to the
next, with teaching fellowships to help bridge the gaps.
Most of her friends are writers. I tell her now that she's
given up cigarettes she has become addicted to workshops.
I wonder when she is going to quit being a student and

become a writer. And she tells me how valuable she finds the close critical attention teachers and students bring to her work—and where else can she find that?

Only twenty-five years ago, people still debated whether writers should be educated at the university or at the school of hard knocks. In 1955, *Atlantic Monthly* carried an article by William Saroyan on becoming a writer. To most of my students today, Saroyan would sound like a man from another planet:

> I did not earn one dollar by any means other than writing . . . I have never been subsidized, I have never accepted money connected with a literary prize or award, I have never been endowed, and I have never received a grant or fellowship. . . .
>
> I am head over heels in debt. I expect to get out of debt by writing, or not at all. . . .
>
> What advice have I for the potential writer?
>
> I have none, for anybody is a potential writer, and the writer who *is* a writer needs no advice and seeks none.
>
> What about courses in colleges and universities in writing?
>
> Useless, they are entirely useless.[6]

Fortunately Saroyan's article was followed by one giving a different point of view. It was written by Roy Cowden, who began teaching at the University of Michigan in 1909 and was director of the Hopwood Awards for twenty years. My mother, who was a student at Michigan while Cowden was on campus but never took a course with him, still speaks of him with awe. "The only way to learn to write," says Cowden, "is to write and write and write and write and write. . . . Where there is no caring, there is no real writing. . . . Great writers are few in the world, but no writer will do as well unless he aims to be among the great ones."[7]

Why is it that so many talented students, when they leave the supportive atmosphere of the university, find it easy to put writing aside? Cowden regretfully recalls that the most promising first-year student he ever taught became not a writer but an interior decorator. And of one of his least promising students, he tells this story. The young man wished to take Cowden's class in creative writing and submitted several short narratives. His work was notably undistinguished. But sensing an unusual degree of tension in the student, Cowden turned to him and said, "How much interested are you in becoming a writer?" The student looked him in the eye and answered, "I'll starve for it." The story has a happy ending. "In the class he wrote a novel that has been published," says Cowden, "and he is now working on another."

When I consider the students of mine who have gone on growing as writers after they left school, I realize how much they have in common. First, they write to be read. They write, of course, for the public. But they also write for one or two readers whose judgment they trust. That trusted reader may be an editor or a friend. For a lucky few, it may be a relative. Jane Austen's trusted reader was her sister, Cassandra; Emily Dickinson's—for a limited time—was her sister-in-law, Susan. I haven't forgotten Keats's claim that even if his poems were burned every morning, unread by anyone save himself, he would continue to write them. A disputable claim; he was never put to the test. What my students want when they take a course in creative writing is an intelligent, sensitive reader. What I want for my students when they finish such a course is that they strike out on their own. And I want them to "write and write and write and write."

To that injunction I should add to read and read and read and read. I don't know a single serious writer who would not include books among the teachers who have influenced him the most. The results of such teaching are entirely different from the results of a workshop. In a workshop the reward is immediate. The poem or story emerges with a new figure and a face-lift. But what you learn from a book may not surface in your writing for years. When I was a graduate student at Stanford, I spent a year putting together an annotated bibliography of the Middle English lyric. While I was working on it, I read everything I could find on that subject in books and scholarly journals. Twenty years later, I have gone back to the forms of those lyrics in some of the poems I want to write now. How useless they seemed to me at the time, and how much I enjoyed reading them!

Remembering my own eclectic education with great pleasure, I hope that Ann Beattie was speaking only for herself and not for her generation when she said in an interview, "I read a lot—mostly modern fiction, nothing before 1960 if I can help it."[8]

The reader for all seasons never knows from what quarter instruction and encouragement may come. A former student of mine who recently published her first novel dreamed that she was walking down a busy street when, to her delight and astonishment, she met Charles Dickens striding toward her on a pair of stilts. She has never forgotten the way he smiled at her as if to say, *Writer, welcome to the family.*

What the members of that family, the community of serious writers, have in common is not their success but their capacity for dealing with failure. Look in the dark corners of the workroom of a writer who has published a good book and you will find an astonishing number of manuscripts that were rejected either by an editor or by the writer himself. To write and rewrite is to grapple with failure, to make the common language do the uncommon things you demand of it. A well-known novelist, while yet unpublished, sent her only copy of her novel to an editor and discovered later that it had got lost in the mail. She never recovered the novel. But she recovered from the loss of it by sitting down and writing another one. I think the best advice I've heard recently for young writers came from Picasso. A critic asked him, "Of all the works you've created, which is your favorite?" And Picasso replied, "My next one."

Angel in the Parlor: The Reading and Writing of Fantasy

The house where I grew up had squirrels in the attic, mice in the pantry, and an angel in the parlor. I never saw the angel, and I only found out about it by accident. My mother had two sisters, both divorced, who hated to cook and who dropped by our house every Sunday for dinner. They never came alone. They brought their boyfriends. Aunt Jessie brought her daughter. Aunt Nellie brought her son and four Baptist missionaries from Detroit bent on saving our comfortable Presbyterian souls. It was not to them that the angel appeared, however, but to the kindly schoolmaster whom my Aunt Jessie had dated for so long that I called him Uncle Bill and assumed that somewhere in the roots of the tree of life we were related.

I remember the first time the angel appeared. We had just sat down to Sunday dinner when my mother, who had been cooking all morning, counted heads and made a perilous discovery.

"There are thirteen at the table," she said. "If we sit down with thirteen at the table, one of us will die within the year."

And she carried her plate to the sideboard. We all knew better than to try to change her mind. So over the clatter of silverware we shouted to her how delicious the chicken tasted, and she shouted back that there were more mashed potatoes in the kitchen, and nobody heard a word.

Then suddenly, for no reason, everyone stopped talking at once. Uncle Bill closed his eyes. Then he glanced at his watch and looked past the dining room into the parlor.

"Ah!" he murmured. "An angel has flown through the room."

I followed his gaze. I, too, looked into the parlor but saw no angel. I could tell from the astonished faces around me that no one else had seen it either. Why, I wondered, would an angel choose Uncle Bill? Why not me? Or the four Baptist missionaries?

Years later I discovered that the angel that flew through the room on that day was a figure of speech, acknowledging the blessing of silence in a room full of voices.

But even after my mother enlightened me about the angel, I still talked about it, still joked about it, and finally, by paying it so much attention, I came to believe in it. That is to say, I came to believe that our house was more than a collection of people, tables, chairs, lost pocketbooks, misplaced spectacles, and back issues of the *National Geographic*. All these things I could see and hear and touch. But there was also an order of life that, like the angel's, was not bound by the laws of the physical universe. And I came to believe that there were two kinds of people in the world, those who believed in tables and those who believed in angels.

In our public library I met representatives of both. There was the plump lady, who worked on Mondays, Wednesdays, and Fridays, and who gave me books on dinosaurs and Abraham Lincoln. The covers of the books she chose bore the label, "This is a Read-It-Yourself Book." That meant I knew all the words and did not have to ask my mother what, for example, a hippodrome was. Then there was the thin lady, who worked on Tuesdays, Thursdays, and Saturdays and gave me books about talking animals and giants and countries at the back of the north wind. The books she recommended had more words I didn't know than words I did, but I felt rather privileged carrying them home, as if I'd just checked out the Rosetta stone.

I do not remember what books I was carrying the afternoon I walked home from the library and saw, high in the clear October sky, a flock of geese winging south over the city. It was their plaintive cry that made me turn, startled at the wild sound over the hum of traffic. Thanks to the plump librarian's selection of books on the migration of birds, I knew how long a journey lay before them. I also knew I would never be happy until I too learned to fly as they did.

Monday afternoon I went to the library and asked the plump librarian for a book on flying. She nodded agreeably. She prided herself on filling all requests, be they ever so peculiar. She gave me a handsomely illustrated book on the Wright brothers. Leafing through it, I could see at once that it did not speak to my condition. So I handed it back and said, "Have you any books on how I can make my own wings and fly like a bird?"

The plump librarian looked distressed but not defeated.

"It is not possible for you to fly like a bird," she answered.

I thanked her and returned to the library on Tuesday. I told the thin librarian I wanted a book on flying but I did not want a book on airplanes. She looked hurt that I should think her capable of so gross a gesture, and after a moment's thought she plucked a small book from the shelving truck. It had only two pictures, neither of them in color. It was the story of Icarus.

I read the story very carefully. I paid special attention to the construction of the wings, but the drawings were not detailed enough to be very useful. I needed a working plan, with measurements. And where on earth could I find so many feathers?

I checked out the book, however, and as the thin librarian was stamping my card I said, "Have you any books that will teach me to fly?"

She considered my question very seriously.

"You want a book on magic," she answered.

"Have you books on magic?" I asked.

She pointed to a section at the back of the room.

"We have plenty of books on how to do magic tricks. However, there is a great difference between mere sleight-of-hand and real magic."

And she waved her hand at the whole section, as if conjuring it to disappear, and led me over to a cupboard. In the cupboard behind windowed doors, which were not locked but looked as if they might be, stood the fairy tales. Here I discovered stories of wizards, witches, shamans, soldiers, fools, and saints who flew by means of every imaginable conveyance, including carpets, trunks, horses, ships, and even bathtubs. It showed me that luck, a virtuous life, or both had something to do with one's ability to fly. As I was born under a mischievous star, I would have to count on luck; virtue would get me nowhere.

It was around this time that I made a curious discovery about my father. He was, by profession, a chemist. For him, to see was to believe. One afternoon I discovered on his bedside table two books I had never noticed before. One was the notebook where he wrote down solutions to scientific problems as they occurred to him during the night. The second was an account of an island called Atlantis, located west of Gibraltar and said by Plato to have sunk into the sea. I sat down on my father's bed and started reading the account of Atlantis, written, according to the title page, by an Englishman who claimed that unbeknownst to geographers the lost island had not sunk but had merely become invisible to ordinary sight. The author knew this for a fact; indeed, he had actually visited Atlantis. In his introduction he took pains to assure his readers that he was telling the truth. He was not, he explained, writing science fiction. A photograph of the island, opposite the title page, showed a woman wearing a snake headdress and a sequined tunic. The caption read, "Queen of Atlantis, taken by the author with a Lecia M-1." I thought she looked like a tired Hedy Lamarr.

This book, I discovered, was part of a secret library my father kept hidden in the springs of his bed, a library that made his mattress so lumpy that no guests ever slept in it and thus no one else except my mother knew about his passion for the fantastic and the occult. In my father's bed-spring library I found numerous books on Atlantis, Shangri-La, flying saucers, and reincarnation. I pored over a book of fuzzy images purported to be the souls of famous men and women photographed during a séance by one Madame Ugo Ugo. These volumes appalled my mother and confused me. They sounded like fairy tales, yet their authors claimed to be telling the truth. Were these books true and my fairy tales false? Were they all false? I knew that the fantasies I read could not be scientifically true. Fantasy, therefore, must be a literature of lies.

I am sure we have all met people who would agree with this view. Fantasy, they will tell you, is a literature of escape from the real world. By the real world they mean the physical world of tables and chairs. A man once asked me if I didn't agree with him that fantasy should be forbidden to children, as it is so difficult for them to unlearn the lies that it teaches. And unlearning, he reminded me, is a painful process, almost as painful as losing one's faith. I thought of my father's books and wondered what this man would make of them. I had long ago decided that my father's books were false because their authors recognized only one kind of truth, the truth of science. Of course, fairy tales are not literally true; their authors make no such claims. But taken as a record of what some call our psychological experience and others call our spiritual history, fantasy at its best is one of the truest forms of fiction we have. Many people have committed the error of taking literally what was meant to be taken metaphorically. Some of the most famous victims of this misunderstanding are those alchemists who tried, several hundred years ago, to turn lead into gold.

I want to look briefly at that lost science, for it is closer to the art of writing than you may have imagined. Surely it is no accident that in ancient Egypt the god of alchemy was also the god of writing. Every Christmas my father received at least a dozen cards showing pictures of alchemists. The details never varied. A man sits in his study, surrounded by beakers, alembics, and the assorted apparatus of scientific discovery. A skull and an hourglass stand on his desk to remind him that he is mortal. A lion dozes at his feet, but the alchemist is not afraid of the lion. Indeed, he seems to have made a pet of it.

Now take away the scientific apparatus. The alchemist undergoes a remarkable change. Posed beside his skull, his hourglass, and his lion, he looks less like a scientist than a saint, meditating on human frailty. Or like an eccentric writer, awaiting the arrival of the muse.

Many years after my interest in flying waned, I came across a chapter on alchemy in a book on magic. It was Albertus Magnus, alchemist par excellence, who kindled my imagination. I particularly liked the story in which he invites a group of churchmen to a garden party in the middle of winter. Albertus Magnus turns winter to summer and the guests dine among blossoms and trees laden with fruit. When they have finished the last course, winter returns. That struck me as rather a neat trick. I went to the public library and asked for a book on alchemy. Alchemy made plain.

The plump librarian gave me an encyclopedia of chemistry. Of alchemy she seemed never to have heard. The thin librarian gave me a book called *Remarks upon Alchemy and the Alchemists* and warned me not to blow myself up with crazy experiments. The book contained directions for turning base metals into gold. But I found these directions quite impossible to follow. How could anyone set up an experiment from the following passages:

> You must so join or mix gold and silver that they may not, by any possible means whatever, be separated. The reader, surely, need not be told that this is not a work of the hands. If you know not how to do this, you know nothing truly in our Art.
>
> Farewell, dilligent reader. In reading these things, invocate the Spirit of Eternal Light; speak little, meditate much, and judge aright.[1]

Further reading gave me the key to this secret language. What many alchemists took to be the science of turning ordinary metal into gold was really a way of describing the spiritual disciplines that turn ordinary people into heroes and saints.

Now think for a moment what we as writers do. We transmute our personal experiences into works of art, which are impersonal and far more orderly and permanent than the lives that created them. The notebook I found by my father's bed testified to his faith in the mystery of this process. He went to bed with the broken pieces of a problem in his head. By what alchemy did he wake in the night with the pieces gathered into a neat solution? By what alchemy do our stories, gathered from our experiences at diverse times and distant places, rise up in our imaginations mended and whole?

So often writing teachers tell their students, Write from experience. Write what you know. This is sound advice, but it is often taken to mean, Write about the people you know and the places you've visited. I believe the breadth of your experience as a writer depends on how well you can focus on whatever it is that humans of all times and places have in common. The range of your experience is less important than the depth with which you can imagine things. I like to imagine Shakespeare, a young writer, signing up for a class in creative writing at some large university and going for his first conference with his teacher. I like to imagine the teacher shaking his head and saying, "Now Bill, this history stuff is all very well, but why don't you write from your own experience? You tell me this play is set in Denmark, but I don't get a very strong sense of place. Why don't you write about Stratford or London?"

But how to begin? How to include in your own experience the secret lives of angels and alchemists, librarians and wild geese? Take as your starting point a story as fantastic as it is familiar: Perrault's version of "Cinderella." Who can forget the scene in which the fairy godmother makes her first appearance?

> At last the happy day arrived. Away they went, Cinderella watching them as long as she could keep them in sight. When she could no longer see them she began to cry. Her godmother found her in tears, and asked what was troubling her.
>
> "I should like—I should like—"
>
> She was crying so bitterly that she could not finish the sentence.
>
> Said her godmother, who was a fairy:
>
> "You would like to go to the ball, would you not?"

"Ah, yes," said Cinderella, sighing.

"Well, well," said her godmother, "promise to be a good girl and I will arrange for you to go."

She took Cinderella into her room and said:

"Go into the garden and bring me a pumpkin."

Cinderella went at once and gathered the finest that she could find. This she brought to her godmother, wondering how a pumpkin could help in taking her to the ball.

Her godmother scooped it out, and when only the rind was left, struck it with her wand. Instantly the pumpkin was changed into a beautiful coach, gilded all over.

Then she went and looked in the mousetrap, where she found six mice all alive. She told Cinderella to lift the door of the mousetrap a little, and as each mouse came out she gave it a tap with her wand, whereupon it was transformed into a fine horse. So that here was a fine team of six dappled mouse-gray horses.

But she was puzzled to know how to provide a coachman.

"I will go and see," said Cinderella, "if there is not a rat in the rattrap. We could make a coachman of him."

"Quite right," said her godmother, "go and see."

Cinderella brought in the rattrap, which contained three big rats. The fairy chose one specially on account of his elegant whiskers.

As soon as she had touched him he turned into a fat coachman with the finest mustachios that ever were seen.

"Now go into the garden and bring me the six

lizards which you will find behind the water-butt."

No sooner had they been brought than the god-mother turned them into six lackeys, who at once climbed up behind the coach in their braided liveries, and hung on there as if they had never done anything else all their lives.[2]

The storyteller focuses on Cinderella. But suppose we change the focus? Suppose we tell the story from the point of view of a less conspicuous character.

If I were to rewrite "Cinderella," whose point of view would I choose? Not the fairy godmother's, for her powers surpass my understanding. Not the wicked stepsisters; I've already met them in literature oftener than I care to remember. I would choose the rat at the bottom of the garden, who for three nights running finds himself transformed into a coachman. I knew very well what the bottom of a garden is like, with its compost heap and broken flowerpots. And by letting the rat tell his autobiography, I can show that the story of the animal who becomes human is as true and familiar as the rags-to-riches story of Cinderella herself.

Consider the rat's predicament. The first night of his human life, his transformation terrifies and astonishes him. The second night he is less terrified but no less astonished; he can hardly believe the miracle has happened to him again. By the third night he is eager to escape from the rot of the garden to the revelry of the palace; all the next day he reviews the events of the nights before, and by the fourth night he is sitting in the pumpkin patch, waiting to be chosen. Nothing happens, not that night, nor the next, nor the next. Never again will the rat turned coachman hand the lovely girl into her coach. Never again will he wait outside the brilliantly lit palace in the evening, chatting with the coachmen of great families who do not know that only hours before, their acquaintance was one of their oldest enemies. Perhaps they shared a bottle of wine while they waited and exchanged gossip about their employers. Did the fairy godmother give our rat coachman a past? Or did he sit silent and bewildered, wondering why he alone arrived at this place without memories?

Did he come to enjoy these summer nights, beating time with his foot to the music as it drifted out the French doors, propped open to cool the dancers? Did he wait eagerly on the fourth night for the amazing change to come over him? Did he think it would happen to him forever? And after Cinderella married her prince, does he find himself exiled by his strange experiences, condemned to live among creatures that can never understand him? Remember, he has acquired human memories and a taste for human pleasures, and he has spoken the language of men and women who like to make jokes and to tell stories. What happens to one who is born at the bottom of a garden, thrust briefly into a life of splendor, and then expected to return forever to the garbage heap that bred him? In changing the point of view, you also change the plot. "Cinderella" contains as many stories as there are writers to invent them.

It is important for writers to know both the uses and the limits of direct experience. The man who never fought in a war may describe a battle much more vividly than the man who did. I remember as a child the day our neighbor's son came home from Europe in 1944. He had won a Purple Heart for surviving the war and half a dozen ribbons for doing the right thing at the right time. His parents invited us over to hear the story of his adventures and to see his souvenirs. I did not know then that souvenir means memory, and that memory, to quote from my first alchemy book, is not a work of the hands.

It was a Sunday afternoon in July. My mother and father and sister led the way. Aunts, cousins, boyfriends, missionaries, and even my grandmother trooped across the yard to the house next door. The hero, a tan young man with short hair, was sitting in a big Morris chair in the middle of his parents' living room beside the coffee table, which held his trophies. There were two trophies, one boxed, the other wrapped in a white handkerchief.

He waited till we were quiet and then he took the little black box from the table and lifted the lid. There on its bed of white satin lay the Purple Heart. To me it looked like a chicken's heart; I had imagined something bigger. The hero said, "I won this in the fighting at Normandy. I got a piece of shrapnel in my leg."

We ooh'd and ah'd. What was shrapnel? I did not know. Before I could ask him, he reached for the second object. Slowly he unwrapped it and held it up for our approval.

"A German Luger," he explained. "I took it from the body of a dead officer."

There were murmurs of "Imagine that!" and "Good God!" I admired the pistol politely and waited for him to tell his story. But all he said was, "I got this at Normandy," and "Yeah, I fought at Normandy." Nothing of how he felt, of whom he fought beside, of what the battle looked and sounded like. And at last I understood that the Purple Heart and the pistol were substitutes for the story he did not know how to tell. They were his souvenirs, his memories.

The first storyteller who made the faces of war vivid to

me was Stephen Crane. At the time of writing *The Red Badge of Courage,* he had no direct experience of life on the battlefield. Here is Crane himself, writing to a correspondent in England about the reviewers who doubted such a feat was possible:

> They all insist . . . that I am a veteran of the civil war, whereas the fact is, as you know, I never smelled even the powder of a sham battle. I know what the psychologists say, that a fellow can't comprehend a condition that he has never experienced . . . of course, I have never been in a battle, but I believe that I got my sense of the rage of conflict on the football field, or else fighting is a hereditary instinct, and I wrote intuitively; . . . I endeavoured to express myself in the simplest and most concise way.[3]

There are two ways of viewing Crane's performance, as a kind of deception or a kind of magic. You know by this time which way I choose. For it seems to me that writers have always been the best magicians, the direct descendants of those true alchemists and sages who tried to refine what is transitory into what is eternal. We take for our medium a language, used and abused by everyone, and we make of it something that has a beauty and permanence not found in ordinary lives.

I still remember the journey that first showed me the power of the storyteller to make the world of tables and chairs as vivid and uncommon to me as the angel itself. When I was a child, I heard a great many fairy stories, not at my mother's knee, but at the cold foot of a large wooden radio. The voices passed through a piece of fine silk covering the speaker, to which I was as attentive as if I were hearing a confession. On Saturday morning my sister and I listened to the fairy stories dramatized for children on a program called "Let's Pretend." From the voices we had a clear image of all the characters. There was a witch voice, a princess voice, a queen voice, an old king voice, and the voices of animals, handmaidens, and churls, as required. We knew every corner of the poor man's hut and the rich man's palace. We knew all the terrors of the enchanted forest. We knew the commercial for Cream of Wheat, which my mother never bought, and we listened till a man's voice announced that this was CBS in New York.

Of New York I knew nothing except that according to Aunt Jessie it was bigger than life, like Jerusalem or Babylon in the Bible. She had lived in New York for two years before leaving her husband and taking up with Uncle Bill, the schoolmaster who first saw the angel in our parlor. My mother called her stories "fantastic," and indeed they were.

In New York, said my aunt, everything is better. She bought the *New York Times* on Sunday, yearned over the advertisements, and wrote away for bath towels and dresses. She told stories about climbing up a skinny stairway right into the Statue of Liberty's stomach. The streets of New York, she said, had more taxis and more people than any other city in the world. And the department stores! You could live in Macy's for six months and want for nothing.

When I was five, Aunt Jessie won a hundred dollars on a radio program called "Name That Tune." A few days before the New Year, she dropped in to announce her good fortune. As the holiday approached, the house filled up with relatives. The night before New Year's Eve, I heard Aunt

Jessie telling my mother about the wonders of Times Square. She was very persuasive. When my mother woke my sister Kirsten and me the next morning, we saw two suitcases in the hall.

"Eat fast," said Mother. "We're taking the train to New York."

The train left at six. Mother had risen at four and turned on the electric heater in our room and brought up our breakfast on a tray so we could dress and eat at the same time. All over the house we heard the muffled commotion of aunts and cousins thumping out of bed, running water, flushing toilets, and exhorting each other to hurry. It was understood that my father would stay at home, for he preferred to travel alone. The rest of us traveled in a flock that included all able-bodied relatives, even my grandmother, though she was senile and could not always remember where she was.

The taxi that morning crept down icy streets to the train station. Snow had nearly erased it from the landscape.

In the waiting room the stationmaster was building a fire, parrying it with a poker. Kirsten and I stood as close as we dared and stretched out our hands. Grandmother asked my mother why Grandfather was not coming with us, and my mother reminded her that he had died two years before. A few old men and one elderly couple dozed on the benches, as patiently as if they were sitting in a doctor's office.

Suddenly the old men stood up.

"Train coming!" shrieked my cousin John. He was younger than I but he could yell louder.

Everyone rushed outside to the platform.

"When the train comes—" shouted my mother over the mounting roar, but the hissing of the train swept her words away. The conductor swung through a cloud of steam, threw down the steps for the car nearest us, and helped us inside.

How dark, how quiet everything looked! In the first four cars we passed dozens of soldiers, huddled together or sprawled across the seats. The windows wept steam, the light from the tracks touched a knee here, an elbow there. My mother led the way to the civilian cars, where we found seats but not together.

Because of the darkness, I slept. Day never broke at all. The snow lightened the air outside, but no one could assign it a time or call it afternoon. My cousins and my sister and I played "Old Maid" while Aunt Jessie cheered us with stories of the Automat, where you could choose your own lunch from behind hundreds of glass doors. And Chinatown, where you couldn't read the newspapers, but you could eat your breakfast with chopsticks. And the throngs of people and cars on the streets—ah, she assured us, then you'll know you're in a real city.

At ten that night, the train arrived at Grand Central Station. The main lobby was dark save for one ticket window and the clock over the information booth. Aunt Jessie herded us to the exit, where she reminded us that hundreds of taxis would be swarming like a salmon run. As we stepped outside, she gave a sharp cry of amazement.

Not a single car passed us. Not a person either. Between walls of snow the streets shone like a glacial tunnel. Aunt Jessie asked the ticket seller where she could call a taxi. Behind silver bars he shook his head.

"No taxis, lady, on account of the storm. You got to walk."

It was at this moment we discovered that nobody had remembered to make hotel reservations.

"I know a good hotel in Gramercy Park," said Aunt Jessie. "Let's go."

We walked briskly down the middle of the empty street. My mother and Aunt Jessie skillfully propelled Grandmother between them. The snowbanks on both sides of us seemed to exhale a ghastly breath that numbed my face and hands. We walked to the hotel without meeting another soul and found ourselves in a deserted lobby. Aunt Jessie left us to collapse into the overstuffed chairs and stepped up to the desk and rang for the clerk, who appeared at last, rubbing his eyes. After a brief, inaudible discussion, she returned to us, frowning.

"All the rooms are taken on account of the convention."

"What convention?" asked my mother, bewildered.

"The convention being held here," explained Aunt Jessie. "Of chefs," she added.

The desk clerk, seeing our distress, came forward.

"I can offer you one room, if you're really desperate."

We all felt better at once.

"A storeroom in the basement is empty now, and I could have cots brought in."

The storeroom had no windows, only chunks of glass in the ceiling, which formed part of the sidewalk overhead; sometimes the shadows of a lone passer-by's feet darkened them, clicking closer and closer, then farther and farther away. Two bellhops rolled in eight cots. There was no other furniture, save a large cardboard Santa Claus holding a bottle of Coca-Cola, leaning against one wall. Mother inquired about the bathroom, and the bellhops pointed into the vast darkness beyond our door.

"If you walk to the end of the boiler room, lady," said one, "you can use the janitor's toilet."

We pattered down the dark corridor in our nightgowns, through a place that fitted almost perfectly my primitive idea of hell. Men sat by roaring furnaces, stoking them and watching us sullenly. Waiting.

My mother closed the door and turned off the light and everyone climbed into bed.

We lay on our cots in the darkness, sweating and staring up at the bottoms of boots and galoshes. The disembodied voice of my Aunt Jessie described the excitement of New York at that hour as clearly as if she were seeing it with a third eye, a magic one, that the rest of us lacked. Now crowds were gathering in Times Square, now Guy Lombardo was playing "Auld Lang Syne." And here we were in New York City, where the new year touched land first, before it flowed out to the rest of America. In spite of the heat, I shivered.

"What would you most like to do in New York?" asked Aunt Jessie suddenly.

As nobody could see to whom she was speaking, nobody answered. Finally I said, "I want to see 'Let's Pretend.' "

The next morning we set out for CBS to watch the program my sister and my cousin and I had faithfully followed for so many years. I do not remember how far we walked, only that I lost all feeling in my hands and feet, and

I saw nothing of note except high hummocks of snow under which, my aunt assured me, lay secret Cadillacs and magnificent limousines.

I had never visited a radio station. Certainly I did not expect to see an empty stage and an empty auditorium. The music that opened the program every Saturday suggested an orchestra and the applause promised huge crowds, not these rows of silent seats. I looked around. Suddenly I realized that on this snowy morning our family was the entire audience of "Let's Pretend."

Now the actors were gathering around the two microphones standing at either end of the stage, and a man who called himself Uncle Ted was welcoming us to New York and warning us not to whistle as this would unsettle the microphones.

"But when I give you the signal," he said, "you can clap. Clap as hard as you can. Think of all those kids out there, listening to you. Clap like you were a thousand."

The story began. It was Hans Christian Andersen's story of the little mermaid who trades her beautiful voice for the chance to be human. To be human, says the mermaid's grandmother, means to be immortal. Only humans have souls.

I watched the actors with growing astonishment. The voices I knew so well did not belong to witches and princesses but to men and women. How I had been deceived into believing in a world more splendid and tragic than this one! Even New York City itself, so hidden from my sight by the snow, seemed an outrageous lie. Why, then, did I feel a rising excitement at being here?

A burst of music announced the end of the story. Now Uncle Ted was waving for us to clap. The mermaid had lost her prince but won her soul. From mermaid to angel. That story. I clapped for the story. I clapped for the lost city, hidden under its shroud of snow, and for my aunt, who made me believe in it anyhow. I clapped till my palms ached for the children all over America who heard the voices and saw the mermaid. I clapped for the actors on their bare stage. In a world of tables and chairs and very human beings, I clapped for the angel, for the supreme illusion that is art.

∽9∾

The Well-tempered Falsehood: The Art of Storytelling

_____ When I was a child, my older sister and I had a game that we played on the long summer afternoons when supper was still hours away and we had nothing to do. We sat in our swings, too hot to move, until one of us started the game, and then we would forget the heat, the small yard with its mosquitoes, the impending supper, everything.

The game was simple. It required two people: the teller and the listener. The teller's task was to describe a place as vividly as possible. The object of the game was to convince the listener she was there. The teller had to carry on the description until the listener said, "Stop. I'm there."

I do not remember all the places we visited in the course of this game, but I do remember the very last time we played it. I was the teller and the place I wished to evoke was paradise. I did not know then that the damned are generally livelier than the saved, and that even Dante and Milton had wrestled with the problem of making virtue entertaining. Emboldened by ignorance, however, I began.

First of all, I filled paradise with the rich furniture of our own church. I put in the brass angels that held the candles and the stained glass windows in which old men read the Gospel to lions, dragons, and assorted penitent beasts. For how could I make paradise pleasant unless I made it comfortable? And how could I make it comfortable unless I made it familiar?

So I put in the hum of the electric fan behind the pulpit and the smell of peppermint that the head usher gave off instead of sweat. I fear it was a rather tedious description, and if I were to describe paradise for you today, it would be something like spring in San Francisco. And hell would be some bone-melting heat wave in New York City.

But however conventional the line I handed my sister, it was a lot more concrete than any account of the kingdom of God I'd heard in Sunday school, where heaven was treated the way my parents treated sex. Yes, it exists. Now don't ask any more questions.

At the height of my telling, something unforeseen happened. My sister burst into tears.

"Stop!" she cried. "I'm there!"

I looked at her in astonishment. I knew she cried at weddings and funerals. But to cry at a place pieced together out of our common experience and our common language, a place that would vanish the minute I stopped talking! That passed beyond the bounds of the game altogether. I knew I could never equal that performance, and we never played the game again.

The joy of being the teller stayed with me, however,

and when people asked me, "What do you want to be when you grow up?" I answered, "I want to tell stories."

And the people to whom I said this always remarked, "Oh, you want to work on a newspaper, do you?"

I grew up thinking that if you wanted to tell stories, you had to go through the initiation rite of working on a newspaper, and that all writers had to do this before they could become proper storytellers. When I was ten, I asked my mother, "How do I get a job on a newspaper?"

For it seemed sensible to get past this hurdle as quickly as possible.

"You apply for the job," said my mother. "But, of course, nobody will hire you without experience."

"But how can I get experience if I need experience to get a job?"

"You could start your own newspaper," said my mother. "You could start it this summer."

In the summer we lived in a small town on the edge of a lake. On the opposite side of the lake stood a gravel pit, which employed nearly all the men in the town. The quality of life in this town did not encourage reading. There was no library and no bookshop. There was not even a Christian Science reading room.

At night people went fishing or fighting. Lying on my stomach at two in the morning, my face pressed to the bedroom window screen, I watched the man across the street drag his wife by the hair down the front steps of his house while her lover fled out the back window. I wondered how these people would like a neighborhood newspaper. I wondered if they would read it. I knew it would have to be free, as nobody in the whole town would be willing to buy it.

But there was an even bigger problem than finding readers. I hadn't the faintest idea how to gather news. Census takers were badly treated in these parts, and even the Jehovah's Witnesses had learned to leave us alone.

So I put the idea of a newspaper aside, until one night the lady next door dropped by for a visit. She was a large woman who made it her business to know everybody else's. She plunked herself down in our best chair to exchange gossip with my mother, who never had any but who knew how to listen to the great events of the day. What were these events? Ray Lomax was out casting for bass and hooked Mrs. Penny's baby through the ear lobe, John Snyder had been drunk five nights running, Tina O'Brien was pregnant by somebody else's husband, and so it went. These were the plain facts. Our neighbor's description of these facts would have done credit to the *New York Post*.

She paused long enough to smile at my sister and me. We were sitting at the dining-room table with our paper and crayons, and we smiled back.

"You like to draw?" she asked.

We nodded. She did not know that we had quit drawing the minute she opened her mouth and were transcribing every word she said. Here was news enough for ten newspapers! After she left, my mother censored what could be construed as libel, and my sister copied out the news in that anonymous schoolgirl hand she saved for thank-you notes and party invitations. We ran off our first edition on the wet face of a hectograph press, and we hung twenty-five copies of the *Stoney Lake News* in the living room to dry. The next day I went forth to deliver it.

We were an instant success. There is nothing people

enjoy reading about so much as themselves. To see yourself in print—it gives you a kind of status. You are worthy of notice to someone besides your mother.

When I look over those newspapers now, I see the real news was not the events themselves but the people who lived them and who narrated these events to me. I heard some wild stories and I wrote them as I heard them. And I have all those people to blame for my prejudice toward fiction that is to be heard as well as read. In my mind, writing a story for a reader cannot be separated from telling a story to a listener.

I still marvel at how easy it is to tell a story, as opposed to writing a story. Collecting the news in that small town, I met people who could tell stories. Stories that left you breathless with suspense. Stories that made you laugh till your stomach hurt. All my storytellers had one thing in common, however. They would have balked at writing their own words down. They would have found writing stories very nearly impossible. But telling stories was for them as simple as conversation. Many years after the *Stoney Lake News* went the way of all pulp, I was reading *Tristram Shandy* and I came across a statement that brought back my brief career as a journalist. "Writing," says Laurence Sterne, "when properly managed, is but a different name for conversation." And I remembered, ironically, all those men and women who told me stories and who read little and wrote nothing.

The very old and the very young are natural storytellers. When you are very old, you narrate your past and it sounds like fiction. And when you are very young, you invent a past and it sounds like fact. Either way, all it takes is a listener to get you going.

I still envy the ease with which my son, at the age of seven, could tell a story. He would begin with no idea and no rough draft and no plan. But at ten minutes of eight, with bedtime in view, he would start spinning his tale. If he made it very exciting, he could prolong bedtime a whole hour. The problems of dialogue and character and plot did not trouble him. He moved swiftly from one crazy episode to the next. And listening to my son, I remembered the original goal of the storyteller: to entertain.

Let me say right now that there are many ways of entertaining a reader. Kafka and Joyce and Borges and Pynchon show us just how complex and diverse are the entertainments we choose. But I am dealing here with simpler fare, with the process of storytelling in a less subjective form. I am going to start with the first book that kept me up all night because I couldn't put it down. That book is *Household Tales of the Brothers Grimm*.

I still go back to folk tales and fairy tales when I want to lose myself for a few hours and come back to myself refreshed. Always the same thing happens. I read perhaps two stories and resolve to read no more, for I have to do the laundry or scrub the kitchen floor. But I happen to glance at the opening sentence of a third story, and the pull is irresistible:

> One day an old man and his wife were sitting in front of their poor hut, resting from their work, when a magnificent carriage drawn by four black stallions came driving up and a richly dressed gentleman stepped out.[1]

And now I can't put the story down until I know who the stranger is and why he has come.

Or take another story, which opens not with an un-familiar guest but with a familiar grief:

It is a long time ago now, as much as two thousand years maybe, that there was a rich man and he had a wife and she was beautiful and good, and they loved each other very much but they had no children even though they wanted some so much, the wife prayed and prayed for one both day and night, and still they did not and they did not get one.[2]

And with that sentence I am hooked. I know the story will tell me how she did get one. Fairy tales generally start at the point when somebody's fortunes change, for better or worse. And I know that the woman in this story will not get her child the way most of humanity gets children. Fairy tales deal with exceptional events rather than ordinary ones. And as I read on, I am not disappointed:

In front of their house was a yard and in the yard stood a juniper tree. Once, in wintertime, the woman stood under the tree and peeled herself an apple, and as she was peeling the apple she cut her finger and the blood fell onto the snow. "Ah," said the woman and sighed a deep sigh, and she looked at the blood before her and her heart ached. "If I only had a child as red as blood and as white as snow." And as she said it, it made her feel very happy, as if it was really going to happen. And so she went into the house, and a month went by, the snow was gone; and two months, and everything was green; and three months, and the flowers came up out of the ground; and four months, and all the trees in the woods sprouted and the green branches grew dense and tangled with one another and the little birds sang so that the woods echoed, and the blossoms fell from the trees; and so five months were gone, and she stood under the juniper tree and it smelled so sweet her heart leaped and she fell on her knees and was beside herself with happiness; and six months had gone by, the fruit grew round and heavy and she was very still, and seven months, and she snatched the juniper berries and ate them so greedily she became sad and ill; and so the eighth month went by, and she called her husband and cried and said, "When I die, bury me under the juniper." And she was comforted and felt happy, but when the nine months were gone, she had a child as white as snow and as red as blood and when she saw it she was so happy that she died.

And so her husband buried her under the juniper tree and began to cry and cried very bitterly; and then for a time he cried more gently and when he had cried some more he stopped crying and more time passed and he took himself another wife.[3]

Now consider for a moment what a miracle of economy you have just read. In two paragraphs a year passes but is not glossed over carelessly, one character dies, another is born, and a third remarries, and the storyteller shows all this so simply yet so concretely that I think nobody could wish for more details. There is something about the process of telling a story that forces you to come right to the point. When you are writing a story, how often does the simple action seem insufficient? And how often do you feel you must analyze or explain it? But when you are telling a story, your first impulse is to create your characters through what they do. You, the author, become the invisible medium through which they live.

I am, to be sure, dealing here with a kind of fiction that emphasizes a linear plot. I know there are many kinds of storytellers and many writers who write as if they were talking to us. I have already mentioned Laurence Sterne. I could also have mentioned Mark Twain.

But the great books of these men were written, first of all, to be read, not just heard, and although they can be read aloud magnificently, a clear understanding of their work comes only when you have the books in your hand and can reread some chapters and compare others, and follow themes and characters over many pages. These are the pleasures of long fiction. When I speak of storytelling here, I am talking about the story as it is told to a listener.

I think it is good for writers to have that experience of telling a story. In my writing classes at Vassar, I sometimes try an exercise designed to give students that experience. We make up a story together. It's rather like making a crazy quilt. You tell your episode, and when your imagination fails, you pass it on to your neighbor, who picks up where you left off. I start by giving my students a list of ten or fifteen characters, which they may use if they are desperate or which they may abandon if they wish to make up their own. The list might go something like this: man, daughter, son, grandfather, magician, devil, car salesman, banker, angel, thief. I start the story by introducing a character whose strong passion for someone or something is likely to get him into difficulty. I say, "Once upon a time there was a woman who loved cars more than anything else in the world. And one day she—" Then I pinpoint a student with my nearsighted stare and say, "Miss Smith, you take it from there."

And though Miss Smith looks back at me as if she has just seen the last Judgment, she generally finds she *can* take it from there. Since the story is a communal affair, she isn't afraid of failure, which I think is often the underlying cause when writers can't write. And since the characters are given to her, she doesn't have that feeling so many of us have when facing a blank page: in the beginning was the void, and darkness was upon the face of the page.

Most important, she has a main character whose ruling passion—in this case, a passion for cars—will create the action of the story. And thereby hangs the tale. I have found the experience of telling a story in this way gives us the rare chance to be objective narrators. For once in our lives we are not talking about ourselves.

Let me go back to the woman who loved cars and remind you that characters with an obsession or a passion for something they don't have are common enough in folk tales. "The Juniper Tree," from which I quoted earlier, opens with a woman's overpowering desire to have a child. I could have picked dozens of other examples.

And we all know writers far more sophisticated than the tellers of folk tales who choose to write of such characters. Take, for example, Chekhov's story, "The Man in a Shell," which deals with a character who is obsessed with isolating himself from the world around him. Chekhov describes him as follows:

> There are not a few people in the world, temperamentally unsociable, who try to withdraw into a shell like a hermit crab or a snail. . . . Why, not to go far

afield, there was Belikov, a colleague of mine, a teacher of Greek, who died in our town about two months ago. You have heard of him, no doubt. The curious thing about him was that he wore rubbers, and a warm coat with an interlining, and carried an umbrella even in the finest weather. And he kept his umbrella in its cover and his watch in a gray chamois case, and when he took out his penknife to sharpen his pencil, his penknife too was in a little case; and his face seemed to be in a case too, because it was always hidden in his turned-up collar. He wore dark spectacles and a sweater, stuffed his ears with cotton-wool, and when he got into a cab always told the driver to put up the hood. In short, the man showed a constant and irrepressible inclination to keep a covering about himself . . . which would isolate him and protect him from outside influences. Actuality irritated him, frightened him, kept him in a state of continual agitation, and perhaps to justify his timidity, his aversion for the present, he would always laud the past and things that had never existed, and the dead languages that he taught were in effect for him the same rubbers and umbrella in which he sought concealment from real life.[4]

Now why choose such a character for the subject of a story? Because the story begins at the point when such a character meets someone or something that brings him out of his shell. When the man's friends conspire to marry him off, what do you think he does? I will not spoil your pleasure in reading the story by giving away the ending.

I once tried to write a story about a man ruled by a passion for telling lies. I called it "The Tailor Who Told the

Truth," because in the last scene, he was cured of his passion for lying, and why hold a penitent man's past failings against him forever? Descriptions of stories are always awkward, so let me quote the opening paragraph:

> In Germantown, New York, on Cherry Street, there lived a tailor named Morgon Axel who, out of long habit, could not tell the truth. As a child he told small lies to put a bright surface on a drab life; as a young man he told bigger lies to get what he wanted. He got what he wanted and went on lying until now when he talked about himself, he did not know the truth from what he wanted the truth to be. The stories he told were often more plausible to him than his own life.

I found the process of writing this story very different from writing about my own experience or my immediate observation of someone else's. In the first place, the tailor was born with a peculiar autonomy, a sort of arrogance, as if I hadn't created him at all. He had already selected the details about himself he wished me to know, and I found myself describing places and situations quite foreign to me. The first half of the story is set in Germany before World War I, up to World War II. I have not visited Germany for at least twenty-five years, and my impressions of Germany between these wars come primarily from the old photograph albums kept by my parents, who lived there briefly during the twenties.

My ignorance did not deter the tailor, however. One night I dreamed that the tailor and I, his creator, had an awful row about the direction I wanted the story to go. I told him the plot, the action as I saw it. He told me that I had my story all wrong, it hadn't happened that way at all, and why did I insist on changing the truth?

Well, he won and I wrote the story his way. Let me remind you that "The Tailor Who Told the Truth" is a written story; that is, I did not tell it out loud to a listener and write it down afterward. Though for me there is a close connection between telling and writing, they are, in the end, two different processes. But I believe that the more you tell stories, and the more you listen to stories, the more it will affect the way you write stories.

How?

First, you find yourself creating characters who are not just individuals but also types. I do not mean stereotypes, those unrealized abstractions on which so many stories have foundered. I mean types of people. The misanthrope. The miser. The martyr. The woman who wants a child. The man who lives in a shell. A character who is both an individual and a type is larger than life. Let us call him an archetype; he is some facet of ourselves that we have in common with the rest of humanity.

Second, you find you are not dealing with individual situations but with the forces that created them. I call these forces good and evil, though I would not name them as such in a story. Stories that develop archetypal situations have the truth and the authority of proverbs, no matter how fantastic the particular events they describe.

Third, you find yourself using fewer adjectives and more verbs, because verbs make the story move. You don't develop your character by describing the kind of man he is—a bad man, a good man, an indifferent man; you develop him by showing what he does. It's up to the reader to pass judgment.

Fourth, you the writer, become less important than the story you have to tell. And thank heaven for that. Which of us doesn't enjoy telling tall tales where we can lie outrageously without having to justify ourselves?

So far, so good. But we are readers and writers, not storytellers sitting around a fire, spinning tales out of a common heritage. I suppose it's the desire to bring the two together that leads some writers to put a story into the mouth of a narrator, at one remove from the writer himself. In "The Man in the Shell," from which I quoted earlier, Chekhov uses a narrator, so that we have a story within a story.

Let me suggest two reasons for using a narrator to tell your story. First, you may want a limited point of view rather than an omniscient point of view. Second, you may want the economy that a story has when it is told rather than written. Isaac Bashevis Singer once explained to an interviewer why he so often puts his story into the mouth of an old village woman instead of narrating it himself. He says:

> Why I like narrators? There is a good reason for that: because when I write a story without a narrator I have to describe things, while if the narrator is a woman she can tell you many things almost in one sentence. Because in life when you sit down to tell a story you don't act like a writer. You don't describe too much. You jump, you digress and this gives to the story speed and drama . . . it comes out especially good when you let an old woman tell a story. In a moment she's here, and a moment she's there. And because of this you feel almost that a human being is talking to you, and you

don't need the kind of description which you expect when the writer himself is telling the story.[5]

To illustrate Singer's point, I want to quote from the opening paragraph of one of his stories. It is called "Passions."

"When a man persists he can do things which one might think can never be done," Zalman the glazier said. "In our village, Radoszyce, there was a simple man, a village peddler, Lieb Belkes. He used to go from village to village, selling the peasant women kerchiefs, glass beads, perfume, all kinds of gilded jewelry. And he would buy from them a measure of buckwheat, a wreath of garlic, a pot of honey, a sack of flax. He never went farther than the hamlet of Byszcz, five miles from Radoszyce. He got the merchandise from a Lublin salesman, and the same man bought his wares from him. This Lieb Belkes was a common man but pious. On the Sabbath he read his wife's Yiddish Bible. He loved most to read about the land of Israel. Sometimes he would stop the cheder boys and ask, 'Which is deeper—the Jordan or the Red Sea?' 'Do apples grow in the Holy Land?' 'What language is spoken by the natives there?' The boys used to laugh at him. He looked like someone from the Holy Land himself— black eyes, a pitch-black beard, and his face was also swarthy."[6]

Singer's story is a long way from "The Juniper Tree," but a number of things in that paragraph will show you that their roots grow in the same place, the archetypal obsessions of man. The opening sentence directs me to the point of the story, which, like a fable, demonstrates a simple proverb: the man who persists can do the impossible. The man who wants to go to the Holy Land will find a way to get there.

Singer recognizes that a man's actions are often inseparable from the objects that make up the fabric of his life. He also knows that we cannot see or touch an abstraction. And so he gives us garlic and perfume to smell, and honey and buckwheat to taste, and jewelry and kerchiefs to please the eye, and speech to please the ear. The speech is what I call essential speech in a story; that is, I could recognize this character by his speech later on, even if Singer chose not to identify him. The opposite of essential speech is small talk, which does not directly express a man or woman's deepest needs, but which is really a way of avoiding them.

Now suppose you have resolved to try writing as if you were telling a story. You are ready to simplify your style and to emphasize action and plot more than you may ever wish to do again. But there is one more problem you will have to confront, and I have saved it for the last because it is the most unsettling and, at the same time, the most exhilarating. When you tell a story, you find that without knowing how or why, you cross over easily from the natural to the supernatural as if you felt absolutely no difference between them.

By supernatural, let me hasten to add, I do not mean ghosts, although ghosts of one kind or another may blow through your story and make themselves at home there. I mean the visible, tangible world released from the laws that, in ordinary experience, separate time from place. You know from your own experience that the supernatural is no farther away than your own dreams at night. I do not think there has ever been or ever will be a writer who does not draw on the healing chaos of dreams for the material of stories. Here is a world of wild and fearful happenings, which mercifully vanish when we open our eyes. But occasionally these happenings shine through our daytime lives and illuminate them.

When I am writing stories, I forget that many people do not read fiction, because they believe a book that is neither truthful nor instructive is a waste of time. And fiction, they believe, is not truthful but only made up. It is not instructive but only entertaining. Though my father read stories as a child, when he became a man he put away childish things. He died at the age of ninety-two, he was nearly sixty when I was born, and I believe he read his last piece of fiction in freshman English when he was eighteen. All the years of my growing up, he read nothing of mine except an occasional poem I wrote for his birthday when I didn't have enough money to buy him my standard present of black socks.

Then one day, in his ninetieth year, he picked up a book of my stories and he started to read it. To his astonishment, he found himself in that book, a character in my stories, and like all characters, a fabricated being and yet a real one. In that book I was still trying to describe paradise, but now it was not a place. It was an experience occurring in time but not bound by it.

My father sat in his chair and read. He read one page for an hour. He never said a word to me, he never made a sound, and though he never cried in my presence when I was a child, now the tears were running down his face. He never said, "Stop, I'm there," the way my sister did when we played our game so many years before, but it was the same game nonetheless, and we are all players. It requires two people, the teller and the listener. The teller tells the story he has made out of bits he has seen and pieces he has heard. His telling brings these fragments together, and in that healing synthesis, he gives the wasted hours of our lives an order they don't have and a radiance that only God and the artist can perceive. We get up, we go to work, we come home dead tired, and sometimes we wonder what we are doing on this planet. And we know that in the great schemelessness of things, our own importance is a lie. Is the object of the game to tell that lie? Yes, to tell the lie. But in the telling, to make it true.

❧ 10 ❧

The Spinning Room:
Symbols and
Storytellers

————————————— When a friend asked me recently who
my ancestors were, I told her they were farmers, clock-
makers, aristocrats, and scoundrels. I did not tell the truth.
My ancestors were squirrels. How else could the members
of my family have acquired such a passion for hiding
things? Once my mother forgot where she'd hidden the family silver, as squirrels forget where they have buried their
acorns. The loss of a dozen place settings was cause for
inconvenience but not for alarm.

"They're not lost," she said. "They're in the house."

The place settings came to light when the piano tuner
was summoned to find out why our piano rasped like a snare
drum.

"You can't imagine the number of people I know
who hide their silver in the piano," the tuner told her.
"You've got to do better than that."

My father hid nothing except his private tube of toothpaste, which he kept under the handkerchiefs in his bureau drawer. After brushing his teeth, he always rolled up the tube, neat as a window shade, for he could not bear to use the tube that the rest of us had squeezed and punched out of shape. But except for his toothpaste, it seemed he had nothing worth hiding. Or so I believed until some years after he died, when I was reading through the pocket diaries he kept for sixty years. Here are some representative entries:

April 2: Today it rained half an inch.
April 6: Today I walked downtown and back.
April 10: Temperature today 65°.

He was, I knew, a man of few words. No man ever had fewer words to say about his own wedding day than my father, who on that occasion wrote in his diary, "Today I married Marge Sheppard."

To my mother he explained that he never put down anything personal. Years later I realized that in his brevity he too was a hider. There are two ways of hiding something in writing. You leave it out, or you disguise it. What is left out is lost. What is disguised is saved, but only for those who can see through the disguise. Nevertheless, disguises themselves can be very attractive. Parables, allegories, satires, and a good many fairy tales are disguises, for they contain ideas more complicated than the surface story that hides them.

When you hide something, you often return to find more than you hid. I learned this not from literature but from my favorite, all-purpose hiding place in the house where I grew up, my parents' closet. On the upper shelves over the tops of the hangers I once found five purses, three heating pads, a roll of toilet paper, a foot massager, a framed picture of Jesus calling Lazarus from the tomb, five vacuum cleaner bags, a small Maypole, a humidifier, a box of cough drops, assorted eyeglasses, several cameras that did not work but were too attractive to throw away, and a dozen Mason jars.

But the only things my mother consciously hid in the closet were Christmas presents. My sister and I found them one year, to our great dismay. The next year I hid my presents there, and my sister, without anyone else's knowledge, hid hers there as well. So when my mother went to the closet to fetch the presents she'd hidden for us, she found they had multiplied, in a sort of reversal of the parable of the talents. That is often the way with hiding places. What you hide suffers a sea change. What you find is not exactly what you hid.

I felt very much as my mother must have felt when I finished my last book for children, *The Island of the Grass King*. It tells of a child who travels to an enchanted island and rescues a king whose kingdom is an earthly paradise, the Garden of Eden before the Fall. Because an imaginary island must be real before you can write about it, I took for my model the most enchanted island I knew: the one on which Shakespeare set *The Tempest*. Here magic and nature are inseparable—a natural abode of witches and magicians.

So I read Shakespeare and the sources he might have used to invent his island before I tried to invent mine. I wondered if my editor would ask me, Why hide literary allusions in a story for children, who probably won't recognize them? She did not ask. But if she had, I would have answered that reading Shakespeare helped me to shape my own story and that the snatches of Shakespeare's songs and speeches are part of the story I want to tell. And although the child reading my book won't recognize them, I hope they will be obvious to a well-read adult reader. Children's books should be big enough for children to grow into. When I grew up, I did not put my favorite children's books away with other childish things. I enjoyed them on a different level. But in spite of the allusions I hid in my book, my purpose in writing was to entertain. I was writing an adventure story, not an allegory. Or so I thought when I sent it off to my editor.

She wrote back an enthusiastic letter, which included the various interpretations of the book given by her staff. One reader claimed that the trip to the island was a hallucination. The Grass King, of course, was marijuana. Another saw it as an allegory about the political conditions in Cuba. Nobody noticed Shakespeare. I was amazed. How did Cuba and marijuana get into my book? Because someone had found them, were they really there? How much came from craft, how much from inspiration, and how much from pure accident? And how consciously can a writer use symbols without becoming self-conscious and pedantic?

The first books that made me ask these questions were *Alice's Adventures in Wonderland* and *Through the Looking Glass*. Lewis Carroll is a hider after my own heart. The house where he grew up had a loose floorboard in the nursery, under which later occupants found the treasures he hid there: a child's white glove, a thimble, a left shoe, a fragment of a poem scrawled on a piece of wood. Glove, thimble, left shoe, poems—all these things turn up years later in the Alice books, where the author himself hides behind a pseudonym. Behind Lewis Carroll, storyteller, is the Reverend Charles L. Dodgson, logician and Oxford don.

Fortunately for us, Dodgson tells us something about how his books came to be written. It is well known that *Alice's Adventures in Wonderland* began as a story told during a boating expedition to amuse the three daughters of the dean of Christ Church. "In a desperate attempt to strike out some new line of fairy lore," says Dodgson, "I . . . sent my heroine straight down a rabbithole, to begin with, without the least idea what was to happen afterwards."[1] His ideas for stories, he claimed, would come of themselves like unlooked-for gifts. When a friend of Dodgson's who was part of the expedition asked if this was an extemporaneous romance, Dodgson replied, "Yes, I'm inventing as we go along."[2]

Alice Liddell, one of the three little girls, asked him to write the story down for her, and that very evening he returned to his rooms and began to record the adventures as well as he could remember them. Although the story was quickly told, it was not quickly written. Five months after the boating expedition that prompted the story, Dodgson noted in his diary, "Began writing the fairy-tale for Alice, which I told them July 4th going to Godstow—I hope to finish it by Christmas." This version was called *Alice's Adventures Underground,* and he did not finish it until February. "In writing it out," he said, "I added many fresh ideas, which seemed to grow of themselves upon the original stock; and many more added themselves when, years afterwards, I wrote it all over again for publication. . . . Sometimes an idea comes at night, when I have had to get up and strike a light to note it down . . . but whenever or however it comes, *it comes of itself* . . . 'Alice' and the 'Looking Glass' are made up almost wholly of bits and scraps, single ideas which came of themselves."[3] He did not know when he wrote out the fairy tale for Alice that it would grow from eighteen thousand words to thirty-five thousand words before it was published. Much was added to the final version: the Mad Tea Party, parodies of the popular songs Dodgson had heard Alice and her sisters sing, parodies of the lessons their governess had inflicted on them. When he revised the original version, he cut out most of the private jokes, leaving only those allusions that served the artistic ends of a book intended to please not merely three little girls but readers of all ages.

Through the Looking Glass was also a long time in the making. "It will probably be some time before I again indulge in paper and print," Dodgson wrote to his publishers. "I have, however, a floating idea of writing a sort of sequel to 'Alice.' "[4] The idea floated for three years. When Dodgson knew that Tenniel would be available to illustrate the new book, he set out to write it, drawing on the stories he had told the three little girls when he was teaching them chess. The problems of writing a text to be illustrated are unknown to most writers of adult fiction. Chapter Thirteen of *Through the Looking Glass* introduced the character of a wasp in a wig, which Tenniel declared he could not draw. "A wasp in a wig," he informed Dodgson, "is altogether beyond the appliances of art."[5] The chapter was omitted from the book.

Some critics have read the Alice books as satire; others have called them allegories. The truth is, Dodgson set out to write neither. He did, however, write stories in which he hid ideas, people, and events familiar to him, though he did not do so in a systematic way. He also took his time writing down his stories, and time seems to have a great deal to do with how successfully a writer changes the parochial into the universal.

I learned the hard way how awful a story can be if you have not waited until it is ready to be written. Let me go back to my book, *The Island of the Grass King*. Four years ago I tried to write that book. It was meant to be a sequel to a collection of stories, *Sailing to Cythera*, about the adventures of a boy named Anatole. In *The Island of the Grass King* one of the characters is a pirate. To help me create that character, I read an enormous number of books on pirates. One of the scenes takes place in the sky. To help me describe the sky, I read a vast number of books on astronomy.

I read too much. I had the trappings of characters but not the characters themselves. I had the details of a setting but not the story to give it significance. Innocent of these weaknesses, I wrote the first fifty pages and sent them to my editor. She was appalled but polite. There are some things that cannot be conveyed over the telephone or in a letter. She invited me to meet her in her office in New York. I agreed. This meant finding a babysitter for the day and riding for two hours on a train that always broke down both coming and going. When my editor heard the obstacles I had overcome to keep our appointment, she could scarcely bring herself to deliver her message. The writing was abysmal. All the reports of the readers agreed. How, asked one, could anyone capable of writing *Sailing to Cythera* have written so badly?

The next morning I took up a copy of *Sailing to Cythera* and asked myself, What did I do so effortlessly in this book that I failed to do in the second? Effortlessly— that was the secret. I had not written *Sailing to Cythera* out of months of research. I had written out of the memories of my own childhood. When I was a child, I greatly admired the wallpaper in a restaurant to which I was sometimes taken as a reward for memorizing a difficult piano piece. It showed shepherds and shepherdesses dancing under willow trees, courting under rose arbors, and piping to one another across flocks of immaculate white sheep. Whenever I saw that idyllic country, I wanted to walk on that grass and hear those birds, rare as nightingales and twice as beautiful. Perhaps all fairy tales are really ways of making impossible wishes come true. As I could not go into the wallpaper myself, I sent my character into it, where he learned a little about magic and a lot about love.

Years after the restaurant had been converted into a pizza parlor, I was a student at the University of Michigan; I was dozing in an art history lecture when there flashed across the screen the very country that the wallpaper had imitated so badly. The painting was *The Embarkation for Cythera* by the eighteenth-century French painter Antoine Watteau. It showed a party of aristocrats preparing to set sail for the island of Cythera, named for the goddess of love. The art history instructor called these people pilgrims, and he drew our attention to the autumnal light, the sunny distances, and a great many other things that I have now forgotten. How long ago I first saw that painting, and how little I thought of it afterward! But when I wanted to describe what things looked like on the other side of the wallpaper, the painting came back to me.

Remembering this, I looked again at my disastrous fifty pages. They had come into the world trailing clouds of research; they were born of other people's books, not my own experience. So I put *The Island of the Grass King* away and wrote instead a book about a girl who plays baseball, and to the best of my knowledge there isn't a symbol in it. Not a trace of satire, not a smidgen of allegory. I forgot about the book I'd wanted to write and couldn't.

But the wonderful thing about failures in writing is, although you forget them, they do not forget you. Left alone, they assume their proper shape. Like children who survive all their parents' plans for them, they grow up in their own way. They return, not when you call them, but when some trivial episode wakes them.

The story I had wanted to write in *The Island of the Grass King* returned two years later when I was polishing my mother's silver, those forks and teapots so often lost in the corners of our house. I was polishing a coffeepot whose handle was a griffin with a tail that twined around the spout and somewhere along the way burst into leaves. Half the pot was bright from my diligence. The other half was dark, and I could not make out the design at all. It was as if one side were awake and the other side asleep, and so it is with us, I thought; we spend half our lives doing things and the other half dreaming about them. Outside the rain began to fall, though the sun was shining, and my mother said, "Rain and sun together! The devil is beating his wife."

And I remembered, suddenly, the wise woman of my childhood whom I believed caused both weather and seasons: Mother Holle. I first met her in one of Grimm's fairy tales, and I did not know that her name means hell in German. I only knew that she lived under the earth and that she sometimes hired mortal girls to help her with her house-work. Their chief duty was to shake out her featherbeds, for this shaking of feathers below caused snow to fall on the surface of the earth. From this memory sprang the three wise women who run the world in *The Island of the Grass King*. The first is the Maker; she makes all the creatures, and as the old ones wear out, she makes new ones. The second is the Mender; she keeps everything in repair, and she heals the torn and broken. The third is the Breaker, who destroys whatever the Mender cannot save.

So out of that odd recollection grew the finished version of my book. My reading on pirates and astronomy was there, but it had got so mixed up with my own memories that what came forth was quite different from either. With children's books, as with adult books, writing is a matter of words and silence, of pounding the material into submission and letting go of it, of trying to finish so many pages a day while telling yourself that you have all the time in the world. It's important to keep in mind the story you want to write. But it is even more important to forget it. Kafka understood this when he told a friend why an artist's material "must be worked on by the spirit."[6] The writer not only gathers experience, he masters what is experienced.

I believe that for most writers there are three kinds of stories. The first is the story that you choose to write and that you believe you understand. The second is the story that chooses you, and where it comes from you don't know, for the material seems to have been worked on out of your sight and hearing. The third is the story that starts out as the first kind and ends up as the second. What you know is changed into more than you know. When the author of *Alice's Adventures in Wonderland* was asked to explain a poem he had written, he excused himself with the remark, "Words mean more than we mean to express when we use them; so a whole book ought to mean a great deal more than the writer meant."[7]

An example of this peculiar transformation is Hans Christian Andersen's story, "The Nightingale," about a little wild bird who saves the life of the emperor of China. When the emperor falls ill, she sings so beautifully that even Death is enchanted and persuaded to give up his victim for a song. But until that moment of triumph, the emperor prefers the music of an artificial nightingale because it is obedient and predictable. The story was inspired by real people. Jenny Lind, the opera singer who became known in this country as "The Swedish Nightingale," is the singer taught by nature. The artificial nightingale is the singer taught by tradition. For Andersen, this meant the Italian opera company that lived at the Danish court. Although real people stand behind this story, it is not an allegory, for the message it carries is independent of them. C. S. Lewis's distinction between myth and allegory describes what the greatest writers of fantasy have always done. "Into an allegory a man can only put what he already knows; into a myth he puts what he does not yet know and would not come to know in any other way."[8]

How can a writer set out to write what he does not yet know? For many writers such stories are triggered by accidents. If Alice Liddell had not asked for a story, would Dodgson have written *Alice's Adventures in Wonderland*? A great many books for children started out as stories told to children when the writer wasn't particularly worried about structure, characters, plot, or niceties of style. I believe that being asked for a story can bring familiar material together in unfamiliar ways, whether the one asking is a child or an editor.

In the case of one of my favorite books, *The Little Prince* by Antoine de Saint-Exupéry, the one asking for a story was an adult. While Saint-Exupéry was having lunch with his publisher in a New York restaurant, he began doodling on the tablecloth. His publisher asked him what he was drawing.

"Oh, nothing much," answered Saint-Exupéry. "Just a little fellow I carry around in my heart."

"Now look, this little fellow—what would you think of making up a story about him . . . for a children's book."

So Saint-Exupéry agreed to try it. The character of the little fellow had had plenty of time to get worked on by the spirit. Saint-Exupéry had first drawn him when he was a little fellow himself and had gone on drawing him on menus, letters, and scraps of paper, in all sorts of disguises. Although Saint-Exupéry had not written books for children, he loved those that hid ideas more serious than the plots that concealed them. In one of his notebooks he writes, "Reread children's books, entirely forgetting the naive part which has no effect, but noting all along the prayers and concepts carried by this imagery."[9] Fairy tales have taught nearly all the great writers of fantasy how to work with symbols.

It's no surprise that many writers of stories for children heard fairy stories long before they heard the word *symbol.* So did many of us, and so it will always be, as long as there are grown-ups to tell stories and children to ask for them. Of all the writers for children whose imaginations were fed on fairy tales, Hans Christian Andersen was surely one of the most fortunate. The place where he heard fairy tales has long since vanished from our world, yet for centuries it was one of the great storehouses of folk literature. This was the spinning room, where women sat spinning at their wheels and working together during the long winter. To make the time pass more pleasantly, they told each other stories. The brothers Grimm assure us that many of the stories brought together in their *Household Tales* were perfected in the spinning room before being set down for our entertainment.

The spinning room Andersen visited was attached to a hospital in Odense, where his grandmother worked as a grounds keeper. The spinners were the local paupers. They listened to the tales that the boy Andersen composed for them and gave him their stories in return. "And thus," says Andersen, "a world as rich as that of the Thousand and One Nights was revealed to me."[10]

I like to imagine that I have found my way to that room where stories as well as wool are spun. By the light of a candle an old woman is spinning, but it isn't wool she winds on her wheel. She is spinning straw into gold, so I know that this is the lady whom Andersen called his muse, his wise woman, the bringer of fairy tales. Her name is Anonymous. Her wheel hums, her shadow looms large on the wall. I like to imagine that our conversation goes something like this:

ANON: So you want to write a story that means something. A story with symbols in it. In this place we learn by doing. Tell me a story.

ME: Give me some ideas for a story, please.

ANON: Story first, ideas later. Set off on your story as if you were taking a journey. "There was once upon a time a soldier who for many years had served the King faithfully, but when the war came to an end he could serve no longer because of the many wounds which he had received. The King said to him: 'You may return to your home, I need you no longer, and you will not receive any more money, for he only receives wages who renders me service for them."[11] Now see how far I've taken you in two. sentences?

ME: You haven't told me where the war happened or who the king was.

ANON: No, and I'm not going to, either. It's true that my stories are full of bears and wolves, water and wine, sun and moon, sea and stars—all palpable things of this world. But my stories are not of this world. I show life from the inside, as dreams do, and for that reason I leave out a great many details. Now, tell me a story.

ME: There was once upon a time——

ANON: Wait a minute. Why imitate me? I don't make up stories, I only pass them on. I gave you the soldier. Now you give him a personality. But don't muddle the story with details of what he had for supper or who his parents were. Just let me see him and hear him. Do you remember a fairy tale called "The Tinder Box"? My old friend Hans Andersen wrote it. He didn't like the way I told the story. Too bare, he said. So he started his story this way:

Left, right! Left, right! . . . Down the country-road came a soldier marching. Left, right! Left, right! . . . He had his knapsack on his back and a sword at his side, for he had been at the war, and now he was on his way home. But then he met an old witch on the road. Oh! she was ugly—her lower lip hung right down on her chest. "Good evening, soldier," she said, "What a nice sword you've got, and what a big knapsack! You're a proper soldier! Now I'll show you how to get as much money as you want!" "Thank you very much, old dame!" said the soldier.[12]

ME: That old witch moves pretty fast. They haven't even been introduced yet.

ANON: You think that's fast? Listen to the scene where he chops her head off:

So he cut off her head . . . . . . There she lay! But the soldier tied up all his money in her apron and made a bundle of it, to go on his back. He put the tinder-box in his pocket and went straight on into the town.[13]

I told that part to a gentleman who visited me some years ago—now what was his name? I believe he called himself "K."

ME: Not Franz Kafka?

ANON: That was the man. When I told him that part, he shook his head gravely. "There are no bloodless fairy stories," he sighed. "Every fairy story comes from the depths of blood and fear."[14] He was right. But he failed to notice one thing. Though the witch loses her head, not a drop of blood is spilled. But you look—disappointed. Don't you like the story?

ME: It's very entertaining. But I was hoping for a story with a deeper meaning.

ANON: All fairy tales have deeper meanings. Tell me, what happens in fairy stories? Witches turn people into beasts. Love turns them human again. And that should remind you, my dear, that for all our human accomplishments, we too can be turned into beasts. We can kill each other like the beasts of the field, but we can save each other as well. When you read a fairy tale, isn't it remarkable how much you recognize? Fairy stories are like rituals. What is a ritual but a simple act that stands for a more complicated one? Sit down. Let *me* tell *you* a story.[15] Once upon a time there lived a king who had three daughters. Now it happened that he had to go out to battle, so he called his daughters and said to them, "My dear children, I am obliged to go to the wars. During my absence be good girls and look after everything in the house. You may walk in the garden and you may go into all the rooms in the palace, except the room at the back in the right-hand corner." Now, what's going to happen?

ME: His daughters will go into that room.

ANON: Oh, you've heard this story?

ME: No. But it sounds familiar.

ANON: It's the story of the Garden of Eden, it's the loss of paradise without God and the serpent. And thereby hangs the tale. Well, the girls got bored and one day they did indeed enter the room and found nothing it it but a large table on which lay an open book. The first girl stepped up to the book and read, "The eldest daughter of this king will marry a prince from the east." The second daughter stepped forward and read, "The second daughter of this king will marry a prince from the west." But the youngest daughter did not want to go near the book. Why not?

ME: Because the youngest is always obedient and virtuous?

ANON: Right again. But why is the youngest always obedient and virtuous? Because in the world of magic, innocence is a virtue. A worldly man does not share his last crust of bread with a beggar. He has bills to pay, he has promises to keep. But the innocent—and it is easier to believe that the hero is innocent if he is young—takes no thought of the morrow. He lives in the present tense, and so he befriends the beggar who turns out to be——

ME: A helpful wizard in disguise?

ANON: Right again. Kindness in the fairy stories is properly rewarded. Now back to the princess. We left her quailing before the book that had predicted such good fortunes for her sisters. They dragged her up to the book and she read, "The youngest daughter of this king will be married to a pig from the north." Her sisters tried to comfort her. "When did it ever happen," they said, "that a king's daughter married a pig?"

ME: It happens all the time in fairy tales.

ANON: So she marries the pig and settles down and lives unhappily ever after?

ME: No. The pig is really a prince in disguise.

ANON: Since you already know this story, I don't suppose you want to hear any more.

ME: I don't know the story. I only know the rituals in the story. Or should I call them symbols?

ANON: Call them whatever you like. You are not listening to my story because it has symbols. You are listening because you care about the world I've invented and the characters who people it. And if I bring on a six-foot pig with a wedding on his mind, it's not to make your blood run cold, it's to make the youngest daughter wiser for having to face him. And if I add a witch who offers to break the spell for her, it's not to make all the girl's wishes come true but to help her choose between good and evil. The greatest writers for children know that fairy tales are not only for children. One evening Hans Andersen was leaving the theater after a play, and he overheard someone say that the play ought not to be taken seriously as it was only a fairy tale. "I was indignant," exclaimed Andersen. "In the whole realm of poetry no domain is so boundless as that of the fairy tale. It reaches from the blood-drenched graves of antiquity to the pious legends of a child's picture-book."[16] Isn't it odd that so simple a story can carry our deepest fears and desires in so small a space?

So our conversation ends. I think of the story of the princess and her pig. None of the ideas in it are new to me. Is that why I like stories that hide ideas, so that I can find them again, like a ring lost in the house, all the more precious when I find it because I had forgotten it? When I was a child, my sister used to blindfold me and lead me about our house, letting me guess through which rooms we passed before she took off the blindfold. In that brief moment of surprise when I saw where I was, everything looked strange to me. Is it for the pleasure of discovering what we already know that we hide familiar things in fantastic stories where straw turns into gold, words into spells, and ourselves into heroes?

The Game and the Garden: The Lively Art of Nonsense

———————— I once had an aunt whom everyone admired as a fountain of good sense, except in matters of travel. She bought tickets to well-known places—Paris, Bermuda, Berlin—but she seemed never to arrive in them, for on her postcards she always wrote of places that could never be found on any map. Portapooka. Pannyfanny Islands. And what she did in these places was a perfect mystery:

> Arrived in Portapooka last night and had a delicious feel of mesh bears. Have taught a new crock to take me up in the morning.

My mother explained to me that my aunt's secret life in these places was the result of her bad handwriting, and when we'd translated this nonsense we would find out what she'd really been up to.

Arrived in Puerto Rico last night and had a delicious meal of fresh pears. Have bought a new clock to wake me up in the morning.

I found her nonsense much more entertaining than her sense. How delightful to feel a mesh bear and to travel by crock every morning! Even after the misunderstanding was explained to me, her encounters with crocks and bears seemed quite as real as her purchase of clocks and pears, perhaps because I had already picked up the habit of hiding common sense with nonsense. If, for example, our family was entertaining guests and either my sister or I saw anything resembling a cockroach, we had been instructed to say, "There is a Turkish mosquito in the pantry." Because of the braces on her teeth, my sister found it hard to close her mouth and sometimes during conversation would sit with it hanging open. This gave her a vacant air that did not at all reflect the liveliness of her mind. Whoever noticed this first was to say, "Good morning, Mrs. Smith," at which signal it would snap shut like a steel trap. If I chattered too much in the presence of guests, anyone in on our game would say, "Go fetch the long matches," and I instantly fell silent—and fetched nothing.

Sometimes a single remark became shorthand for a complicated event that we all remembered. Who could forget the day my father nearly peeled the paint off an adjacent car while trying to park his own? Who could forget my aunt calling out from the back seat, "You haven't got space for a sheet of toilet paper!" Custom shortened her advice to a single phrase, and what made sense to us must have confounded the sideswiping taxi driver to whom my aunt shouted, over the roar of traffic in downtown Detroit, "Toilet paper! For God's sake, toilet paper!" Though she may never have read *Through the Looking Glass*, my aunt was a faithful disciple of Humpty Dumpty, who tells Alice, "When *I* use a word . . . it means just what I choose it to mean—neither more nor less."[1]

I especially treasured one postcard from my aunt that no one could ever reduce to sense. The picture showed a formal garden: an elegant maze of shaped hedges, arbors, beds of herbs and flowers. On the reverse side she had scrawled her message:

> You'd love this place. The roaring shillilies san sea whet all and the pappasnippigoo are zooming.

It's right and fitting that a sensible garden and a nonsensical message should be two sides of a single card. Nonsense is both logical and absurd, like the games we play as children. Some years ago I was out walking and found myself treading on a game of hopscotch, chalked out on twelve squares. The last square, which we called "Home" when I played the game, was marked "Heaven" in this one. I am told by those who play this version of hopscotch that it's harder to get into heaven than to go home. You must throw your stone into heaven, jump to the eleventh square, pick up the stone, jump to the spot where it landed, and recite at top speed the alphabet forward and backward, your name, address, and telephone number, your age, and the name of your boyfriend or girlfriend. If I were to tell a clergyman that I got into heaven by throwing a stone into it, he would say, "Nonsense!" In life, yes, but in the game, no. In the game it makes perfect sense. Nonsense too is a game, and a great part of learning to write it is learning to play it.

When I was little and the prospect of reaching heaven seemed closer than it does now, I heard the story of the Minotaur, half man, half bull, whom King Minos kept in a maze and to whom every year the most beautiful young Athenians were sacrificed. I didn't know that when Theseus killed the Minotaur, the Athenians celebrated by drawing the maze on the ground and dancing through it. I didn't know that hopscotch may have come down to us from that custom.[2] Where else but in children's games and nursery rhymes do the ancient and the modern so amiably link hands?

The grandmother of nonsense is Mother Goose, and many a modern poet writing for adults has acknowledged his debt to her. Auden praises her songs for being almost infallible as memorable speech. Roethke, defending the difficult poems in his sequence, "The Lost Son," claims for their literary ancestors German and English folk literature, "particularly Mother Goose."[3] But none praises her so well, I think, as Muriel Rukeyser:

> Mother Goose does not come into our lives when we are young children just having learned to speak. She is there before, before language. We come to language through her, and to mystery and laughter and action. To poetry. She is only one of many ways, of course, and she has her equivalent in all cultures. . . . It is this figure, Mother Goose, who bends over the early days of many of us . . . with her babble . . . It is syncopated, to both white children and black children, and must be read that way. . . . Who, having heard "Thislittlepig-

wenttomarket," can say as an adult that he can't get the rhythms of contemporary poets or Gerard Manley Hopkins?[4]

Of what is this nonsense made? When John Newbery published *Mother Goose's Melody* in 1760, the rhymes were already old. Nevertheless, we find in them a highly domesticated society with customs similar to our own— courtships, weddings, feasts, fashions, and funerals—but with this difference: everything is alive and can speak for itself. The moment you allow your dishes and spoons to elope and your cats and mice to converse, all social conventions are turned on their heads. Dogs read newspapers, spiders have parlors, hens long for shoes, pots play with ladles, flies marry bumblebees, wrens conduct funerals, hawks build churches, barbers shave pigs, and ladies fall in love, not with the barber, but with the pig. Everything is alive and anything can happen:

> *Hoddley, poddley, puddle and fogs,*
> *Cats are to marry the poodle dogs;*
> *Cats in blue jackets and dogs in red hats,*
> *What will become of the mice and the rats?*[5]

The meter in this little poem would do any poet proud. It skips along in anapests, a foot that Edward Lear and Lewis Carroll made good use of many years later. Even the meaningless "hoddley, poddley, puddle and fogs" dances in strict time. That well-regulated babble is as essential to the poem as abracadabra to the magician. Like the wizard's charmed circle, it draws a boundary between the game and the real world and lets us make light of the most dreadful events:

The cat she seized the rat by the crown,
  Heigh ho! says Rowley,
The kittens they pulled the little mouse down.
  With a rowley, powley, gammon and spinach,
  Heigh ho! says Anthony Rowley.[6]

Some fine books have been written on the connections between nonsense and play, and I recommend them to you.[7] My task here is much humbler: to look at two of my favorite nonsense writers for children, Lewis Carroll and Edward Lear, and to consider a few of the ways they can teach writers how to start on the downward path to wisdom. It's not the wisdom of Solomon we're after here, but Blake's wise foolishness: "If the fool would persist in his folly he would become wise."[8] Perhaps if I ever translate the babble on my aunt's postcard, I'll find her saying that she's having a wonderful time in the Garden of Eden, and the roses are lovely but not as fragrant as the ones in her garden in Detroit. I wish this revelation about the roses would turn out to be true. I wish paradise was all around us and finding it was as easy as recognizing it. I hope Blake is right when he says, "If the doors of perception were cleaned every thing would appear to man as it is, infinite."[9] The proper name of that celestial cleaning person is Faith, but perhaps the nickname for Faith is Nonsense.

Eighty-six years after the publication of *Mother Goose's Melody*, Edward Lear published his first book of nonsense poems and was dismayed when reviewers thought he had merely recycled Mother Goose. In a letter he writes, "I was disgusted at the *Saturday Review* Dec. 21 talking of the Nonsense verses being 'anonymous, & a reprint of old nursery rhymes,' tho' they gave 'Mr. Lear credit for a persistent absurdity.' I wish I could have all the credit due to me, small as that may be." And he adds, "If you are ever asked about that Book of Nonsense, remember I made *all* the verses: except two lines of two of them . . . I wish someone would review it properly & funnily."[10] Lear gave himself the title of "Lord High bosh and nonsense producer."[11] In 1865, twenty years after Lear's first book of nonsense poems appeared, Lewis Carroll published *Alice's Adventures in Wonderland*, and now if in some heavenly roll call the Lord High bosh and nonsense producer were summoned, I am sure both Lear and Carroll would rise to answer.

Though Lear by profession was a painter of landscapes and birds, and Lewis Carroll, alias Charles Dodgson, was an Oxford don and a logician, there are important similarities—important, I think, to the making of nonsense. Neither man ever married, but both greatly enjoyed the company of children and wrote their best work to please their child friends. Lewis Carroll told many stories to Alice Liddell and her sisters long before he told the story that was to make him famous. The grown-up Alice Liddell gave this description of Carroll the storyteller:

> We used to sit on the big sofa on each side of him while he told us stories, illustrating them by pencil or ink drawings as he went along. . . . He seemed to have an endless store of these fantastical tales, which he made up as he told them. . . . They were not always entirely new. Sometimes they were new versions of old stories; sometimes they started on the old basis, but grew into new tales owing to the frequent interruptions

which opened up fresh and undreamed-of possibilities.[12]

And Gertrude Chataway, another child friend of Carroll's, remembers:

One thing that made his stories particularly charming to a child was that he often took his cue from her remarks—a question would set him off on quite a new trail of ideas, so that one felt one had somehow helped to make the story, and it seemed a personal possession.[13]

Lear too was the "Adopty Duncle" of children whom he met on his travels or the children of friends with whom he stayed. Daisy Terry, recalling how she met Lear at a hotel, gives us a picture of a man who "glowed, bubbled and twinkled," and sang her "The Owl and the Pussy-cat," and every day left on the lunch plate for her brother and herself a new letter of a nonsense alphabet, which was later published under the title, "The Absolutely Abstemious Ass."[14] The limericks in Lear's first book of nonsense were composed for the grandchildren of Lord Derby, who had commissioned him to draw the birds and animals in his private menagerie. Lear lived on his patron's estate during this time but took his meals with the servants. A friend of Lear's recalls how his sense of humor got him out of the servant's hall into society:

Old Lord Derby liked to have his grandsons' company after dinner, and one day complained that they con-

stantly left him as soon as dinner was over. Their reply
was, "It is so much more amusing downstairs!"
"Why?" "Oh, because that young fellow in the steward's room who is drawing the birds for you is such
good company, and we like to go and hear him talk."

Like a wise man, instead of scolding them and
after full inquiry, he invited Lear to dine upstairs instead of in the steward's room, and not only Lord
Derby, but all his friends were equally delighted with
him.[15]

If you want to play the game of nonsense, the best way
to start is by playing with words. Imagine that nonsense is
like hopscotch and to reach the first square you must invent
twenty-five words, all recognizable as parts of speech. That
is, the reader or listener must be able to recognize a verb,
an adjective, and so on. To Lear, the gift for playing with
language came so easily that it overflows from his poems
into his letters. Of the weather he writes, "The day is highly
beastly & squondangerlous" and "The views over the har-
bour are of the most clipfombious and ompsiquillious
nature."[16] From his "Nonsense Cookery" you may learn
how to make crumbobblious cutlets and an amblongus pie
—easy, if you can find an amblongus. And what is an
amblongus? Lear never tells. It is not customary for a
writer of recipes to stop and define his ingredients; he
merely tells you what to do with them. If you invent imaginary things, you must also invent names for them. Lear's
long poem "The Quangle Wangle's Hat" introduces a con-
gerie of imaginary creatures so matter-of-factly that you feel
in some far corner of the known world they must have always existed:

I.

On the top of the Crumpetty Tree
        The Quangle Wangle sat,
But his face you could not see,
        On account of his Beaver Hat.
For his Hat was a hundred and two feet wide,
With ribbons and bibbons on every side,
And bells, and buttons, and loops, and lace,
So that nobody ever could see the face
                Of the Quangle Wangle Quee.
                . . .
And besides, to the Crumpetty Tree
        Came the Stork, the Duck, and the Owl;
The Snail and the Bumble-Bee,
        The Frog and the Fimble Fowl
(The Fimble Fowl, with a Corkscrew leg);
And all of them said, "We humbly beg
We may build our homes on your lovely Hat,—
Mr. Quangle Wangle, grant us that!
                Mr. Quangle Wangle Quee!"

V.

And the Golden Grouse came there,
        And the Pobble who has no toes,
And the small Olympian Bear,
        And the Dong with a luminous nose.
And the Blue Baboon who played the flute,
And the Orient Calf from the Land of Tute,
And the Attery Squash, and the Bisky Bat,—
All came and built on the lovely Hat
                Of the Quangle Wangle Quee.[17]

The Pobble, the Attery* Squash, the Bisky Bat—fantastic creatures all—could I have met them in dreams? Not likely. There's nothing dreamlike about their appearance here. Strict meter and form keep each thing in its place, much as the squares in hopscotch order the moves of the players. None of these images are allowed to run together, the way images do in dreams; they are introduced, one by one, in a stanza that is both a litany and a catalog.

Lear writes in conventional forms about unconventional things. A useful exercise for writers who wish to do the same is the nonsense recipe. The conventions are familiar enough. Turn to any cookbook: *combine and mix well, chop, season the mixture with, beat these ingredients until they are blended.* Following a complicated recipe always makes me feel a little like a magician preparing a potion. Lear's recipe for Gosky Patties persuades me that the connection between cooking and magic is closer than Julia Child would have us believe:

TO MAKE GOSKY PATTIES

Take a pig three or four years of age, and tie him by the off hind-leg to a post. Place 5 pounds of currants, 3 of sugar, 2 pecks of peas, 18 roast chestnuts, a candle, and 6 bushels of turnips, within his reach: if he eats these, constantly provide him with more.

Then procure some cream, some slices of Cheshire cheese, 4 quires of foolscap paper, and a packet of black pins. Work the whole into a paste, and spread it out to dry on a sheet of clean brown waterproof linen.

---

* Attery: Venomous, poisonous. (*C.E.D.*)

When the paste is perfectly dry, but not before, proceed to beat the pig violently with the handle of a large broom. If he squeals, beat him again.

Visit the paste and beat the pig alternately for some days, and ascertain if, at the end of that period, the whole is about to turn into Gosky Patties.

If it does not then, it never will; and in that case the pig may be let loose, and the whole process may be considered as finished.[18]

If you play by the rules—that is, if you follow the rules of syntax and grammar and if you write in a regular meter and stanza form—you can walk the thin line between chaos and nonsense without a qualm. When Lewis Carroll included "Jabberwock" in *Through the Looking Glass*, he could scarcely have imagined what James Joyce would borrow and transform in *Finnegan's Wake*. For every unfamiliar word in "Jabberwock," Carroll has not only a definition but an explanation:

> *'Twas brillig, and the slithy toves*
> > *Did gyre and gimble in the wabe;*
> *All mimsy were the borogroves,*
> > *And the mome raths outgrabe.*
>
> *"Beware the Jabberwock, my son!*
> > *The jaws that bite, the claws that catch!*
> *Beware the Jubjub bird, and shun*
> > *The frumious Bandersnatch!"*[19]

Some of Carroll's neologisms are, like Lear's Quangle Wangle, names for things that never were. Having never seen a tove, I take Carroll's word for it that it is something like a badger, a lizard, and a corkscrew, which nests under sundials and lives on cheese. But "slithy" is an invention of a different kind. It means lithe and slimy. It is, we are told, like a portmanteau; there are two meanings packed up into one word. Nonsense was never so clearly taught, I think, as in this passage from Carroll's introduction to *The Hunting of the Snark*:

> . . . take the two words "fuming" and "furious." Make up your mind that you will say both words, but leave it unsettled which you will say first. Now open your mouth and speak. If your thoughts incline ever so little towards "fuming," you will say "fuming-furious"; if they turn, by even a hair's breadth, towards "furious," you will say "furious-fuming"; but if you have that rarest of gifts, a perfectly balanced mind, you will say "frumious."[20]

Playing with words leads to playing on words and a whole range of puns, malapropisms, and intentional misunderstandings. One of the commonest misunderstandings among children—and one that Carroll makes use of—is taking a figure of speech literally. When my son was about five or six, we were finishing our dinner at a restaurant and the waiter glided over to our table and magnanimously announced, "Dessert is on the house." A look of panic came over my son's face. Was that dish of chocolate ice cream worth the danger of scaling Howard Johnson's orange roof? Such logical misunderstandings run through both the Alice books. In *Through the Looking Glass*, the White King asks Alice if she can see either of his messengers on the road:

"I see nobody on the road," said Alice.

"I only wish I had such eyes," the King remarked in a fretful tone. "To be able to see Nobody! And at that distance too! Why, it's as much as I can do to see real people, by this light!"[21]

The inappropriate word as a literary device comes into its own with Edward Lear. We have all heard people misuse words, often choosing not the right word but a word similar to it in sound. A passage from Lear's "The Story of the Four Little Children Who Went Round the World" shows this device in its glory, with a few of Lear's invented words thrown in for good measure:

The Moon was shining slobaciously from the star-bespangled sky, while her light irrigated the smooth and shiny sides and wings and backs of the Blue-Bottle-Flies with a peculiar and trivial splendor, while all Nature cheerfully responded to the cerulean and conspicuous circumstances.[22]

The more high-flown the rhetoric, the greater the incongruity between what the writer seems to say and what he actually says.

When Lewis Carroll uses the wrong but similar-sounding word, he depends on our knowing the right word so that we can enjoy the incongruity, just as we enjoy the parody of a poem more when we know the original. In the Alice books, a word that seems wrong to the reader may be exactly the right word to the speaker. How the Liddell sisters must have enjoyed the Mock Turtle's discussion of his schooling in *Alice's Adventures in Wonderland*. For them, a proper education included reading and writing; the different branches of arithmetic—addition, subtraction, multiplication, and division; geography; history, ancient and modern; Latin and Greek; drawing; sketching; and painting in oils. And what did the Mock Turtle study?

> "Reeling and writhing, of course, to begin with," the Mock Turtle replied; "and then the different branches of Arithmetic—Ambition, Distraction, Uglification, and Derision," ...
>
> Alice ... said, "What else had you to learn?"
>
> "Well, there was Mystery," the Mock Turtle replied, counting off the subjects on his flappers,"—Mystery, ancient and modern, with Seaography: then Drawling—the Drawling-master was an old conger-eel, that used to come once a week: he taught us Drawling, Stretching, and Fainting in Coils."
>
> "What was *that* like?" said Alice.
>
> "Well, I can't show it to you, myself," the Mock Turtle said: "I'm too stiff. And the Gryphon never learnt it."[23]

The Classical master, we are told, taught "Laughing and Grief," and the lessons lasted "ten hours the first day ... nine the next, and so on." When Alice observes that this is a curious plan, the Gryphon explains, "That's the reason they're called lessons ... because they lessen from day to day."[24] The only connection between what the Mock Turtle studied and what the Liddell sisters studied is the sound of the words themselves. But in nonsense that connection is an essential one.

The secret heart of nonsense is the amiable incongruity. One of the ways I first discovered this was through a game, "Peter Coddle's Trip." The game involves a printed story and a pack of cards on which are named a miscellaneous assortment of things: a yellow nightcap, an insane bedbug, an intoxicated clam, an old hairbrush, a red wig, an elderly porcupine, and so on. The leader reads the story aloud until he comes to a blank. One of the players draws a card and what is written on that card fills the blank and becomes part of the story. The story describes Peter Coddle's trip to New York, and if the player were to draw the cards I have just mentioned, Peter's description of the Statue of Liberty would read as follows:

> Squire Mildew wanted to go down to the Statue of Liberty, which loomed up down the bay like an elderly porcupine . . . As we came near the statue the hand holding the torch seemed about the size of an old hairbrush. We landed and went up into the head. On the way up we met some people coming down the narrow winding stairs; one of them said it was as close as an intoxicated clam. I thought the lights were no better than a red wig. From the head we had a splendid view. We saw a steamer passing out of the harbor; . . . she was going like an insane bedbug.[25]

Literary nonsense differs from the game I've just described in this way: the nonsense writer needs a reason other than chance for linking incongruous things together. He needs an arbitrary convention that will free the words from the categories of everyday use and from our sense of what belongs with what. One of the most useful of these conventions is alliteration. In *Through the Looking Glass*,

Alice plays a game that both Carroll and Lear use in their poetry:

> "I love my love with an H," Alice couldn't help beginning, "because he is Happy. I hate him with an H, because he is Hideous. I fed him with—with—Ham-sandwiches and Hay. His name is Haigha, and he lives——"
>
> "He lives on the Hill," the king remarked simply, without the least idea that he was joining in the game . . . [26]

Lear builds many of his nonsense alphabets around alliteration, which leads him to some very odd combinations:

> The Melodious Meritorious Mouse,
> who played a merry minuet on the
> Piano-forte.

> The Visibly Vicious Vulture,
> who wrote some Verses to a Veal-cutlet in a
> Volume bound in Vellum.[27]

Students in search of subjects for nonsense can turn to the yellow pages of the telephone directory and read the categories at the top of adjacent pages. In our directory I discovered a Burglar Bus, a Calculating Canvas, Chimney Churches, Cleaning Clergy, Dancing Dentists, Karate Kindergartens, and Musical Nurserymen. Sometimes when I bring nonsense poetry into a class of very sensible people, I say, "For the next hour I am going to ask you to make some

changes in your vocabulary. Instead of the word *door*, I
want you to use the word *rainbow*. Instead of the verb *to
open*, please use the verb *to skin*. For the word *light*, please
substitute the word *cat*. And for the verb *to turn on*, use the
verb *to hassle*. Remember: the door is the rainbow, to open
is to skin, the light is the cat, to turn on is to hassle. Now, in
this new language please tell me to open the door and turn
on the light."

A deep silence follows. And then very slowly, somebody says, "Skin the rainbow and hassle the cat. Please."

"Thank you. What else can you say about the door
and the light?"

"The cat is by the rainbow."

"The rainbow is already skinned," adds another student.

Though we would sound like lunatics to a visitor, we
understand each other. Following the rules of nonsense, we
speak a common language. The most inspired example of
this double talk I know occurs in a Spanish folk tale, "The
Shepherd Who Laughed Last," which I will quote nearly in
full, since it is brief:

> Tomas, the owner of a little roadside inn in Spain,
> loved to have a good laugh. . . .
> One night a shepherd came to the inn. . . .
> After he had served some wine to the shepherd,
> Tomas winked at his cronies.
> "Here is one who will be easy to fool," he whis-
> pered.
> The others watched delightedly as Tomas, set-
> tling himself before the charcoal fire and lighting his
> pipe, said to the stranger:

"In this part of Spain, you know, we have different names for things. You had best learn them before you go any farther. . . . For example, here we call a bottle a Fat Boy. The blood pudding we call Johnny. The rooster we call the Singer; the hen, the Dancer; the cat, Our Neighbor; the chimney chain, Forbearance. We call the bed, Your Honor; the fire, Happiness; and the master of the house, Always With Us." . . .

They were still laughing and the shepherd was still repeating the names when the inn closed for the night. Tomas went upstairs to bed, and then the shepherd lay down beside the fire to sleep. He kept one eye open, however, and when the black cat came in, he watched her. She went over to the fire for warmth and, getting too near it, set fire to the end of her tail. The pain maddened her, and yowling loudly, she began to climb up the chain into the chimney.

The shepherd rose, took two bottles of wine and the blood pudding from the cupboard, the hen and the rooster from their corner, and thrust them into his pouch.

Then walking to the door he called out:

"Arise, Always With Us, from the heights of Your Honor. For there goes Our Neighbor up Forbearance pursued by Happiness. As for the Fat Boys, Johnny, the Singer, and the Dancer, they go along the road with me!"

"What can the simpleton be saying?" Tomas thought opening his eyes for a moment. Then he turned over and went to sleep again.

And the shepherd unlatched the door and went off into the night, laughing.[28]

Suppose all the story were lost except the shepherd's final speech. What would we have? The private ravings of a madman? The broken speech of the brain damaged? In the first formal speech actress Patricia Neal gave after recovering from a stroke, she describes how she passed through nonsense while learning to speak again:

> I became an expert at double-talk. Once when I was very cross with Roald, I said, "Get out! Get out! You . . . you jake my dioddles!" And instead of saying. "Tell me once more," I would say, "Inject me again!"
>
> A cigarette was an oblogan. "A dry martini" came out "a red hair dryer, please." And so on. Mind you, this was after weeks of practice, when I was getting really good at talking.[29]

The writer who uses double talk has taken a road that, followed far enough, leads to surrealism. It should come as no surprise that when André Breton wrote his pamphlet, *What is Surrealism?* in 1936, he named Lewis Carroll among its patron saints.[30] What especially interested Breton was Carroll's ability to invent stories without knowing where they came from or where they would end: "Sometimes an idea comes at night, when I have had to get up and strike a light to note it down . . . but whenever or however it comes, *it comes of itself*. I cannot set invention going like a clock, by any voluntary winding up; nor do I believe that any *original* writing (and what other writing is worth preserving?) was ever so produced . . ."[31] Breton tells an anecdote that would have delighted Carroll. "Saint-Pol-Roux, in times gone by, used to have a notice posted on the door of his manor house in Camaret, every evening before he went to sleep, which read: THE POET IS WORKING."[32]

Breton recommended automatic writing as a way of bringing to the conscious act of writing the unconscious freedom of dreaming. "Forget about your genius, your talents, and the talents of everyone else. . . . Write quickly, without any preconceived subject, fast enough so that you will not remember what you're writing and be tempted to reread what you have written."[33] In automatic writing, the freedom of association found in dreams becomes the ability to make connections between remote parts of one's experience. Robert Bly calls this "leaping," and what he says about "leaps" in poetry would have interested Lear and Carroll. "In a great ancient or modern poem, the considerable distance between the associations, the distance the spark has to leap, gives the lines their bottomless feeling, their space . . ."[34] He takes Wallace Stevens as an example of a poet in whose poems the content is the distance between what the poet was given as fact and what he made of it. The spectacle of a Yale commencement may have started Stevens writing "On the Manner of Addressing Clouds." But what started with hoods and mortarboards ends up, in the poem, as "Gloomy grammarians in golden gowns," a line that Carroll and Lear would have admired.

God only knows what Kenneth Patchen was watching when he wrote "because the zebra-plant bore spotted cubs":

> He grabbed the beanpot off the clothesline
> And poured hot maple syrup into his parade sneakers;
> And still it was a mess! (Hear footnote above.)—
> Like frantic horsemen trying to exchange nightgowns
>   on a lake.

"Today," announced the kindlingwood, "September
    begins."
And the sinkstopper growled: "Wha-at! on April
    10th!"
"It is a mite late this year," admitted a swansnail,
Ruffling up its shell and trying ineffectually to scowl.
"Shut up!" commanded Grover Clevewater Giraffe.
    "Let's
Everybody get on this here blade of grass;
Then the one with the handsomest neck will
Be given all the jellybuns. How's that?"
The old philosopher slowly lowered his stone:
"Suppose," he said, "you were a wisp of sour loneliness
Stuck to the wrong side of a life; would you right away
Have someone locked up for trying to lap your hand?
Someone, that is, who had spent thirty-five years
Pasting vile-tasting labels on cans in
A dog-meat factory. Yes, they say there are rooms;
That there are reasons; that things make sense . . . Yes,
    woof! woof!
But it will all come right; yes, it will end.
The last cruel wag to a cruel tale.
Ah, no . . . life is not a story that children
Should ever be allowed to hear about."[35]

Free of the order imposed by meter and rhyme, the
images run together, as in a dream. Even the White Queen,
who maintained she could believe as many as six impossible
things before breakfast, might find herself taxed by Patchen.
Believing the impossible isn't easy. While sitting in the waiting room of a doctor's office recently, I overheard a mother

trying to entertain her young daughter with a game in a children's magazine. The game was, How many things can you find wrong with this picture? I could not see the picture, but the conversation had me riveted.

MOTHER: What do you mean there's nothing wrong with the picture? Look at the tree. It's full of carrots.
CHILD: Maybe it's a carrot tree.
MOTHER: You know carrots don't grow on trees. Now, what's wrong with the train?
CHILD: Nothing.
MOTHER: You don't see it? The train has wings. Choo-choo trains don't have wings.

I felt sure the child knew the right answer, but who among us would not like to see a carrot tree or ride a train with wings? And I thought of the child Stephen in *A Portrait of the Artist as A Young Man*, who muses on red roses and white roses, cream and pink and lavender roses. "But you could not have a green rose," he tells himself, adding wistfully, "But perhaps somewhere in the world you could."[36]

Perhaps among the roaring shillilies and the pappasnippigoo on my aunt's postcard, a green rose is growing. I've never been to the Garden of Nonsense to see for myself. But one night I dreamed myself in a very different garden, and persisting in my folly, like the fool in Blake's proverb, I woke a little wiser. Since the dream took the shape of a story, let me tell you the story.

Once upon a time at the edge of town grew a garden about which I knew nothing except that some called it the Garden of Reason and I was forbidden to go there. Eve conversing with the serpent was not more curious than I, and I headed straight for the garden the first chance I got. The gatekeeper was a magician, and the gatehouse was his cottage. He let me into the house and told me I must wait to be admitted but I might sit at his table and drink a cup of tea while I waited. This I declined to do, as the table was cluttered with papers and dirty dishes, and I could not find a clean cup. Suddenly a young woman rushed in, clutching a book and pounding the title with her fist: THE LIFE AND DEATH OF SHEILA HOROWITZ.

"Don't tell me this is the way it's got to be!" she shouted. "Tell me there's more to my life than this book!"

The magician folded his hands over his chest, unmoved. If to be admitted I had to accept the magician's version of my life, then I would go back the way I came. But now I saw that the front door had vanished and the only door open to me led into the garden itself. The magician turned his back on me for an instant, and I jumped up and fled through the door.

The garden was as formal as that in my aunt's picture: a maze of hedges, beds of herbs, long walks under wisteria arbors. But hers was empty and this one was full of people. I knew from their clothes that some had come here a long time ago. Those old men in Greek togas—how many hundreds of years had they wandered these paths? That handsome woman in flowered brocade skirts and a farthingale— what was she looking for? Weren't we all looking for the same thing, the way out?

Far behind me I could hear the magician beating down bowers and running through rosebeds, shouting, "You have not been admitted! You have not been admitted!" Suddenly I spied two familiar figures ahead of me,

Martin and Alice Provensen, who in our waking lives had just finished the illustrations for our book A *Visit to William Blake's Inn.*

"If we don't hurry, the magician will catch us," I said.

"If we don't look back," said Alice, "the magician won't catch us."

A high, smooth wall let us know we had reached the back boundary of the garden; reason has its limits. Against the wall leaned an old ladder, which was not even suitable for apple picking; the rungs were broken.

"Let's put our feet where the rungs were," suggested Martin.

My common sense said, What nonsense! But my uncommon sense whispered, If a fool persists——

One by one, under our feet, the rungs healed themselves and grew whole enough to hold us. Now we stood on top of the wall. Facing us was an angel so tall that we brushed the hem of its gown like grasshoppers.

"You are free," said the angel. It pointed over trees and fields, to the far-off world-town we'd started from, sparkling on the horizon. Sunlight slanted from its sleeve, touched down in the world-town. On that broad road of sunlight we slid like children playing, all the way back to the beginning.

12

The Rutabaga Lamp: The Reading and Writing of Fairy Tales

——————————— Before I learned to read, I thought all people were divided into two sorts: explorers and dreamers. I had a clear image in my mind of both, and I still remember the source of that image. Two weeks before Christmas, my Sunday school teacher gave us little canisters in which we were to put money for the poor. Painted on these curious banks were the three wise men. I supposed it was for these three indigents that we were saving, and I thought it very odd that men so wise should be reduced to taking alms from children.

But it was easy to see why they were poor. They had spent all their money on expensive clothes, gifts, and travel. They had, I was sure, prudent wives waiting for them at home in leaf-brown hoods and homespun gowns, three wise women who would never get *their* pictures on banks, because, like the wise women in fairy tales, they would never travel to the far corners of the earth and bring back tales of adventure. The wise women of the fairy tales are not tourists. They travel invisible roads. Their journeys are inward: their destinations belong to the uncharted territory of dreams. Because these places are not found on maps, the stories about them are called fantasies. I imagined that wise men wrote geographies and histories of real places. They were the explorers. Wise women wrote fantasies and fairy tales. They were the dreamers.

The more I read, the more I understood that the best writers are both explorers and dreamers. And nowhere is this truer than in the stories we call fairy tales. I have always thought of fairy tales as one of the highest forms of truth, like parables, or the *koan* which, repeated and taken to heart, help Zen monks along the road to enlightenment. Their truth is hidden, and therein lies their power.

I remember my first encounter with this sort of truth. Once upon a time, if I had been asked to describe an egg, I would have said "An egg is hard and smooth and fragile on the outside, but inside you will find a yellow yolk and a white, which isn't white but a sort of pale slippery yellow." Hard. Smooth. Fragile. Yellow. White. The egg has vanished. I have covered it with labels. I can see it no longer and can give you no further account of it.

What shattered these labels for me was a riddle. The egg was the answer, yet knowing the answer did not keep me from enjoying the riddle:

> *In marble walls as white as milk,*
> *Lined with a skin as soft as silk,*
> *Within a fountain crystal-clear,*
> *A golden apple doth appear.*

> *No doors there are to this stronghold,*
> *Yet thieves break in and steal the gold.*[1]

When I first heard riddles, I soon realized that I did not need to know the answer to enjoy the riddle. Indeed, not until I grew up did I learn that one of my favorite poems was a riddle for snow:

> *White bird featherless*
> *Flew from paradise,*
> *Pitched on the castle wall;*
> *Along came Lord Landless,*
> *Took it up handless,*
> *And rode away*
> *to the King's white hall.*[2]

But now I hear somebody ask, "What have riddles to do with fairy tales? Where are the fairies, the wizards, the witches?" To answer, I must borrow a definition of fairy tales from Tolkien, who takes pains to distinguish between *fairy*, meaning elf, and *fäerie*, the realm or state in which fairies have their being. "Fäerie itself may perhaps most nearly be translated by Magic," he explains. "And though it keeps elves, dragons, and trolls, it also holds the sun and moon, the earth and sea, and ourselves, when we are enchanted. A fairy story, says Tolkien, is "one which touches on or uses Fäerie, whatever its own main purpose may be: satire, adventure, morality, fantasy."[3]

Though children read fairy tales, fairy tales are not only for children. The brothers Grimm took their tales from German peasant women who took them from each other. A hundred years before the publication of those tales, Charles

Perrault, a French academician at the court of Louis XIV, published—under his son's name—*Tales of my Mother Goose*. The frontispiece to the 1697 edition shows an old woman warming herself at the hearth and telling stories to a young child. Who is this old woman? The child's grandmother? A peasant nurse? "If she were a peasant Nanny, rather than a blood grandmother, she must have remained forever a stranger to everyone in the household but the children . . . ," suggests one critic. "No wonder such old women appear in their own tales as creatures from another world . . ."[4]

Perrault's book set the women at court writing fairy tales, not only for children, but for each other, to be read in the salons. Madame de Sévigné mentions in a letter that she spent the evening listening to fairy tales with great pleasure.[5] "If fairy-story as a kind is worth reading at all it is worthy to be written for and read by adults," says Tolkien, who did not develop a taste for fairy tales until after he was grown up. "They will, of course, put more in and get more out than children can."[6]

Certainly many of the literary fairy tales published in Europe during the nineteenth century are for adults. Both Hans Christian Andersen and George MacDonald wrote fairy tales for adults as well as for children. Charles Dickens adds the subtitle, "A fairy tale of home" to his adult story, "The Cricket on the Hearth." E. T. A. Hoffman's "The Golden Flower Pot" is subtitled "A Fairy Tale of Our Time," yet the only tale by Hoffman most children know today is "Nutcracker and the King of Mice" and few know it except as a ballet. And in our own time, who reads James Stephens's *The Crock of Gold*? Children or their parents? Or both?

Since I have always assumed that fairy tales are as necessary to both children and adults as dictionaries, I was much surprised to receive a letter from a former student at the Bread Loaf Writers' Conference, asking if the fairy tale was dead. She writes as follows:

> I have been informed that what I have to offer the world is unpublishable. Blanket statement to cover all fairy tales. Told in this case by an agency (paid in cold hard cash) who advertises that they solicit picture book manuscripts. . . . If it is true that fairy tales . . . are unpublishable, then I had better know it now. And give the whole thing up.

> That's the way my mind runs—to gnomes and fairies, witches and warlocks, with side trips to the ancient gods. . . . It has occurred to me that if the agency is right, I am as extinct as the dodo. . . . Please, please tell me, is "Little Red Riding Hood" all there is?

The best way to answer her question, I thought (for I did not know her work), was to ask Barbara Lucas, who was then editor of children's books at Harcourt Brace Jovanovich, the publisher of two of my favorite fantasies for children, *The Little Prince* and *Mary Poppins*. And very soon I realized how different an editor's point of view is from a writer's.

"Fantasy represents the worst of several thousand manuscripts we get a year," she told me. "People put some consideration into writing an adult book, but they'll sit down and write a children's book on a rainy afternoon. They think writing for children is easy. It's the hardest thing in the world."

Why, I wanted to know, do so many of these manuscripts fail?

"Fantasy is very structured," she answered. "You introduce your main character. You show who the leading characters are and what they want to achieve. You make your promises and you follow through. You've got to have your audience believe that those characters are never going to get what they want. And then, either they get what they want, or they get what turns out to be better."

That sounded to me like good advice for the writer of realistic fiction. Surely there were problems peculiar to fantasy.

"Most people don't understand fantasy," said Barbara. "They think it is an exercise for stream-of-consciousness. They confuse two things: fantasy and to fanatisize. Fantasy has to be rooted in logical, familiar things. First you have to get your reader comfortable. Along the journey you've got to have things connect, to make the journey meaningful. Otherwise there's no point of reference."

"Do you think more adults than children read fantasy?" I asked, remembering how many of my favorite writers for adults have tried their hand at fairy tales.

"Adults love fantasy," answered Barbara. "They help to keep it alive. Most children are TV bred. *Watership Down* was submitted as a children's book and sent upstairs. If we want to get both markets for a book, we market it as an adult book and let it filter down. If we market it as a children's book, adults won't buy it."

And what advice did she have for the student from Bread Loaf?

"She should study the market," replied Barbara.

Market? I had a lunatic image of bookshelves lined

with carrots and cauliflowers. I thought of rainbows fading into ticker tape, of stocks rising and falling on the invisible backs of gnomes. When I write a book, I never think of the market for it. But though our views differed, Barbara and I agreed on one thing: the more fairy tales you've read, the more skill you bring to writing your own. The best writers of fairy tales have always had a deep knowledge of the stories handed down by our ancestors, like a thread binding us to some innocent part of ourselves that might otherwise be lost.

I reread the letter. "Is 'Little Red Riding Hood' all there is?" How could I answer this writer? Should I tell her to read Perrault's *Tales of My Mother Goose,* in which "Little Red Riding Hood" was first published? Would it not be better to ask, Why has Little Red Riding Hood endured so long? What in that simple story moved Charles Dickens to confess that Little Red Riding Hood "was my first love. I felt that if I could have married Little Red Riding Hood, I should have known perfect bliss."[7]

Perrault's stories are witty and elegant versions of traditional fairy tales. Over and over we recognize the traditional motifs: the quest, the animals who offer advice, the witch who hurts the hero, the wise woman who helps him. When my students use these motifs, they often apologize for their stories. A story can't be good, they fear, if it is not original. They forget that writing, like many other things, can be both original, and traditional. When I go to a wedding, I do not judge the occasion a paltry affair because the bride walked down the aisle on her father's arm in the last wedding I attended, and therefore the wedding is not original.

If the peasant grandmother who first told Little Red

Riding Hood—and Little Red Riding Hood herself has many different names—could listen to a few of the stories written by the writers who claim they are writing fairy tales, how astonished she would be! First of all, she would see no connection between her art and those fanciful failures of which Andrew Lang writes, "they always begin with a little boy or girl who goes out and meets the fairies of polyanthuses and gardenias and appleblossoms. . . . These fairies try to be funny, and fail; or they try to preach and succeed. At the end, the little boy or girl wakes up and finds that he has been dreaming."[8] Who knows better than our peasant grandmother that fairy tales are moral but not moralistic, instructive but not didactic? At some of our best-known fairy tales she would shake her head in bewilderment and murmur, "How things have changed! In my time, the fairies never came to christenings. Why, you could frighten them off with the Lord's prayer! Tell, me, do people still turn into beasts and beasts into people? Are there still ghosts and spirits and wishing caps? And do you still tell stories of kings and queens and princesses? And have you made these things your own, as I made them mine when I told my stories?"

To make them your own; that is the difference between the archetype and the stereotype in fairy tales. The stereotype starts and ends in abstraction. Of the stereotype we say, "I've seen that before" and we tire of it. But of the archetype we say, "Where have I seen you before? Was it in a dream we met?" The archetype begins in experience. Before it becomes impersonal, it is intensely personal. And this transformation, from the personal to the impersonal, from the particular grandmother to the archetypal wise woman, involves as much waiting as willing.

It is a long journey from what we know because we've lived it to what we know because we've invented it. I made that journey backward, from story to source, when I asked my husband to read the manuscript of a fantasy novel for children, *Uncle Terrible.** He read in silence until he met a character whom all the animals in the world called Mother. At her waist she wears the cord of life and the cord of death, and every morning she sings the song of strong knots to keep them together. She runs an inn for animals under a cemetery. Seen in the right light—or the right dark—the shadows cast by the gravestones are her windows:

> The windows, which kept the odd shape of the stones themselves, looked right down into Mother's house. The shadow of an angel gave Anatole a clear view of the living room. . . . The lamp on the great round table was carved from a rutabaga, and the oil in the lamp threw such an amber light on the floor that the rushes scattered there seemed washed in honey.

And here is Mother herself:

> A giant of a woman was striding toward them. The face that smiled out of her sunbonnet was as lumpy and plain as a potato. She wore corn shucks gathered into a gown, over which shimmered an apron of onion skins. Through her bonnet poked antlers that branched out like a tree, and at the end of every branch danced a flame, which lit the ground before her. She was carrying a laundry basket, and every now and then she

---

*Published by Harcourt Brace Jovanovich in 1982.

threw out a handful of snowdrops which vanished as soon as they touched the ground. A thin glaze of frost sparkled in their place.

My husband put down the manuscript.

"Where," he said, "did you find her?"

I did not know. Had I found her in fairy tales? I have long loved the character of the wise woman in the old stories. Yet my wise woman was not borrowed from these. She took her shape from my work and my wishes. I have gathered corn shucks into dolls, toted laundry baskets, scattered snowdrops, and peeled onions and longed for a gown such as onions wear, of some shiny pale gold silk, thinly striped with green. But had I found her or had she found me?

More miraculous than any fairy tale is the significance of the detail that can start a story going. Henry James recalls a dinner party in which the lady beside him made "one of those allusions, that I have always found myself recognizing on the spot as 'germs.' The germ, wherever gathered, has ever been for me the germ of a 'story,' and most of the stories straining to shape under my hand have sprung from a single small seed, a seed as minute and wind-blown as that casual hint . . . dropped unwillingly by my neighbor."[9]

The germ from which my wise woman grew was the lamp, carved long ago from a rutabaga by my immigrant ancestors to light their first home in the new world. I never saw the lamp. But I heard about it from a great-uncle, who, after retiring from his job as a salesman in St. Paul, Minnesota, wrote a family history, which he published at his own expense. Uncle Oscar did not care for fairy tales. Every year I gave him the same book for Christmas: the updated edition of the *World Almanac*. To converse with my uncle was to learn the number of deaths caused by tidal waves since 1807 or who won the championship in softball for the slow pitch for any given year. He called his book *The Tales of Two Eyes and Ears for Seventy Years,* and in his preface he announced that he would tell the truth and nothing but the truth. "This book relates to incidents that I have seen, or that were told to me in my boyhood days," he wrote. "The names of characters, dates, and locations are true to the best of my knowledge."

The rutabaga lamp lit a small corner of the chapter called "Honeymoon trip from Sweden to America by Mr. John Martinson, born in Fagelsjo, Helsingland 1842 and Miss Anna Halverson, born in Sveg, Jamtland 1842." It unfolds the story of how a young man and his bride, both twenty-five years old, sail from Sweden to New York; of how Mr. and Mrs. Martinson lose their name because too many Swedes named Martinson have already arrived; of how they receive new names and how they leave the immigration sheds as Mr. and Mrs. John Hedlund; of how they make their way by train and by riverboat to St. Cloud, Minnesota, which, says my uncle, "was the end of the line."

What happened to them there reminds me of the fairy tales in which the youngest son sets off down the road to make his fortune, and it is always the right road, for he meets those who offer to help him, and if he follows it far enough he meets the princess he must rescue and the troll he must rescue her from. The road is more than a road; it is his destiny. In my uncle's history, however, destiny is not mentioned. He writes:

> Mrs. Hedlund's relatives were supposed to meet them there, but none were to be found. A Norwegian who

was ready to start home with an empty wagon, offered them a ride as far as he was going, which was a little village by the name of Cold Springs. There they rented a little house by the roadside where they could watch for their relatives. They remained there more than a week, before the expected relatives arrived. . . .

The mansion into which they were cordially invited by their relatives was an underground cellar, the very best and only habitation in their possession. While in St. Paul, they had secured some good warm clothing and shoes, so with plenty of ammunition they were able to secure deer and other game . . . For lighting purposes they hollowed a large rutabaga for a lamp, filled it with skunk oil, with a strip of rag for a wick. That winter they cut logs and built a small log house.

Like all fairy tales, the story has a happy ending. Mr. Hedlund opened a gun shop and earned enough money to build a comfortable home and raise a large family. My great-uncle adds, "I was lucky enough to marry one of his fine daughters."

This was my first introduction to Mrs. Hedlund. It would not be accurate to say I forgot her, yet I ceased to think of her after I put down my uncle's book. And so she fell asleep in the dark cellars of my mind, taking her rutabaga lamp with her. And over the years, the storeroom that hid her filled up with myths and fairy tales, goddesses and witches and wise women. And Mrs. Hedlund, living among them, took on their light and their look, as partners in a long and happy marriage are said to resemble one another. When she turned up many years later in the fairy tale I asked my husband to read, her root cellar had become an enchanted place and she herself was as ancient as the old woman so often celebrated in nursery rhymes:

> *There was an old woman lived under the hill,*
> *And if she's not dead, she lives there still.*

Only the rutabaga lamp remained unchanged, casting its light both on the cellar in my uncle's history and the dwelling that my dreaming had made of it. Thank goodness that did not change. How could I show the imaginary house if not by the natural light of the rutabaga lamp? How can we see an imaginary world except by the light of this one?

If you could hold the rutabaga lamp to one of the oldest stories in the world, that of the human child stolen by the fairies, you would find as many tales in that plot as there are people to tell them. Among modern versions I've always admired Mary Lavin's "A Likely Story." To her, the lamp shows, first of all, the everyday world of country Ireland. It shows her the pump in the village, the gloss of a blackbird's wing, the bread cooling on the window sill in the morning, the clatter of rain on a tin roof. The fairies who lure the boy Packy from his home are as natural as the birds, the bread, and the rain. And why should they be otherwise? As Tolkien points out, "it is man who is . . . supernatural (and often of diminutive stature); whereas they are natural, far more natural than he. Such is their doom. The road to fairyland is not the road to heaven; not even to Hell . . ."[10]

Perhaps the failure to see fairyland is a human failure, for which a good writer can atone by describing it with loving attention to detail. Of the little man in green who kidnaps the boy Packy, Lavin says that "his shoes . . . were so fine his muscles rippled under the leather like the muscles of a finely bred horse rippled under his skin." While showing us the beauty of the other world, she shows us the beauty of this one. For Packy, everything rare is weighed against the commonplace and found wanting. In the fairy's chambers under the earth, he sees gold basins and ewers and pails. The fairy tells him the advantages of gold utensils. "Nothing ever gets cracked down here; nothing ever gets broken." Packy is unimpressed:

> Not that he thought it was such a good idea to have cups made of gold. When you'd pour your tea into them, wouldn't it get so hot it would scald the lip off you?
>
> One day in the summer that was gone past, he and the Tubridys went fishing on the Boyne up beyond Rathnally, and they took a few grains of tea with them in case they got dry. They forgot to bring cups though, and they had to empty out their tin-cans of worms and use them for cups. But the metal rim of the can got red hot the minute the tea went into it, and they couldn't drink a drop. Gold would be just the same?
>
> But in fact, there were no cups at all it appeared.
>
> "One no longer has any need for food, Packy," said the little man, "once one has learned the secret of eternal youth!"
>
> "You're joking, sir!" said Packy, doubtful. At that very minute he had a powerful longing for a cut of bread and a swig of milk.[11]

Most of the traditional changeling stories show the fairy world through human eyes. But what if we look at the human world through the eyes of the fairies? Sylvia Townsend Warner's novel *Kingdoms of Elfin* opens at the moment of kidnapping. No praise of rustic pleasures here; her fairies are more at home in the court than in the country. Though fairies are invisible to mortals, she knows that they must not be invisible to readers. Rain and oak, birch and fir, heath and hill, wind and fire—of such familiar stuff are their lives made. Enchantment begins in the commonplace:

> When the baby was lifted from the cradle, he began to whimper. When he felt the rain on his face, he began to bellow. "Nothing wrong with his lungs," said the footman to the nurse. They spread their wings, they rose in the air. They carried the baby over a birchwood, over an oakwood, over a firwood. Beyond the firwood was a heath, on the heath was a grassy green hill. "Elfhame at last," said the nurse. They folded their wings and alighted. A door opened in the hillside and they carried the baby in. It stared at the candles and the silver tapestries, left off bellowing, and sneezed.
>
> "It's not taken a chill, I hope," said the footman.
>
> "No, no," said the nurse. "But Elfhame strikes cold at first." She took off the swaddling clothes, wrapped the baby in gossamer, shook pollen powder over it to abate the human smell, and carried it to Queen Tiphaine, who sat in her bower. The Queen examined the baby carefully, and said he was just what she wanted: a fine baby with a red face and large ears.
>
> "Such a pity they grow up," she said. She was in her seven hundred and twentieth year, so naturally she had exhausted a good many human babies.[12]

Once you begin to see human lives from the point of view of nonhumans, you are on your way to writing *The Lord of the Rings* and doing away with the human altogether. Who knows better than Tolkien the pitfalls here?

"Anyone inheriting the fantastic device of human language can say *the green sun,*" he points out. But "to make a Secondary World inside which the green sun will be credible . . . will certainly demand a special skill, a kind of elvish craft."[13]

Fairies, princesses, wizards. The writer who wants to make them his own takes none of the traditional characters and motifs for granted. Take, for example, the good fairy godmothers who bring so much happiness to the kind and virtuous. Are they happy themselves? Thackeray's sketch of the Fairy Blackstick in *The Rose and the Ring* holds the conventional duties of good fairies up to the light of common sense, with amusing results:

> Between the kingdoms of Paffagonia and Crim Tartary, there lived a mysterious personage, who was known in those countries as the Fairy Blackstick, from the ebony wand or crutch which she carried; on which she rode to the moon sometimes, or upon other excursions of business or pleasure, and with which she performed her wonders.
>
> When she was young, and had been first taught the art of conjuring by the necromancer, her father, she was always practising her skill, whizzing about from one kingdom to another upon her black stick, and conferring her fairy favours upon this Prince or that. She had scores of royal godchildren; turned numberless wicked people into beasts, birds, millstones, clocks, pumps, bootjacks, or other absurd shapes; and in a word was one of the most active and officious of the whole College of fairies.
>
> But after two or three thousand years of this sport,

I suppose Blackstick grew tired of it. Or perhaps she thought, "What good am I doing by sending this Princess to sleep for a hundred years? by fixing a black pudding on to that booby's nose? by causing diamonds and pearls to drop from one little girl's mouth, and vipers and toads from another's? I begin to think I do as much harm as good by my performances. I might as well shut my incantations up, and allow things to take their natural course." . . . So she locked up her books in her cupboard, declined further magical performances, and scarcely used her wand at all except as a cane to walk about with.[14]

And the boons that fairies bestow on those they love; are they really so desirable? Jay Williams shows the logical consequences of a reward often given to good girls: every time you speak, gold will fall from your lips:

The floor was covered with gold pieces which had piled up against the door like a drift of yellow snow. Four bright gold pieces fell from her mouth and clinked to the floor.

The girl clapped her hand to her forehead and said, "Drat!"

Another gold piece dropped from her lips. She took down a large pad that hung on the wall and began writing busily on it. Marco and Sylvia came and looked curiously over her shoulders.

"I am Roseanne. Welcome," the girl wrote. "As you see, I have something of a problem. Some time ago, I saved the life of the good fairy Melynda. As a reward, she said to me, 'My child, since you are poor but kind, a gold piece shall fall from your mouth with every word you speak.' . . . I'm sorry about the floor. I had some friends in for a party last night, and I haven't had a chance to sweep up yet."[15]

How much can you tinker with the traditional fairy tale before it changes into something else? It's easy to tell why a fairy tale has gone wrong, harder to tell why it has gone right. It's easy to see why George Cruikshank failed to improve on Grimm's fairy tales when he rewrote them twenty years after he illustrated the first English edition. Cruikshank, now a confirmed teetotaler, assures his readers that at Cinderella's wedding "the King gave orders that all the wine, beer, and spirits in the place shall be collected together, and piled upon the top of a rocky mound in the vicinity of the palace, and made a great bonfire of on the night of the wedding . . .[16]

Dickens, who admired Cruikshank the illustrator did not admire Cruikshank the editor. "In an utilitarian age, of all other times, it is a matter of grave importance that fairy tales should be respected," he observes. ". . . Whoever alters them to suit his own opinions . . . appropriates to himself what does not belong to him."[17] What would Dickens think of Anne Sexton's retelling of Cinderella in *Transformations*, her collection of Grimm's tales retold as poems? For those unacquainted with this book, I give two stanzas from "Cinderella":

> *Once*
> *the wife of a rich man was on her deathbed*
> *and she said to her daughter Cinderella:*
> *Be devout. Be good. Then I will smile*

down from heaven in the seam of a cloud.
The man took another wife who had
two daughters, pretty enough
but with hearts like blackjacks.
Cinderella was their maid.
She slept on the sooty hearth each night
and walked around looking like Al Jolson.
Her father brought presents home from town,
jewels and gowns for the other women
but the twig of a tree for Cinderella.
She planted the twig on her mother's grave
and it grew to a tree where a white dove sat.
Whenever she wished for anything the dove
would drop it like an egg upon the ground.
The bird is important, my dears, so heed him.

Next came the ball, as you all know.
It was a marriage market.
The prince was looking for a wife.
All but Cinderella were preparing
and gussying up for the big event.
Cinderella begged to go too.
Her stepmother threw a dish of lentils
into the cinders and said: Pick them
up in an hour and you shall go.
The white dove brought all his friends;
all the warm wings of the fatherland came,
and picked up the lentils in a jiffy.
No, Cinderella, said the stepmother,
you have no clothes and cannot dance.
That's the way with stepmothers.[18]

Has Sexton meddled with what does not belong to her? No. She grinds no axes, preaches no sermons. Let no one be deceived by her comic tone; the poems start from a deep understanding of fairy tales and a respect for the dark pools of consciousness from which they rise. Between the peasant grandmother and the poet who calls herself Dame Sexton lie Jung, Freud, and the magic of modern science.

When I took my son to see a Walt Disney movie called *The Cat from Outer Space*, I was struck by how much science fiction has borrowed from the fairy tale. A cat from a far planet arrives in a spaceship that looks very much like a crystal ball. The cat understands our language, and by means of thought transference, it makes its wishes known without speaking. A jeweled collar gives it the power to fly. Like the clever animals in the fairy tales, this space-age descendant of Puss-in-Boots helps the hero and confounds the villain. To the hero it gives the words he needs to run the spacecraft. Though they are a jargon of technology and mathematical formulae, they sound magic to children, who do not understand them. The power of science is ours when we understand its laws. But the power of abracadabra—what has that to do with laws and logic? To be told that abracadabra is a corruption from a Hebrew phrase that means "I bless the dead"—what power does that give you but the power of faith that the dead are alive and no mathematical formula on earth can tell us how?

Science fiction often carries the same spiritual truths that fairy tales have always carried. But science belongs to a universe of cause and effect, of laws that we could understand if only we were clever enough. Magic, on the other hand, is man's way of confronting a mystery that is beyond human understanding. "The wind bloweth where it listeth, and thou hearest the sound thereof, but canst not tell whence it cometh, and wither it goeth; so is every one that is born of the Spirit" (John, 3:8). When science masquerades as magic, it may give us spiritual lies such as this one, which recently caught my eye in a toy shop. On a box that claimed to hold Snow White's talking mirror was written the following:

> *Snow White's*
> *Talking Mirror*
> *ages 3½ to 10*
> *It's a Real Mirror*
> *But just tilt it and*
>   MAGICALLY
> *Snow White's Face*
>   Appears
> *and she really*
>   TALKS TO YOU
>
> *Snow White says*
> *6 different phrases.*
>
> *Advertised on TV.*
> *Requires 1 C cell and 3 D cell.*
> *Batteries not included.*

If magic is only in the eye of the beholder, then to God, magic and science are indistinguishable. But to a child who touches a switch on one wall and causes a light to shine in the next room, surely electricity is magic. Out of such a maze of innocence the Nigerian novelist Amos Tutuola, who has written so vividly about his sojourns among ghosts, has invented a television-handed ghostess. As her name indicates, her hand is a television set that shows the narrator events in far places. The magic mirror in traditional fairy tales did no less. Of the narrator's encounter with this ghostess, Tutuola writes:

> I was hearing on this television when my mother was discussing about me with one of her friends. . . . So as I was enjoying these discussions the television-handed ghostess took away the hand from my face and I saw nothing again except the hand. . . . I told her again to let me look at them. . . . Immediately she showed it to me my people appeared again . . .[19]

When Tutuola wrote *My Life in the Bush of Ghosts*, he had not yet seen television. Those who do not believe in the miracles of magic will speak of the miracles of science, forgetting that the rising of the sun is a miracle until you learn to take it for granted. "Try to be one of the people," says Henry James, "on whom nothing is lost!"[20]

I must confess that when choosing marvels, I prefer ghosts to fairies, terror to beauty. I believe the chipmunk in Randall Jarrell's *The Bat Poet* speaks for lovers of fantasy as well as poetry when he says, "It makes me shiver. Why do I like it if it makes me shiver?" One of my favorite ghost stories, *A Christmas Carol*, has always seemed to me so flawlessly written that I was much surprised to learn it had its beginnings in a much less successful ghost story. To read "The Story of the Goblins Who Stole a Sexton," published as Chapter 24 in *The Pickwick Papers*, and then to read what Dickens made of the same material in *A Christmas Carol* is to understand how a great writer uses traditional material to shape his own vision.

Before Ebenezer Scrooge came Gabriel Grub, the sexton who keeps Christmas so badly that he is willing to dig a grave on Christmas Eve. "Who makes graves at a time when all the other men are merry?" calls the chief goblin. "We know the man with the sulky face and grim scowl, that came down the street to-night, throwing his evil looks at the children . . ."[21] The goblins carry him to hell and show him edifying scenes from everyday life, and he hears his own life judged: "men like himself, who snarled at the mirth of cheerfulness of others, were the foulest weeds on the fair surface of the earth . . ."[22] Gabriel Grub repents, leaves his village, and returns many years later as "a ragged, contented, rheumatic old man."

Throughout the story Grub has neither a personal past nor idiosyncrasies by which we can remember him. "The Story of the Goblins Who Stole a Sexton" is the story of the Cheerless Man rather than a particular person, and for that reason Dickens can draw what moral he pleases; it does not arise from the changed life of Grub. ". . . as Gabriel Grub was afflicted with rheumatism to the end of his days, this story has at least one moral, if it teaches no better one— and that is, that if a man turns sulky and drinks by himself at Christmas time, he may make up his mind to be not a bit the better for it . . ."[23]

Seven years later Dickens reshapes the cheerless man's repentance into the selfish man's journey to find the love of his fellow man. Grub's graveyard has given way to Scrooge's counting-house, and the sights, smells, and sounds have a local habitation and a name: London.

Once upon a time—of all good days in the year, on Christmas Eve—old Scrooge sat busy in his counting-house. It was cold, bleak, biting weather: foggy withal: and he could hear the people in the court outside, go wheezing up and down, beating their hands upon their breasts, and stamping their feet upon the pavement-stones to warm them. The city clocks had only just gone three, but it was quite dark already: it had not been light all day: and candles were flaring in the windows of neighboring offices, like ruddy smears upon the palpable brown air. The fog came pouring in at every clink and keyhole, and was so dense without, that although the court was of the narrowest, the houses opposite were mere phantoms. To see the dingy cloud come drooping down, obscuring everything, one might have thought that Nature lived hard by, and was brewing on a large scale.[24]

The goblins of traditional folklore have blossomed into Marley's ghost and the three spirits appropriate to Scrooge's past, present, and future. Marley's chain clanks with "cash boxes, keys, padlocks, deeds, and heavy purses wrought in steel." The ghost of Christmas past is both an old man, like Scrooge, and a child, which Scrooge must become if he is to be saved from his own selfishness and skepticism:

It was a strange figure—like a child: yet not so like a child as like an old man, viewed through some super-natural medium, which gave him the appearance of having receded from the view, and being diminished to a child's proportions. Its hair, which hung about its neck and down its back, was white as if with age; and yet the face had not a wrinkle in it. . . . But the strangest thing about it was, that from the crown of its head there sprung a bright clear jet of light, by which all this was visible; and which was doubtless the occasion of its using, in its duller moments, a great extinguisher for a cap, which it now held under its arm.[25]

The moral and the happy ending are earned, both by Scrooge and by the writer. A happy ending is the heart of the fairy tale, and if you tinker with the form, this must not be tinkered with. Fairy tales are a wish unrolled into a story, a wish that when we disappear under the great extinguisher of death, we may not go out forever. More impossible wishes than this have come true in the stories told by our peasant grandmother, in whose stories strange things are common: wands, wishing caps, eight-headed trolls.

But the stories we write today are literature, not folk tales. And as writers, we take common things and make them strange, just as the rutabaga lamp did in Anna Hedlund's cellar. Do you see the shadows it throws on the wall? The shadow of Anna's pitcher rises like a bird. The shadow of her husband's gun sleeps like a snake. Anna Hedlund lifts her hand and bends her fingers and makes the shadow of a strange animal. Would she mind what I made of her in my story, an earth goddess in a subterranean hotel? I think not. Who among us does not want to be saved? What storyteller will not try to see in an aging grandmother the eternal woman? And to evoke in a weary reader the ageless child?

13

"Who Invented Water?": Magic, Craft, and the Making of Children's Books

I grew up in a house full of books. And once, during a long illness when I was nearly nine years old, I set out to read all of them. What stopped me almost immediately were the books that the previous owner of the house had bought to fill his empty shelves, so that he should appear at least as well educated as his neighbors. Among his stately volumes of Dickens and Swift was a Victorian novel dealing with pregnancy, in which that word was not once mentioned, and a treatise on the human body written for the young, which claimed that all my bodily functions were governed by magic dwarfs. One dwarf inhabited my liver, another lived in the chambers of my heart, a third guarded my kidneys. When I threw up, I could be certain that the dwarf who occupied my intestines was throwing a tantrum. An illustration showed him scattering gumdrops and chocolates still wrapped in foil, like a maddened child.

On the bottom shelves stood the etiquette books. There were several dozen of these. The chapters on servants included the correct liveries for your groom, your coachman, your butler, your page, your parlormaid, your nursemaid, your lady's maid, and your chambermaid. To me, these books were as exotic as the descriptions of court life in "The Sleeping Beauty" or "Cinderella." Reading the model letters for all occasions in the *Encyclopedia of Etiquette: What to Do, What to Say, What to Write, What to Wear*, I felt like the chambermaid who surreptitiously reads her mistress's postcards:

40 Garden Place
November 24th 19—

My dear Mrs. Carroll:

I return with great regret the cards for the first Assembly Ball, thinking you may wish to pass them on to someone more fortunate than I am. While out riding last week I severely injured my knee and the doctor gives me no hope that it will be sufficiently strong for dancing on the fifth of next month. This is a grievous disappointment, for the Assembly Balls are always such brilliant and successful affairs.

Believe me with many thanks sincerely yours,

Flora Dabney.

The most tantalizing book on the shelf was a textbook on music appreciation. Its chapters described in great detail the major works of Palestrina, Bach, Beethoven, Brahms, Schubert, and others whose names meant nothing to me. The chapters were to be read after you had listened to the recommended selections. Unfortunately we had not a single classical record in our house. Searching among the fox trots and Al Jolson's greatest hits, I did find Act I of "The Student Prince," but the opening bars of the overture had got chipped off. I tried to imagine those opening bars along with the symphonies and oratorios described in the book, like a deaf man watching an opera and reading the program notes.

Among the discoveries I made in this haphazard course of study was *Alice's Adventures in Wonderland*. It was number two in a set of ten books that had "Children's Classics" stamped in gold on the bindings. My mother immediately shelved the entire set in my room. This canonized company among my "Little Lulu" comics and my Mickey Mouse flip books was as attractive as a delegation of missionaries at a cocktail party. How, I thought, could any book given the adult seal of approval be entertaining? But the pictures in *Alice* were attractive, and I read the book. Indeed, I read it twice. Then I looked at the other nine volumes in the set. They included *Gulliver's Travels*, *The Arabian Nights*, *The Odyssey*, *The Iliad*, *The Pilgrim's Progress*, *Kidnapped*, and *Huckleberry Finn*. Many of these were the same books I had run across in the grown-up library downstairs, bound in red leather, with a frontispiece showing the author or one of his characters hiding behind a piece of tissue paper, waiting to be unveiled like a commemorative statue.

Our local bookseller only made matters more confusing. In his shop *David Copperfield* and the *Collected Poems of Robert Frost* shared a shelf with *Winnie the Pooh* and *Mary Poppins*. Today I am not surprised. For years children have been appropriating books intended for adults and adults have appropriated books intended for children. In his essay on Lewis Carroll, Auden writes, "There are good books which are only for adults, because their comprehension presupposes adult experiences, but there are no good books which are only for children."[1]

As a writer of children's books, I have asked myself, What qualities give the best books for children this broad appeal? Thinking back over the books I read with as much pleasure now as I did when I was eight or nine, I realize that my favorite writers never limited their vocabulary because they were writing for children. A writer's vocabulary is part of his style. His favorite words, however peculiar, become our favorite words. If a child wants to know what happened next, he is not going to be put off by an unfamiliar vocabulary.

I know this from experience. When I was ten years old, I sang in a church choir for children. The lady who directed the choir believed that children should be seen and not heard. We sang at Easter and Christmas services, and the rest of the year we lay fallow. I remember one rehearsal in particular. It was the day before Christmas Eve. The kids in Sunday school who couldn't carry a tune were pressed into service as shepherds and wise men for the annual pageant. I sat, bored and restless in my white taffeta wings and white robe, with eleven other angels in the choir stall. The girl next to me was allergic to tinsel and had already gotten a rash from her halo. We were singing the first verse of "Away in a Manger," the only one we could be counted on not to mumble, when she slipped me, from behind her hymnal, a small brown book. Slim, plain-covered, discreet.

I opened it eagerly. It was a sex manual, sneaked into church not by the devil but by the blond, curly-haired boy playing Gabriel, whom my mother called a holy terror. The sex manual was not illustrated and the account of what grown-ups did when we weren't looking was set forth in admirably scientific language. I didn't know much about sex, but motivation can do a lot, even for the most ignorant; I read it avidly and came away feeling much as Alice felt when she has finished reading "Jabberwocky" and remarks, "Somehow it seems to fill my head with ideas—only I don't know exactly what they are!"

But I noticed that, given unlimited freedom of vocabulary, the best writers for children use simple words instead of complicated ones, short words instead of long ones, not because children won't understand them but because simple language is the most effective. I once heard John Gardner tell a group of students at Bread Loaf to go through the dictionary and make a list of all the simple words they knew but didn't commonly use. I tried it and didn't even finish the A's. I already had more words than I could use in a lifetime. And if I'm ever tempted to choose a long word over a short one, I remember this passage, not from children's literature, but from the book of Ecclesiastes:

> I returned and saw under the sun, that the race is not to the swift, nor the battle to the strong neither yet bread to the wise, nor yet riches to men of understanding, nor yet favor to men of skill: but time and chance happeneth to them all.

And here is George Orwell's translation of the same passage into complicated English:

Objective consideration of contemporary phenomena compels the conclusion that success or failure in competitive activities exhibits no tendency to be commensurate with innate capacity, but that a considerable element of the unpredictable must invariably be taken into account.[2]

When I tell people that I write books for children and that I do not believe a writer should limit his or her vocabulary, I am sometimes asked, "Has an editor ever wanted you to change a word because children might not understand it? And have you done it?" Yes. The one word I've never been able to sneak past an editor is icebox. I am told that modern children will not know what an icebox is, and that I must say refrigerator. I've changed it, but regretfully; to my ear, icebox is the better word. In the house where I grew up, behind our icebox was a little door that could be opened by the man who delivered the ice. We didn't have to depend on his deliveries, as our icebox was electric. But what can I say to the reader who thinks I'm talking about a box of ice?

The question of what makes a book appeal to both adults and children goes well beyond vocabulary, however. Here I want to look at that question using fantasy rather than realistic fiction, since the books I loved best were fantasy. Nevertheless, I grew up aware of two ways of looking at the world that are opposed to each other and yet can exist side by side in the same person. One is the scientific view (my father was a scientist). The other is the magic view (my mother is a storyteller). Most of us come round at last to the scientific view. When we grow up, we put magic away with our other childish things. But I think we can all remember a time when magic was as palatable as science and the things we can't see were as important to us as the things we can.

From my own childhood, one such scene stays with me above all others. Every Easter morning my great-grandmother would rise before sunrise, cross the cold fields of her husband's farm in Deep River, Iowa, kneel beside the muddy river and dip water into a small bottle, chanting as she did so the words she believed turned common water into holy water. The words that brought about this miraculous change were a sort of garbled Latin, and I doubt that my great-grandmother, who spoke and read only German, understood them any better than I did. When I asked her why she used those words and no others she answered, "They always worked for my mother."

"But that was in Germany. This is America!"

"Water is water," said my great-grandmother.

"But why can't you speak plain, like I'm talking to you right now?"

Indignantly she answered, "Do you think water will listen to you if you get up and talk to it just any old way? That is no time to make personal remarks. You have to keep yourself out of it."

Years later, as a graduate student slogging my way through a course in Anglo-Saxon, I came across a charm for healing that reminded me of my great-grandmother's riverbank soliloquies. According to the textbook, the charm was a relic from the days when people believed that spirits lived in rivers and wells. My great-grandmother, a staunch Lutheran who kept her burial clothes in her room to remind her of her mortality, would have been shocked if I had told her she was really indulging in a pagan charm used by her ancestors to heal horses and their masters:

> Sing this thrice nine times, evening and morning, above a man's head, and in a horse's left ear, in running water, and turn his head against the stream: "In domo manosin inchorna meoti, otimimeoti quoddealde otuuotiua et marethin . . ."[3]

In these rituals my great-grandmother was a magician, and like the magicians in the fairy tales, she was dealing with invisible powers. The water of life looks no different than the water of death. The water she brought back from that muddy river was used only for emergencies of the spirit, not afflictions of the flesh. The last time I can recall its being used was at a family dinner. A child who had not yet been baptized choked on a chicken bone. My great-grandfather seized the water, baptized the child, and then called the doctor. Perhaps the water really was charmed, for the child recovered before the doctor arrived. Language was the instrument that brought about this transformation from the insignificant to the powerful, and so it has always been, ever since the first Maker said, "Let there be light," and there was light.

This belief that everything is alive, this faith in the power of what is invisible, I call the magic view of life. And I believe that all small children and some adults hold this view at the same time that they hold the scientific one. I also believe that the great books for children come from those writers who hold both.

I have recently had a chance to observe how the magic

view shapes our understanding of the most common events. Over a period of several years I kept a notebook in our kitchen where I jotted down the questions my son asked me. I kept it in the kitchen because I have noticed that the great revelations between parents and children occur most often there, in the hectic half hour before dinner must be put on the table. Many of the questions an adult could have asked; they could be answered with facts, that is, with a scientific or historical answer. Did the Pharaohs brush their teeth? Who was the first person to think of using a fork? Who invented the pretzel?

There is a book in our public library that answers such questions, and it is so popular that I am lucky if I can find it on the shelf once in six months. It is called *The Stone Soup*, by Maria Leach, and it is the history of common things. The table of contents reads like an abbreviated index of the Sears Roebuck catalog. There you will find the name of the woman who first introduced the fork to England. And if you turn to another book, *The Book of Firsts*, by Patrick Robertson, you will find that the Chinese claim to have invented the first toothbrush in 1498 and that the earliest mention of toothbrushes in Europe occurs in a letter, sent to one Sir Ralph Verney in 1649, asking him to bring back from Paris some of those "little brushes for making cleane of the teeth, most covered with sylver and some few with gold and sylver twiste . . ." And I always assumed that pretzels had no history until *Cricket* magazine ran an article on them several years ago. Pretzels are said to have been invented in the thirteenth century by a monk who gave them as a reward to children for learning their prayers. In the shape of the pretzel a sharp eye can discern the shape of the children's folded hands. Which all goes to show that there are a good many stories in the world that need not be made up but only found out. Cats, dogs, flowers, seashells, presidents, wars, knives, eyeglasses, shoes—everything in the world has a history, and to a child, for whom these things are new, every history is worth telling.

But there is another kind of question that children ask, which comes not from a scientific or historic interest in things but from a magic view of them. I will give you a selection from the questions I jotted down in my kitchen, as I believe they speak for themselves:

When a mouse falls on its knees, does it hurt?
Can I eat a star?
If I stand on my head, will the sleep in my eye roll up into my head?
If I drop my tooth in the telephone, will it go through the wires and bite someone's ear?
Who tied my navel? Did God tie it?
When my grandpa died, did he get young again? Will he be an invisible baby? Does everything have a birthday, even air?
Does the sun give you freckles? How long do I have to hold out my hand to get one?
When Grandma broke her arm, did it come right off?
How soft can loud be and still be loud?
Am I growing all the time? Even when I'm walking?
Do moths eat the wool off lambs?
Where does time go? Into the air?
Do the years ever run out?
Do caterpillars play like children? Do butterflies make a noise?
Are they part of our family?

Who invented water?
Could we xerox the moon?
Am I in my life? Are you in yours?
What happens if I open a clock and touch the ticky
    part?
Have all the kinds of shells in the sea been discovered?

These questions arise from a belief that practically everything in the universe is alive and that there is more than one way of being alive. Things that pass out of sight and hearing do not pass out of existence, and the failure to see and hear them is our failure. When my son, at the age of four, asked me if he could marry our cat, he really did believe that animals could understand human speech and only some defect in himself kept him from understanding theirs. Further, he had heard a great many stories about animals that turned out to be human beings in disguise. He is still especially fond of a fairy tale called "The White Cat," in which a king sends his three sons off on a journey to see who can find the most beautiful wife. The youngest son comes to a castle in which all the courtiers are cats. The princess, though a cat, is so lovely and wise that he chooses her for his wife and takes her home to meet his father. The last scene, in the version of the story my son knows, runs as follows:

Crowds gathered again around the king's palace to see the prince's return.

The two elder princes presented their brides to their father. The king welcomed them politely, but the two ladies were equally beautiful and he did not know how to choose between them.

"Where is my youngest son?" the king asked.

At that moment the youngest prince appeared, leading the White Cat. The courtiers looked at her in amazement.

"My son," the king said, "what does this mean? I asked you to bring a beautiful bride and you have brought a white cat. A beautiful cat, I admit, but do you want her to be your wife?"

The prince looked at the White Cat; she only smiled and said nothing. "I know she is a cat, Father," he said, "but I love her and want her to be my wife."

At the prince's words the Cat put her paws to her face and furled back her fur like a cloak. "An evil fairy cast a spell on me," she said to the prince, "but your love has broken it. Now I am a woman again." And so she was.

"You are the most beautiful woman in the world," the king said, "and now you shall be a queen."[4]

The White Cat is not the first whom love has changed from a beast to an angel. Though the metaphor is fantastic, the story is true, as the best fantasies for children always are. You have only to leaf through Grimms' fairy tales to see that fantasy need not be an escape from the problems of what we like to call the "real world," and you won't find a better collection of stories about murder, poverty, child abuse, and abandonment.

Nothing could be further from the "problem" books now being published on these subjects than Grimms' fairy tales. There are books about divorce for children whose parents are getting a divorce, books about going to the hospital for the first time for a child who is about to have his tonsils out, and so on. A problem book is first cousin to those jokes that the traveling patent medicine man would tell when he wanted to collect a good crowd. He'd start out telling you a good story and end up trying to sell you something. And once you saw the ulterior motive, you felt cheated. The problem is a sort of Procrustean bed and the story is cut to fit it. You and I know that the best stories are like rivers, which cut their own channels. The only problems the storyteller should worry about are narrative ones. How do I start my story? How do I keep my reader interested? How do I end my story?

As a child I loved Grimms' fairy tales, not because they instructed me or enlarged my understanding, but because they kept me sitting on the edge of my chair. Their makers never forgot their audience wanted to be entertained and would just as soon go out and climb a tree as listen to you. It's no accident that some of the most popular children's books started as stories told to or written for real children. Lovers of the Alice books know that Lewis Carroll invented Alice's adventures for the entertainment of the three young daughters of the dean of Christ Church at Oxford, during a boating expedition. A friend of Carroll's says of that expedition:

> I rowed *stroke* and he rowed *bow* . . . the story was actually composed and spoken over my shoulder for the benefit of Alice Liddell, who was acting as "cox" of our gig. I remember turning round and saying "Dodgson, is this an extempore romance of yours?" And he replied: "Yes, I'm inventing as we go along."[5]

Johnny Gruelle claims to have told the Raggedy Ann stories to his daughter Marcella and to have written them down afterward. And Beatrix Potter says of her picture books, which often got their start in illustrated letters for her child friends, "It is much more satisfactory to address a real live child: I often think that was the secret of the success of Peter Rabbit, it was written to a child—not made to order."[6] The first draft of *The Story of Peter Rabbit* is to be found in a letter to Noel Moore, the son of the young woman who had been her own governess:

> My dear Noel,
>
> I don't know what to write to you, so I shall tell you a story about four little rabbits whose names were Flopsy, Mopsy, Cottontail and Peter. They lived with their mother in a sand bank under the root of a big fir tree.
>
> "Now, my dears," said old Mrs. Bunny, "you may go into the field or down the lane, but don't go into Mr. McGregor's garden."[7]

But I believe that in all these cases the child was as much the catalyst that got the stories going as the shaper of the tales themselves. Beatrix Potter makes it plain in her letters and conversations that she wrote chiefly to please herself.

> I have just made stories to please myself because I never grew up! . . . I think I write carefully because I enjoy my writing, and enjoy taking pains over it. . . . My usual way of writing is to scribble, and cut out, and write it again and again. The shorter and plainer the better. And read the Bible (*unrevised* version and Old Testament) if I feel my style wants chastening. . . .

I think the great point in writing for children is to have something to say and to say it in simple direct language. . . . I polish, polish, polish! to the last, revise.[8]

Christopher Robin Milne's remarks on the way his father created the world of Winnie the Pooh are not so different from Potter's. "There was no question of tossing off something that was good enough for kiddies," he writes. "He was writing first to please and satisfy himself."[9]

I think what Maurice Sendak says about the source of his own work holds true for all makers of children's books. For Sendak, the child for whom he writes is the part of himself that still believes in magic:

. . . all I have to go on is what I know not only about my childhood but about the child I was as he exists now. . . . You see, I don't believe, in a way, that the kid I was grew up into me. . . . He still exists somewhere, in the most graphic, plastic, physical way. It's as if he had moved somewhere. I have a tremendous concern for him and interest in him. I communicate with him—or try to—all the time. . . . The pleasures I get as an adult are heightened by the fact that I experience them as a child at the same time. Like, when autumn comes, as an adult I welcome the departure of the heat, and simultaneously, as a child would, I start anticipating the snow and the first day it will be possible to use a sled. This dual apperception does break down occasionally. That usually happens when my work is going badly. I get a sour feeling about books in general and my own in particular. The next stage is annoyance at my dependence on this dual apperception, and I reject it. Then I become depressed. When excitement about what I'm working on returns, so does the child. We're on happy terms again.[10]

The child is the imagination at its most free, the adult is the disciplined craftsman who shapes it into a book. In the end, what really makes a book beloved both by children and adults is the high quality of the writing itself. When I reread the books I loved as a child, I always notice the scenes and characters that stayed with me. That is, I notice first of all the parts I remembered. Then I notice the parts I forgot. And the passages that time did not touch are insignificant, unexciting, and unessential to the plot. But they are vividly written and often symbolic, a single metaphor, perhaps, that brings the many strands of the book together. The writing, not the action, fixed them in my mind.

Here are three passages from three favorite stories of mine. They are, in fact, the opening paragraphs:

"Are you quite sure he will be at home?" said Jane, as they got off the bus, she and Michael and Mary Poppins.

"Would my uncle ask me to bring you to tea if he intended to go out, I'd like to know?" said Mary Poppins, who was evidently very offended by the question.[11]

"Perhaps she won't be there," said Michael.

"Yes, she will," said Jane. "She's always there for ever and ever."[12]

"And be sure you don't drop it!" said Mary Poppins, as she handed Michael a large black bottle.

He met the warning glint in her eye and shook his head earnestly.

"I'll be extra specially careful," he promised. He could not have gone more cautiously if he had been a burglar.[13]

What these three beginnings have in common, of course, is a situation that only the rest of the story can resolve. The first opens with a question: "Are you quite sure he will be at home?" The second opens with an argument, a sure-fire way of getting your reader's attention. The third involves danger. If Michael drops the bottle, there will be serious consequences. How serious? What's in the bottle? Will he drop it? Further, they all start with dialogue that puts you into the middle of an ongoing conversation, so that you feel the action has already started. No slow warm-up here. But the slow warm-up can also be a powerful beginning. Here is the opening of *Alice's Adventures in Wonderland*:

Alice was beginning to get very tired of sitting by her sister on the bank, and of having nothing to do: once or twice she had peeped into the book her sister was reading, but it had no pictures or conversations in it, "and what is the use of a book," thought Alice, "without pictures or conversations?"

So she was considering in her own mind (as well as she could, for the hot day made her feel very sleepy and stupid), whether the pleasure of making a daisy-chain would be worth the trouble of getting up and picking the daisies, when suddenly a White Rabbit with pink eyes ran close by her.

There was nothing so *very* remarkable in that; nor did Alice think it so *very* much out of the way to hear the Rabbit say to itself "Oh dear! Oh dear! I shall be too late!" (when she thought it over afterwards, it occurred to her that she ought to have wondered at this, but at the time it all seemed quite natural); but when the Rabbit actually *took a watch out of its waistcoat-pocket*, and looked at it, and then hurried on, Alice started to her feet, for it flashed across her mind that she had never before seen a rabbit with either a waistcoat-pocket, or a watch to take out of it, and, burning with curiosity, she ran across the field after it, and was just in time to see it pop down a large rabbit-hole under the hedge.

In another moment down went Alice after it, never once considering how in the world she was to get out again.[14]

In the first paragraph Alice is bored. Why isn't the reader bored? Because from Alice's discontent springs the story. If her sister's book had had more pictures and conversations, Alice would never have noticed the White Rabbit. By the fourth paragraph, she is off on a journey.

The more I read, the more I am convinced that nearly all the great stories for children start out with people taking journeys. In that set of classics I discovered as a child, the journey was so common that one could almost have accused the publisher of being in league with a travel agency. Another favorite book of mine, *Five Children and It*, by E. Nesbit, opens with the conclusion of a realistic journey that is the beginning of a whole series of imaginary ones:

The house was three miles from the station, but before the dusty hired fly had rattled along for five minutes the children began to put their heads out of the carriage window and to say, "Aren't we nearly there?" And every time they passed a house, which was not very often, they all said, "Oh, is this it?" But it never was, till they reached the very top of the hill, just past the chalk-quarry and before you come to the gravel-pit. And then there was a white house with a green garden and an orchard beyond, and mother said, "Here we are!" ...

The children had explored the gardens and the outhouses thoroughly before they were caught and cleaned for tea, and they saw quite well that they were certain to be happy at the White House. They thought so from the first moment, but when they found the back of the house covered with jasmine, all in white flower, and smelling like a bottle of the most expensive scent that is ever given for a birthday present; and when they had seen the lawn, all green and smooth, and quite different from the brown grass in the gardens at Camden Town; and when they found the stable with a loft over it and some old hay still left, they were almost certain; and when Robert had found the broken swing and tumbled out of it and got a lump on his head the size of an egg, and Cyril had nipped his finger in the door of a hutch that seemed made to keep rabbits in, if you ever had any, they had no longer any doubts whatever.[15]

And I, as a reader, no longer had any doubts that I wanted to read the book and go exploring with them. But something else contributes to the power of this beginning: the rhythm of the sentences, the sounds of the words themselves. Nesbit is mistress of the long sentence, which speeds forward and gathers events together. Here it is not the events but the syntax that keeps you in suspense, all those dependent clauses piling up, one after the other. On what main clause do they depend? An entirely different kind of suspense results when you use the long sentence to catalog events, poeple, or things. In this passage from Charles Kingsley's *The Water Babies*, the catalog is used to suggest that everyone has come together pell-mell, in the greatest confusion:

> . . . never was there heard at Hall Place—not even when the fox was killed in the conservatory, among acres of broken glass, and tons of smashed flower-pots—such a noise, row, hubbub, babel, shindy, hullabaloo, stramash, charivari, and total contempt of dignity, repose, and order, as that day, when Grimes, the gardener, the groom, the dairy-man, Sir John, the steward, the ploughman, the keeper, and the Irishwoman, all ran up the park, shouting "Stop thief," in the belief that Tom had at least a thousand pounds' worth of jewels in his empty pockets; and the very magpies and jays followed Tom up, screaking and screaming, as if he were a hunted fox beginning to droop his brush.[16]

None of the books from which I have just been quoting tell realistic stories. They are all fantasies. It is one of the paradoxes of writing for children that the more fantastic the events you describe, the more you must convince your reader that you are not making anything up. To borrow an image from Marianne Moore, if you make up imaginary gardens, you must put real toads in them. Beatrix Potter claimed that she never made anything up. I did not realize the truth of this until I visited her house in Sawrey and recognized the chimneys, cupboards, lanes, barnyards, and pastures of her own farm as the very places I had come to love in her books. The writers of the greatest fantasies for children could not have written as convincingly of other worlds without a thorough knowledge of this one. Beatrix Potter started out as a naturalist. Lewis Carroll wrote nonsense, but Charles Dodgson was a logician. The creator of hobbits was a medieval scholar. (When I used his texts as a graduate student, I knew nothing of his fiction.) The greatest fantasies for children come from a fullness of knowledge of human nature, of science, of history, of life.

Anything made to last is not made quickly. You are writing for the child who will pick up your book a hundred years from now and for the child who may read it tomorrow. A friend of mine, Lore Segal, once told me the effect of the *Iliad* on her son, Jacob, when he was a child. She had read up to the chapter in which the Greeks enter Troy, concealed in the belly of the wooden horse. The revelation of what this meant for the Trojans came to Jacob as he was riding with his mother on a bus, in the middle of Manhattan. The Trojans were doomed. Jacob burst into tears. What a tribute to Homer! In the twentieth century, on a bus in the middle of Manhattan, a child was weeping for the lost Trojans. A classic is a book that makes you weep or laugh more than twenty centuries after it was written. What writer could possibly ask for more?

Notes ✍

The One Who Goes Out at the Cry of Dawn:
The Secret Process of Stories.

1. "Notes on Writing," in *The Collected Essays and Occasional Writings of Katherine Anne Porter* (New York: Delta, 1973), pp. 449–450.
2. *The Complete Grimm's Fairy Tales*, intro. Padriac Colum, comment. Joseph Campbell (New York: Pantheon, 1972), pp. 237, 244, 326–327.
3. "The Lass Who Went Out at the Cry of Dawn," in *Thistle and Thyme, Tales and Legends from Scotland* (New York: Holt Rinehart and Winston), p. 62.

Becoming a Writer

1. *The Autobiography of William Carlos Williams* (New York: New Directions, 1951).
2. From Marianne Knight's reminiscence, quoted by C. Hill, *Homes and Friends*, p. 202, in Mary Lascelles, *Jane Austen and Her Art* (Oxford: Clarendon, 1939), p. 32.
3. J.E. Austen-Leigh, *Memoir of Jane Austen* (Oxford: Clarendon, 1926), p. 102.
4. M. D. Herter Norton, trans., *Letters to a Young Poet* (New York: Norton, 1954), pp. 18–19.
5. R. Brimley Johnson, ed., *The Novels and Letters of Jane Austen, Letters*, Part II (New York: Holby, 1906), pp. 339–340.
6. "Twenty Years of Writing," *Atlantic Monthly*, May 1955, pp. 65, 68.
7. "Teaching Creative Writing," *Atlantic Monthly*, May 1955, pp. 69, 70.

8. Joyce Maynard, "Visiting Ann Beattie," *The New York Times Book Review*, May 11, 1980, p. 91.

Angel in the Parlor: The Reading and Writing of Fantasy

1. Ethan Allen Hitchcock, *Remarks upon Alchemy and the Alchemists*, indicating a method of Discovering the True Nature of Hermetic Philosophy; and Showing that the Search After the Philosopher's Stone had Not for Its Object the Discovery of an Agent for the Transmutation of Metals. Being also An Attempt to Rescue from Undeserved Opprobrium the Reputation of a Class of Extraordinary Thinkers in the Past Ages (Boston: Crosby, Nichols, 1857), pp. 171–173.
2. A. E. Johnson, trans., *Perrault's Fairy Tales* (New York: Dover, 1969), pp. 69–70.
3. Letter to John W. Hilliard, in the *New York Times, Supplement*, July 14, 1900, p. 466. Reprinted in Robert Wooster Stallman, ed., *Stephen Crane, An Omnibus* (New York: Knopf, 1952), p. xxix.

The Well-tempered Falsehood: The Art of Storytelling

1. Lore Segal, trans., "The Master Thief," in *The Juniper Tree and Other Tales from Grimm*, vol. I (New York: Farrar, Straus and Giroux, 1973), p. 113.
2. Segal, "The Juniper Tree," vol 2, p. 314.
3. Segal, "The Juniper Tree," vol 2, pp. 314–315.
4. Avrahm Yarmolinski, ed., *The Portable Chekhov* (New York: Viking, 1973), pp. 355–356.
5. David M. Andersen, "Isaac Bashevis Singer: Conversations in California," *Modern Fiction Studies*, vol 16, 1970, p. 436.
6. *Passions and Other Stories* (New York: Farrar, Straus and Giroux, 1975), p. 296.

The Spinning Room: Symbols and Storytellers

1. " 'Alice' on the Stage," in Stuart Dodgson Collingwood, ed., *The Lewis Carroll Picture Book* (London: Unwin, 1899), p. 165.

2. Derek Hudson, *Lewis Carroll* (London: Constable, 1954), p. 128.

3. Collingwood, *The Lewis Carroll Picture Book*, pp. 166–167.

4. Hudson, *Lewis Carroll*, p. 173.

5. John Pudney, *Lewis Carroll and His World* (New York: Scribner's, 1976), p. 76.

6. Gustav Janouch, *Conversations with Kafka, Notes and Reminiscences* (New York: Praeger, 1953), p. 88.

7. Pudney, *Lewis Carroll and His World*, pp. 18–19.

8. Peter Milward, "C. S. Lewis on Allegory," in *The Rising Generation*, ed. J. J. Smith (New York: Macmillan), p. 20.

9. The anecdote is given by Curtis Cate in *Antoine de Saint-Exupéry* (New York: Putnam's, 1970), p. 461. The quotation from the notebooks is found on p. 463.

10. *The Story of my Life* (New York: Hurd and Houghton; Cambridge: Riverside, 1876), p. 8.

11. "The Blue Light," in *The Complete Grimm's Fairy Tales*, intro. Padriac Colum, comment. Joseph Campbell (New York: Pantheon, 1972), p. 530.

12. "The Tinder-Box," Svend Larsen, ed., R.P. Keigwin, trans., *Hans Christian Andersen, Fairy Tales* (New York: Scribner's, 1950), pp. 35–36, 40–41.

13. Larsen, *Hans Christian Andersen, Fairy Tales*, pp. 40–41.

14. Janouch, *Conversations with Kafka*, p. 59.

15. The following is retold from "The Enchanted Pig," in Andrew Lang, ed., *The Red Fairy Book* (New York: Random, 1960), pp. 145ff.

16. Elias Bredsdorff, *Hans Christian Andersen* (London: Phaidon, 1975), p. 358.

The Game and the Garden: The Lively Art of Nonsense

1. Edward Guiliano, ed., *The Complete Illustrated Works of Lewis Carroll* (New York: Avenel, 1982), p. 136.

2. Patricia Healy Evans, *Rimbles: A Book of Children's Classic Games, Rhymes, Songs and Sayings* (Garden City, N.Y.: Doubleday, 1961), pp. 55, 75.

3. Ralph J. Mills, Jr., ed., *On the Poet and His Craft: Selected Prose* (Seattle: University of Washington Press, 1965), p. 41.

4. "Mother Geese," *New York Times Book Review*, November 14, 1971, p. 8.

5. Iona and Peter Opie, eds., *The Oxford Nursery Rhyme Book* (Oxford: Oxford University Press, 1967), p. 24.

6. Opie, *The Oxford Nursery Rhyme Book*, p. 174.

7. See Susan Stewart, *Nonsense, Aspects of Intertextuality in Folklore and Literature* (Baltimore: Johns Hopkins University Press, 1979) and Elizabeth Sewell, *The Field of Nonsense* (London: Chatto and Windus, 1952).

8. David Erdman, ed., *The Poetry and Prose of William Blake* (Garden City, N.Y.: Doubleday, 1970), p. 36.

9. Erdman, *The Poetry and Prose of William Blake*, p. 39.

10. Constance Strachey, ed., *Letters of Edward Lear to Chichester Fortescue, Lord Carlingford, and Frances, Countess Waldegrave* (New York: Duffield, 1907), pp. 219, 222.

11. Strachey, *Letters of Edward Lear*, p. 289.

12. Roger Lancelyn Green, *Lewis Carroll* (London: The Bodley Head, 1960), pp. 29–30.

13. Green, *Lewis Carroll*, p. 51.

14. Thomas Byrom, *Nonsense and Wonder, The Poems and Cartoons of Edward Lear* (New York: Dutton, 1977), p. 35.

15. Strachey, *Letters of Edward Lear*, p. xlvi.

16. Strachey, *Letters of Edward Lear*, pp. 58–59, 267.

17. Edward Lear, *Nonsense Books* (Boston: Little, Brown, 1888), pp. 355, 356–357.

18. Lear, *Nonsense Books*, p. 137.

19. Guiliano, *The Complete Illustrated Works of Lewis Carroll*, pp. 95–96.

20. Guiliano, *The Complete Illustrated Works of Lewis Carroll*, p. 181.

21. Guiliano, *The Complete Illustrated Works of Lewis Carroll*, p. 143.

22. Lear, *Nonsense Books*, pp. 107–108.

23. Guiliano, *The Complete Illustrated Works of Lewis Carroll*, pp. 61, 62.

24. Guiliano, *The Complete Illustrated Works of Lewis Carroll,* p. 62.
25. "Peter Coddle's Narrative," *Peter Coddle's Trip* (Springfield, Mass.: Bradley, 1970), p. 5.
26. Guiliano, *The Complete Illustrated Works of Lewis Carroll,* p. 143.
27. Lear, *Nonsense Books,* pp. 313, 321.
28. Ralph Steele Boggs and Mary Gould Davis, "The Shepherd Who Laughed Last," in *Signals,* ed. Alma Whitney (New York: Macmillan, 1975), pp. 25–28. Reprinted from Boggs and Davis, *Three Golden Oranges and Other Spanish Folk Tales.* © 1936 by David McKay Company, Inc. for Longmans, Green & Co. Copyright renewed 1964 by R. S. Boggs and P. R. Davis.
29. Valerie Eaton Griffith, *A Stroke in the Family* (New York: Delacorte, 1970), p. 87.
30. See Jeffrey Stern, "Lewis Carroll the Surrealist," in *Lewis Carroll: A Celebration,* ed. Edward Guiliano (New York: Potter, 1982), p. 133. See also André Breton, "Limits Not Frontiers of Surrealism," in *Surrealism,* ed. Herbert Read (London: Faber and Faber, 1937): "With Swift and Lewis Carrol [sic], the English reader is more fitted than anyone to appreciate the resources of that humour which . . . hovers over the origins of Surrealism . . ." (p. 103).
31. Green, *Lewis Carroll,* p. 50.
32. Breton, André, *Manifestoes of Surrealism,* trans. Richard Seaver and Helen R. Lane (Ann Arbor: University of Michigan Press, 1969), p. 14.
33. Breton, *Manifestoes of Surrealism,* pp. 29–30.
34. *Leaping Poetry: An Idea With Poems and Translations* (Boston: Beacon, 1975), p. 4.
35. *Because It Is* (New York: New Directions, 1960), p. 11.
36. James Joyce, *A Portrait of the Artist as a Young Man* (New York: Viking, 1957), p. 13.

The Rutabaga Lamp: The Reading and Writing of Fairy Tales

1. Iona and Peter Opie, eds., *The Oxford Nursery Rhyme Book* (London: Oxford University Press, 1967), p. 152.
2. Opie, *The Oxford Nursery Rhyme Book*, p. 153.
3. *Tree and Leaf* (Boston: Houghton Mifflin, 1965), p. 10.
4. Leslie Fiedler, "Introduction," in *Beyond the Looking Glass*, ed. Jonathan Cott (New York: Stonehall, 1973), p. xiii.
5. Madame de Sévigné, August 6, 1677, *Correspondance*, Vol. II (juillet 1675—septembre 1680). Texte établi, présenté et annoté par Roger Duchêne (Paris: Editions Gallimard, 1974), p. 513.
6. Tolkien, *Tree and Leaf*, p. 45.
7. "A Christmas Tree," in *Christmas Stories* from "Household Words" and "All the Year Round" (London: Chapman & Hall and Henry Frowde, n.d.), p. 15.
8. "Preface," *The Lilac Fairy Book* (New York: Dover, 1968), p. viii.
9. "Preface to 'The Spoils of Poynton,'" in *The Art of the Novel: Critical Prefaces* by Henry James, intro. Richard P. Blackmur (New York: Scribners, 1934), p. 119.
10. Tolkien, *Tree and Leaf*, p. 5.
11. *A Likely Story* (Dublin: Doleman, 1967), p. 25.
12. *Kingdoms of Elfin* (New York: Viking, 1977), p. 1.
13. Tolkien, *Tree and Leaf*, pp. 48–49.
14. *The Works of William Makepeace Thackeray*, vol. 21 (London: Smith, Elder, 1879), pp. 297–298.
15. *The Practical Princess and Other Liberating Fairy Tales* (New York: Scholastic, 1978), pp. 2, 3.
16. *George Cruikshank's Fairy Library* (London: Bell, [1877]), p. 27.
17. "Frauds on the Fairies," in *Plays, Poems and Miscellaneous* (Boston: Houghton Mifflin, 1894), p. 488.
18. *Transformations* (Boston: Houghton Mifflin, 1971), pp. 54–55.

19. *My Life in the Bush of Ghosts* (London: Faber & Faber, 1954), p. 164.
20. Henry James, "The Art of Fiction," in *The Portable Henry James*, ed. Morton Dauwen Zabel (New York: Viking, 1975), p. 399.
21. *The Posthumous Papers of the Pickwick Club* (London: Chapman & Hall and Henry Frowde, n.d.), p. 479.
22. *The Posthumous Papers of the Pickwick Club*, p. 483.
23. *The Posthumous Papers of the Pickwick Club*, p. 485.
24. Michael Slater, ed., *The Christmas Books*, vol. 1 (Middlesex, England: Penguin, 1975), p. 47.
25. Slater, *The Christmas Books*, p. 24.

"Who Invented Water?": Magic, Craft, and the Making of Children's Books

1. "Today's Wonder-World Needs *Alice*," in Robert Phillips, *Aspects of Alice* (London: Gollancz, 1972), p. 11.
2. *A Collection of Essays* (Garden City, N.Y.: Doubleday/Anchor, 1953), p. 169.
3. J. H. G. Grattan and Charles Singer, eds., *Anglo-Saxon Magic and Medicine* (London: Oxford University Press, 1952), p. 193.
4. Erroll LeCain, ed. and illus., *The White Cat* (Scarsdale, N.Y.: Bradbury, 1975), n.p.
5. Phillips, *Aspects of Alice*, p. 4.
6. Leslie Lindner, *History of the Writings of Beatrix Potter* (London: Warne, 1971), p. 110.
7. Lindner, *History of the Writings of Beatrix Potter*, pp. 7–8.
8. Lindner, *History of the Writings of Beatrix Potter*, p. xxv.
9. Christopher Robin Milne, *The Enchanted Places* (New York: Dutton, 1975), p. 13.
10. Nat Hentoff, "Profiles: Among the Wild Things," *The New Yorker*, January 22, 1966, pp. 42–44.
11. P. L. Travers, *Mary Poppins* (New York: Harcourt Brace Jovanovich, 1962), p. 29.
12. Travers, *Mary Poppins*, p. 103.

13. P. L. Travers, *Mary Poppins Opens the Door* (New York Harcourt Brace Jovanovich, 1943), p. 148.
14. Edward Guiliano, ed., *The Complete Illustrated Works of Lewis Carroll* (New York: Avenel, 1982) pp. 5–6.
15. London: Ernest Benn Ltd., 1902. p. 1.
16. *The Water Babies* (New York: Dodd, Mead, 1910), p. 24.